Wrong in All the Right Ways

wrong

in all

the

right

ways

**TIFFANY
BROWNLEE**

Christy Ottaviano Books
HENRY HOLT AND COMPANY
New York

Henry Holt and Company, *Publishers since 1866*
Henry Holt® is a registered trademark of Macmillan Publishing Group, LLC
175 Fifth Avenue, New York, New York 10010 • fiercereads.com

Library of Congress Cataloging-in-Publication Data is available.
ISBN 978-1-250-13053-2

Our books may be purchased in bulk for promotional, educational, or business use. Please contact
your local bookseller or the Macmillan Corporate and Premium Sales Department at (800) 221-7945
ext. 5442 or by e-mail at MacmillanSpecialMarkets@macmillan.com.

First edition, 2018 / Designed by Danielle Mazzella di Bosco

Printed in the United States of America
1 3 5 7 9 10 8 6 4 2

To my mom, Benfordnetti; my siblings: Kenny, Brittny, Tyler, Kennedy &
Colston; and my love, Will. Thanks for never getting annoyed when I
would constantly ask you to listen to my stories. And also to bacon
cheeseburgers and french fries, for being the greatest food combo to eat
while writing.

chapter 1

L ET ME BE clear: I am not the biggest fan of small children. Now, I don't dislike all of them—the cute ones are hard to hate, and my seven-year-old brother is sort of awesome, too—but most of them I actually do loathe. They're obnoxious, they're messy, and they have not yet acquired the level of self-discipline I think is necessary to function in this world. Like I said, I hate them. So when my parents told me they were thinking of fostering a young kid, I wasn't exactly overflowing with joy.

And rightfully so. I mean, they already have two lovely and highly intelligent children. Do they really need another one? No, they don't. But it's not my place to tell them that.

Why not? Well, because I'm a people pleaser. I believe that there are two kinds of people in this world: those who live to make others happy, and those who live to make themselves happy. You can't be both; you have to choose one. Because let's face it: you can't please everyone and yourself at the same time. It's impossible. If that *was* in the realm of possibilities, we would all be living in a problem-free world, and God knows that's never going to happen.

I fall into the first category, which brings me back to square one: I'm a people pleaser. Actually, let me correct that: I'm a *parent* pleaser. I like to make my parents happy, and my acquiescing, being compliant, makes them happy. So even though my insides completely object to their decision to foster some wrong-side-of-the-tracks kid, I wear a smile as if everything is okay, because it's what I'm supposed to do. It's what they expect me to do.

"Time to wake up, Emma," my mom says on the intercom system that is hooked up in my room. When my parents first told me that they were fostering a kid, I volunteered to give up my room for him or her. I didn't want anyone else to have to sacrifice one of their rooms. My dad would die if he had to give up his socially primitive man cave, and my mom and I didn't want Matthew to have to give up his playroom. According to my mom, "a playroom is essential to the growth of cognitive and motor skills in a child, and *blah blah blah* . . ." So I relocated to the pool house. I told them that it would free up a room so they could keep an eye on my new sibling, and that because I'd be moving out of the house for college soon, this arrangement would make the transition easier on them, and on me. That's what I told them, anyway. Truth is, I don't want to be anywhere near the kid who is replacing me in their hearts, and twenty feet of distance is going to achieve just that.

"I'm getting up now," I lie as I pull the covers back over my head to block out the sunlight. This is the point in my day that I love the most, and I'm not going to let her wake-up call ruin it.

According to Folgers, the best part of waking up is having their coffee in your cup, but I beg to differ. It's actually the stage right before we wake up, or the Middle, as I like to call it. To me, it's as if my mind has registered that I've lived to see another day but it's not ready to pull away from its dreamland yet. It's the overlapping of waking and dream states, and every day, I take a few minutes to relish this moment.

I use this time to do my deepest thinking. It's usually something nonsensical or philosophical, like how many stars are in the sky, or why glue doesn't stick to the inside of the bottle. I never really answer these questions, but they wake my mind up just enough to get my day started.

Today's Middle topic is death. People die every day, and we all will die one day. It's an inevitable truth that we have to overlook if we want to live a happy life. I mean, think about it: the world would be a morbid place to live in if all we ever thought about was death and when it was coming and how it would happen. I'm not really scared of dying, but I'm kind of afraid of what happens after that; it's the only unknown that humans will never be able to figure out. I believe that death will come when it's supposed to, but I just want it to come after I've experienced a few life-changing moments—well, one in particular.

I want to fall in love. Who doesn't? In movies, it's made out to be a defining moment in our lives. Girl meets boy, and they share a season of love. He does something stupid to lose her, then wins her back with a grand gesture at the end so they can live happily ever after. Now, I'm not so naïve as to think this actually happens in real life. I know it doesn't. Somewhere between the first kiss and falling in love, life happens. Messy entanglements ensue, summer flings end, hearts break, et cetera, et cetera. That's just the way it is. Falling in love sounds agonizing, but if it means I find the other half of my heart in the end, I think it's worth it.

I roll over and look at the calendar on my wall. It's Monday, September 3. This day marks not only my last first day of high school, but also the day that I'll get to meet my possible new foster brother or sister. My parents are going to bring them to live with us for a while, and if all goes well, the courts will make them an official member of our family . . . well, eventually. Apparently, getting parents to sign over their rights can be a long process.

It will be nice for Matthew to have someone to keep him company, but having another sibling—technically—around is only going to force my parents to divide their attention even more. I don't want to come off as selfish, but aside from my brother, my parents are all I have, and I don't want some ungrateful brat coming in here to take them away from me. Especially not when I only have this year left with them before I leave for college.

I drag myself out of bed and saunter over to my closet. "What to wear?" I ask myself as I place my hands on my waist. I was supposed to figure this out last night, but I got distracted by the book I'm reading. A love story, if it's compelling enough, has the ability to make you forget that you have a life outside its fictitious world. And that's exactly what happened to me last night. I got lost between the pages of a story with a messy love triangle. So much so that I forgot all about today being the first day of school.

Figuring out what to wear is an impossible decision today. What you wear on the first day of school can make or break your year. At least, that's what most teen magazines preach to their readers. You are what you wear, they say. Wear too much black and you're a gothic freak. Show too much skin and you're a slut. To be popular, you have to find the perfect blend of casual and cool—with a hint of sexy and sassy—and I've gotten it wrong every year.

Now, I'm not drop-dead gorgeous, but I'm not completely unfortunate-looking either (thank you, Mom and Dad). I'm stuck in the plain-Jane middle of the spectrum, and most of the time I'm okay with that, except when it comes to one aspect of my life: boys.

Even though I'm decent-looking, I still haven't been able to land a boyfriend. I want that to be because I'm brilliant and my intelligence intimidates the boys at school—I skipped two grades in middle school (which just screams *socially well-adjusted*)—but I know it's not. It's more likely because I'm the "freaky genius girl" who cares more about my grades than how many points the football team scored in their last game. It's the things I care about, like intelligence and individuality, that make me invisible to them. All of them.

"I'm ready," I say as I enter the kitchen through the back door. My mom is waiting with a Polaroid camera in her hand, just as I expect her to be. We've done first-day-of-school photos for as long as I can remember. When she spots me, she pulls the camera away from her eye, and I see her thin lips press into a tight, straight line.

"Jeans and a T-shirt?" she asks. Her eyebrows are raised so high that they disappear behind her low-cut blond bangs. "I thought you were gonna wear that dress you bought last weekend. You know, the one that brings out your eyes?" As she says that, I pull my glasses out of my bag and slip them onto my face. "No contacts today either, huh?"

Well, it's not like I have anyone to impress. "Nope." I don't mean it, but it comes out in a moodier tone than I intended. "Sorry," I say as her eyes drop to the floor. "The first day of school always stresses me out." I grab an apple and swing my bag over my shoulder. It has only a notebook, a pen, and my wallet inside it, but it feels heavier than usual, because I'm not looking forward to going to school today. Not because I don't like school—I actually love learning—but because I don't really have any friends right now. Most of the girl cliques at school have already been established, and I don't think they're looking to add anyone else to their unwritten roster, which means I have to sit at the loner table at lunch. Yay me.

"Well, it's nice to know the hundreds of dollars your father and I spent on your corrective contact lenses are getting put to good use." I fold my arms across my chest and sigh. I've heard this speech so many times that I can probably recite it verbatim. "I don't get it. You beg us for contacts, and then you never wear them."

I didn't beg you for them. *You* decided to buy them all on your own. "They itch my eyes, so I'm going for recreational use only."

But that was a lie. My contacts don't bother my eyes at all. I just feel more comfortable wearing my glasses at school. They give me something to hide behind.

"Well, excuse me," she says, pointing the camera at me once again to take my picture. The flash temporarily blinds me, and it isn't until I see her fanning herself with the photo that my vision returns to normal. "Are you happy with this?" she says, showing me the photograph.

I don't have to look at the photo to know that I don't look good enough for the first day of school. I never have and never will. That's just the way it is. I take another look at my mom's camera in her hands and sigh. This is our last first day together; I can't disappoint her.

"On second thought, I'll go change." I come back ten minutes later in a white button-down blouse and a pair of black shorts. I almost never wear shorts in public—they are so revealing!—and putting them on to appease my mother kills me. "Better?" I ask upon returning. After receiving a nod of approval from my mom, I reach for my keys on the wall. As I do, I spot an old picture of my dad hoisting me in the air at the end of one of my softball games. I used to be really into softball, but that was only because my dad wanted me to be. "Did Dad leave for his morning run already?"

My father used to play professional baseball back when I was younger, but he had to retire early after he hurt his back sliding into home plate during a World Series game. So now he's the coach of an unstoppable junior baseball team in the neighborhood, and when he's not focused on that, he's trying his best to be a father to my brother and me.

"No, he skipped it. He's upstairs getting ready for our meeting with the group home." I see my mother tighten her ponytail, which can mean only one thing: she's worried that the kid won't like her. Why that would be, I have no clue. To me, she's pretty awesome— aside from the unspoken-pressure-to-please-her thing. "We don't get to choose, but we told them that we're looking for a child between the ages of eight and sixteen, so hopefully he or she is on the younger side of that spectrum."

"That'll be good for Matthew," I say. "He'll have someone to play with when I leave for college." I look over at my little brother. He's at the table eating a bowl of oatmeal. I imagine he's devising an elaborate plan to get out of having to go to school today. He says he hates it there, but the Fulton Academy of Advanced Math and Science is the only school in our area that will challenge him. Last year, when we were informed that he was gifted in mathematics, we were advised to send him there. I know this is what's best for him, but I can't help wondering if he misses being a normal kid sometimes. I know that I missed being normal when I skipped two grades four years ago.

"You sure you're okay with this?" my mom asks, tucking a couple strands of my hair behind my ear. I get almost all of my physical features from her: hair color, eye color, and height, just to name a few. From my father I get my intelligence, and that's about it. "I know the idea of having another sibling probably has you feeling unwanted, but I need you to know that that's not the case at all. Your dad and I will still love you just as much as we do right now."

"I'm fine, Mom, really. This is a good thing." It's not exactly a lie, but it's not exactly the truth, either. I'm happy that they're going to give a kid with a troubled past a second chance at what their life should have been. But at the same time, I don't want this new family member to replace me. After all, I *was* here first. "I'm gonna be late. Give Dad a hug for me."

I don't breathe until I escape out the front door. The only reason they're fostering this kid is because of my early graduation, and that kind of makes me ineligible for righteous birth-child indignation. No, I refuse to lose it in front of her. I'm the one who's leaving the nest two years ahead of schedule, prompting them to refill it as quickly as possible. This is basically my fault, but we're in too deep with the fostering process for me to beg her not to go through with it now. We're in too deep for me to break her heart with a confession.

After fighting for a good parking space at school, I get out to see tons of other students smiling and laughing with their friends. There are girls running across the courtyard, flinging their arms around each other, and guys fist-bumping buddies that they haven't seen all summer. The sight of their giddy reunions unfolding before me puts a bitter taste in my mouth; I've never been able to do any of those things on the first day of school.

Instead of reuniting with the friends I wish I had, I head to the counselor's office. From down the hall, I can see the white pieces of paper taped to the inside of the glass window on the door. Two big, bold words typed across the top of it come into view as I creep closer to the window: CLASS RANKINGS. I don't have to search for too long before I find my name. It's sitting at the top of the list, next to the number one. *Top in my class. That should make Dad happy.* He hates it when others beat me out. The warning bell rings, signaling that I should begin to make my way to class, and as I do, a proud smile creeps its way across my face. *I'm number one. Valedictorian, here I come.*

The school day is very uneventful. It's the same as every other first day in high school: the teacher introduces him- or herself, goes over the syllabus with us, distributes the class books, and then opens up the floor so that we can say a few things about who we are. Name, favorite pastime, and something interesting about ourselves. After third period, I'm so sick of this monotonous routine that I instinctively cringe when it starts all over again.

"I'm Emma Ellenburg," I mumble when it's my turn, adjusting my glasses. "I like writing and going to school." I get crickets from my classmates, but a nod of approval from my teacher. "Anyways, um, an interesting fact about me is that I'm the daughter of the youngest record-holding retired baseball player in America, Daniel Ellenburg."

There are times when I wish I had a different factoid to share about myself—something that is actually about me—but this is all I have.

My statement usually sparks a conversation about baseball, which I have no interest in anymore, and ends with a sports-obsessed boy jumping in to tell the class about an upcoming football or basketball game and why everyone in the entire school should attend. The jocks here are always looking for an opportunity to promote their sports teams, but I don't blame them. I would probably do the same thing if I were in their position.

The day drags on in this boring and repetitive cycle. But things change at lunch when a girl I have never spoken to sets her lunch tray down beside me. She doesn't have any food on her tray, but she does have a rather large stack of papers.

"Hey." She smiles at me, her dark green eyes glowing. She's too peppy for my liking, and before she speaks again, I almost leave the table to finish reading my book in peace. But I don't. That would be rude, and my parents taught me better than that.

"Hi." I don't mean for it to come out as flat as it does, but I can't help it.

"Karmin Ortega," she says, extending her perfectly manicured hand toward me. She flips her silky dark brown—almost black—hair over her shoulder, and that's when it hits me. She's the captain of the dance team, vice president of the Hispanic Heritage Club, and possibly the best dancer in our entire school.

The longer I stare at her, the more tiny snapshots of her come to mind. She's the girl that I used to see making out with some surfer guy in between classes last year. I always used to think that their PDA was gross and intrusive. I mean, they never came out and said it, but the way their hands roamed over each other's bodies screamed that they were having sex on a regular basis.

"You performed at the dance benefit concert last year, right?" she says, pulling me out of my mental rant. "The one that helped raise money to save the Cedar Pointe Dance studio?"

"Yeah." *Finally, someone notices me. Maybe I'm not so invisible after all.* "I'm Emma Ellenb—"

"I know who you are. I wanted to invite you to try out for the dance team in two weeks. That lyrical routine you did last year was mind-blowing. We could really use your skills."

Her compliment catches me off guard. Before the dance benefit, my feet hadn't touched center stage in years, but when my parents signed me up to perform in it—"You need to pay your respects to CPD. They taught you everything you know!"—I had to throw something together last minute. "Really? You . . . you think I'm good?"

"Definitely." She lifts her phone, which is acting as a makeshift paperweight, off the stack of papers and slides one of them to me. The highlighter-yellow color of the flyer makes me squint as I read the information about the tryouts. "I hope to see you there."

"Dance team? I thought you were going to give tennis another shot this year?" my mother says when I call her at the end of the school day. She lowers her voice, and I expect she's trying to hide it from my dad, who is probably close by. "You know your dad's not going to be too happy with you switching it up again." The disappointment in her voice almost tears me up inside. My mom and dad like to think they know what's best for me, and my divergence from their plan isn't going to sit well with them.

"I know." I can see my dad now: stretching out his tie and unbuttoning the top button on the collar of his shirt as he turns red with anger.

"I'm not going to tell your father. I'm leaving that up to you. But if I were you, I'd do it sooner rather than later."

"How about this: if I make the team, I'll tell him."

She goes silent on the line for a moment, and I imagine her weighing the options in her head. "Fine. But again, you have to tell him. I'm not getting in the middle of this. You know how he is."

I feel my stomach knot and twist as I think about telling him. He's not exactly going to be delighted when I do, and so I'm going to have to make sure he's in a semi-good mood when I fess up.

"And I still expect you to stay on top of your grades. I expect nothing less than what you're giving right now."

Of course you do. "I will. I promise."

"I didn't think you liked school enough to want to join a spirit team of any kind. But if it's something you really want to do, I'm behind you all the way."

I love how empowering my mom is. Whenever I want to pursue something, she always hears me out. Once, when I was ten and wanted to learn how to play the guitar, she bought me one of the most expensive ones *and* paid for a year's worth of lessons. I quit after two classes, but that's beside the point. The point is, she has always been willing to invest in my dreams, no matter how pipe-dreamy or irrational they may seem.

But my dad is the complete opposite. He hates that I switch activities so much, and he has no problem showing it. I've started and quit too many things—softball, guitar, gymnastics, soccer, tap and jazz dancing, ballet, and now tennis—for him to just sit back and accept it. The way I see it, he should be happy that I'm actually getting out to do something, instead of sitting on my ass all day, watching Netflix. But of course, he doesn't take that into account.

"I'm on my way to pick up Matthew from school, but I just wanted to call and run that by you."

"Okay, honey." I can hear a muffled sound in the background; it's someone talking, but I can't tell if it's a woman or a man, an adult or a kid. *Is that my new brother or sister? Or is that just Dad?* "That's the social worker," she says, answering the question before I can ask it. "We're going to be here for maybe another hour or so. There's a ton of paperwork that we have to read through and sign, but we should be nearing the end of it all pretty soon."

"Is everything okay?" I ask as I pull up to Matthew's school.

"Everything is fine, Emma. We'll be home with Dylan in about an hour." I can hear her smiling through the phone. "You're gonna love him." *Dylan*, I repeat in my head. *So it's a boy. I guess I'm okay with that. This means that I'll still reside as the only princess in the Ellenburg residence.*

A ton of questions that I want to ask her pulse through my mind, but I decide to keep them to myself. I don't want to ruin the surprise. "I'll see you soon, Mom."

Matthew's school reminds me of some of the best times in my life. In elementary school, I used to have a lot of friends. Back then it was easy. Nobody was competing to be the best athlete or the prettiest or the smartest. All you had to do was be yourself, and people liked you for that. I would give anything to return to that time.

When he sees me enter his classroom, Matthew runs up and gives me the biggest hug that he can. He's in a room full of parents trying to ask how their kid's day went, and it must be nice for him to finally see a familiar face. I don't want a conversation with his teacher like everyone else coming through the door; I just came to grab him and go. I'm tempted to tell him about our new brother, but I'm not sure how much he knows, so I choose to wait until he brings it up first.

"Where's Mom and Dad?" he asks as I strap him into his booster seat. He was a premature baby and has always been smaller than other kids his age. It wasn't until I saw his classmates that I realized how much smaller.

"They're out running errands."

"Does 'errands' mean picking up our new brother or sister?" He must see my eyes widen, because he quickly tacks on a reason for how he knows what's going on. "I heard you guys talking about that this morning, and Dad told me things would start happening soon. So is today the day?"

"That's not exactly 'errands,' I guess. But yes, they told me that they're going to be home soon, and that's when we'll get to meet him. Or her," I throw in to keep the gender a mystery to him. "So, are you ready to meet the newest member of our family?" He gives me a goofy grin, as if to say, *Hell, yeah,* in kid language, and then spends the entire ride home bombarding me with his thoughts on how our new sibling is going to look and act.

"It's definitely going to be a boy. I can feel it."

I have to choke back my grin as he speaks. He's going to be convinced he's psychic when he finds out that we really are fostering a boy.

"I think he's going to have brown hair and brown eyes, just like me," he says. "And he's going to love playing hide-and-seek with me, too."

His excitement for our new brother is contagious, and before I know it, I'm giddy, too. But even that moment doesn't last. After a while, my resentment resurfaces, as if it never left my heart to begin with.

We head home, but the idea that I'm going to be a big sister again doesn't officially hit me until I hear my dad jingle his keys outside the front door. I set my homework aside and flex my fingers to get the feeling back into them. I don't want this new kid to think we're slobs, so I fluff and karate-chop the top of each pillow that I was sitting on. That's the way Mom likes to fix them; she says it makes them look like they belong on a spread in a furniture magazine.

My dad once told me that there's a thin line between love and hate, and sides are chosen when two people meet for the first time. The crossing of two paths, he called it. "The first interaction is what people will remember most about you, and it will be the basis of your relationship with them," he said in a serious tone. In about ten seconds, my path and the path of my future foster brother will collide, and all I can think is *I hope he likes me, and I hope I like him.*

When I see the door handle start to turn, I feel time stand still. Like, for a moment, I'm frozen in space and I can choose whether I really want to go through with this, or run and hide under my bed. But that would be cowardly, and I don't want this kid to feel anything but welcomed.

Matthew and I stand in front of the sofa closest to the door and wait. First, our parents walk in, drawing out the anticipation. There is a sparkle in my mom's blue eyes and a grin across my dad's face. "Hey, guys. This is Dylan," he says as he extends his hand toward the door.

I expect to see a rambunctious eight- or nine-year-old race through the door, grinning from ear to ear, but instead, a teenage boy walks in—a very cute teenage boy, I might add. I fold my arms across my chest and wait for him to speak, but he doesn't say a word. He just keeps shifting his weight from one foot to the other as he looks us up and down.

Plot twist.

chapter 2

THIS ISN'T REAL. This can't be real, I repeat in my head as I pinch myself. There is no way that my parents have brought a teenage boy—again, a very cute teenage boy—to live under the same roof as me. There's just no way.

I squeeze and squeeze until the skin just above my elbow glows a deep shade of pink, but nothing happens. The image of Dylan standing next to my parents doesn't fade into darkness. It stays there. *This is not a dream.*

"This is Emma," my dad begins as he leads him toward me. "You guys are around the same age, and you'll be going to the same school now." He fails to mention that I skipped two years of school and won't be in the same grade as him, but I figure it's so that Dylan doesn't feel insecure.

"Nice to meet you, Emma," he says in a voice that's not too high and not too low. "I'm Dylan. Dylan McAndrews." The corners of his mouth twitch upward for a split second, and his dimples flash across his cheeks so fast that I would have missed it if I had blinked. I'm glad I didn't blink.

"It's nice to meet you, too, Dylan." I extend my hand to give his hand a shake, but he catches me a little off guard when he pulls me into a hug. Leaning in, I catch a whiff of his soapy scent. It's so potent as I inhale that I can visualize the manly scented suds on his tan body. As we embrace, I feel my parents' eyes on us. I was the one who showed the most discomfort with the entire fostering process, and now that he's here, I'm sure they're trying to see how I'm taking it. Their facial expressions don't change, so I'm guessing that they approve of this awkward welcome hug.

"This little guy down here is Matthew. Go ahead, Matt. Say hi." My dad is trying his hardest not to make this awkward for us, but from the way Dylan keeps fidgeting and cracking his knuckles, I can tell that my dad is failing miserably. Dylan's hardly meeting any of our gazes, and when he does, it's so brief that I start to wonder if it's because we're not as disarming as I think we are.

"I have one question and one question only," Matthew says, wagging a finger in Dylan's direction.

"What's that?"

"Do you like to play hide-and-seek?"

"I love hide-and-seek. We can play after I'm settled in. Okay, buddy?" He extends his pinky finger toward Matthew, who nods his head feverishly and then looks at me.

"I think I'm gonna like him," he tries to whisper, though everyone can hear him. "He already knows our secret sign for promises, and

I didn't even have to teach him." When Matthew was four, I taught him how to make a pinky promise. I said that no one else in the world knew about it, or how to do it. I guess he still believes that.

Matthew hooks his tiny pinky finger around Dylan's, and that's when I see it. A full smile emerges across Dylan's face, and in an instant, I can tell that he feels like one of us. Like he belongs.

"Daniel and I are gonna grab your bags out of the car for you. You guys," my mom says, turning to Matthew and me, "should show him around the house."

We speed through a tour, showing him the basics: the garage—which we never use because it's cluttered with dusty family photos, trophies, and other memorabilia—the kitchen, the bathrooms, the bedrooms, the office, and the living room area. Along the way, Matthew tries to show him where all of the best hiding places are. He points out the nooks and crannies that can drag a game of hide-and-seek on for hours.

"I don't want you to think I'm cheating because I've lived here all my life," he says, giggling.

"Good looking out, Matt."

Matt? Dylan has been here for less than an hour, and he's already using our nickname with Matthew. *Are they* that *close already?* Out of the corner of my eye, I see them bump fists, and I feel my stomach twist and knot with discomfort. Matthew's only seven, and he already has better social skills than I do.

"I'm going to go pick out my pajamas for bed," Matthew says as we prepare to descend the stairs. "Wait for me."

As I stand along the railing, I try to think of something good to say to Dylan. *So, how are you doing this evening? Do you like everything so far? Do you need me to get you anything?* Everything I come up with sounds as if we are running a bed-and-breakfast and he's a guest for the weekend rather than my new brother, so I give up on conversation starters and just look up at him and smile.

When I raise my eyes, I see that he's already looking at me. But the second our eyes meet, he looks away. I take it he's embarrassed that I caught him gawking.

"You guys have an amazing house," he says, now staring at the floor.

"Well, it's yours, too. Seeing as you're technically part of this household now."

"I guess you're right." Another awkward silence fills the gap in our conversation, and I feel obligated to keep it going—I don't want him to think that I'm callous or socially inept—but as I open my mouth to speak, so does Dylan. "I hope you don't feel threatened by me. I'm not here to step on your toes." As he says the word *toes*, I see his gaze travel over my feet, and his eyebrows scrunch up in disgust.

"I was betrayed by the beach," I offer as an explanation, curling my toes under. "Last summer, I stepped on some sharp shells, and they cut into my foot. One week later, I found out it was infected, and I guess my feet are still recovering from the trauma of it all."

"Damn," is all he says, but I get it. My freak accident story is a little too involved to share on his first day here.

"I know. Poor me."

"Poor you? More like poor me for having to look at them," he jokes. "I think I just lost my appetite." He chokes back a laugh, and before I know it, we are both giggling uncontrollably. "It's okay. I've got plenty of scars, too."

I know I shouldn't, but the words spill out before I can command them to stay put. "Let me see."

He checks over his shoulder—I guess to make sure Matthew isn't around. *Are they* that *gruesome?*—and then pulls at the collar of his T-shirt to show me the heavily scarred skin just below his collarbone. He casts his eyes down as I run my fingers over the raised lines on his skin, as if he's ashamed of the marks on his body.

"What made you do this to yourself?" I whisper into his dark brown eyes. The room starts to spin as I imagine him taking a razor blade and slicing into his skin, and I have to hold on to the railing to keep my knees from buckling. I can't imagine ever marking my body up with the intent of leaving scars.

"What makes you think I did this to myself?" he spits at me. And just like that, the fire in his eyes dissolves. The guy who was clutching his stomach in a fit of giggles two minutes ago is gone.

"I just thought—"

"That I'm a foster kid, and so I *must* be messed up enough to want to cut myself, right?"

"I didn't mean it like that. I—"

"I get it. You think I'm troubled and traumatized, and so you expect me to do things like this." He releases the collar of his shirt and takes a step closer to me, making me flinch. Even the aroma of the soap I smelled on him earlier isn't enough to calm the fright in my heart. "I've seen stuff that no person, let alone a kid, should ever have to witness. Horrors that I couldn't unsee even if I tried. You don't know my story, and you don't know me. So I would appreciate it if you didn't jump to conclusions, because your assumptions are only making an ass out of you, not me."

My heart is beating too loud for me to think of a good comeback, and my mouth has gone dry from the mini panic attack I'm having, but somehow I still manage to whisper, "Got it."

"It's my first day. Please, don't ruin this for me," he says, backing away from me. The hurt in his eyes is almost tangible, like the scars near his collarbone.

"I'm sorry. For assuming, I mean."

"Yeah, I know." It's only been twenty minutes, and I've already gotten him to hate me. *How is that possible?* When Matthew rejoins us at the top of the stairs, I try to keep to myself. If I open my mouth, I'll only make things worse.

"And that concludes the tour," I murmur as we make our way back to the kitchen.

"What's over there?" Dylan asks, pointing outside the back door. There's no trace of a lingering rage in his voice and no flickers of fury left over from his blood boiling over, either. It's steady, as if he didn't just jump down my throat a minute ago.

"Oh, that's the pool house, where my room is," I say, my voice cracking beneath my words. He's acting as if the conversation we had at the top of the stairs didn't happen, but unlike him, I don't have the luxury of forgetting that easily. "I volunteered to give up my room when they decided to adopt you, so my parents let me have it." His thick eyebrows furl when I say the word *adopt*. Surely, he must know that adoption is a possibility. If my parents have anything to do with it, he won't stay in the system forever, but it's not my place to tell him this. At least, not after the scolding I just got about jumping to conclusions.

"Foster," he corrects. "I'm not your brother yet."

But eventually you will be, I start to say, but I flash back to our conversation on the stairs, and decide not to.

My parents are finishing up with his things when we complete our tour. "I don't want you to think that I never cook, because I do." My mom laughs. "But we figured you'd like something simple for your first day here." She hands me two boxes of pizza, and I lead the way to the kitchen table.

We pass around plates and then the boxes of pizza, each person taking two slices for themselves. It's not the usual Ellenburg family dinner that's filled with random banter about how everyone's day went. Tonight, all of the attention and interest are on Dylan.

"I'm sorry about your room," my mom says. "Emma took her queen mattress and wrought iron bedframe to the pool house. We were expecting to bring home a boy around Matthew's age and thought a smaller bed would be more fitting. Now obviously, that twin bed isn't going to do you much good, so I've ordered you a bigger bed, which should be in tomorrow. But for tonight, is it okay if you take the couch?"

"No worries, Mrs. Ellenburg. Believe me, I've slept on worse." He laughs, but no one else joins in with him. Once again, it occurs to me that I know nothing about him or his past. I'm curious to know what horrific thing happened to him that led to him being placed in foster care as well as how many foster families he's had, but I don't ask about it now. His deep, dark secrets are hardly appropriate for dinner conversation, especially with Matthew listening. He's still young and so impressionable that we're not even allowed to curse in front of him— even though I know for a fact that both of my parents love to use colorful words.

"You can call me Mom, if you want." Mom's trying to bridge the gap of awkward silence with something light and fluffy; she doesn't handle discomfort well. "Or Lauren, if Mom doesn't feel right. Whatever makes you comfortable."

"Thanks." Dylan's mouth stretches into a grin that resembles that of a clown: deceiving and full of secrets. *What's he hiding?*

As he looks away from Mom, he catches my eyes. I mouth the words *I'm sorry* across the table, and I see him make an arc motion with his hand, as if to say that it's water under the bridge. I lean back in my seat, finally able to relax again.

"What's your favorite color?" Matthew asks, pointing his half-eaten pizza crust at Dylan. We've told him a million times that pointing is rude, but then again, he's only seven. We can't expect him to be as refined as the rest of the family yet.

Blue, I answer for him in my head. I know I'm right just by looking at him. The blue in his T-shirt and shoes is a dead giveaway. People always wear their favorite color the most.

"It's blue."

"Mine is green. What's your favorite book?"

"I'm a big Harry Potter fan." Dylan holds up his pizza crust as if it's a wand and casts a fake spell on Matthew. "That series will always be close to my heart."

"Emma has all of the movies. Maybe we can watch them together sometime," Matthew suggests.

"Maybe." Our eyes meet again, and a flutter jolts through me. But it doesn't last long; Matthew's asking his next question before a full smile can spread across my face.

"What about your favorite—"

"Matthew, let's ease up on the interrogation. We haven't even touched on his hobbies yet. What are you into, son?"

Dylan swallows hard when he hears the word *son* come out of my father's mouth. I know my dad doesn't mean it *literally*—he calls Matthew's friends *son* as well, but something about it feels alarming now. "I-I'm not the biggest sports fan," he admits after taking a sip from his glass. "I'm more into the arts. Painting, sketching, sculpting. That kind of stuff. More painting than anything, though." I watch as my father sets down his piece of pizza and clasps his hands, darting his eyes toward Dylan, who quickly edits himself. "Not saying I *don't* like to play sports. It's just that it's always come second to my art." He stuffs a piece of pizza crust into his mouth, and I can't help but snort, trying to hold back a laugh.

"Well, Dad, I guess Matthew is your last hope for a baseball star. Hopefully he has good hand-eye coordination." I pat my dad's shoulder, faux apologetically, and sneak a look at Dylan. *He's smart. He got out early*, I think to myself.

"Did you used to play baseball in high school and college?" Dylan asks, ignoring my interjection and turning the conversation back to my dad.

"Here we go," I whisper under my breath. "You've done it now."

"Speak up, Emma. I've told you about the mumbling. It's not very ladylike," my dad snaps.

"Just wondering if you'd like me to start cleaning up, Dad." Before he can answer, I pick up his plate, which has four pizza crusts on it, and head to the kitchen to avoid his walk down memory lane. I've heard my dad's stories so many times that I know them by heart now.

"I went pro when I was only nineteen years old, played for seventeen years, and became the youngest batter ever to get over two hundred hits in a single season . . ."

Out of the corner of my eye, I catch sight of Dylan. He's nodding his head and grunting every once in a while, but I know he's not into it. I mean, he *did* just say that he's not a sports person. But my dad has no clue that this is happening; he just keeps going on and on about the "good ol' days" like he usually does when we have a new guest in the house. I don't blame him, though. He hardly ever gets to talk baseball with us anymore. Mom and I have outgrown his stories from the big leagues, and Matthew is too young to fully understand them all, so my dad must be ecstatic to have someone new to tell them to.

I shuffle through the kitchen, eavesdropping on their conversation until I can no longer hear what they are saying. I expect they are talking about his adjustment here and going over the rules, so I start to clean up the kitchen. As I fill the sink with dishwater, I let myself get lost in thought. The only thing that keeps passing through my mind is Dylan. He seems like he's gonna be a good fit for our family, and I'm surprised that I'm kind of all right with having him here, since just this morning I was still on the fence about the whole thing. And aside from the confrontation we had at the top of the stairs, he seems to be pretty nice, too. I mean, I haven't seen my dad talk and smile this much in a long time.

The "welcome home" festivities don't last much longer, and after Mom and Dad remind us that it's a school night, we take our showers and retire to our bedrooms—well, Matthew and I do. Dylan has to get comfortable on the sofa tonight.

I'm just about to crawl into bed, when I notice that the pool lights are still on. Dad has been on my case about remembering to turn them off, and if I'm going to get (and stay) on his good side, I need to start remembering to do my only chore.

My fingers are a second away from flipping the switch when I see Dylan exit the back door of the house and lie down in the grass near the edge of the pool, his arm hooked over the back of his head. After a minute or two, he closes his eyes.

Confused, I rush outside. "I know Mom messed up your sleeping arrangements, but come on, the sofa isn't *that* bad," I joke as I approach him.

"I'm just admiring the sky. It's been a long time since I've seen the stars. Too much light pollution in Los Angeles."

"Yeah. They are pretty amazing, aren't they?" He closes his eyes once again, and I can't help but wonder how he's "admiring the sky" if his eyes are closed. Maybe some of his screws really are loose, and he failed to mention that to my parents before they brought him home. "I'm sorry, again," I say to fill the silence between us. "I know I said it earlier, but I just wanted to reiterate it. I don't know why I assumed that about you. It was very wrong of me."

"You haven't gotten over that yet?" he asks, opening his left eye and patting the ground, inviting me to sit with him for a moment. "I was over that when the conversation ended. I don't hold grudges. It's emotionally draining."

"I agree. It is." I lie back on the grass and look up into the sky in silenced bewilderment. *Why are we lying in the grass when we've both taken showers already? Isn't this defeating the purpose?*

"I don't remember much from the actual accident. I blacked out from blood loss before we even made it to the hospital," Dylan rattles off as if I know what he's talking about. It takes me a minute to realize that he's talking about his scar again.

I feel my breath start to shorten as he talks about his old wounds. There's a reason that I never dreamed of becoming a doctor, and I'm reminded of the impossibility of this career option whenever I hear someone talk about blood and broken bones and other gory things like that.

I'm so busy trying to redirect my thoughts away from the image he's creating that I don't catch the end of what he's saying. Instead, I'm wondering whether I should take another shower when I get back inside.

It's quiet, I observe after a moment. *Should I say something so things don't get too weird?* I pull my hair over my left shoulder and begin to braid it while I think of something to say to fill the void. *I wonder what he's thinking about. Is he thinking about his family? Is he thinking about us? Is he thinking about . . . me?* I'm halfway down my mane when I figure out how to start a conversation with him. "So how does it feel? Has it all sunk in yet?"

In his set of navy blue pajamas, he looks over at me and then shakes his head. His hair is wet from the shower, and a couple drops find their way to me as he answers my question. "Nope. I still feel like I'm gonna wake up tomorrow and have this all be a dream. Like I should still be in LA. It just doesn't feel real yet."

"Well, believe it, bro," I say leaning up on my elbows. *Bro?* That was a weird thing to say; I've never called Matthew bro. "This is your life now, so start enjoying it." He's quiet for a moment, and out of the corner of my eye, I catch him looking at me. When I meet his gaze, he doesn't look away. "What?"

He closes his eyes once more, before answering. "What's our school like?"

"Oh, it's nothing special. Just a place where a bunch of popular, yet dumb, girls and guys convene to cheat off of each other to matriculate into their dream party-central, I mean college. Not too different from any other high school, I'm sure."

"Matriculate," he repeats. "Big-word points for you." I smile and wait for him to speak again. "Sounds like fun. So . . . you're not popular, I'm guessing?" I furl my eyebrows and tilt my head to the side as if to ask why he would say such a thing. "I'm only asking because you called them dumb. Nobody would describe themselves as dumb to a total stranger, new foster sibling or not."

He's wittier than I initially gave him credit for, I think to myself.

"No, I'm not. Quite the opposite, actually," I admit with a frown. "But I don't care. Pretty soon, I'm going to graduate and move on to college, while they learn how to shotgun a beer."

"You don't like it? School, I mean."

"The social part of it, no. I'd rather walk slowly across hot coals every hour, on the hour, for the rest of my life than to go to that place every day. It's mostly a hellhole, aside from the learning-new-things part. I like that part very much." I don't feel like venting my feelings anymore, so I turn the conversation back on him. "You're gonna be the center of attention tomorrow, so get ready."

"Why?" he says, opening his eyes once more.

"Because you're new and mysterious, and you kind of look like pre-Miley Liam Hemsworth—so without the beard—and with brown eyes instead of blue."

I imagine him coming home with a notebook full of girls' numbers, and another wave of jealousy washes over my body. *He's going to be popular. I just know it.* He's going to spend one day at my high school and end up doing the one thing that I couldn't for four whole years.

"Yep," I say, rolling my eyes, "they're gonna be all over you."

"Who's Liam Hemsworth?"

"Ha, very funny," I say, pushing his shoulder playfully. I'm surprised that I can feel his muscles; for a guy who isn't into sports, he's sure built like an athlete. "You know, the little brother of that actor who plays Thor in all the superhero movies with the perfectly messy brown hair, toned biceps, and dreamy blue eyes."

" 'Dreamy blue eyes'? You mean like yours?" The hair on my arms rises slowly as the aura of electricity settles around us, and it isn't long before I feel my cheeks and ears grow warm.

"Yeah, sure." I look away from him, but I can still feel his eyes dancing across my face, as if he's trying to memorize the precise placement of every freckle on my nose and cheeks. "It's getting late. I'll, uh . . . I'll see you in the morning. Okay?"

"Sounds good."

Leaving him to lounge on the ground, I set the pool lights to turn off in two hours, just in case he wants to lie out there and gaze—with closed eyes—at the stars a bit longer.

I toss and turn all night, my mind alternating between thinking and dreaming about Dylan and the last seconds of our conversation by the pool. I know that he's going to be my official brother on paper one day, but a piece of me wants to explore the side of Dylan that I saw before we parted ways tonight. The side that I think was flirting with me.

chapter 3

Surprisingly, I'm okay sharing my school with Dylan. Throughout the day, I am so engrossed in my schoolwork that I forget he is even here with me. That is, until lunch.

"I don't know. Sorry," I say to yet another girl who comes up to ask about Dylan's relationship status. If he was on Instagram, I could just redirect them to stalk his account. Alas, he is not. "Why don't you ask him yourself?" I don't mean to sound as harsh as I do, but she is the fifth girl today who has come up to ask me the same question, and my tolerance level is dropping.

"I figured you knew if he was dating anyone. You *are* his sister, anyway." *Sister? Not yet*, as Dylan made clear to me last night.

"I just met him yesterday. So that brings the amount of time of me knowing him to, I don't know, seventeen hours. But wait, subtract the eight hours we spent sleeping last night and the five I've spent at school today, and that leaves me with four. Four hours. Now, do you think that his romantic involvement with another girl was at the top of my list of things to find out about him?" I don't know why I'm all of a sudden overcome with rage, but once I start talking, the words spill out uncontrollably. "Well?"

"Sorry I asked." She grabs her tray and leaves without another word, and I do the same. I'm not going to continue to eat my lunch out in the open and put myself in a position to be showered with questions about Dylan's love life. I retreat to the only open classroom in the school during lunch hours: the art room.

"You know, you'd probably have more friends if you actually stuck around to talk to people during your free time," someone says from behind an easel as I set my backpack and calculus book down on the table. I don't need to see their face to know that it's Dylan. Though I've only known him for about seventeen—or, okay, four—hours, I'm able to recognize his voice pretty easily.

"I'm sorry. I didn't know anyone was in here." I grab my things and start for the door. "I'll just go. Sorry."

"Oh, please, stay. I like a little company when I'm working on something."

I set my things back down and make my way around the easel to take a look at his creation. It's the image of someone's eyes. At first glance, it looks like any other picture of blue eyes, but as I stare longer, I see another image emerge: in the center of the eyes, where the pupil should be, is the reflection of a night's sky. The way he captured the swirls of the clouds and the sparkle of the stars and moon within the blue irises is so detailed that I get lost in it. I knew that he was artsy, but he is much better than I imagined him to be.

"Wow" is all I can get out, and even then, it comes out as a whisper.

"Thanks," he says, raising his arms above his head to stretch. "This image has been in my mind since yesterday. I couldn't sleep last night because of it."

"I couldn't sleep last night, either." I'm a little embarrassed now that I've seen his painting. He wasn't trying to flirt last night when he was staring into my eyes, but rather trying to study the image in them long enough so that he could artistically regurgitate it onto his canvas. "I hope you don't mind me asking, but shouldn't you be out mixing and mingling with your future friends and girlfriends?"

"There will be plenty of time for that. But right now, this has my attention." He starts to mix some colors together, and as he does, his tongue pokes out between his lips. The concentration on his face is intense, yet inspiring. "So what about you? Why aren't you chatting it up with your clique, or posse, or whatever you girls call yourselves these days?"

"I would be with my *crew* . . . if I had one." I can feel his eyes on me as I start to pick at the dark purple polish on my nails. "It makes no sense to start making any friends now. I mean, I'm graduating soon. I'll hang out with them this year and then forget all about them once I leave this place. Seems like a waste of time and emotion."

"I guess that makes sense." He must have finished mixing, because he picks up his brush again and starts adding more stars and constellations to the reflection of the sky with the newly created color. "So is that why you've elected to come here? To avoid making friends?"

"Well, actually, I'm hiding. Girls have been harassing me all day trying to get me to spill the juicy details of your love life. I guess they're too intimidated to ask you themselves."

He lets out a laugh and picks up a smaller brush to add some detail to the shape of the moon. "So, your ideal way to spend lunch on the run is doing homework?" I follow his eyes to the calculus book on the desk.

A flash of burning red flushes across my cheeks and up to my ears. "You probably think I'm a huge nerd—"

"Your words, not mine." He chuckles, turning back to his canvas. "Is it not going to get done at home?"

"No, it will. I never don't do homework." I blink hard at my last comment; nothing coming out of my mouth is helping to refute this nerd status I've established.

"Then I'm sure you won't mind breaking away for an art lesson. That is, unless you have other nerdy obligations to tend to." I purse my lips as he tosses a smock in my direction, which I catch with one hand. "Looks like you *have* inherited your dad's hand-eye coordination. Matt isn't his last hope after all."

"Whatever," I say, rolling my eyes playfully. "Just hand me a brush."

He takes me through the basics of mixing colors and then teaches me a couple brushstrokes. It isn't until he's guiding my hand over the canvas that I really take notice of how he looks. He has a square jaw, which he clenches and unclenches when he's concentrating on a stroke. And his eyes are a lighter shade of brown than I originally thought they were. Last night, they looked dark and full of secrets, but today, they are honey-colored and relaxed, almost carefree. I zero in on a scar just above his left eyebrow. *He wasn't lying; he does have a lot of scars. Where could he have possibly gotten them all?*

"You're supposed to be watching my hands, not my face," he says as his eyes pierce through the lenses of my glasses and into mine. The pink in my cheeks returns, and I avert my eyes, killing the curiosity, but it's too late. He's already seen me staring. "Go ahead. Say what's on your mind. I can see those wheels turning."

I pause. *Should I ask him about his past home life?* He looks so happy right now, and I don't want to be responsible for shattering that feeling. "What happened to your family?" I say, looking directly into his eyes. I see his broad shoulders droop, and instantly I regret asking. Setting down his paintbrush, he starts to clench his jaw again, as if he's fighting the urge to tell me the truth.

"My mom—" he starts, but gets cut off by the PA system.

Ding. Ding. Ding. "Please excuse the following announcement," a woman's voice booms through the intercom in the art room.

Dylan frowns. "I guess we'll have to finish this conversation another time."

"All students currently taking Ms. Harper's fifth- and sixth-period English II classes need to report to room 306 for class today. I repeat, all students currently taking Ms. Harper's fifth- and sixth-period English II class need to report to room 306 for class today."

I can't help but wonder how anyone sitting out by the lunch tables can hear this announcement. Lunchtime can get pretty loud and wild; sometimes it's hard to hear the intercom even on a tame day.

A look of concern passes over Dylan's eyebrows, and I can't tell whether it's directed at his painting or the announcement, but when he drops his brushes in the sink and charges toward his backpack to pull out the cream-colored sheet of paper with his schedule on it, I figure it's the latter. "Everything okay?"

I watch in silence as he gnaws at his lower lip while his eyes graze the front of the sheet of paper. "I guess I'll head to room 306 after lunch today. I wonder what's going on."

"There's always something going on in this school. It's probably just a schedule mix-up or misprint. Wait, what room did they say to meet in?"

"306."

"Hold on," I say, pulling my folded-up schedule from my back pocket. "I could have sworn that that's where my AP English class was meeting next period. Well, where are we supposed to go, then?"

"AP English, huh?" He smirks, ignoring my question. "Classic over-achiever." The way he says the word *overachiever* makes it sound as if it's a disease that he doesn't want to catch.

"Yeah." I hand him my schedule so he can see how full my plate will be this semester.

"Are you aware that three out of your six classes are AP courses?" he asks, his voice caked with disbelief. "Chemistry, English, *and* calculus. *And* you're taking honors civics, too?"

"What's wrong with that?"

"Nothing. It just sounds like a lot of work."

I have to laugh. "I'm number one in my class right now, so if graduation was tomorrow, I'd be walking across that stage with the valedictorian title." I see his eyebrows rise in surprise as I speak. "Valedictorians get early admissions and free rides to college, and if AP and honors classes are going to earn me that, then I'm just gonna have to suck it up and power through them, no matter how much work I have to do."

He heads back to the sink and smiles, shaking his head. "Well, aren't you something."

I'm not sure if it's a compliment, but I blush at his words anyway. Before I can think of a sassy comeback, the bell rings, commanding us to make our way across campus to the 300 building, where all English and foreign language classes are held.

"It's been a helluva day—let me just start with that," Mr. Lawrence, my AP English teacher, says, taking a deep breath as if he'd just run a mile before starting class. He rounds the front of his desk and plops down on top of it, crossing his ankles like someone waiting to be checked out by a general practitioner. "I began today thinking that I was going to be teaching five AP students after lunch each day, but, as evidenced by the number of students in here with me right now, that isn't going to be the case this semester."

Dylan must be a lot more vocal in his classes than I am because while I sit back and wait to hear the reason for the combining of two classes, his hand is the first to shoot into the air with a question. "Your backstory is nice and all, Mr. Lawrence, but can't you just tell us what happened to Ms. Harper?" It's not the way I would have worded it, but still, it's the question everyone in this room wants answered.

"She quit." A few students start to chatter at his announcement, and it isn't until he raises his hairy hands, as if surrendering, that we quiet down. "I know. I know. You were all looking forward to an easy breezy semester with the young and fun Ms. Harper, but unfortunately for you—and me, I guess—she checked her lottery tickets during third period. Apparently, she won, and immediately after, she decided that she didn't need, and I quote, 'this headache anymore.' Unquote. Now—"

"How much did she win?" It's Dylan again.

"Enough to never have to work again a day in her life." Mr. Lawrence loosens his tie a bit before continuing, obviously bothered at Dylan's incessant interruptions. "Now, as luck would have it, it just so happens that the first book you all were going to read in her class was going to be *Wuthering Heights* by Emily Brontë. The same book that my AP students were going to dive into later this semester." He raises a medium-sized, fragile-looking softcover book above his head for everyone to see. "Administration was in a bit of a tizzy over her sudden departure, so to buy them some time, I said I'd take on you guys. You will spend the first half of this semester with me, and finish it out with the new teacher they hire."

A few boys in the back—football players, judging by the patches on their letterman jackets—start a slow clap, and I have to stop myself from rolling my eyes. This was the madness I tried to get away from by taking an AP class.

"Yes, I know, I'm like Superman coming to save the day, but we have no time to waste. You two," he says, pointing to the slow-clapping boys, "pass around these books, and please, people, be careful with these. They're a little worn."

The first thing Mr. Lawrence tells us to do is pull out a notebook and put the date on the top of the page. "Now, obviously, the AP students can't do the same assignments as you English II folks. My AP angels will have to do a little more work than you guys, but there is one exercise I would like both classes to do as we read this book together. journaling. In order to elevate your thinking with this novel, I want each of you to compile a first-person journal relating to this text."

The feeling of déjà vu clouds my mind as I think back to freshman year. We had to do a journaling activity in English I, too, but obviously, with our teacher reading them at the end of each week, we couldn't be very truthful in what we wrote. Fearing that history is about to repeat itself, I raise my hand, hesitantly. "Mr. Lawrence, are you going to read these?"

"Not exactly. At the end of each week, you will submit your journals to me, and I'll check to make sure you are indeed using the ten minutes I allot at the beginning of each class to write. But no, I will not read them. If you're that worried about it, change the names, but

I can assure you, Ms. Ellenburg, there's nothing that's going on with you that I haven't seen before.

"Quite frankly," he says, running his fingers through his head of receding brown hair, "your lives are filled with way too much drama for me . . . who's going out with whom, who broke up with whom, and all of the other hormone-induced nonsense that prevents you guys from focusing on your studies. I'd lose my mind if I chose to read every one of your journal entries. God, you couldn't pay me to go through high school again." He pauses for a second, probably to recall the good and bad that happened during his high school years. After a minute, he rolls up his sleeves, claps his hands twice, and says, "All right, let's write."

Mr. Lawrence allots us only ten minutes to write in class, which I spend coming up with a recipient name. I can't just journal without a purpose; I need someone to write to. At the end of my ten minutes, I scrawl two words across the top of my page: *Dear Catherine.* Catherine Earnshaw is the protagonist in *Wuthering Heights,* so it only seems fitting to share my private thoughts with her, a complete and total fictional character.

When time is called, I close my notebook with the promise of picking this back up later at home, and I look over at Dylan's journal. With a full page of barely legible handwriting sitting before him, he flips through his copy of *Wuthering Heights.* I can't help but wonder what he chose to write about. He could have written about his life before us, but he also has many other topics to choose from: his fostering situation . . . my family . . . his first day at Cedar Pointe High . . . me.

What could he possibly have to say about you? I ask myself as I twirl a few strands of hair around my index finger. *Well, he did kinda flirt with you last night,* the voice in my mind responds. *Very true. Very true, indeed.*

I go back and forth a few more times, but when my curiosity overpowers my better judgment, I decide to sneak a peek. I lean over a little more and squint my eyes to see if I can recognize my name in his microscopic writing, but Mr. Lawrence begins teaching before I can scan my way down his page. *Maybe I'm not meant to know* is the idea I settle on.

"This novel may be a classic, but I promise you'll be surprised at just how much this book will relate to your own lives."

"Doubt it," Dylan disputes under his breath.

After reading the back cover of my copy and getting a peek at the messy love-hate relationship between Catherine and her adopted brother, Heathcliff, I have an answer of my own, too: *I hope not.*

chapter 4

W HEN THE FINAL bell rings, I rush from the gym to my car and wait for Dylan. Most of the students have already left by the time I see him exit the building with two girls in tow. I want to gag as I watch them follow behind him like a couple of puppies. They've rolled their PE shorts up so far that if they bend over, everyone within fifty feet of them will get a peep show. *Tasteful.*

After he waves good-bye and thanks them for walking him to my car, he gets in. The first thing he does is dig his hands into his pockets and pull out two handfuls of tiny slips of paper.

"You weren't kidding," he says, letting the slips fall through his fingers and into my lap. "The girls here love fresh meat."

I scoff and let out a laugh at the sexual undertones. Once I compose myself, I turn to Dylan and say, "I don't want to hear about your sexual escapades, especially on your first day here."

"As if," he wheezes, stuffing the numbers back into his pockets.

"They're pretty hot, don't get me wrong, but most are dumb as door-knobs."

"I told you," I say, cranking the engine. "So no one caught your eye?"

"One girl did, briefly, but she's off-limits."

"She's got a boyfriend, huh?" My question goes unanswered as he stares out the window. I imagine that he's daydreaming about the girl he can't have. "Yeah, most of the good ones are either taken or don't care to mess around in high school because they know it's not going to last. I, myself, fall into the second category."

"So you've never dated . . . anyone?"

"Nope." I see his thick eyebrows rise up. "Boys are not part of the plan."

" 'The plan'?"

"If I'm going to be a big-time novelist by the time I'm twenty five, there is no room for dating. It'll mess everything up. And plus, no one here is worth a second glance. At least not at our school, any-way." We ride in silence the rest of the way home until he mentions our journaling assignment in English class.

"Saw you trying to poke around in my journal during class today. Did you find what you were looking for?"

Flustered, I stutter around, trying to string a good excuse together, but his laughter cuts me off.

"I get it. I haven't exactly told you much about myself."

My thoughts exactly.

"One day, though," he says, unbuckling his seat belt after I pull into our driveway. "One day."

"Deal," is what I end up saying, but what I'm really thinking is, *What's wrong with today? Why not now?* We hop out of the car and as we walk up to the house, my dad appears at the edge of the driveway. He waves at us with a grin so large that it looks like his face is going to break if it stretches any wider.

"Hey, how was school?" At first, I think he's talking to me, but when he slaps his arm around Dylan's shoulder and walks him up the driveway, I fall back. "Come inside the garage. I have a surprise for you." *Am I being replaced already?*

I've been jealous of plenty of people before, but never at home. At school, there are hot popular kids to envy everywhere. That's normal. But not here. Our house is my safe place.

I would never resent Matthew for stealing the spotlight, mainly because it's never been something that could be stolen. We share it; that light shines on both of us all the time. Over the years, the love and praise we receive from our parents has always been split evenly between the two of us. But now that Dylan is here, I'm starting to feel that pressure behind my eyes grow as the amount of attention I get from them diminishes.

"Your very own art studio," my dad says as he opens the door. There are two easels in the center of what used to be our garage, and around that, tons of art supplies. "We haven't parked our cars in here in years due to all of the clutter. Someone might as well make use of the space, right?"

I run my fingers over the soft paintbrush bristles and smile, remembering the way Dylan's hand guided mine over the canvas at school today. The memory overtakes me for a moment, and I almost forget why I was mad a second ago.

"I got a little bit of everything. Over there, on that back wall, are your paints—acrylic, oil, *and* watercolor—and in that bin are some bags of charcoal in case you like to sketch with them. In this," he says, patting his hands on top of a blue-and-gold chest, "is pastels. I've hung some of your paintbrushes on the wall, and you have backups in those drawers over there." He crosses his hands over his chest and sighs, proud of his hard work. "You like it? The guy at the store said these were the best artsy items they had."

"Like it? This is amazing!" He wraps his arms around my father to give him a manly hug, and then circles the room to gape at the art supplies that he's been gifted.

I personally feel like my dad overdid it on the art studio, but Dylan doesn't seem to think so. The crater-like dimples in his cheeks cannot contain the warmth radiating through his body, and neither can the caramel-colored gleam in his eyes. I watch as he forces his trembling fingers into his pockets, and bites his bottom lip to hold back tears of happiness.

"Well, I'm gonna go get cleaned up now. Your mom should be here with Matthew soon, so be on the lookout."

"Thanks again, Daniel."

"Oh . . . ," my dad says as his lips press together into a slight grimace. He never lets Matthew and me call him by his first name; he finds it disrespectful. "Oh, it's nothing. I'll see you both later."

"This is crazy, right?" Dylan breathes when Dad leaves.

"Yeah. It's really cool," I say, trying to match his enthusiasm. "Complete with your own stereo system and everything."

"I know, I can't believe it."

"So, what kind of music are you going to blast to channel your artistic abilities? For some reason, I'm getting this electronic techno vibe from you. Am I right?"

"Not even close." He side-smiles. "I like classic and urban rock and roll."

"That was my second guess."

"But I probably won't be listening to much music down here. I think I paint better with conversation than with music. And speaking of painting, now we can continue your art lessons here." He grabs the two stools from the corner and then pulls on a smock before handing one to me. "You want to join me?"

His amber eyes are hard to say no to, so I give in. He walks me through the strokes that he taught me earlier and then lets me loose to try it on my own, freeing him up to get started on his own piece.

"That's perfect, but ease up on the pressure. You don't want the paint to bleed through." Turning away from his canvas, he places his hand over mine to show me the amount of pressure I should be using, and when he does, I flinch.

"No need to be scared. I don't bite." He's so close that I can smell the soap on his skin. *He smells good*, I think to myself. But then he reclaims his seat beside me and takes his scent with him, leaving only traces for me to inhale into my memory. Out of the corner of my eye, I watch as he picks up his brush to continue working on a painting of a woman with a young boy sitting on her lap. I still haven't been able to figure out how he is able to paint so fast and have his paintings turn out as beautiful as they do. At this rate, his studio will be filled with at least a hundred paintings by the time Christmas rolls around.

"Who are they?" I ask, overstepping my boundaries again.

"My mom and me."

"She's gorgeous."

"Of course she is. I mean, have you seen me? Runs in the family."

I can't stop the chuckle in my throat from escaping. "I don't think I've ever met someone who is as cognitively aware of their good looks as you are, Dylan."

"I'll take that as a compliment." His witty responses make it hard to fault him for being so vain.

"So, how long has it been since you've seen her?" I ask, trying to ease back into the conversation that I'm dying to have with him. I don't want to seem too pushy, though. His breathing already seems to be deeper and heavier than it was ten seconds ago. Nothing but silence echoes throughout the reorganized garage, and I try my best to act like it doesn't bother me. "Where is she now? Do you know?"

"I don't want to talk about this," he says, slapping his paintbrush down. I see his jaw clench and unclench again. "Just drop it. Please."

I see the hurt in his watering eyes and do as he requests. Is it wrong of me to want to know a *little* bit about him? If I were in his position, I would want to let my new family know a little about me. But he's not me.

The silence is almost too much for me to take, and I start to look for ways that I can end our painting lesson without offending him. Just then, my mom's car pulls into the driveway and I no longer need to search for an excuse. "My mom probably wants help with dinner, so I'm gonna go wash up to help her."

As I get up to hang my smock on the wall, he grabs my wrist. At first, his grip is tight, but I feel it loosen as he pulls me toward him. There's a fretful look in his eyes, like he doesn't want me to leave his side, but I know that's not the reason behind it. "I didn't mean to lash out at you. I . . . I just miss her."

I suppress the urge to ask him why he doesn't live with his mom now and secure my hands around his waist to pull him into a hug. "Whenever, if ever, you want to talk, I'm here." As his muscles wrap around my body, I feel an adrenaline rush. *Whoa! What is that?*

"I appreciate that, Emma." As I pull away from him, he tries to put on a smile, but it comes out more like a scowl. "I'll see you at dinner."

As I cross the grassy backyard, heading for my room to wash up, I can't help but wonder what that feeling in my stomach was all about when I hugged Dylan. I'm not hungry, I'm not on my period, and I don't feel sick, so I know it's not related to any of those. No, it's something else. I don't know what it was, but I've never felt something like that before and my insides are longing to feel it again.

$$\backsim \diamond \smile$$

I AM USUALLY NOT ONE TO BRING ADULTS INTO MY PROBLEMS, SIMPLY FOR the fact that I think it's a cop-out. I like to learn my own lessons, even if it means making the same mistakes over and over before I master them, so when I find myself alone with my mom after dinner, I know that this is serious.

"Mom, can I ask you something?"

"Anything." She's adjusting the temperature to make a lukewarm soap water for the dirty dishes to soak in. I expect her to think that I'm coming to her with a boy problem, because I never have before, and I know she is excited for the day that I do.

"It's about Dylan."

"What's wrong? Is everything okay?" Her eyebrows draw together with worry, and I start to question if she reacts the same way when she thinks something is wrong with me.

"He's fine. I just want to know how you guys came to fostering him." She breaks eye contact with me, and I see her swallow hard before turning her attention back to the dishwater. "Not that I don't like that he's here, but we were all expecting a little kid, right? So how did we end up with him?"

She stops in the middle of testing the water and looks at me, letting the suds run down the sides of her arms and drip onto the floor. "You want to know what happened to him before we took him in, don't you?"

"Well, yeah. I feel like we're owed that much. I mean, we *did* bring him in to stay with us. It's only fair that we know his backstory."

"Did you ask him?"

"Yeah. Kind of. But bringing it up only makes him upset. And I want to help him adjust, but it feels like he takes three steps back every time we come close to talking about his past."

"Have you stopped to ask yourself why it's so important to you? You've always told me that someone's past doesn't define them."

"Very true."

"So why does it mean so much to you to hear every little detail about his?"

I have no answer to this. His past shouldn't matter because his future with us is what's important now. "I don't know. Like I said, I guess I feel like he owes this to me. To us, I mean." Our eyes meet, and I know what she's going to say before her lips form the word. *No.*

"No. I'm not going to tell you his story just yet. It's dark, and I want him to be a little more comfortable in this house before we divulge his demons to you and Matthew."

"Oh," I say, the lightbulb going off in my head. "You don't want his past to influence how we feel about him while we're getting to know him."

"Exactly. And if I were you, I'd quit prodding. It might cause him to slip into a depressive state. He was a mess when he first entered the system, and I don't want him to relapse into that. You might want to reconsider having that conversation altogether."

"So you're saying just forget about it?"

"For now, yes. And for God's sake, Emma, it's his second day in the house. Let him get adjusted before you start digging for secrets." I see Dylan zoom around the corner, carrying Matthew on his back. They have already created a bond based on fun and laughter, and I'm still sitting here trying to play Nancy Drew with his backstory. "Start thinking of him as your brother, not some random stranger that you need to run a background check on."

After taking another look at Matthew and Dylan, I beam. "Maybe you're right."

I pocket her advice, and, after grabbing *Wuthering Heights* from my backpack, head to the pool to lounge. The California heat has cooled to a more bearable temperature, and the reflection of the sunset-colored sky on the surface of the pool has created the perfect, romantic atmosphere to read. I've read through three chapters of *Wuthering Heights* when Dylan appears by my side, wearing swimming trunks and a T-shirt.

"The writing's a bit pretentious," he says, pulling his shirt over his head in an I'm-a-sexy-lifeguard kind of way. "I mean, the story's okay, but Emily Brontë probably could have written it without using words like *vexatious* and *lachrymose*."

"Y-yeah," I manage to get out, averting my eyes as he reveals his upper body to me. The scar beneath his collarbone reminds me of our conversation on the stairs last night, and I swallow hard when I feel an uneasy warmth travel up my neck. I'm thankful for the orange glow that the sunset is casting on me; it makes the flushed color in my face harder to detect. I close my book, making sure to use my finger as a bookmark, and try to clear my throat. "You've got a point there."

"I'm just going for a swim, but don't stop reading on my account."

I reopen my book and peek over the top of it to see his muscular figure, which demands attention, standing on the edge of the diving board. "And you might want to go sit over there. This could get messy, and I don't want to hear anything about you or your precious book getting wet."

"I'm fine," I say, settling even deeper into my seat. "I've cannonballed into that pool enough times to know that I'm nowhere near the splash zone. You won't damage my 'precious book.'"

"Suit yourself. But believe me when I say that I'm an expert." Balancing on the edge of the board, he gives me a daring smirk. "CANNONBALL!" he screams, and a second later jumps into the pool, sending a rush of waves crashing down toward the feet of my lawn chair. He must know that he has failed to send the chlorine water far enough to get me wet, because when his tan, muscular frame resurfaces in the center of the sunset's reflection, he slaps at the water.

"I told you so," I shout over his splashing. "I should have had you put money on it."

I'm almost positive that he didn't have a pool in his last group home or foster home—or wherever he was living before he came into our lives—because it's as if he's regressed to the age of four and has discovered the fun of playing in the pool for the first time. He splashes and flops around theatrically. I turn my attention back to *Wuthering Heights* and tune him out. That is, until I hear him speak again.

"Emma," he gurgles with a mouthful of water as his head bobs up and down on the surface. "Emma!" I hear him scream once more as he disappears under the water.

I don't have enough time to form a coherent thought about what's going on. My mind is set on only one thing: saving him.

I underestimate how much he weighs, and it takes me almost five minutes to drag him to the shallow end and out of the water. *He could be dead by now*, I think as I lay him on his back in the grass and place my head on his chest, hoping to still hear a heartbeat.

"Please don't die, Dylan. Please don't die," I repeat as I pump his chest three times, then lift his chin and pinch the bridge of his nose.

My lips are an inch away from his when I hear him snicker and say, "God, I wish I could have gotten that on camera." It takes me a moment to realize what's going on, and when I do, my first instinct is to hit him.

"What. The hell. Is wrong. With you?" I say, slapping his defined abs. "I thought you were drowning! I almost had a heart attack!"

"You should have seen your face. 'Please don't die, Dylan! Please don't die,'" he imitates as he clutches his stomach with laughter.

"Something is wrong with you." Standing over the edge of the pool, I wring the water out of my hair and imagine that it's Dylan's neck. "Like, seriously wrong if you think that's funny."

"Oh, come on, Em. Can't you take a little joke?" he says, brushing the grass off of his back as he gets up. "I was only trying to get you to laugh. You've been distant since our painting lesson earlier."

"And with good reason. Oh, and would you look at this?" I race to the lawn chair I was just at and pick up my copy of *Wuthering Heights* from the edge of the pool, the pages dripping from the water that splashed up as I dove in to save him. "Mr. Lawrence is going to kill me."

I return to my room, plug in my hair dryer, and turn it on its highest setting before pointing it at the pages of the book. I watch the blue-inked, cursive-lettered margin notes expand into unreadable blots as the moisture settles in. The words on the delicate pages begin to dissolve next, and before long, they disappear altogether, almost as if they were never there to begin with.

"How's the book?" Dylan says, poking his head through the crack of the door. "I was going to knock, but the door was already open. How's it looking?"

"Ruined. Thanks, Dylan," I say, tossing the soggy book into the trash can and moving in front of my dresser to dig out a set of dry clothes. "I'm gonna have to get a new book for class."

"Why not just get the e-book or read it for free online?"

"Because print books are better—everyone knows that. Plus, Mr. Lawrence won't allow electronics in class. He's old-school when it comes to education."

"Damn," he whispers as I slip past him and behind the dressing screen in the corner of my room. "You can use mine for now. I know how important your schoolwork is to you, and I'll pay for another one so Mr. Lawrence doesn't eat you alive. I promise." I find it hard to stay mad at him while he's standing half-naked and dripping wet in the middle of my bedroom. "Deal?"

"Yeah. Sure." When I reappear from behind the screen, his eyes are bouncing around the walls of my room.

"Well, this is different. Much cooler than my room, I'll give you that."

"Oh. Thanks," I say, grinning. "I've always wanted a room with vintage décor, and when I moved out here, I finally got the chance to change things up."

"Complete with a vanity mirror and room divider." He stands with his hands on his waist a little longer, admiring the contents of my bedroom more before saying, "Anyways, before my incredibly stupid fake drowning joke—"

"I'm glad you see the error of your ways."

"I wanted to talk to you about what happened in the art studio earlier. Those memories affect me in a way that's hard to explain to those who don't know what happened."

"It's fine. You don't have to tell me anything if you don't want to. I was being overly insistent earlier, anyway. I'm sorry."

I look up to see his piercing brown eyes locked on mine as if I'm a target that he's trying to throw a spear through. "They were your eyes, do you know that?"

"What?"

"In the painting at school today? They were your eyes."

"Oh, I know. And I'm quite flattered that you chose me to be your muse. I didn't think you liked me that much. But then again, I haven't been the most welcoming family member."

"Why wouldn't I? You're beautiful and smart. Any guy would be lucky to have you in his life." Our eyes lock again, and this time, I don't look away. I let myself get lost in his words and the side-smile that he's wearing. "As a sister, I mean."

"I know." *Why would I expect you to think of me in any other way? That would be wrong. Wouldn't it?* "I mean . . . thanks."

"You're never going to die now. You'll live forever."

"Huh?" I ask, tilting my head to the side in the quizzical way I used to do when I was a child. "What do you mean?"

"I mean, physically, you will die. That's inevitable. But spiritually speaking, you can't die. If you ever become the muse of a writer or artist, you can never die. Well, at least that's what my mom used to tell me." He grins to himself as if he can hear her voice in his head, repeating the words he just said to me. "A piece of you will live forever in their art, touching whoever it comes in contact with. You can never die."

"That's beautiful," I breathe, so low that I can barely hear it myself.

His words are so abstract and philosophical that I find myself wondering if he's a poet, too. When I bring myself back to reality, I see his bronze eyes staring into mine again. It feels as if he's trying to pry into my soul by sheer force of eye contact.

There he goes again, I think to myself. Is he trying to see how long I can go before I cave and have to look away? Or does he just enjoy looking into my eyes? Or maybe it's simpler than that. Maybe he just likes to have staring contests. Whatever the reason, I don't want him to stop doing it. The intensity is a high.

I'm the one who breaks contact first, and I let my eyes fall to the circular scar just above his left pec. My hand reacts too fast for me to stop it, and before I know it, my fingertips outline the circle of smooth skin. "What happened there?"

"I got shot."

"Okay, that's enough jokes for one night. Have you not learned your lesson from the pool incident?"

"I'm serious."

I give him a look to test his statement.

"For real this time! But it's a long story, and since I don't want to be blamed for ruining your book *and* your antique carpet, I'll have to tell you another time." The *squish-squish* of the carpet beneath his feet distracts me enough to take my eyes away from his bullet wound. "Well, I'll see you tomorrow."

"Good night, Dylan. And, I look forward to hearing that story."

"Yeah. Good night, Emma." He lingers for a little while longer, like he wants to say something more, and that's when I feel it: a series of flutters in the pit of my stomach. I think back to the magazines I used to read religiously when I was twelve and pinpoint the feeling. Butterflies. With the thought fresh on my mind, I race to my journal and open it to the page I began in class today.

Dear Catherine,

I can't believe this is all I was able to get down in class today. Then again, if I'd written more earlier, I wouldn't have this blank page to unpack what just happened between Dylan and me. So, job well done, Emma.

It's only Tuesday, the second day of my supposed-to-be-simple senior year, and I already have a huge problem. You see, my parents decided to foster this boy, Dylan, and we're the exact same age. At first I wasn't too excited about the whole thing—we even had a bit of a disagreement on his first night—but now, things have . . . changed. Let me get this out of the way now: he's very easy on the eyes. And speaking of eyes, he has these chocolate-brown, puppy dog ones that make my insides crawl when they meet mine. It's all kind of crazy.

Flirting was never a talent of mine, but there have been moments in the past two days when he looked at me, and I started to . . . feel . . . something for him. Not something sisterly, but something else. Something more. Something like I've never felt before. I get nervous, and tongue-tied, and I start to sweat in places I didn't think I was even able to sweat. And just now, he was standing in my room, and when he said my name, I swear I felt my stomach do somersaults.

I think . . . I think I might like him. I mean, that

would explain why I can barely go a couple hours without thinking about him and why I'm so obsessed with learning about his past. I think I'm . . . attracted to him. Now, I'm hardly an expert on the rules of foster siblinghood, but I'm almost certain we can't date. It's unacceptable . . . and improper . . . and a crime? At least I think it's a crime. Wait . . . no. Not a crime, but definitely unethical. There are rules against this kind of thing, right? Right?!

I'm not sure what's going on with me—for all I know, this is just some weird phase brought on by reading this book—but it looks like it's going to be an interesting senior year. I'll be sure to keep you posted on everything.

 Emma

chapter 5

"I KNOW THIS ISN'T going to make up for not having the physical book in front of you," Dylan says, handing me a CD when he arrives at my car after school the next day, "but it will allow you to keep up until I can buy you another book. The CD's a little retro, but after seeing your room I don't think that'll be a problem for you. Plus, I think you might enjoy the different voices."

My heart almost jumps out of my chest when I see him approach. Last night, the caseworker faxed my parents the paperwork for Dylan to get his license, and in order to take the driver's test, he had to miss class today. Somehow he found a way to make it back to school for the last two class periods of the day, though. I try my best to hide the smile on my face, but the closer he walks toward me, the harder it is to conceal my excitement at his proximity to me. "What is it?"

"It's the audio version of *Wuthering Heights*. They were out of physical copies—I guess this book really is a hot commodity—but I figured this would be better than nothing, especially since you're allergic to e-books."

"How sweet of you. Thanks." I grin, taking the thin plastic case from him. When I do, my fingertips caress the inside of his hand, sending a surge of static electricity through my body. It's so little contact, but even those short seconds of us connecting is enough to hold me over until the next time we touch. "So, how'd your driver's test go?"

"See for yourself." He pulls his wallet out of his front pocket and nonchalantly hands his license to me as if I'm a club bouncer asking for ID. In the picture, his face swells with excitement until it can't stretch any wider.

"You passed? That's great!" I hold back my urge to wrap my arms around his shoulders and give him a hug, so I search my backpack for my car keys to distract myself.

"Yeah, and do you know what would be a great congratulatory gift?" Dumbfounded, I flip my hair over my shoulder and wait for the response I know is coming. "To let me drive your car home today."

"I don't know, Dylan. This car is my baby. No one else has ever even sat behind the wheel."

"All the more reason to try something new." Again, his dimples make me melt like a Popsicle in the middle of summer, and I have no choice but to hand my keys over.

I keep trying to convince myself that this is a good idea as we zip out of the school parking lot, but when I see the speedometer inch higher and higher, I have to say something. "Don't you think you should slow down? You're going forty in a thirty, you know?"

"We'll be okay," he says, meeting my eyes as we zoom by another car.

"Are you crazy? Keep your eyes on the road!" I yell, motioning to the bikers in front of us, though in the back of my mind, I don't want him to stop looking at me. "Please try your hardest not to hit anyone. I'd love a casualty-free afternoon."

"Yes, Mommy Dearest," he laughs. "And I suppose next you're gonna tell me to put on my seat belt."

"You're not wearing a seat belt?!" I reach over him to pull the belt across his waist, struggling to not seem as if I'm fondling him; though, with my nerves all over the place, I'm sure I'm failing miserably.

"Emma Ellenburg," he gasps, peeking in my direction. "We just met a few days ago—not to mention, I'm your foster brother—and you're trying to undo my pants? And while driving, no less? I am appalled at this kind of reckless behavior, young lady." He bursts out laughing, causing us to swerve just a little bit.

"You're unbelievable." When I hear the belt click into place, I sit back in my seat and fold my arms across my chest, hoping that the burning sensation in my cheeks isn't here to stay.

"I know. Sometimes I amaze myself." He puts on his left turn signal, cuts off yet another driver, and takes a hard right into a parking lot. I want to tell him something about his improper use of a signal—he should use the right one, not the left, to merge right—but I opt to keep my mouth shut. He's only going to shove his license in my face as proof that he can indeed drive, though I'm a bit doubtful. "I hear this place has the best frozen yogurt in town. I guess we'll see."

I know all about the Silver Spoon and the famous frozen yogurt they sell beyond the doors of the pink, lime-green, and orange building before me. My family and I used to come here all the time after my softball games, and although it was only a few years ago, it feels like it's been much longer than that since I've set foot inside this place.

When we enter, the girl at the front counter perks up a bit. She throws back her shoulders and arches her back as she leans over the counter. "Welcome to the Silver Spoon! Just let me know if you want to sample anything." I know that her hospitable tone is meant for the both of us, but by the way she bites her bottom lip and flutters her eyelashes at Dylan, I can tell that she's a lot more interested in assisting him than me.

"This one's on me," Dylan whispers, handing me a bowl and then turning to the girl. With a glimmer in his eye and a half smile across his pouty lips, he asks, "Can I taste the vanilla bean flavor, please?" Suddenly I don't feel so special anymore. Obviously, he smiles at all girls like that, not just me. I wipe the look of disappointment off my face and begin to pull the levers of the yogurt machines.

While I finish making and topping mine in under three minutes, Dylan takes almost ten minutes to perfect his creation, rotating between the yogurt dispensers and the toppings bar several times. When he finally makes it to the counter to pay, mine is already half melted.

"Together, right?" the girl at the counter asks, frowning.

"Yeah." For a sliver of a second, a wide smile appears on my face. His answer makes it seem as if we are a couple. But Dylan recognizes this, too, and adds a bit of clarification. "The yogurt, I mean. She's my foster sister, so obviously, we can't date."

"Gotcha. Your total is ten seventy-six." While waiting for the payment, she looks Dylan up and down, the lust in her eyes returning. "I've never seen you around here. Are you new? I'm Vanessa, but everyone calls me Nessa."

"Pleasure to meet you, Nessa. I'm Dylan," he flirts back, grabbing her hand just like he did mine at our first meeting.

My eyes burn with envy as I watch Dylan charm his way into Nessa's heart right in front of me. To spare myself from even more heartache, I retreat to one of the outside tables as he hands her a couple of bills to cover our total.

"What was all that about?" I ask when he joins me, trying to sound more like a genuinely curious sibling than a jealous wannabe girl-friend.

"Nothing." After setting his bowl of yogurt down, he slides his receipt across to me. "Tell me what's wrong with this."

I admire the scrap of paper for a second and then look up to meet his gaze. "There's no way she's that dumb. There's just no way," I say, suppressing my urge to thrust a fist into the air. Suddenly, I don't feel so threatened by the girl anymore. The note reads, *If you ever need a special friend*, followed by *248–633*. "How do they expect her to run the cash register if she can't even count out seven numbers to give to someone?"

"Your guess is as good as mine." He throws his head back and laughs, revealing the perfectly white molars in the back of his mouth. "I guess I'll add this one to the growing stack of hell-no's I've got at home."

His comment reminds me of how popular he is among the girls at school. Not because of his smarts or his painting, but because of his glowing amber eyes, male-model smirk, and thin-but-muscular frame. When changing into my PE uniform for sixth period, I now have to pretend I don't hear the way the other girls talk about how much they love being around him and listening to his laugh, and how badly they want to run their fingers through his hair and kiss him until their lips grow chapped. It's nauseating to know that at any moment, he can choose one of them and break my heart into a million pieces.

"Well, in her defense," I offer, pushing those thoughts from my mind, "you did take thirty minutes to make your yogurt. She may have gotten all hot and bothered while watching you brew your concoction and forgotten a number."

"I did not take thirty minutes."

"Okay, twenty."

"Five."

"Ten. And I'm not going any lower."

"Okay, Drew Carey." He laughs. I pull my spoon from its plastic wrapper, and I'm mid-first-bite when he sticks his hand in front of my face. "What are you doing?"

"What does it look like I'm doing? I'm eating my fro-yo."

"But, you're missing out on the best part," he says, removing the wrapper from his spoon. "We have to taste each other's creation and rate it on a scale of one to ten. Winner gets five bucks." Before I can ask any questions, he's digging his spoon into my bowl.

"Hey!" I whine as I take a spoonful from his bowl and bring it to my lips. The vanilla bean yogurt melts in my mouth as I turn the sweet flavors over on my tongue. "Eight. The banana bits are a nice touch, but you should have added some whipped cream on top of it."

"I'll give it to you, Blondie," he says, licking his spoon. "Eight and a half. Adding strawberries and blueberries to the cheesecake-flavored one? Genius." He smiles at me again, this time revealing his gorgeous dimples.

"Thank you." Now I'm beaming. Since the first time I saw them, his dimples have always been a weak point of mine. "Can I change my prize?"

"It's contingent upon what you want." He raises his eyebrows in anticipation.

Impressed by his correct usage of the word *contingent*, I lick the back of my spoon and ask, "How about a round of Twenty-Any-Questions instead?" The crinkle in his eyebrows clues me in on the fact that he's unfamiliar with the game, just as I was with his taste-testing ritual a moment ago. "Ten questions each. Twenty total. And other than the topics we establish as off-limits at the beginning of the game, you get to ask anything you want."

With his spoon hanging halfway out of his mouth, he takes a minute to consider the trade before finally saying, "I feel like I'm going to regret this later, but okay. My off-limits topic is my family. Go there, and I'm done with this game of yours."

"Fine. No limitations for me. I'm an open book."

He spoons yogurt into his mouth and leans back in his seat, waiting for the first question. "Ladies first."

"What's your middle name?"

"Alexander." *Dylan Alexander McAndrews.* It sounds regal, as if he should be part of an imperial family somewhere.

"Birthday?"

"April tenth. Greatest date of all time."

"Okay, I'm going to kick it up a notch. What is your calling in life?"

"Come on. Challenge me a little, Em." *Em.* I like the little nickname he has given me. "Obviously, I want to be a famous artist one day."

"That one *was* supposed to be a challenge. Are you sure it wasn't?"

"Not even in the least. I've known what I want to be since I was ten years old." He stuffs a spoonful of yogurt into his mouth, but not before reminding me how many questions we've burned through. "And that was question number four, by the way."

"Shoot." *Don't let his big brown eyes distract you, Emma,* I pep talk inside my head. *Stay focused.* I find it hard to ask him questions when there's so much I want to know about him regarding his feelings toward me. I'm not one of his off-limits topics, but still, I don't want to push the envelope. "Okay, how about this one: Who's your celebrity crush?"

"Five." He's taken to using his fingers to keep track of my questions, and I find it rather odd that he can comprehend dense works, such as *Wuthering Heights*, but still needs to count on his fingers for something as simple as this. "Selena Gomez. She's so hot."

We speed through the next few questions, where I learn that if he could eat only one food for the rest of his life, it would be pepperoni pizza; that his biggest pet peeve is when people improperly use the word *literally* for things that are, in fact, not literal; and that he name-dropped to get a passing score on his driver's license test today.

"My proctor was in the middle of penalizing me for my crappy parallel parking, which was going to cost me my license. But that was before she saw me wave to your dad. 'That's my foster dad, Daniel Ellenburg,' I told her as we got out of the car. I guess she recognized him because she asked me if I could get her an autograph once we walked back up to the DMV. I agreed, and the next thing I knew, I was standing in front of a blue backdrop, taking my license photo."

"Life just isn't fair," I whisper, taking another bite of yogurt. I had to take the test three times before I was awarded my license, and to hear that all it took to pass was a name-drop makes my chest burn with resentment.

Dylan holds up nine fingers in front of my face and grins mischievously. "Okay, Em. You're down to your last question. Better make it count." He winks at me, and I feel my pulse pick up.

Ask it, the voice in my head hisses. *You know you want to.* "Do you think I'm pretty?"

"Pretty? No," he says frankly, getting up to throw his now-empty bowl away. Out of disappointment, my heart rate begins to decline back down to its regular hum, the electricity in my fingertips now gone. I'm a second away from shooting back a cunning retort when he reclaims his seat beside me. He's so close that I can see my own reflection in his amber irises and feel the warmth emanating from his body. "You're more like mesmeric. Resplendent. Heart-stopping. Captivating."

I open my mouth to say thank you, but nothing comes out. I mean, what am I supposed to say to follow that? Nothing. Nothing I say can match his level of flattery, so I just sit and smile. My mother taught me that not everything needs a response. Sometimes the simplest way to tell someone that you appreciate their words or actions is to smile, which I can't stop myself from doing now.

"I'm obviously reading too much *Wuthering Heights*. So much that Emily Brontë—and her lavish language—just took over my body," he confesses as a rosy color rises at the base of his neck. "It's getting late. I'll ask you my questions on the ride home. That okay?"

Anything you want, I swoon inside my head. But what comes out is "Yep. Sounds good."

A BRAND-NEW BLACK CAMARO IS SITTING IN OUR DRIVEWAY WHEN WE arrive home, and it's pretty obvious who it belongs to, as Matthew is too young to drive, I already have a car, and my mother and father just purchased new vehicles last summer. Leaning on the trunk of the shiny, sleek automobile, my mom waits, twirling the keys around her right pointer finger.

"Wait, you still have two questions left," I scream through the window when Dylan jumps out before my car can even stop rolling. But he doesn't hear me. Too much excitement, I guess.

By the time I pull the key from the ignition and get out of my car, Dylan is already behind the wheel of his, disturbing the peace as he revs his engine. "We bought this car so you don't have to rely on others to get around. I know how busy Emma gets with school, and I want you to have another means of transportation. But just because you have this car doesn't mean that you are allowed to break curfew. It's still ten o'clock as usual," my mom shouts over the noise.

"Yes, Mrs. Ellenburg," Dylan says, turning on the radio. I find it strange that he calls my mom Mrs. Ellenburg and my dad Daniel, but Dylan seems to be the king of oddities, so maybe this is just another one of his quirks.

"I'm serious, Dylan," my mom emphasizes with pointy eyebrows and wrinkles in her forehead. "Break curfew, and you'll be back to riding with Emma."

What's wrong with that? I ponder, secretly wanting him to come home late so I don't have to wait too long for his soap-and-paint scent to fill my car once more.

"Once or twice around the block, Emma?" Dylan begs from the front seat.

"I have homework to finish," I say, trying not to sound too eager to be alone with him, though there's nothing I want more right now. "But once around the block won't put me behind too much."

With my mother still watching, Dylan fastens his seat belt as I slide into the passenger's seat. "Be back shortly," he says to her.

"Okay. Be safe."

We ride in awkward silence for a few seconds before he glances at me, his toothy grin almost too big for his face. "I can't believe your parents bought me this car."

"Me neither." The words come out flat and caked in jealousy, but I don't mean for them to. I just don't know how to handle my parents spoiling this relative stranger. "First an art studio and now a brand-new car. I wonder what they'll get you next."

Amused, he shakes his head in disbelief. "Most foster kids don't get their license, let alone their own car, and your parents made both of those things happen in one day. Unreal."

"So, the people you were with before us . . . they didn't want you to get your license?"

"Nope. And even though the social worker was fine with it, they were afraid that I'd use it to run away. I don't blame them, though. That's how foster kids are portrayed on TV—as if all we care about is rebelling against the system and getting back to our 'normal' lives, whatever that means." Dylan goes quiet for a moment, and I'm not sure if it's because he needs time to concentrate on his driving or if he's just deep in thought. "But I'd never do that. Not with you guys, any-way. You're the best thing that's happened to me in a long time. I mean, look at this car!"

"Yeah, it's pretty amazing. My parents must really like you."

He smiles back.

"Hey," Dylan says, "I still have two questions left, don't I?" He taps his right pointer finger on his lips as he glances over at me. "What should I ask you?"

"Well, you've already asked me about my favorite food, color, and place to go when I'm feeling sad—"

"Grilled lemon and thyme chicken, purple, and the balcony with a good book, if I remember correctly."

"Spot-on. Now how about something a little deeper? There's gotta be something you're dying to know about me, right?"

He turns down his music—I guess so it's quiet enough to think of a question—and he snaps his fingers when he reaches a good one. "What is your greatest fear?"

My first thought is to say that I'm afraid of the dark—which, even though I'm sixteen years old, is the complete and honest truth—but then I think of his big brown eyes and my mind goes blank except for one thing: him. "Not being good enough. Rejection, really." *By you*, I want to add, but don't.

He scoffs at my answer, and I swallow hard to cover up the fact that I'm hurt by his reaction. "Are we talking with guys, or colleges, or something else?"

Brushing over the fact that he just asked his tenth and final question, I take a deep breath and divulge my vulnerabilities. "Both."

"I'm listening."

"I'm not the kind of girl who gets invited to parties every weekend or has a ton of guys chasing after her. Yes, I'm blond, but I'm hardly a social creature, and that seems to turn them off of me. Guys. Or, at least, that's what I've spent the last four years trying to convince myself of. That that's the reason they see right through me." By the time I get through my rant, we've already made it back to the house. Dylan doesn't go for the second lap around the block like he'd originally planned. Instead, he pulls into the driveway and shuts off the engine, but for some reason, he can't meet my eyes. "Love sucks at this age," I continue. "You're either too much this or not enough of that. You can never be just enough. Then again, I guess that shouldn't matter, anyway. With college apps staring me in the face and my future so uncertain right now, I'm probably better off single."

With his hands still at ten and two on the wheel, he stares blankly at the garage door before us. "So what I'm hearing is that you like someone, or someone likes you, and you aren't sure if it's worth pursuing because of the time-sensitivity of your senior status, and this . . . idea . . . that you think that he thinks you're invisible. Am I right?"

Eleven. "I-I never said I liked someone."

"But you do, right?" It's then that his eyes pry into mine, opening the cage of butterflies in my stomach.

Yes. Twelve. "You'd know if I did."

He doesn't pursue the matter any further, but I can tell he doesn't believe me; I don't even believe me, and I'm the one telling the lie. For all I know, he's completely aware that I like him and just wants to see how far I can bend before I break down and tell him. But if he does know, he sure doesn't let it show.

"He must be one hell of a guy if he's got you thinking about breaking your no-dating rule."

He is, I want to tell him as I unbuckle my seat belt. *You are.*

chapter 6

T HE FIRST TWO weeks of school fly by, and when dance team audi-
tions finally roll around, I've not only pulled out a tuft of my
hair at the roots, but I've also bitten my nails down so far that I had to
get fake ones put on just to make them presentable for tryouts. This
Dylan madness has commanded my every thought—both waking and
dreaming—but after the come-to-Jesus moment I had with myself this
morning about him being my foster—and possibly future—brother, I
know that I have to stay away. His tawny eyes and dimples are going
to be hard to resist, but it's the right thing to do.

I block all thoughts of Dylan from my mind and focus on getting
through my dance team tryout. With the worst part of the audition
behind me—the complex turn-and-leap sequences, and the grueling
flexibility tests—I have to stay cool and hope that everything I gave
was enough to make the cut.

This kind of commitment is exactly what I need so I don't have to be home with Dylan all of the time. What I'm feeling is twisted, and I know that the easiest way to put an end to it is to join the dance team. Also, I need to find someone else to crush on.

"The list is up, girls," a woman says as she exits the gym. She's going to be the coach, but I haven't committed her name to memory yet. "Congratulations to those of you who made the team this year, and I encourage everyone else to try out again next year." Her words go in one ear and out the other; this is it for me. It's now or never.

I have to fight my way through the crowd of rabid contenders around the bulletin board. I close my eyes and say a silent prayer before looking at the sheet of paper. *Please let me make the team. Please let me make the team.*

I scan the list and find my name at the bottom. *I made it.*

"I made it!" I scream, wrapping my arms around a stranger who also made the cut.

"Congratulations," I hear Karmin Ortega say from behind me. "I knew you'd make it. You have the best turns I've seen in a while. Well, besides mine, of course."

Thanks, I guess. "Thanks." I glance at the clock outside the gym. It's almost five thirty. "I've got to run, but our first practice is on Monday, right?"

"Yeah. Well, kind of," she says, leaning in closer so that only I can hear her. "It's our fitting session. We're getting new uniforms, but don't tell anyone. It's supposed to be a surprise." *Who am I going to tell? It's not like I have any friends.*

"Okay. I'll be there." I wave her off and dance my way to the parking lot. I finally have a foot in the door to popularity; better late than never.

As soon as I get home, I race to the pool house. We have our first follow-up meeting with a social worker to assess Dylan's adjustment to living here, and my mom and dad will kill me if I present as anything less than perfect. I don't want to come off too casual, so I slip into the dress my mom wanted me to wear on the first day of school. It's not too revealing and not too juvenile, but a sensible mix of both.

Play it cool tonight, I tell myself as I finish straightening my hair. *Just be normal*. Be normal? How am I supposed to do that when I haven't stopped thinking about Dylan every day for the past two weeks. My eyes shift to the laptop lying at the foot of my bed. How am I supposed to act normal when I spent two hours last night brainstorming how to combine our names into a cute couple name? (I landed on Emmylan, rather than Dylemma, because that's just painfully obvious.)

"Emma," my dad's voice booms over the intercom, almost stopping my heart. "It's time."

When I enter the kitchen, I see that everyone is in jeans, looks like this was more casual than I thought. My mom's eyes widen when she spots me. She's probably also wondering what the hell is going on.

"And this is our daughter, Emma," she says to the social worker. "She and Dylan go to the same school and have become quite close over the past two weeks."

I meet eyes with the dark-skinned woman in the pantsuit, and I feel like I'm under inspection. I try to calm my nerves, but when I open my mouth to speak, everything comes out so fast that I'm not even sure I know what I said to the woman. "Not *that* close. I mean, how close are brothers and sisters these days, anyway? We fight all the time. Watch this: Dylan, I hate you."

"Hate you too, Em." Dylan smiles from across the room, where he and Matthew are playing a game of Go Fish.

"She's only joking," my father says, dragging me away from the woman. "Why don't we all sit down for dinner? Tonight we're having steak, baked potatoes, and a tossed salad."

"Sounds good," she says, laughing at my antics.

"Come on, boys. Let's eat." My mom's tone is almost saccharine. She doesn't have to, but I can tell she's laying on the lovability extra thick tonight.

As my dad races to the grill to pull off the steaks, I take my seat across from Matthew, and of course, Dylan takes the seat next to me.

"Nice dress," he snickers in a voice so low that only I can hear. "How nice of you to get dressed up for little ol' me."

"Shut up." I pass the salad bowl to him and prepare myself for a tough night. I mean, my mom and dad are already looking at me as if I'm a psych ward runaway.

I don't say much during dinner. I let my parents, Dylan, and the social worker do most of the talking. This is definitely my best bet, after the performance I gave upon arrival.

"So how are things going at school?" The woman, whose name is so long and complicated that I'd rather not use it at all, has already worked her way through Dylan's feelings about his new home life, and moves on to a new topic.

"School's school," he says after swallowing a piece of his steak. "But I'm thinking about joining art club. The other artists are pretty cool, and I spend most of my time in the art room anyway, so I might as well."

"That's great. I saw some of the pieces you did at your group home, and I'm happy to hear that your love for art hasn't changed over the years." I perk up a bit when she says this. Maybe I'm going to get the scoop on Dylan's old life right now, without having to ask. "And how about you? Are you involved with anything at school?" It takes me a second to realize that she's talking to me; I haven't had a question directed toward me all night.

"I was going to tell you all later, but I made the dance team today." I glow from the inside out as the words leave my lips.

"What happened to tennis?" my dad questions me from the other end of the table. I know he's trying to keep his cool in front of the social worker, but I detect a hint of agitation in his voice. A hint that wants to know why I've decided to quit yet another activity.

"I've been trying to find a way to tell you, but I'm tired of playing tennis. And I've only won a few matches, so I might as well give it up and move on to something that I'm actually good at." I see a small grin slide across Dylan's face. *What's so funny? I'm being serious here.* "I gave up on that about a month ago, and I wanted to find something else to keep me busy. You know, besides college apps." *College apps? Why, oh why, did I bring that up? Here comes the UCLA advertorial again.*

"From what I remember, UCLA's application didn't take too much of my time." *Here we go. Somebody, please step in and change the subject.*

"Well, we're behind you one hundred percent, honey," my mom cuts in before my dad's head explodes. "I can't wait to see you dance at the football and basketball games."

"Yeah!" Matthew agrees, throwing both his hands in the air in a goofy dance.

Following Matthew's lead, everyone congratulates me at the same time, including my dad, even though I know he doesn't want to. I'm so focused on how good it feels to be back in their spotlight for the moment that I don't notice when Dylan leans over to hug me until it's happening.

"Congrats, Em." He's so close that I can smell the soap on him again. It smells woodsy—manly, yet clean. *God, why does he have to smell so good?*

"Thanks. These steaks are awesome. You helped Dad cook them, right?" I ask, turning the conversation away from me. I've had enough attention for the night.

Dinner continues with light conversation, and once we all say our goodbyes to the social worker, I feel like I can breathe again. I retire to my room and let out a sigh of relief. "It's over."

"Yes, it is," Dylan says as he enters my room. He hasn't been in here since that day he fake-drowned. "Do you always leave that door unlocked? You're pretty much asking for a burglar to come in here and kidnap you."

"Burglars don't kidnap, they steal," I say, using my feet to fling my shoes across the room.

"Well, technically, kidnappers steal people."

"Hmm. I guess you're right." A chuckle escapes me, and it's then I realize that I haven't laughed all night.

"There's that beautiful smile of yours. Where was that tonight? You looked like a Barbie doll, but your personality was gone." He sits down on my bed—closer to me than I expect him to—and I feel the butterflies in my stomach take flight.

"Apprehensive, I guess."

"Big-word points."

I let out a small chuckle. "Thanks, but yeah. I just don't want them to take you away."

"Nah. Something really bad has to happen for them to take me away." I focus on his lips as he speaks, and the longer I do, the louder the voice in my head commands, *Kiss him, Emma! Kiss him!* It's what I want so badly, but I'm not ready to die of embarrassment just yet. I know he doesn't feel the same way about me. "So you hate me, huh?"

"No." I giggle as I pull my hair into a messy ponytail. "I can't even begin to tell you what all of that was about."

"Humor me." He turns to me, his tawny eyes smiling, as if he wants to hear the story. I try to hold back my urge to kiss him, but against my better judgment, I end up leaning in anyway.

I close my eyes, but only slightly so I can see my way to his lips. I know that's what I'm supposed to do, because in every movie that I've watched, everyone closes their eyes a little. I pucker my lips, expecting to make contact with his. For a second, I think he's going to lean in as well, but he doesn't. Instead, he turns his head so that my lips catch the side of his cheek. When he realizes what has just happened, he gets up and puts his hands on top of his head. He doesn't even look at me when he speaks; he just keeps his eyes on the ground between us.

"I just wanted to, um, say good night." He has a confused look on his face, and I feel like I can hear him asking himself if that really just happened. "And now that I have, I'm gonna go take a shower. Good night," he says again without looking back.

Oh. My. God. I want to die, I think, grabbing my journal from my nightstand.

Dear Catherine,

I did something really, really stupid tonight. I KISSED Dylan. I know. I messed up. But I took one look into his big brown eyes and lost all of my control. There we were, sitting on the edge of my bed after what I considered to be a successful dinner with the social worker, and I just leaned in . . . and ran straight into a wall of rejection. I'm so embarrassed, I just want to disappear. God should strike me dead now and have me reincarnated as a rock. Nobody likes rocks. Little kids kick them, and bulldozers roll over them. They should just make me a rock, and call it a D-A-Y.

I mean, what am I doing? This is not me. This is not part of the plan. I don't do things like this. What is happening to me, Catherine? I need to figure this out before I completely lose my mind and any relationship with my foster brother all at once.

 Emma

chapter 7

THE FOLLOWING WEEK is filled with enough uncomfortable encounters to last me a lifetime. On Monday, I tripped up the school's front stairs when I saw him heading down the other side. On Wednesday, I unintentionally doodled our initials inside a heart on an English assignment that I turned in to the (thankfully) oblivious Mr. Lawrence. On top of that, with the wrench my kissing ambush threw into the middle of our budding connection, every family dinner and outing felt like a thousand bee stings.

"What do you think? Can you fix it?" I ask on Friday morning, tightening the towel around my body as my dad investigates my shower drain. Without my glasses or contacts, I have to squint to see the numbers on the clock in my bedroom. "It's already seven o'clock, and I'm going to be late for school."

"It's too early in the morning for your whining. I haven't even had my cup of coffee yet," my dad scolds, pulling something long, green, and stringy from the gutter. *Gross*.

"I know, and I appreciate that you're doing this for me, but I really need the shower to work." My buttering up doesn't go over as well as I anticipate because he doesn't even acknowledge my words.

"How many times have I told you to clean out this drain, Emma?" Asking him for assistance is one of the most torturous things I can ever do to myself; lectures and help always come as a package deal.

"I don't know, Dad. Probably a hundred."

"Yeah, because the last time I cleaned it, I pulled so much hair out of it that if I strung it all together, I could make a blond wig." He stands up, puts his hands on his hips, and shakes his head. I know what he's going to say before the words even come out. He can't fix it. Not right now, anyway. "I'm gonna have to go to the store after my run and buy a shower snake for this."

"Well, what am I supposed to do until then? School starts in an hour, and I haven't even taken my shower yet."

"Now, this is a bit of a stretch," he says, laying the sarcasm on really thick, "but maybe—just maybe—you can use one of the showers in the main house." It's completely involuntary, but a disgusted look crawls across my face in response. "What? You used to shower in our house all the time before Dylan got here. It'll be just like old times."

That's just it, I want to tell him. *A lot has changed since Dylan stepped into our house three weeks ago.* "Fine. But will you have it fixed before I come home today?" I bat my eyelashes at him as if that's going to make him get the job done faster, but I know it won't make a difference.

"I will try my hardest, sweetheart." He hands me my shower tote, which holds two different shampoos and conditioners, several shower gels, one bottle of scented lotion, and a brand-new stick of deodorant. "No wonder you always smell like a perfume store when you come out of the shower. You have about thirty different smells in that basket." I roll my eyes and push past him in response. "Have a great day, honey."

I wave him off and tiptoe across the lawn before attacking the stairs two at a time, making sure to hold on to my towel tight. When I finally reach the bathroom door at the top of the staircase, I grab hold of the doorknob and turn. I'm already imagining the steaming waters dripping down my body, cleansing every bit of stress from my system, when I run headfirst into Dylan, who has nothing but a towel wrapped around his lower body.

"Dylan," I choke, almost dropping my shower tote in our collision. His still-wet skin glistens in the bathroom lighting, and I have to look down at the floor to keep my eyes from roaming over his hairless, muscular chest. "Sorry, I didn't know anyone was in here."

"What are you doing over here?" he asks, raising a hand towel to his dripping face.

Um, I live here, too, remember?

"My shower . . . it, um . . . There's something wrong with the, um . . . um . . . It's not working." Unmoving, he stares at me, his eyes glancing over every inch of the little bit of skin I have exposed. When the awkward air between us becomes too heavy to avoid, I speak again, hoping that this time, I can complete the thought. "Can I use the . . . ?" *Nope. Full sentences are not an option right now.*

"Yeah. It's all yours." He brushes past me, and when I catch a whiff of him, my stomach drops as if I'm free-falling without a parachute.

My shower doesn't relax me like I hoped it would. When I rinse the suds from my body and wash the shampoo from my hair, my heart races with the thought that Dylan was just doing the same thing right here, in this same tub, not too long ago.

"Can somebody tell me what time it is?" I yell through the bathroom door as I towel-dry my hair in front of the mirror.

"Seven nineteen," Dylan replies, his voice floating through my ears. I kick things into high gear upon hearing the time, and once my hair is dry enough not to drip all over the carpet, I exit the bathroom, hoping to get one more glance at Dylan before making the journey back to the pool house.

"All finished?" he asks, fiddling with some of the buttons on his shirt. "I gotta brush my teeth."

"I'm all done." *Good job, Emma. You're back to speaking in actual complete sentences.*

"Great." He bends over to tie his shoes, and I take a moment to admire his outfit. As on any other day, he's wearing jeans, but instead of a graphic T-shirt, he has on a blue-and-black plaid polo with the sleeves pushed up to expose his strong forearms. Thanks to the moisture from his shower, the tiny hairs around the edges of his face twist and curl around each other, screaming for the attention of a brush. And even with his hair out of place, he's still so irresistible to me.

"Is that a new shirt?" I smile, small but genuine.

"Yeah. Your mom bought it for me."

"Looks good."

"Thanks." The awkward tension between us returns, and it's so tangible that it feels like a slap in the face as he dismisses me without another word.

You really messed up, Emma. I pout, descending the stairs. The thought that he's probably never going to talk to me again crosses my mind, and that's when the panic sets in. *I have to fix things between us.*

⌘

DYLAN CONTINUES TO AVOID ME FOR THE REMAINING WEEK OF SEPTEMBER, and it isn't until our family takes a trip to the mall to see a movie (per Matthew's special request) that he makes an effort to say anything to me.

"How's your weekend been? Anything new?" At first I'm confused, but I have to stay as cool as he is, so I brush over it.

"It's been okay. I've had a boatload of schoolwork to do, so that's kept me busy most of the time." I know he's just forcing conversation to make me feel better about him being so distant lately, but I can't help feeling like a pity project. He's probably sorry for me and is just hoping that this attempt at small talk will bring us back to where we were before the kiss.

We're supposed to be on our way to the movie theater, but Dad has gotten distracted by a power drill that caught his eye in a display window. He's now in a deep conversation with a salesman, and I fear Mom's foot might catch fire if she taps any faster on the wooden floor panel of the shop.

"Emma and Dylan, can you guys go buy the tickets and find seats for us? There's no telling how long it's gonna take me to pull your father away from that power drill." She uncrosses her arms, digs in her purse, and hands us a fifty-dollar bill. *Great*, I think to myself, flashing back to the moment Dylan turned his cheek on my kiss. *More privacy. Because this ended so well the last time.*

I let Dylan lead the way, attempting to keep my eyes on the

ground. But that doesn't work; I find myself admiring him from behind as we walk. He has a patch of hair that sticks up in the back of his head, and no matter how many times he runs his hands over it, it doesn't lie down. I have to place my hands in my jacket pockets to fight the urge to smooth it down myself, but the thought of running my fingers through his brown hair keeps trying to push its way to the forefront of my mind.

"Damn," I hear him say before he ducks behind a pillar and, to my surprise, pulls me with him. "Play along, okay?"

"What?"

"Just play along." He reaches down for my hand and laces his fingers with mine before coming from behind the column. *What is going on? What are you doing?* "I'll explain later," he says as if he can read my mind.

"Dylan! Hey!" I see a girl prance up to us, her eyes wide with excitement.

"Chelsea, right?" Dylan asks, his voice deep and alluring. When I notice that he hasn't dropped my hand yet, the butterflies in my stomach emerge from their cocoons, fluttering their wings and tickling my insides.

"How are you?" She smiles. She's really pretty. The juxtaposition of her long dark hair against her pale skin makes her green eyes look as penetrating and intense as a lioness in the dark of night. If I were into girls, I'd probably be attracted to her, too.

"I've been okay." *He's such a guy.* Keeping it short and to the point.

I see her eyes drop to where our hands are. "Who is this?"

"This is Emma, my girlfriend." He raises our intertwined hands and kisses the back of mine. "We're trying to catch a movie before it starts to get busy."

Girlfriend. At first, I think I'm hearing things, so I repeat his words again in my head. My mom used to say that sometimes we hear what we want to hear because it satisfies a need deep down inside of us. I fear that this is one of those instances, and so I replay his words a few more times to make sure that I've heard him correctly. *Nope, he said it. He definitely said "girlfriend."*

She looks me up and down as if I'm not worthy to cling to Dylan's arm, and then she giggles. I shudder; even her laugh is attractive.

"This is going to sound embarrassing," she says, "but I thought you were playing the girlfriend card to let me down easy."

"Well, as you can see, my girlfriend does indeed exist." I raise my eyebrows in contentment, and squeeze Dylan's hand a little harder. I expect him to end their conversation and pull me toward the theater, but he continues to stand there, staring Chelsea down. "We're gonna be late for our movie." After a moment of uncomfortable silence between them, I feel his fingers graze the bottom of my chin and lift my face toward his. Before I can register what's happening, his soft lips are on mine.

A million questions pulse through my mind as he grabs hold of my waist to pull me closer. *Am I doing this right? Do I breathe through my nose or my mouth? Or am I not supposed to breathe at all?* As his lips continue to wrestle with mine, I push the questions out of my brain. I don't want them to ruin the moment I've waited my entire life for: my first kiss.

When he finally pulls away and I open my eyes, I realize that I'm out of breath. I search his face for some kind of clue to what just happened between us, but get nothing except a side-smile that says, *Wow,* and a look in his eyes that reads, *Did I really just do that?*

"Well, I'll see you two later," Chelsea says before walking away.

There's a sodden look in her eyes, and her already pale face seems to fade into a lighter shade of white. But her pain is no concern of mine. I got my first kiss, and nothing can bring me down from this high.

"Dylan—" I start before he cuts in.

"Thanks for that," he says, letting go of my hand and putting more distance between us. He's still smiling, but this time it's mischievous, like he just got away with murder or some other heinous crime.

"For what?"

"When I saw her at an art exhibit downtown yesterday, I told her that I was taking my blond bombshell of a girlfriend to a movie, so I couldn't go on a coffee date with her," he says, shoving his hands into the front pockets of his jeans. "If you hadn't been here today, I would have been exposed as a liar, *and* Chelsea would have continued to pursue me."

"So that was all—"

"An act? Well, yeah. What did you think I was doing? You're my foster sister. We can't date."

"But," I begin as my eyes well up. I don't want him to see me cry, so I try to blink the tears away. "You *knew* I liked you, though."

"Yeah, I did," he says after a moment. "Honestly, it wasn't that hard to figure out, especially after you tried to kiss me after our meet-up with the social worker." The suffocating pain of my heart breaking is all I can focus on as I watch a smug grin settle onto his face. "But you should be happy, Emma. I gave you what you wanted, didn't I? Now, can we forget this ever happened and go buy the tickets like we were supposed to?"

"'Gave me what I wanted'? You mean, made a fool of me?" I can't hold back now; the tears start streaming down my face, burning my skin as if they are laced with hydrochloric acid.

"That's not fair, Emma. You know I won't be able to stay if they even think that we're romantically involved." He turns away from me, I guess in disbelief. "Are you really *that* selfish that you're willing to risk my future in this family to get what you want? Everything isn't always about you."

Selfish? I replay inside my head. His words are cold and harsh, and I have to turn away before my face starts to crumple. "You're such an ass," I spit at him, feeling around for the money in my pocket. When my fingers find it, I start toward the theater to buy the movie tickets. I refuse to let him have the satisfaction of getting the last word.

chapter 8

"YOU'RE LIVING WITH the Ellenburgs now, right, McAndrews?" I hear two students grilling him across the hall. As much as I look forward to my English class, it's excruciating today; for an entire hour, I have to share the same space as Dylan, and ever since our falling-out at the mall, it's been hard to face him. I feel my cheeks grow hot with embarrassment and anger when he approaches the group waiting to get inside the classroom. But even the memory of his betrayal can't stop me from thinking about the passion that lit up inside of me when his lips touched mine.

Most days, it's a quiet wait in the hallway, but thanks to the two oaf-looking boys—one tall and gangly, and the other short and plump—poking fingers into Dylan's chest, there's a scene for everyone to watch while we wait. "I saw you pulling into the parking lot this morning. That's a nice car that you have there. Did your new mommy and daddy buy that for you, too?"

"Actually, yes. It was a gift, and I was always taught that it's rude not to accept gifts." Dylan's calmness turns the entire scene into a farce. It seems as if the calmer he stays, the madder the two boys get. "By now, you should know that, but good manners don't seem to be a priority for either of you."

"You think you're funny, huh?" the tall one says, grabbing a fistful of Dylan's button-down shirt. I try hard to ignore the conversation across the hall, but even the anticipation of presenting our close readings of *Wuthering Heights* next period can't pull my attention away.

"So how does it feel, huh?" the shorter one sneers. "You waltz into their lives, and they just supply you with everything you want. How does it feel to be their own little charity case?"

"Yeah, you gonna freeload off of them for the rest of your life?" *Freeloading? I'm sure that thought has never crossed any of our minds. Being an ass? Yes, that's definitely crossed mine, but not freeloading.* I see Dylan open his mouth to respond, but before he can muster up a smart-ass comeback, the bell rings, bringing Mr. Lawrence to the hall.

"Is there a problem, gentlemen?"

"No problem here, sir," the two boys say in unison, walking away as we begin to file inside the classroom.

"Coming in or staying out, Miss Ellenburg?" Mr. Lawrence says, raising an eyebrow in my direction.

"Coming in." I adjust the strap on my bag and make my way toward the door, but not before stealing a glance in Dylan's direction to see his bronze eyes piercing mine through my glasses, pleading for me to stay out of it. *We're not on speaking terms anyway, so it's not like I have much of a choice*, I answer back in my head.

The first thing that Dylan does when he enters the room is

march up to Mr. Lawrence's desk and ask to switch seats. Not entirely unexpected—his seat is right next to mine.

"Give me a good reason, and I'll let you move," the teacher bargains, but Dylan doesn't take the bait. He's cornered, and no one can find out what's going on with us. Without another word, he bolts to his seat and angles away from me, mad at the world.

"I love Mondays," Mr. Lawrence sighs, uncapping a whiteboard marker. "Don't you guys just love Mondays?" I hear the students around me grumble and groan as he scribbles two words on the board: *Metaphysical Monday*. At the start of every week, Mr. Lawrence blocks out the entire class period to have a "creative discussion," as he calls it. This is really just a debate. "But before we get to this, you guys owe me a journal entry." He raises his wrist to expose a fancy pedometer watch, and we all rush to pull our journals and something to write with from our backpacks. "You have ten minutes to write. Get started."

Dear Catherine,

Some say that the worst type of love is a dying one. One that started with a small bud of a crush and blossomed into a beautiful, breathtaking tree. One that stood its ground in the face of every hurricane and flood that crossed its path. One that didn't even know it was dying until it was too late to remedy the broken pieces. But that's not it. The worst type of love is unrequited. A love that never even had the chance to see an end because it never got off the ground to begin with.

_____ doesn't like me in the same way I like _____ found that out the hard way. But knowing that doesn't stunt the feelings I am developing for him. Knowing that doesn't stop him from being the first person I think about when I wake up in the morning and the last thing I long for before I close my eyes at night. It doesn't stop my heart from racing at the mere mention of his name.

I should hate him with every fiber of my being. But I don't.

And I thought things were weird between us before, but now . . . ? He's been dodging me since the mall incident, which sucks because now he's treating me the same way that every other guy does around here: as if I don't exist. As if I'm invisible. That's what hurts most of all. I thought he was different.

I don't know what kind of trouble I caused in my past lives, but I'm sure that whatever I did didn't merit this kind of karmic retribution. Crap . . . my ten minutes are up. Catch you later.

♡ Emma

"Now, where were we? Oh, yeah," Mr. Lawrence says, clapping his hands—he does that a lot. "Here's your Metaphysical Monday question: Catherine loves Heathcliff, but she decides that they can't be together because of the differences in their social classes." He pauses here for dramatic effect, but I fear that no one but me is truly interested. "But what if they were of the same caste? Do you think their love would be more socially acceptable if they belonged to the same class?"

I have to shake my head at Mr. Lawrence's suggestion. It's not explicitly said in the book, but the real reason Catherine and Heathcliff can't be together is not because of their statuses; it's because they are foster siblings and, as Dylan can vouch for, that's not okay. When Mr. Lawrence told us that this book would relate to our lives in ways we would never imagine, I tried to write that off as melodramatic. But now I'm beginning to see a few problematic connections.

Mr. Lawrence starts rattling off the names of our partners, and I cringe when I hear my partner's name. "Emma, I'm partnering you with Dylan for today's discussion. That okay?"

Is he kidding? Mr. Lawrence must have no idea that my family is fostering Dylan. He's not so maniacal as to pair up real foster siblings to discuss literature's most famous lusty foster siblings. I dismiss the thought and nod approvingly, scoot my desk a little closer to Dylan's, and dive right into the task at hand. "Hypothetically speaking, they should be able to date . . . I mean, if they are no longer in different classes, right?" No response. He just sits there balancing his mechanical pencil on the tip of his index finger. "So, what do you think about this?" I probe again, thinking that maybe he hadn't heard me the first time. But still, nothing.

"Well, this is a conundrum," I whisper, half to myself and half to Dylan. Unblinking, he glares in my direction, sending chills down my spine, until it's so uncomfortable that I have to focus solely on my own response just to distract myself from it all. And when Mr. Lawrence opens up the floor for us to share our opinions, Dylan slides his desk away from mine. Clearly, he wants nothing to do with me inside and outside the classroom.

"I say yes," one girl articulates without raising her hand. "It should definitely be okay for Heathcliff to pursue Catherine. She's not his *real* sister, so it wouldn't be incest or anything like that. If they're in the same class, then there is nothing standing in the way of them falling in love with each other. I don't see a problem with it."

"I disagree," another boy interjects. "Heathcliff was brought into their family as an orphan, and it's pretty obvious that he will probably become a real part of the family at some point. Adopted sibling, half sibling, foster sibling . . . whatever. It's all the same. If you live under the same roof and refer to each other as family, then you should act accordingly." I feel my heart shrink when I see some students nod their heads in agreement with him.

"But that's not fair," a different girl—Diem— contests from across the classroom. "Think about how you would feel if you were in their position. I mean, yes, Heathcliff is technically her brother, but he shouldn't have to give up the love of his life just because society thinks that it's wrong for adopted siblings to be together. Society can't dictate the terms of these artificially constructed relationships. There is absolutely nothing wrong with them falling in love with each other."

"Anyone willing to take her on?" Mr. Lawrence asks, looking for more raised hands. Diem is the captain of the debate team, and everyone is always afraid to disagree with her in class. When no one steps up to the plate, Mr. Lawrence doesn't waste any time calling on some one else. "Dylan. I'd like to hear what you have to say."

God, I wish Mr. Lawrence understood the unbearable irony. My heart flutters when I hear Dylan's name pass over my teacher's lips. His opinion is the only one that matters to me, and I'm dying to hear his response, though a part of me feels like I already know the answer.

"I think it's stupid."

Well, there you have it, my mind relays to my heart. *He thinks it's stupid.* Does that mean that he thinks my feelings for him are stupid, too? *No,* the voice in my head answers. *He thinks it's selfish.*

"But why?" I ask, all of a sudden overcome with a mixture of sadness and rage, my mind replaying the scene from the mall again. He cuts his eyes toward me, warning me not to overstep my bounds, but I push the matter anyway. "What makes you think that?"

"Because he's in a lose-lose situation from the moment he walks into her life. No matter which side he chooses, he's going to have to sacrifice something. He'll lose a sister—and a family—if he chooses to love her romantically. He'll lose a partner if he chooses to ignore his feelings for her. It's an inescapable catch-22."

"Good point, Mr. McAndrews."

The bell rings before I can dispute his words, but part of what he says stays with me well into my next class. *It's an inescapable catch-22.* I'm dying to know whether Dylan thinks of me in that same way: if he chooses me, he'll lose my family, and if he chooses my family, he'll lose me. Maybe he really *did* like me, but was in too sticky a situation to follow his heart. Maybe he just chose the option that would cause the least damage for him, even if it meant hurting me in the process. I guess I'll never know.

APPARENTLY, WHEN YOU MAKE THE DANCE TEAM AT CEDAR POINTE HIGH, you also sign up for torturous after-school running sessions on the track with Karmin. We start off every practice with a one-mile run to "build stamina" and get our legs warmed up, but, if you ask me, I think it does more wearing out than warming up.

"Almost there, girls. Push it!" she screams into the wind, leading the pack. From behind, she doesn't appear out of breath or even look like she's breaking a sweat in the eighty-five-degree heat—which, I'm sure, frustrates every girl on our team. We're drenched in sweat from head to toe, our cheeks are rosy with heat exhaustion, and we can hardly breathe, let alone hold a conversation, when she finally calls time. "Five-minute water break and then we're heading inside to start practice."

Taking a seat on the grass, I watch her long, thin legs carry her petite-yet-optimally-curvy frame to the water fountain. Confidence exudes from every inch of her body. I pull at the grass beneath me, imagining how different I would be if I had her life. For starters, I'd have a boyfriend—cute and popular—and a bunch of fabulous friends to surround myself with. I'd never have to eat lunch by myself. There would always be a spot ready to clear for me at the good lunch tables. Life would be so much glossier.

"So, Emma," Karmin says, plopping down beside me as I lie back, closing my eyes, "what's been going on with you and Dylan?"

My eyes snap open, wide like a doe's right after it sees the head-lights of a car coming its way. *Oh, God, she knows! How could she have found out?* "W-w-what do you mean? There—there's nothing 'going on' with us."

She fans at her tan cheeks, the heat from outside finally starting to affect her. *"You sure?" As far as you are concerned, very sure.* "You guys were so close at the beginning of the year, and now, you're . . . well . . . not. What happened?"

I happened, that's what. "I'm not sure. Now that he has his own car and has made a few friends in art club, I guess he doesn't need me any-more or something."

"Hmm. That kinda sucks," is all she says, pulling at the grass now, too. She doesn't push the matter, and I realize that she isn't trying to pry, but rather just keep the conversation flowing. "So, have you heard that the theme for homecoming is 'An Evening in Paris'?"

"I had not, but thanks for letting me know." Truth be told, I don't really care. I'm not going anyway.

"Yeah. I heard they're going to make a balloon Eiffel Tower in the center of the gym and everything. I'm so excited!" She squeals, I guess thinking about how much fun it's going to be, but I can't feign the same enthusiasm. "Sam and I are going together, as usual. Are you going with anyone special?"

"Nope. I don't really *do* homecoming dances. Or . . . any dance, really."

"But why?"

"It's just not my scene. Watching girls grind up on their dates to music that I don't really listen to doesn't exactly sound like a fun time."

"It's all about the people you surround yourself with. I'm telling you, going with your crew is key to having a good time." Mulling it over for a moment, I almost consider asking her if I can be in her "crew," but on second thought, that sounds a little lame. "I know you don't have a date . . . yet . . . but please tell me you're at least thinking of going."

"Sorry," I say running my fingers over my damp hair. "I've gone three years without attending a homecoming dance. What's one more?"

She pouts and gives me a green-eyed puppy-dog stare.

"My answer is still no."

"Why? Is this about not having a date?"

"No. I just—"

"Because if it is, I know plenty of guys who'd be happy to accompany you. There's Paulie Guzman, Jason Kingsford, Daxton Waters. I mean, the list goes on and on. All it'll take is one phone call, and you can have a date like that." She snaps her fingers in front of my face. I want to ask her how she knows that all of these guys are dateless right now, but I know that'll just make it sound as if I'm interested, which won't help my case.

"No, thanks."

One thing I admire about Karmin is her stubborn, never-gonna-give-up attitude. She doesn't take no for an answer: "You sure? Like I said, all it takes is one phone call."

"I'm sure. I don't even know who those guys are, and besides, *if* I wanted to go—I'm not saying that I do, but *if* I wanted to go—there'd only be one person worth going with."

"Ohh, I get it," she says, raising an eyebrow at me. "You *like* someone, don't you?"

My first thought is to lie, but then I figure, what's the harm in admitting that I have a crush? As long as I don't say Dylan's name, my feelings for him are still under wraps. "Maybe."

I thought her squealing was obnoxious before, but when she rolls onto her back, giggling and screaming like a five-year-old who's just learned that she's going to Disneyland, we've reached a whole new level of crazy. "Spill everything."

"There's nothing to 'spill.' He's a guy, and I like him . . . and that's about it."

"What's his name?" She's so close that I can see the microscopic gold specks around the edges of her irises.

I shake my head. "Not going to tell you. Knowing you, you might track him down and threaten to key his car if he doesn't go with me."

"As if." She laughs guiltily. "I'd threaten him with a lot more than just that."

"Which is exactly why I'm not telling you his name. You'd scare him away." I push her shoulder playfully, and she lets out another giggle.

"It'd be for a good reason, though. I mean, you're freaking gorgeous."

"Eh. If you say so."

"Oh, I know so. You could use a little extra mascara here and there, but gorgeous nonetheless. Blue eyes, blond hair, smooth skin, hot body. God, I'd kill for your looks."

Funny, I'd kill for yours. I'm not sure if she's trying to flatter me so I'll open up more, but I don't fall for it. "I can't make any promises, but I'll at least *think* about going to the dance."

"Yay!" She slaps her hands around my shoulders and squeezes me until I can no longer breathe, her sleek brown ponytail slapping me in the face. "So does this mean that you'll go dress shopping with me, too? My mom put my brother in charge of my shopping budget, so he has to tag along"—she mimes sticking her finger down her throat as if the thought of her brother tagging along makes her want to puke— "but I'm going to need a friend's honest-to-God opinion if I'm going to buy a dress that'll outdo that stunning ruby two-piece that I wore last year."

I wasn't at the dance to see the gown in person, but I remember seeing pictures. Her dress exposed her flawlessly flat stomach, and it fit so well with the Arabian Nights theme that they featured her in several photos on the Homecoming Dance page in the yearbook.

"Okay. I'm in."

"Perfect! It's a date," she says, running off to resume practice, leaving me there with a clownish smile plastered to my face. *God, it feels good to finally be a part of something.*

chapter 9

Because *Wuthering Heights* is the only overlap in the regular and AP English syllabi, Mr. Lawrence has been getting us through it slowly, I guess to buy the school more time to find a replacement for Ms. Harper. So even though I want to be invested in his review of chapter eleven—yeah, I know, it's been a month and we're *only* on chapter eleven—my mind is elsewhere, searching for a way to help Dylan shake off the two jackasses. For the past couple of days, they've been looking for Dylan before fifth period and harassing him for no reason. Dylan's not a fighter, so he takes every blow without retaliating. He ended up skipping class today to hang out in the nurse's office—he's milking his "upset stomach" excuse for all it's worth—and I know he probably wants me to stay out of it, but I can't.

Helping him should be the last thing on my mind, given how reckless he can be with me, but I feel morally obligated to do it. Not as the girl who likes him, but as the girl who will eventually become his sister.

Fourth period chemistry doesn't last long enough, though, because when the bell rings for lunch, I still haven't found a way to get Dylan out of this.

"Who pissed in your cereal this morning?" Karmin asks as she approaches the lunch table where I've settled in.

"Huh?"

"You're scooting your peas around your plate, and you have that whole resting bitch face thing going on, too. So clearly, something is wrong. Now, out with it." Karmin places her tray of shepherd's pie and corn down next to mine, giving me time to admire it. The portions on her plate look significantly bigger than what I have on mine, and I can't help but wonder if she's in with the cafeteria ladies, too. She seems to have everyone at this school wrapped around her French-tipped finger.

"Just deep in thought is all."

"Hopefully thinking up ways to make our routine better. Our first game is this Friday, and if things aren't perfectly perfect, I may lose my mind."

"Of course," I say through gritted teeth.

I'm a little worried about Karmin; it seems that up to this point, her main focus has been on dance. And I'm almost certain that she thinks she will be a famous dancer one day, too. Now, I'm not trying to kill her dreams, but I think she has a better chance of getting struck by lightning than achieving that. But who am I to tell her so? We're barely friends. She probably wouldn't even know my name if I hadn't wowed her at the CPD benefit last year.

"Karmin, I've got some bad news," a brown-skinned girl with thick, curly hair—Peyton from the dance team—says after putting a folded-up turquoise shirt on the table. "I'm really, really, REALLY sorry, but I can't work at your family's sub shop anymore. I love working there, and your mom is the coolest boss ever, but it's interfering with Bible study, and if I miss one more time, my parents are going to flip the freak out."

I'm not sure what I find more annoying: her tedious string of *really*s, or her attempt to fake curse.

"Okay, Peyton. No big deal. I'll call my mom and tell her later. Thanks for letting me know." Karmin picks up her fork and starts eating. She's obviously done with the conversation, but Peyton, who's still standing at attention at our lunch table, isn't.

"And I know I'm scheduled to work tonight, but again, I can't miss. My dad's the pastor, and apparently it looks bad if I don't show up to . . ."

I zone out. I've only known Peyton for a couple of weeks, but I know that once she gets started on her church life, we might as well take a seat, because she can go on and on and on.

"Peyton." Karmin stops her after a minute or so. "It's fine. I got it. I'll call my mom to let her know." She waits until Peyton leaves to say, "It's great that she loves Jesus, but she needs to chill with all of that." I can't help but wonder if she has any secret frustrations about me.

While my head is still spinning from Peyton's mini sermon, I see the two boys from the hallway fling open the cafeteria doors. I dart my eyes toward the table in the far corner, where the art kids usually eat; Dylan is in a conversation with someone and hasn't noticed them walking his way yet.

"Can you postpone that call to your mom for like a minute? I've got an idea," I say, picking up the T-shirt. I only have a small window of time to put my plan into action, but if I can make this work, I'll kill three birds with one stone—two of them being the brutes nagging Dylan for being a "freeloader," and the other problem encroaching on the Ortega family with Peyton deciding to quit and leave them short-handed tonight.

"Hey, Dylan," I manage to get out as I hurry across the cafeteria to him. "I think Mom put your work shirt in my dance bag by mistake. Here you go." Before he can say anything, I speak again, this time so only he can hear me. "I got you a job at Karmin's family's restaurant. If you're ever going to get me a replacement copy of *Wuthering Heights*, you're going to need a job to make some money." I wink, projecting confidence to mask my urgency as I see the two bullies move closer. They might lay off him if they hear that he has a job now and a little more local cred, but that depends on whether or not Dylan wants the job. "You have ten seconds to tell me if you want the job or not before I give up on this plan. So what do you say?"

"I'll take it."

"Perfect." I slide the shirt across the table to him and prance back to my seat, waving at the two boys, who respond with questioning eyes.

"What was that about?" Karmin asks mid-bite, when I reclaim my seat next to her.

"Nothing. Just tell your mom to add Dylan McAndrews to the payroll. You guys just hired him."

"Looks good to me," Denise, our dance team coach, says when we finish practicing the routine she taught us. She's a spunky little

dancing powerhouse with gorgeous brown eyes, full lips—
compliments of her Mediterranean background, I'm sure—and long
red-velvet-cake-colored hair that she always pulls into a messy bun
before practice begins. Her voice makes up for her lack of height,
though; it's so commanding that sometimes I think I'm at military
boot camp, instead of dance practice.

"Just good? We don't want to be 'good.' We want to be great,"
Karmin says as she pulls herself off the ground. "I think we need something extra to show off how far we've come. Homecoming is around
the corner, and I want to blow everyone away. I want it to be a teaser
of what we're gonna do when we get to competition season."

"You're right," Coach Denise says after a few minutes. She's very
young and has the demeanor of a levelheaded coach, but I can tell she's
easily influenced by Karmin; whenever Karmin questions Denise's
ideas, she always second-guesses herself and changes her mind. Then
again, maybe she's just trying to find her footing. After all, this *is* her
first year at Cedar Pointe. "Anyone have something that they're dying
to add to the dance?"

"Something that says, 'Look at us, we're hot shit'—I mean 'stuff,'"
Karmin corrects quickly; she knows that she's not supposed to curse
in front of the faculty. "Any ideas, anyone?"

I've never been one to publicly contribute ideas; I'm more of a fol-
lower than a leader. Something about stepping into that spotlight
scares the crap out of me. If you make a mistake, people blame you
for poor judgment; if your followers make a mistake, they still blame
you, but for poor leadership skills. Basically, you're screwed either way.

Still, the need to contribute an idea right now gnaws at my insides.
Just do it. What's the worst that can happen? I raise my hand slowly, and
when Coach Denise calls on me, I have to take a breath before I speak

to calm my nerves. "How about we put emphasis on our turns and leaps by doing side aerials after three *à la seconde* turns? One group goes to the right, one to the left, and then the spotlight dancers can come up the middle."

The girls all tilt their heads to the side as if they are imagining how the dance steps will play out in the routine. I get nervous the longer they stay silent, and when Coach Denise finally speaks, I jump.

"Love that idea. Now, that is the kind of innovation I'm looking for in you girls. Take notes, because I sure am." She dismisses us, but some of the girls stick around to practice the moves with my changes in them.

"I knew you were a good pick for the team." Karmin smiles when we finally exit the gym. "You're a natural."

"Well, I did take a couple years of tap, jazz, and ballet back in the day at CPD." I shrug. "Some things you just never forget how to do." As I'm explaining, I see her wave to a guy across the parking lot. "Who's that?"

"That's just my twin brother. You know, the one who's coming dress shopping with us."

"And he's on the baseball team?"

"Yep. Outfielder, if I remember correctly. But he's not important right now. Our routine is." As she continues to rave on and on about the dance team and how excited she is for our first game appearance and the upcoming competition season, I can't help gazing over at her brother.

I see him toss his bag over his shoulder and nod goodbye to his friends on the field. *For someone who's not important, he sure is cute.* Out of fear of letting this slip to Karmin, I part ways with her and head for my car.

After getting in and strapping on my seat belt, I put my key in the ignition and turn. Nothing. *Maybe I did it wrong.* I take out the key, then put it back in and turn. Nothing again. Every time my mom used to have car troubles, she would get out and go look under the hood, so I do the same. I open the hood and put my hands on my hips. *What am I supposed to do now?*

"You need help?" I hear someone ask from behind me. It's Karmin's brother. Now that he's close enough for me to see his facial features, I see how alike they look. They both have the same dark brown hair, olive skin, and dark green eyes. At first, the only real differences I can spot between them is their height and hair texture. Karmin is significantly shorter and always wears her hair pin straight—I take it she flat-irons religiously every morning before school—while her brother is a little over six feet and has a full head of luscious Puerto Rican curls. Upon closer inspection, I see another difference. Karmin has tiny freckles powdered across her beige cheeks, and he doesn't.

I hand him my keys, and he tries to start it. "Battery's working fine, so I'm guessing that it's an issue with your starter." The way he takes command of the situation makes him instantly more attractive to me. "Do you know what to do?"

I find it hard to form an intelligible sentence with him so close, so I shake my head. My dad told me to get my car checked over a month ago, and I told him that I had it under control. *Eek.* I whip out my phone to call my mom—Dad will be furious, and I'm not in the mood for a lecture—but as soon as I take it out, he puts his hand over my screen.

"No need. My older brother has an auto shop down the street. I can get him to tow it there, and he'll have it fixed for you by tomorrow. Family favors are free." Within twenty minutes, my car has been transported to the shop and I'm on my way home with Karmin's brother. Once I get in his truck, it dawns on me that I don't even know his name.

"I'm Keegan, by the way," he declares, somehow deciphering my thoughts.

"Emma."

"Oh, I know who you are," he says as we drive through my neighborhood. "You're the smartest girl in our class."

How does he know who I am? I always thought I was invisible.

"I saw you compete against my girlfriend in the scholastic decathlon last year." *Of course he has a girlfriend,* I think. *The decent jocks are always taken.* "Well, ex-girlfriend, I should say. She broke up with me for some loser she met last summer."

"Oh" is all I say. I don't want to make it seem like I'm too interested in his love life. The magazines I read say that if you show too much curiosity, the guy will always lose interest. "So . . . why didn't your brother opt to work at your family's sandwich shop? It sounds like a nice place to work. It's always packed in there."

"He got tired of taking orders from people—mainly my mom— and decided to open a mechanic shop. He's happy, I guess."

"Hmm" I hope that my faux disinterest in his personal life doesn't make me come off as self-centered. "It's the navy blue house with the big white columns," I say when he turns onto my street. He pulls up into the part of the driveway that snakes around to the side of the house and comes to a hard stop at the end of it, so as not to ruin my mother's sunflower garden. "Thanks for the ride."

"No problem. We should trade numbers. You know, so I can text you when your car is ready," Keegan adds before I can find the door handle to let myself out.

Sure, that's what you want it for, my overconfident mind thinks as I close the door on his truck. *Easy, Emma. Remember what happened the last time you thought someone was interested.*

"Okay, sure." We trade numbers and say our goodbyes, and before I know it, I'm unlocking the door to the pool house. After I shower and change into something more comfortable, I plug my phone into its charger and turn the ringer up in case Keegan calls or texts me tonight, though I'm almost certain he won't.

"You okay, Emma?" my mom says, when she comes to drop some laundry off in my room. "We missed you at dinner today . . . again."

I turn down the volume on my stereo, which is blasting the passage for our close reading homework assignment, and hold up the CD case of the audiobook—God, how my fingers miss flipping through the yellowed pages of that old print copy—in response. I want her to think that I'm too busy to spend time with them because of my heavy load of homework, rather than simply avoiding Dylan.

"You've hardly set foot inside the house lately. This isn't about Dylan, is it?" she asks.

My eyes widen, and I almost lose my cool as I replay her words in my head. I have to remind myself that she doesn't know anything about what happened when she sent us to buy movie tickets.

"Did you guys have a fight?"

"No. I've just been busy with school and dance practice." She's the person who knows me best in the entire world, so I expect her to call me out on my decently conceivable lie, but she doesn't.

"You sure? You two have barely communicated in weeks." She pulls open my dresser drawers and begins putting folded laundry into them. She recently started doing this, and I know it's probably because she feels me slipping away. Ten months is all she has left with me before I head off for college. With a stack of my pajamas in her hands, she squints her eyes to peer through the semi-sheer floral curtains that match my vintage wallpaper in color. "Speaking of Dylan, it looks like he's headed over this way. What's going on with you two?"

"I guess I'm about to find out." I hit the pause button on my stereo and watch as my mother finishes putting away my clothes.

"Hello, Dylan," she says on her way out.

"Hi, Mrs. Ellenburg . . . er . . . yeah, Mrs. Ellenburg." In his eyes, I see him fight over what to call my mom. She's okay with him calling her Mom, but I know he doesn't want to disrespect his birth mother. "Emma."

"How was work?" I ask.

"It was good, I guess. It's easy money, especially since the people in this town tip very well." I'm probably going to have to take that as a thank-you because he doesn't elaborate on the subject, even though I was the one who, for now at least, got the boys to stop harassing him for being a "freeloader." They're either going to have to find something else to bully him about or refocus their energies elsewhere. "I picked this up for you today. Sorry it took so long."

Before I can thank him for the horribly wrapped package he sets at the end of my bed, he's already exiting the room. Even after looking out for him at lunch today, I guess we're still not on good terms.

When I peel off the dark purple wrapping, I find a brand-new edition of *Wuthering Heights*. It's leather-bound, and the edges of the pages look as if they have been dusted with gold paint. *Is this supposed to be an apology?* I flip through the glittering pages and find a flattened rose in the middle. I can't stop myself from pursing my lips in agitation. *Yep.*

"No offense, but this is half-assed," I fume as I step over the threshold of his art studio. I haven't set foot in here in so long that I almost fall under a dizzy spell as the strong odor floods my nostrils.

"The vintage audio edition was meant to replace the one I ruined. But this one," he says, pointing his brush toward the book in my hand, "is a gift. One that I won't receive a thank-you for, I guess."

"Thanks," I mumble, feeling a flush of color run across my face. "But you buy a book and just expect things to go back to normal? Really, Dylan?"

"Why are you holding such a grudge? Just let this go," he says, his voice tensing up.

"I'm not mad that you rejected me," I retort, lowering mine. I don't want my parents and neighbors knowing that I made a move on him. Although he's not my brother on paper yet, I'm still supposed to treat him that way. "Yes, I told you that being rejected is my biggest fear— and it still is—but that's not why I'm upset. I'm mad about the way you did it. You led me on and used me."

I hear the backyard screen door slide open, and a wave of panic washes over me. Someone's coming. *Did they hear us?*

"Hey, kids. Your mother's apple pie just finished cooling if you want a slice," my dad announces when he appears at the studio entrance. *Good. He didn't hear a thing.* "Oh, and Dylan, I'm glad I caught you. I have some big news for you."

"What's up, Daniel?"

"I was down by the art museum the other day, and I saw that they were taking submissions for the county-wide art showcase. It's this big art show that they have in December, and only the best kids are selected to showcase their work. From the twenty kids selected, only one will receive a ten-thousand-dollar scholarship for college. Cool, huh?"

"Sounds like a blast, but I think I'm going to pass this time around. I don't really paint for competition. I paint just because I like to."

"Oh, you don't have to worry about it. I already entered you."

"How? You don't have any of my artwork." Dylan's eyebrows curl in confusion.

"I submitted the piece that was over there in that corner. The one with the boy sitting on the woman's lap. It is so powerful and intimate, and that's exactly the kind of work they're looking for." I know which painting he's talking about, and I feel my stomach drop. He took the one of Dylan and his mother.

"You did . . . what?"

"Yeah. I figured you wouldn't mind. And with your talent, you'll win for sure."

All of a sudden, I see a beet-red flush across Dylan's cheeks. He throws his brush down and stands up, his breathing deep and heavy. "You took my stuff without asking me?"

"Dad—" I start, but Dylan overpowers me.

"That one was personal! Why are you touching my stuff?"

My dad looks taken aback. Matthew and I never yell at him . . . or any adult for that matter. "I just thought—"

"That you were helping me?"

"I just want you to get some exposure. No one is ever going to know how good you are unless you put yourself out there for the world to see."

"Dad! Dad, just stop!" I shout at him from across the room. They are both deep into their argument and must have forgotten that I was still present. "You're doing it again."

"Doing what?"

"Taking what we love and turning it into something competitive and ugly. We can never follow our passions because you put so much pressure on us to win." He looks at me as if I don't know what I'm talking about. "Haven't you ever wondered why I quit playing softball?"

"You were the best batter on the team."

"Yeah, and the pressure you put on me to win drove me away from the one sport that I actually enjoyed."

"I had no clue," he says, lowering his voice.

"Just because you don't have a life anymore doesn't mean that you can control ours and ruin the love we have for our hobbies." My words sting me as they take flight off of my tongue, so I can only imagine how they feel to him as they land. I know I've hurt him, but he needs to hear this before he ruins someone else's passion. I wish I could tone it down a little, but he's out the door before I can do so.

When I turn back to Dylan, he's washing paint off his hands in the back corner. "You didn't have to do that, you know? I can take care of myself," he says.

"I know. But I care about you, and I wasn't going to stand by and let him ruin your one true love in this world."

I see him chuckle. "Interesting. That was the reason I turned you down. Because I care about you."

"What? That makes no sense. I mean, if you care about me, why would you . . . At the movie theater, you . . ."

"I did that because I care about you and your family. I love it here, but the agency will take me away if we get caught. It's the one rule they hammer into our heads in group homes. Don't fall for your foster siblings. Don't fall for your foster siblings." He reaches for the towel and dries his hands. He didn't do a very good job washing because I can still see traces of paint beneath his fingernails. "I never thought that would be a problem for me until I met you." I hold my breath as he continues to talk. Now, this? This is an apology. "I like you, Emma. A lot."

"Then why publicly humiliate me? Why would you put me through that?"

"Because I thought it'd be easier to stay away from you if you hated me. But that's not working, either." He reaches for my hand, but I flinch, hesitant to let him touch me. When he laces his fingers with mine, it's as if an electric current starts to pulse through my body. But it doesn't hurt like people say it does when they get struck by lightning. It feels . . . well, I can't put into words just how remarkable it is. All I know is that it feels good, and I don't want him to let go.

"Dylan," I breathe. *Don't do this. We shouldn't*, is what I'm supposed to say, but I can't get the words out.

"I know," he says, untangling his fingers from mine. "If we do this, things will end badly. That's how it happens in all the stories that I've heard." He lets go and turns away from me, replacing the electricity running through me with chills. "This isn't how things are supposed to be. I must be clinically messed up to feel this way for you."

"You're not messed up, Dylan."

"But I am. I was the one who found her," he says. "My mom. Ever since then—"

I put a finger to his lips, halting him mid-thought. I don't want him to think that he needs to tell me about his past just because I protected him from Dad. "You don't have to tell me now," I say as I feel his arms envelop my shoulder, the heat returning to my body. "But if you really want to tell me, I'm here."

I see him look down at me and smile. "You're right. I don't want to talk about it right now." He grabs my face with both of his hands and brushes his lips against mine. It's the same kind of kiss that he gave me in the middle of the half-empty mall, but this time it feels different. This time it feels real.

I force my brain off. Not only because the logical portions of it will stop me (which is clearly not happening), but also because I'm over-thinking everything: my lips, my tongue, my hand placements, the angle at which my head is tilted—everything. But that doesn't last for long, because when he pulls away and I open my eyes, he's headed for the door, leaving me to think that I've done something—though I'm not exactly sure what that something is yet—wrong.

chapter 10

WHEN I WAS eleven years old, I had to attend my grandfather's funeral. He died the day before his fifty-ninth birthday, and from what I can infer from the massive attendance at the service, he was deeply loved. His was the first dead body I had ever seen in my life, and to this day I pray that I never have to see one again; it's not something you can forget so easily. I mean, his body wasn't disfigured in any way, but it felt weird to see my family members openly viewing, crying over, and sometimes kissing his lifeless figure. It just didn't seem right.

I don't have many memories of my grandfather, but I know that when we went to church on Sundays, he would always give me three peppermints to suck on during the service and a dollar to put into the offering plate. He smelled of cinnamon all the time and gave me hugs so tight, sometimes I couldn't breathe. It wasn't until I turned thirteen that I learned the real reason behind his death. My mother told me that he died of Alzheimer's and could barely remember his name, let alone her, in his final days. She said that he would wake up in a stupor every morning, and she would have to remind him who and where he was.

This is what it feels like when I wake up now. It's like I've developed teenage Alzheimer's and I have to reconvince myself of what happened between Dylan and me every morning. When I lie in my bed reliving the kiss we shared in his studio, I grow giddy and anxious with anticipation for what will happen next. And everything would be perfect . . . if only Dylan felt excited about this, too.

His feelings for me operate on a rotating schedule: some days he likes me and others he doesn't. On the latter days, I wish that I could just freeze him out completely; it wouldn't hurt so much to have him ignore the situation altogether. I just wish he would make up his mind. I don't want to keep obsessing over whether he wants me or not. I need a definite answer, and I need it now.

"Hey," he says to me from the breakfast table when I walk into the kitchen. It's been ten days since we kissed, and to my disappointment, he hasn't brought it up once. *Was it not memorable enough? Did I do it wrong?*

"Hey," I respond, pulling a bowl from the cabinet and the milk from the refrigerator, but there's so much more I want to say to him: *Are we going to talk about this, or what? Do you have plans to pick up from where we left off that night? Do you even like me still?*

Dear God, please let him like me still.

I'm so distracted with my thoughts that I end up pouring the milk into my bowl before I even grab the box of cereal. At least I'm the only person in the house who eats cereal, and since I haven't eaten any in a while, I know there's enough to cover the amount of milk I poured.

"How are you?" he asks. *Here we go with the small talk again.* Out of the corner of my eye, I see him roll his neck around a few times, and I have to suppress the impulse to give him a massage, but it's so hard. "Do you have plans for the weekend?" *Yep, we're back to that.*

"Karmin is going homecoming-dress shopping downtown this afternoon, and I promised her I'd come with." *Ugh, you should have sounded more available. Maybe he was trying to find time together!*

"Sounds fun." He licks his lips, smiling, and I almost melt into the floor just looking at him. "I think I might visit the Literary Lovers Festival downtown today. Maybe we'll run into each other." He's not asking me out, but his words still make my insides squirm with excitement.

Again, my thoughts distract me, and it isn't until I see cereal crumbs falling out of the box that I realize there's not enough of it to balance out the milk I have in my bowl. "What in the world?"

"What?"

"I could've sworn that there was a half box of cereal last week. Who ate—" I stop midsentence when I find the answer to the question I was just about to ask. "Is that . . . Did you eat my cereal?"

"My bad," he says with a grimace, as if in pain. "I didn't know it was yours."

As he speaks, my eyes fall to the now-empty bowl sitting in front of him. *First my parents, then my attention span—kind of—and now my cereal. What else is he going to steal from me?*

"It's okay. I wasn't really hungry anyway." I pour the milk down the drain, hoping he isn't going to call me out on being wasteful, and grab two apples before starting toward the back door. I still have homework to do before dress shopping.

"Emma." My heartbeat hastens the second I hear my name pass

over his lips. I don't turn to face him, struggling to play it cool. I don't want him to know how excited I am for us to finally talk about the elephant in the room.

"Yeah?"

"About the other night . . . I—I don't think we should do it . . . Date, I mean."

The smile has barely settled in on my face before it fades, and my heart starts to sink. "Okay."

"Don't get me wrong, I care about you. I really do. It's just not what's best for us now. I hope you understand."

"Yeah. I understand completely. It was stupid to think that it could work, anyway." I don't believe a word that's coming out of my mouth, but I don't want him to see how truly disappointed I am.

☙

When I arrive at She's So Chic Formalwear, Karmin and Keegan are already there, leaning up against the white truck I rode in not too long ago. I glance at the clock on my dashboard. *Twelve o'clock on the dot. I'm not late; they're just early.*

"I thought you'd forgotten," Karmin whines when I get out of the car. "I was starting to think that the only opinion I was going to have on my dress was going to be my brother's. But, crisis averted. Let's shop."

Keegan and I exchange a look as we follow behind her. "I hope you're ready for this. We're both in for a wild ride." He grins, but I can't return the pleasantries. With Dylan's words still fresh on my mind, I don't have much to be happy or excited about.

Upon entering the store, Karmin has the clerk grab a handful of dresses and lead us all to the waiting room. She's modeled and discarded four different gowns by the time I decide to break out a book and catch up on my reading.

"*Wuthering Heights*, huh? You must be in that combined English class with Lawrence."

"Yep." I know that he's just trying to be friendly, but I'm not in the mood for it today. Over the top of my book, I watch his eyes flicker back and forth between the book in my hands and my face.

"It's crazy how they had to combine your class with the English II class, isn't it?"

I mumble something in agreement and continue reading.

"Are you okay?" he asks, leaning over to let his elbows rest on his knees. Behind him, through the viewing window, I watch a family of four wander across the street to the Literary Lovers Festival. *I wonder if Dylan has made it there yet. Wait*, I counter, *I'm not allowed to care about what he's doing.*

"Perfectly fine, actually." I turn the page of the book and focus on making my eyes skim across the page in a believable manner.

"I'm fine, too. I'd be a lot better, though, if I wasn't here watching Karmin play dress-up. But, hey, at least I have you to keep me entertained." I purse my lips in an attempt to hold back my smile, but after a while, it sort of slithers onto my face.

"Is that a smile I see?" he says, tilting his head to the side as if trying to get a better view of my grin. "So you *do* have one of those."

"Do you have nothing better to do than stare at me?" I ask, gently smirking.

"Well, I've gotta pass the time somehow. This"—he waves his hands encompassingly—"could last for hours." He struggles to get comfortable in his seat, but gives up when he realizes that it's an impossible task. "You going to homecoming?"

More questions. "Haven't decided yet."

After a long pause, he says, "It's okay. I don't have a date either."

"What makes you think I don't have a date?"

"Because you're not trying on a dress."

I don't want him to think that I haven't at least been asked out by someone, but I also don't want to give him any ideas about trying to ask me to the dance, so I close my book and set it aside. "I'm going to go check on Karmin."

Walking through the perfume-scented store, I see Karmin throw a short white gown over the top of her changing room. That must be her "No" pile.

"Hey, how's it going in there?"

"So far, not very good. I swore I'd found *the* perfect dress, but it was a little too small for my boobs. These Puerto Rican genes—they're a blessing and a curse." She cracks open the door and pokes her face through the opening. "It'll probably look really good on you, though—not saying that your boobs are small, but you know what I mean. You should try it on!"

"Karmin, I—"

"I don't want to hear any buts. Try on that dress!" Before I can get another word out, she slams the door in my face. I've only been Karmin's friend for a few weeks, but I know that if I go against any one of her wishes—especially when it comes to fashion—I'll be getting hell for it later. So I pull the dress from the top of her changing area and ask the clerk for a room.

In my dressing room, I sit and stare at the gown for a full five minutes before taking it off the hanger. It's a strapless minidress made of white satin and tulle, with a carefully draped bodice, puffy-but-not-too-fluffy tutu bottom, and lace-up backing. I don't know how I've gone my entire life without it. I slip it on without too much effort, and when it falls over my body, I feel my fingers tingle with excitement. *It's perfect.*

"Emma!" I hear Karmin call from just outside the fitting rooms as I twirl in front of the mirror. "Come quick! I think I've found *the one!*"

My dress isn't laced yet, but I exit anyway, with hopes that someone will help me tighten things up.

Karmin is standing on the circular pedestal in a floor-length lavender cut-out dress when I emerge from my changing room. "I can hear my mom now. 'Oh, Karmincita, you look so pretty.'" Even in a mocking tone her Spanish accent is beautiful, with rolling *R*s gingerly dispersed like punctuation.

"Yeah," I say, pulling my dress closer to my body. "That color is gorgeous on you."

"Gorgeous is nice and all, but more importantly, this dress makes my boobs look amazing!" I hear Keegan cough uncomfortably from the corner. I'm sure discussing his twin sister's boobs wasn't something he planned on doing today—or ever. "Without a doubt, Sam's going to love me in this . . . out of it, too."

With that, Keegan hops up, not exactly sure what to do. He can't leave because he's Karmin's ride, but listening to her joke about her homecoming sex plans with her boyfriend is more than he can handle.

"Do you need some help with that?" he asks me, pointing to the corset on my dress. I nod and he rushes to my aid. He must do this a lot with Karmin, because he effortlessly tightens the back of the dress until it hugs me in all the right places.

"Wow," Keegan breathes, causing me to blush. He grabs my hand and twirls me around slowly like I'm a princess at a grand ball.

"What did I tell you?" Karmin chimes in. "You look killer in that dress. It's like it was made for you. You have to get it."

Flipping over the price tag, I frown. "Not exactly in my price range for a one-wear homecoming dress." I run my fingers over the tulle bottom and smile, but not for too long. "And I'm not even sure if I'm going yet." I motion for Keegan to undo the corset ribbons and sigh. "Maybe if I *do* decide to go, this dress will still be here."

"Nobody looks that good in a dress and puts it back on the rack. Now, say it with me: 'I'm going to the dance.'" Karmin stares me down, waiting for me to repeat her words, but I look at the price tag again.

"I'm still not sure."

"Fine." Karmin shrugs, uncaringly. "Well, I think I've found my dress, so let's pay and head off for lunch. I'm starving."

I return to my dressing room and say my goodbyes to the most perfect dress I've ever seen on my body. Keegan is in charge of their mother's credit card, so while he handles payment, Karmin and I head to the car.

"You should really think about going to homecoming. That dress fits you like a glove. Even Keegan thought so."

Yeah. I noticed, I want to tell her, but don't. I saw the way Keegan's green eyes lit up when I walked out of the dressing room. It's the same way Dylan looked at me right before he kissed me in his studio last week.

"Still on the fence," I tell her, but what I really mean is *Still waiting on Dylan to ask me.*

I haven't even been home for five minutes when I hear the engine of Dylan's car in the driveway. It's almost nighttime; I spent the rest of my day at the Literary Lovers Festival, purchasing a hefty haul with hopes that it would heal my broken heart, and more devious hopes that

I'd run into Dylan. But I didn't. The pain of my rejection had subsided when I was with Karmin and Keegan, but now that I'm home, it's back for round two. Right before I head to the shower, I hear three small knocks at my door.

"Emma?" Dylan calls from outside. I'm sure he's surprised that it's locked this time. "Can I come in? I want to talk."

What more could he possibly have to say to me? I'm pretty sure I understood everything crystal clearly the first time. You don't want me, and it's time to move on.

"What is it?" I ask through the door.

He's quiet at first, but then I hear him take a deep breath and ask, "Were you and Karmin at She's So Chic Formalwear today? I think I saw your car there."

"Yeah."

"And . . . that guy there? The one who helped you lace up your dress? Is he . . . like . . . your homecoming date?"

I roll my eyes and put my back to the door. "It's really none of your business who I spend my time with."

"It just looked . . . I don't know . . . like you like him."

"Were you spying on me or something?"

"No. I . . . I just," he stammers before sighing again. "Can you please open the door so we can talk? It's important."

"Yeah. Give me a second." Turning around to look at my vanity mirror, I run my fingers through my hair and groan; there's no need for me to try to look good for him anymore. I open the door, and before he can step over the threshold, his hands are cupping my face and his lips are on mine again. *God, I don't want this to be a dream.*

"Dylan," I try to get in, but can't seem to with his tongue weaving in and out of my mouth. "I thought—"

"I know," he says, finally letting me catch my breath. "I know what I said earlier, but . . . I don't know. When I'm with you, something . . . something just feels right."

"Dylan," I breathe in a voice so low that even I can barely hear it. I spent the entire day trying to convince myself that we were wrong for each other, and now that he's flipped the script again, I don't know what to think. I search his face for answers, but his honey-colored eyes leave me hanging, and I come up short. "Aren't you worried that something bad might happen? That they will take you away?"

"I don't care what happens." He's gotten pretty good at reading my mind, and before I can squeeze in another word, he says, "I just want you."

Dear God, please let this not be a dream. Please.

I GO BACK AND FORTH A MILLION TIMES IN THE FOLLOWING DAYS, BUT I finally settle on the idea that everything that's happening between Dylan and me is real. Dreams don't last this long, and they usually stop just when it's getting good. This got good way too long ago to be a dream.

I find it hard not to smile nowadays. I wake up with it on. I go to school with it on. I even have it on when I'm hungry—and I am usually not the happiest person in the world when I've missed a meal or two. I wish I could attribute this to something more than just a boy, but I know it's all Dylan. When he's on my mind, which is about ninety percent of the time, I beam. I can't help it.

So this is what I've been missing out on? This is how it feels to have a guy you like, like you back. No wonder girls get so attached to their first boyfriends—Dylan and I aren't even a couple yet, and I'm already attached. I know I'm falling fast, but it's hard to put the brakes on this high; whenever he's around or on my mind, it's as if someone has turned off the gravity and I'm floating.

"So what do you think, Emma?" I hear my mom say from across the dinner table.

"Sorry. What?" I'm too busy playing footsie with Dylan to hear what her question is even about. It's been a while since I've been able to catch dinner with my family, and they probably think that I'm bored out of my mind with them.

"I'm thinking about writing a book. What do you think?"

"Oh, right. Just curious, what is it going to be about?"

"My experience being a foster parent. The highs, the lows, and things like that."

My fork clinks against my plate when I drop it, mid-bite. "This isn't going to be a tell-all book, is it? I'd rather not have my personal business out there for the world to read about."

"Oh, no. Nothing like that. I promise, it'll be about me, not you guys."

"But, what if—?"

"Oh, for goodness' sake, Emma," my mom says, cutting me off. "It's not about you, but in the event that I *have* to talk about you, I'll make sure it's something nice."

Across the table, Dylan sends me a look that reads, *Be supportive.* I thought I was, but I guess I need to make it more obvious. "You're right, Mom. It's not about me, so you know what . . . follow your dreams. Don't let anyone or anything stand in your way. If it feels right, go for it."

She gives me a look. "When did you start becoming so idealistic? You used to be a lot more jaded about those aphorisms."

"Well, that was before I wanted to become a writer. And I guess I'm changing inside."

I see my father drop his fork and slip into a fit of oh-God-my-daughter-is-a-woman coughs.

"Not that way, Dad." I laugh, though it's partly true. "I just mean that there are so many obstacles that keep us from the things we love. If you can find a way to keep that thing in your life, make it happen."

"Remind me to have you make the toast at my book release party. You're becoming quite the motivational speaker."

"Yeah, Emma," Matthew says, extending his cup into the middle of the table. "Cheers." He has already finished his juice, and the cup in his hands is empty.

"Matthew, you have to have something in your cup to toast." Dylan chuckles as he refills Matthew's cup to the halfway mark. I haven't seen him stop smiling since he knocked on my door and kissed me passionately in the moonlight. And it seems like everything else has fallen into place since that moment. I'm finally starting to fit in at school, my GPA is going strong, and I feel like nothing can go wrong.

"Excellent dinner, honey," I hear my dad say as I continue to daydream about Dylan.

"I agree, Mrs. Ellenburg," Dylan says. "Dinner *was* really good, but I have some chemistry homework to finish. So I'm going to head upstairs." In his eyes, he asks me if I'm coming, too.

"Oh yeah. I have to show him how to draw some of the Lewis structures. I gotta go too, Mom." I pick up my plate and give my mom and dad a good-night kiss on the cheek. "I'll see you all in the morning."

"Nice lie," Dylan says when I walk into his room. I've barely entered when he draws me close and kisses me. "I've been waiting to do that all day."

"Me too." As I pull away from him, I stare into his golden eyes and feel a bolt of guilt zap through me. I haven't really seen him all day, thanks to my rigorous dance practice schedule. "I'm sorry, Dylan," I whisper into the space between us. "Since homecoming's only three weeks away, Coach Denise has extended practice for an entire hour this week so we can nail our performance." Breaking his gaze, I grab his chemistry book from his desk and lie down beside him, my feet dangling off the edge of the bed. "But enough of my boring dance team talk. Let's get down to business. Chapter Seven: Lewis Structures."

"Oh, you were serious about doing homework? I thought you were kidding."

"Well, if anyone walks in here, we have to make it look believable, don't we?"

"Pass. I'd rather do this." He steals another kiss, and I push him away.

"I'm serious. You should study."

He rejects my advice by playfully hitting me with a pillow, and then the wrestling commences. Before I know it, we're on the floor, I have my legs straddled across him, and I'm choking down laughter, trying to keep him from tickling me. The longer we wrestle, the harder it becomes to stifle my laughter, and I fear that my parents will discover us.

"I want in," Matthew yells as he bursts through the door. "You guys sound like you're having so much fun in here. I want to play, too."

"Matt," Dylan says, pushing me off of him, "we were just taking a break from studying." He picks himself up off of the floor and races over to Matthew. "Do you want to play a game of tickle tag? It's just like regular tag, but instead of tagging the person, you have to tickle them."

"Awesome! I'm first!"

"Okay, cool. We'll be right down as soon as we put our books away." I love how big-brotherly Dylan is with Matthew. It's like he knows exactly what to say to keep him smiling. "That was a close one," he says when Matthew is out of the room.

"That was my fault. I don't think I pushed the door closed all of the way."

"We need to be more careful. That could have easily been your parents."

"I agree. After Matthew gets put to bed, let's meet in your studio." It comes out as if I'm planning a sexy rendezvous, but it's a lot more serious than that.

"Listen," he says when I enter his studio an hour later, "we have to establish some ground rules if this is going to work."

"Definitely. That was a close call earlier."

"Here's what I'm thinking: we act like normal brother and sister when it's daylight, and the only time we can hug and kiss or whatever is if it's after hours when we're in a closed-off room. Like your room, or in here. But not my bedroom. It's too close to them."

"I'm with you," I say. And I am. I just wish we didn't have to do so much sneaking around. When I imagined my first relationship with someone—not that we're a couple yet—I imagined that I would be able to show it off to the world. I didn't expect it to be so suffocated. But this is better than nothing, right? "Um, also all daytime flirty conversations should be through text message only. My mom and dad never go through our phones, so that will be our best mode of communication if we are dying to tell each other something."

"You mean, like this." He pulls his phone from his pocket and sends me a quick text.

"I didn't bring my phone. And we're in your studio, our safe zone."

"I know. But I want you to smile when you read it before you go to sleep."

He's being so sweet right now, I can't take it. "Who would have guessed that my foster brother would be the first guy that I like, and the guy to give me my first kiss?"

"Ohhhhh," he says with a chuckle. "So that's why you were so mad at me for the incident at the mall. You thought you wasted your first kiss on me."

"Well, yeah. There are three guys that a girl will always remember in her life: the guy who gives her her first kiss, the one who takes her virginity, and the first one she ever falls in love with. I didn't want to have to grow up and tell my children that my first kiss was with a guy who used me to make another girl back off."

"Is that what you think I was doing?" His eyes catch the light, and I see that they are honey again.

"Yep."

He doesn't correct me, so I know that my assumption about his intentions at the mall is right. "Well, you're still screwed. Now you have to tell your children that your first real kiss was with your foster brother."

"Well, I guess I'm going to have to make something up, then. Any suggestions?"

"Your first kiss was in a pool? How does that sound?"

"I can deal with that. Keep going."

"The guy was a total amateur, and you hated every second of it."

"Pool. Bad kisser. I hated it. Got it."

"And I promise to take your secret to my grave." He laughs, and I can tell he wants to kiss me by the way he keeps looking at my lips. It's weirdly nice to know that he finds me attractive and tantalizing enough to risk so much. "So do you want another art lesson?" he says as he replaces the small canvas he's working on with a bigger blank one.

"Of course." I grab a smock while he pulls the other barstool up to the easel. "We're sharing?"

"Yep. This is going to be an abstract piece where each artist tries to mirror what the other has done. The only catch is that you will use the opposite color of what I use. Remember the color wheel we went over on the first day?" He must see my face twist into a frown. "Don't freak out. I'm not going to do anything difficult." He takes the brushes and sets them on the table near us. "Besides, we're not going to be using brushes; we'll be using our fingers instead."

Our fingers? "But I just took a shower."

"We're not *body* painting, we're finger painting. Like kindergarten. You won't get *that* dirty, and it'll be fun. I promise."

"You're lucky I'm not a girly girl who gets her nails done every other week." I see him dip his fingers in the paint and draw a red sun, and then I do the same in green.

"No, I'm lucky to have a girlfriend who doesn't mind getting a little messy for me." Dylan sneaks in a kiss as I mirror his finger painting. "You're so beautiful. Do you know that?" he says out of the blue, once we've gone through a few rounds of drawing and mirroring. Overwhelmed, I don't respond, but I know he can see his effect on me through the grin on my face.

When we finish, the red, blue, and green paint has found its way underneath my nails, and he catches me looking at them. "Don't worry, it's just paint. And now you look like an artist," he says, grabbing my hands. He leans in for a kiss, but gets denied when a yawn escapes me.

"Sorry, it's getting late," I say as I cover my mouth, heading to the sink to scrub the paint off my fingertips. "How are you able to stay up so late every night?"

"I can't sleep. Actually, I usually don't sleep more than a few hours. I can't even remember the last time I was able to get a full night's rest."

I want to ask him why he can't sleep, but I know it has something to do with whatever he wanted to tell me the night he first kissed me in here. The night I defended him against Dad. I should have just let him tell me; I don't know when he'll open up to me like that again.

"Well, I'm going to go to bed. It's almost eleven and I'm super tired." With pruney, almost-clean hands, I reach to kiss him good night and exit the studio.

"Don't forget to check your phone," he says, and I don't. It's the first thing I do when I get back to my room.

Dylan: I like you. Want to be my girlfriend? Text back yes or no.

It reminds me of the notes I used to see kids pass around in middle school. I never got one, but I always used to think that they were so cute. I text him back without thinking because it's such an easy answer.

Me: Of course.

Me: I mean yes 😊

Dylan: You sure? I don't want you to regret anything if things don't go as planned.

Me: No regrets.

Dylan: No regrets!

For a moment, all is right with the world, but then a thought occurs to me. *What if all of this backfires on us? What if this doesn't go the way we plan, and the social worker takes him away?*

Me: Truth . . . I'm scared. I don't want to lose you. Not as a brother or a boyfriend.

Dylan: Not possible. You're never gonna lose me. No matter what happens, I'm always gonna be here 🩶

Me: Promise?

Dylan: I promise.

chapter 11

I

F SOMEONE EVER decided to make a movie of my life, this would
be where the honeymoon sequence begins—aka the first weeks of
a relationship, all set to a romantic and touching piano ballad. There
would be scenes of Dylan and me holding hands as we frolic through
the flower gardens of San Diego, and scenes of us laughing uncontrollably at some inane inside joke. Oh, and let's not forget the scenes of
me wearing his sweatshirt as he gives me a piggyback ride.

But that's not real life. There's been a lot of laughing and hand-
holding (in secret, of course), but definitely no frolicking or piggyback
rides. Still, public mushiness or not, Dylan is the best thing to ever
happen to me.

I finish my AP calculus homework as soon as Dylan reappears
behind the counter and sets a ham and cheese sandwich down in front
of me. I couldn't bear to go another day without spending a little
bit of time with him, and his work seems to be the only place we can

meet up nowadays. Between his shifts and all-night painting sessions, and my crazy dance and early sleep schedules, we barely get to see each other, and when we do, everything has to be done in secret. I can't kiss him when I want to, and he can't hold me when *he* wants to. As much as I hate it, I know we can't afford to get caught. Not with his adoption still hanging in limbo.

"Enjoying your sandwich?" Dylan says, handing me a napkin. "I made it with love."

"Corny," I say, grabbing the napkin to wipe the crumbs from the sides of my mouth.

"You like it, though."

"Maybe."

"'Maybe'? Fine, we're done." A laugh escapes him as I ball up my napkin and pelt it at him. "It sucks that I can't see you that much," he says in a more serious tone. I feel his fingertips brush up against mine when I set my hand back down on the table. *Sister, Emma. You're supposed to be his sister right now.*

"I know." My lips shape into a grimace as I pull my fingers away and tuck my hands under the seat of the barstool I'm sitting on. *This sucks.* My eyes fall on the journal to the right of the plate holding my ham and cheese sandwich.

"What do you write in this thing? Poems?" he says, extending his fingers to touch the navy blue felt cover of my English journal, which I scramble to get hold of before he can.

"Well, what do *you* write about? I mean, we both have the same assignment."

"I asked you first. So, do you write about me?" His Cheshire cat grin and glowing eyes—thanks to the glare on the window—almost win me over, but I refuse to give in.

"Stop that."

"What?"

"That thing you do with your eyes. Like, you're trying to get me to fall in love with you or something."

"Is it working?"

Maybe.

"Aww, brother and sister bonding. How cute," I hear a familiar voice say before I can answer. The bell above the door is still ringing when I swivel around in my seat to see Karmin and Keegan walk through the front door of the shop. "Is my mom here?"

"She's in the back."

"Great. I got the lady at Petite Feet to hold this amazing pair of strappy heels for me. They match my homecoming dress perfectly, and I need her to give me—well, Keegan—her credit card to buy them." She looks over her shoulder before advancing behind the counter, like she's on some type of covert mission and doesn't want to be followed. As she enters the back, the bell rings again. Another customer has arrived to steal Dylan away from me.

"Mrs. Chesterfield, nice to see you again," Dylan's voice booms from behind me. I've never met the woman, but judging from the way Dylan drops everything to get the door for her, I'm guessing she's a regular customer. The withered woman, with different shades of graying hair, takes Dylan's hand as he leads her to the corner booth.

"That's Mrs. Chesterfield," Keegan leans in to whisper in my ear. "She and her husband were the first customers to ever eat at my family's restaurant, almost forty years ago." He points to a black-and-white photo behind the counter; a girl and a boy, probably not much older than I am now, smile at the camera as they prepare to take a bite of their sandwiches. "They were only high school sweethearts then, and they probably had no clue that they would live out the latter half of their lives as husband and wife. He proposed to her in that very booth, you know?"

"How romantic."

"Yeah. My grandparents were the godparents of their first child, Elianna. From all of the pictures I've seen, she was really pretty. Long blond hair, bright blue eyes, and a smile so intense, it could cure cancer if it wanted to. Unfortunately, her smile couldn't cure her of her own, though. She passed away a few years ago."

"Aw, that's too bad. Elianna sounds like she had a beautiful soul."

"She did. She kind of reminds me of you." Our eyes lock for a moment, and it's as if someone has flipped a power switch because the electric current that I feel running through me almost knocks me out of my seat. I thought that Dylan was the only one who had the potential to do that. I guess I was wrong.

Look away, a voice bellows inside my head. *Bad Emma. Bad, bad, bad*, it shouts again, making me break the connection.

"Mrs. Chesterfield hasn't been the same since the funeral," he continues. "Sometimes, she even forgets that her daughter died."

"How horrible." I frown.

Karmin reappears, holding her mother's card high above her head as if it's the key that unlocks the door to paradise. "Got the card, Keegan. Let's go before she changes her mind."

"Looks like you been summoned," I tease.

"Indeed, I have."

"But it was nice seeing you again."

"Yes. It *was* nice." Keegan smiles, ignoring his sister's demand. "I'll see you later."

"Dylan, I'm headed out," I say as he gestures for Mrs. Chesterfield to stay put and rushes over to me.

"Trying to make me jealous, are you?"

"Wouldn't dream of it. Keegan and I were just talking."

"That better have been all." He says this in a pleasant tone, so I'm not sure if I should play along with him or be frightened by his sudden territoriality. I don't have the luxury of thinking too long about it, though. A light tap on my shoulder stops my thoughts dead in their tracks.

"Elianna?" Mrs. Chesterfield says, continuing to pat my shoulder with her frail fingers. "Elianna, is that you?"

"Umm . . ."

"Please, honey. It's been so long." I see Dylan mouth the words *play along*, and despite my brain's efforts to conjure up the bad memories from the last time I "played along," I follow her to the corner booth and take a seat.

"Somehow you look even younger and prettier than last time you came home." She places her glasses on the end of her nose and peers down them to look at the menu. "Let's decide what we want before the waiter comes back. We don't want to keep him waiting."

Out of the corner of my eye, I see Dylan approaching with two glasses of water. As he sets one down in front of me, he leans low and whispers, "She sometimes forgets that her daughter passed away. Just sit and talk to her. You'll make her day." He straightens himself up, and smiles at Mrs. Chesterfield as she looks over the menu. "So what will it be, ladies?"

"A small turkey and Swiss for me."

"The water is fine. I'm not hungry," I say, taking a sip from my glass. Dylan nods and walks away, stealing a glance at me over his shoulder before disappearing behind the counter to ring in the order.

"You're not hungry? There was once a time when we couldn't stop you from eating. Lucky for you, that metabolism of yours hasn't slowed down yet. You're still as skinny as a toothpick." I watch as her weathered hands struggle to open her straw wrapper. "So how's Joshua?"

Since I have to play along, I figure I might as well make things interesting. "He's okay . . . I guess. He's been working a lot, but what else is new?"

"I was never a fan of that boy. I don't think he's good enough for you." She finally gets the wrapper open and takes a long sip of her water before continuing. "I come here almost every day for lunch, and at first, I kept trying to set you up with that young man over there. But unfortunately he has a girlfriend."

"H-he told you that?"

"Oh, yes. He says that she has eyes like two aquamarine stones framed with flaxen eyelashes. A blue so crystal clear that he can see straight through to her—"

"Heart of gold," Dylan finishes as he approaches with Mrs. Chesterfield's sandwich. "And don't even get me started on her laugh."

"You're going to love this, Ellie. Tell her!" Mrs. Chesterfield eggs him on excitedly.

"It's not how it sounds. It's how it makes you feel. Like that hair-raising moment that you experience when you hear a song on the radio that seems to speak directly to you." He pauses to look into his hands and meets my gaze once more before saying, "She's radiant . . . inside and out."

"And brilliant, too—right?" Mrs. Chesterfield adds.

Suddenly all of this is too much, and I have to hold my breath to keep myself from crying. He's shared so much of his feeling for me with this woman that I can't help but feel overwhelmed.

"She's a walking SAT study manual. She uses words like *pulchritudinous* to describe pretty flowers, and *conundrum* when talking about her problems. She dreams out loud about impossible things and encourages others to believe in them, too. It's hard not to be dazzled by how her mind works." Dylan's bronze eyes catch hold of mine, and I almost lose it. No one has ever been drawn to me for my vocabulary. "I better get back to work. You enjoy your sandwich, Mrs. Chesterfield."

I watch as Dylan makes his way back to the front counter and starts wiping it with a damp rag. It isn't until I feel Mrs. Chesterfield's cold hands grab my arm that I realize that I'm still sitting before her, acting as if I'm her daughter. "Sweet, isn't it?"

"Very," I say, wiping away a tear before it can fall from my eye.

"Does your Joshua talk about you like that, Elianna?"

I don't know how to answer that question, so I sit silently, waiting for her to continue. I mean, I don't want to badmouth this Joshua guy. I don't even know him.

"Well, I'd make sure that he does before you decide to take his name. And that's all I'm going to say about that."

THE BLISS IS STILL TINGLING IN MY FINGERTIPS WHEN I ARRIVE BACK AT the pool house thirty minutes later. With Dylan's words still resonating in my head, I fall back onto my bed to soak it up in private. *He likes me,* I repeat to myself over and over as I lie there with my eyes closed. *He really likes me.*

"Delivery for Miss Emma Ellenburg." My mom's fluid voice echoes through the room, bringing me to my feet. Before I can get up to open the door, she's bursting through it with a long yellow box.

"I could have totally been naked, Mom. I mean, for goodness' sake, have you never heard of knocking?"

"Get over yourself, Emma. We have the same parts." She sets the box down beside me and pauses, lifting an eyebrow. "Unless you have something to tell me, that is."

Slapping my palm to my forehead, I feel my cheeks flush with embarrassment. "You said I had a package? From where?"

"Some fancy boutique called She's So Chic Formalwear. And with homecoming looming in the air, I'm guessing that you've finally decided to go?"

"Uhh . . . no. I haven't bought a dress, because as far as I know, I'm not going."

My mom looks at the box again to make sure my name is indeed on it. "Well, someone must be dying for you to go. Especially if they went out of their way to buy you a dress."

"Karmin is relentless," I say through clenched teeth, though I'm touched that she thought of gifting it to me. "I . . . uh . . . guess I'm going to homecoming, then." I know what's about to come next, and so I sit in silence, waiting for her to burst into tears of happiness, which she does, as if on cue.

She hands the canary-yellow rectangular package to me and pulls two tissues from the box on my side table. "Well, what are you waiting for? Try it on. Let me see your dress," she says, dabbing at her eyes. I can't believe she's getting all blubbery over homecoming. It's not like I'm getting engaged or anything like that. It's just a school dance.

I vanish behind my dressing screen. It takes me all of two minutes to slip into and lace up the dress I've dreamed about at least three times since I first tried it on. The satin fabric awakens the same intoxicating feeling that I had at the boutique. I feel proud, beautiful, and unrelentingly visible.

"Try your hardest to keep the waterworks to a minimum," I warn as I peek around the screen. My mom nods, but I know that the second I step in front of her, she's going to lose it. Again.

Her gasp is so great that she has to cover her mouth with both hands to conceal it. "Honey," she breathes, "you look absolutely amazing." She signals for me to turn and I do as I'm told, like I'm one of those TLC pageant girls. *Spin left. Pause. Shoulders back. Smile. Eyes on the judges.* "So which lucky guy are you going to go with?"

"Mom, I literally just decided that I was going. What makes you think I have a date lined up?"

"Your excuse for not going the previous three years was that you couldn't go without a date, and seeing as Karmin went out of her way to buy you this gorgeous dress, I'm willing to bet that the two of you at least have *someone* in mind for your date." Before my mom married my dad, she had every intention of going to law school. Nothing gets past her; she is, and always has been, according to my grandmother, very observant. "And by the way, I'm glad you have such a generous and thoughtful friend, but you need to make arrangements for us to pay her back."

I feel my temperature rise as my tongue goes dry—sticking to the roof of my mouth—and a warm sweat breaks through to the surface of my skin. There *is* someone I want to go with, but telling her that it's Dylan will cause more trouble than it's worth. And I don't have enough time to think up an elaborate lie that will get her off my case. I'm stuck.

I scrounge up some saliva to wet my mouth enough to spill everything that's been going on with me these past few months: my feelings for Dylan, the many kisses that we've shared, what just happened at the sub shop, even the possibility of him being in love with me. Until—

My cell phone screen lights up, and Karmin's name flashes across it. "We're gonna have to postpone this conversation. I've got to thank Karmin for the dress. But I'll tell you later, Mom." *When I've thought up a good enough lie, that is.* I shoo my mother out of the room and wait until she's halfway back to the house before I answer the phone. "Hey, Karmin. What's up?"

"Did you get the package?"

"I did, and I cannot believe you bought me this dress!"

"I didn't. Keegan did. Apparently, he's as interested in who your date is going to be as I am. Speaking of, that's why I'm calling. Now that you have the dress, there is absolutely nothing holding you back from asking this mystery man of yours to the dance."

"Karmin, I don't know if—"

"You'll thank me later. Call him!" *Click.*

Tossing my phone onto the bed, I take another look in the mirror at me in my homecoming dress, and smile. *Dylan is going to love me in this. Now I just have to figure out how to ask him without setting off too many foster-brother-etiquette alarms.*

chapter 12

Dear Catherine,

Six days. There are six days standing in between now and my first-ever homecoming dance, and I must say that I'm proud of myself for keeping cool about everything. I asked Dylan to be my secret date the night I got my dress and he said yes, which I'm ecstatic about. I haven't told a soul who my date is, and no one but Karmin even knows that I like a guy. I'll call this a win.

Dylan and I agreed that we wouldn't go with anyone else, because we will be each other's secret date, even though I won't get the chance to dance with him until we're hidden away back home. Thursday we're going to decorate his studio with lights and candles, so we have somewhere private to slow dance afterward. That was actually his idea. God, he's so thoughtful, and sweet, and just . . . perfect. Would I love to scream that I'm his girlfriend from the rooftops? Of course. But this clandestine arrangement will have to do for now. Having to hide our feelings for each other is better than not being able to be together at all. Wouldn't you agree?

♡ Emma

"So," my mom says to me when I come into the kitchen after school, smiling. Dylan is upstairs, and he's just texted me a lame joke that I can't help but laugh at.

"So . . . what?" I ask her once I look up from my phone. My cheeks are hurting from smiling so hard, and I try to calm myself down in front of her, but no matter what I do, my grin won't go away. I get the sinking feeling in my stomach that she can tell something's up, but I know I have to play it cool.

"Who's the boy?"

"What boy?"

"The one who's got you walking around here giggling like a grade-school girl. Now, you skillfully evaded my question the other day in your room, and I've decided to pick up where we left off. So, who's the boy?"

"What makes you think it's a boy? I mean, can't a person just be happy about life?"

"You're right. Maybe it's not a boy. Is it a girl?"

"Mom, please don't."

"Okay, okay. It's true that a *person* can just be happy about life, but a *teenager* can't. Or have you forgotten that I, too, was young at some point in time?"

I give her a look like I don't know what she's talking about, and she grins.

"Oh, come on, Emma. The signs are all there. I see the way you've been skipping around the house with a permanent smile plastered to your face. And every time your phone buzzes with a new text, you light up even more."

She has a point; I have been *a lot* more chipper than usual. I guess my mouth kept everything concealed, but my face couldn't hide anything. What am I going to say? *Hey, Mom, I'm falling for the teenage boy who's going to be my brother in about five months, and by the way, he's my secret homecoming date?* I think not.

"You can tell me. Who am I going to tell?"

I don't say a word. My best bet is to keep quiet—and if that fails: Deny. Deny. Deny.

"Okay, fine, at least tell me that you guys are being safe."

"MOM!" I feel my face burn red. I cannot believe she's about to have the sex talk with me in the middle of our kitchen. *Gross.*

"What? I know how teenagers are. Hooking up and making out." She leans against the refrigerator and gives me a raised-eyebrow glance, like she has everything figured out.

"Well, you don't have to worry about that."

"About which one? The hooking up or making out?"

"Both. I'm not doing either, because I'm not dating anyone."

I see her eyes relax as another small smile graces her face. "So no boyfriend?"

I shake my head again. *Deny. Deny. Deny.*

"You may have postponed my sex talk, but don't think you're off the hook."

I breathe a sigh of relief and lean against the kitchen counter.

She has turned her attention back to cooking dinner, giving me a tiny window to escape out of the kitchen, but I fail to do so before she starts back again. "Well, there's a guy in your life. Maybe not as a boyfriend, but as some kind of love interest. You're too smitten for there not to be. I may be getting old, but I'm not dumb."

"Well, there's no one."

"Hmm" is all she says as she adds a couple seasonings to the pot she's hovering over. "I don't believe you." She places a lid on the pot and looks down at my phone as it vibrates on the counter. "Is that him?"

I don't want to look at it, but I find myself unable to resist the magnetic pull of our secret inbox. I glance down, expecting to see Dylan's response to my text. But the name that flashes across my screen is not Dylan's; it's Keegan's. *Oh God*. He probably wants to talk about that extravagant homecoming dress, just like Karmin already did.

Keegan: Did you like your homecoming surprise?

Yep. They really are twins. I reread the word *homecoming* in his text, and a brilliant idea slams into my head with the force of a category-five hurricane.

"Yeah. It's him," I lie. I figure it's better to tell her that I'm dating another guy, so if she ever suspects Dylan, I will have someone else to cover my ass. *So much for "Deny. Deny. Deny."*

"I knew it," she squeals. "You can't hide the 'in like' smile from me."

I pour myself a glass of apple juice, and grin with relief. I've escaped her interrogation for now. I'm safe.

"What's his name?"

"Keegan Ortega. He's Karmin's brother."

"So he's the one who bought you the dress, huh?" she teases as she adds salt to the now-boiling pot. "When can we meet him?"

"You want to . . . what?" I say, almost spitting out the apple juice in my mouth.

"I want to meet him. Invite him over for dinner with the family one of these days." My mom is pushing the situation too far now. First she thinks that I'm having sex, and now she wants to invite Keegan into the house to meet everyone. She's messing everything up. "I'm making my special shrimp pasta tomorrow. Invite him over." Before I can find a way to weasel out of it, she exits the room. *Great*. This is a mess. *Dylan is going to kill me.*

BEFORE I HIT SEND ON MY PHONE, I SEND UP A SILENT PRAYER, HOPEFUL some divine intervention will block the message from going through. Right now, it's the only chance I have left.

> **Me:** I ADORE this dress, but I don't feel comfortable accepting an extravagant gift like this. I will pay you back for it, I promise.
>
> **Keegan:** Absolutely not. A gift is a gift.
>
> **Me:** True, but I'm still going to pay you back.
>
> **Keegan:** If that's what you really want, but no obligation.
>
> **Me:** I will. But I'd also like to thank you for the dress, so do you want to come over for dinner tomorrow? My parents are making shrimp Alfredo pasta.

Before he can text back, I send him another one.

Me: I know it's weird and last minute, so you don't have to come if you're busy. After the whole dress delivery, my parents wanted to meet you, but we can postpone this or forget it altogether if you don't want to do it.

He doesn't text me back for ten minutes, and I pace the room until he does. *Is he trying to find a way to let me down easy?* I sure hope so. I want him to tell me that he already has plans or is allergic to shrimp or that he's getting back together with his ex. Something. Anything to get me out of this tangled web.

Keegan: Is that even a question? I'd never turn down an invitation to eat. I have practice but can be there by 6ish. Sound okay?
Me: Sounds great.

Yeah. Just great.

❦

I KEEP TRYING TO FIND THE WORDS TO TELL DYLAN, AND IT ISN'T UNTIL five minutes before Keegan shows up that I finally do.

"Don't freak out, but I had to invite Keegan over for dinner tonight."

"Why?" Dylan still isn't too fond of Keegan, but he needs to get over it. I'm with him, not Keegan.

"Because I kind of told my mom that I'm into him to cover up why, according to Mom, I've been so 'smitten' lately. Apparently, I've never been this happy in my entire life." I see his jaw begin to clench and unclench again, telling me that he's not pleased. "Anyways, Mom

146

wanted to meet him and he's going to be here any minute . . . for dinner."

"So you're into him, too, now?" This is a loaded question, and I know I have to answer it carefully.

"No. But I have a plan, and we need him for it. It's kind of crazy, but hear me out, okay?" I take a breath before continuing, not to steady my thoughts, but to prepare myself for the blowup that's about to happen. Dylan's a very territorial person, and if he even thinks that another guy is stepping in to take me away from him, this could escalate fast. "How about I get him to ask me out and we become a couple?"

"But you're with me." I can almost see the question mark of confusion hovering over his head. Maybe he thinks that I'm having second thoughts about us.

"I know that. But my mom knows that I'm into someone, and if they find out it's you, they'll take you away. And that can't happen. But if they *think* it's Keegan, we can fool them."

He doesn't say anything. He just stares at me, his big, brown eyes fuming.

"I know it sounds crazy, but we have to throw them off our trail somehow."

He's going to need some convincing, I think, so I grab his head with both my hands and pull it toward mine. Before I know it, my hands are playing in his hair, his are exploring my body, and our lips and tongues are playing tug-of-war. I've never kissed him like this before, so I hope it's sending the message clearly.

"I want you, and only you," I say once I catch my breath. "This arrangement will just make it easier to conceal us. You have to trust me."

"Fine." His voice is low and cold. I know he doesn't like it, but he's going to have to. "I'll go get changed for dinner." He pecks at my neck before he leaves and then rushes inside. He's on board, or at least he seems to be, but something inside of me feels like I just planted a ticking time bomb.

I don't have much time to think about Dylan and how he's feeling because as soon as I make it outside, Keegan's white truck pulls into our driveway. When he gets out of the car, I can see that he's dressed up for the event, like I hoped he would. He has on black pants and a light blue collared shirt, the same color as the blouse I'm wearing. All I can think is, *I hope Dylan doesn't think that we planned to match.*

"Are you trying to copy me?" Keegan says as he leans in for a hug.

"Great minds think alike, I guess." Though I've already had three encounters with him, it isn't until now that I look deeper into his eyes. They're a dark green, just like Karmin's, with hints of gold in the center, almost as if it were dusted on. I find myself staring into his eyes for longer than I intended, and the electricity between us that I felt at the restaurant returns.

"You look gorgeous tonight, by the way."

"Thank you." I don't know why, but as I accept his compliment, I feel my insides curl into a ball. But it's not a ball of nerves; it's more like a ball of bliss. "So do you. Handsome, I mean . . . not gorgeous."

His smile turns into a tiny but deep-voiced laugh. "You're really cute when you're nervous."

Blushing, I try to keep the conversation going. "Do you like shrimp Alfredo?"

"Is that even a question?" A smile stretches across his cheeks, and as it does, a laugh escapes me. That rhetorical question is his catch-phrase and I've heard him use it numerous times. "My mom grew up in the south—Baton Rouge, Louisiana, to be exact—and seafood is its own lifestyle down there. I came out of the womb as a shrimp lover." He chuckles as he rests his hand on my lower back.

I remember reading in a magazine that a girl can always tell if a guy likes her by the way he touches her back. If it's too high, he wants to just be friends, but if it's low, then he wants something more.

I lead him around to our side deck, and while trying to hide my excitement for the lower-back touch he just gave me, I wait for the rest of the family to join us. Out of the corner of my eye, I see my dad approaching, and I'm instantly worried about Keegan's safety; I expect my dad to grill him like I've seen some fathers do in movies, asking what his goals are after high school and what his intentions with me are.

"Is this Keegan?" he asks, extending a hand. "I'm—"

"Daniel Ellenburg," Keegan finishes before my dad can get the words out. "I used to watch you play when I was a kid. You're a legend. I'm a huge fan, sir." Keegan is such a charmer. Before I know it, he's bumping fists with my dad and talking all things baseball as if they've known each other for years.

"They seem to be getting along pretty well," my mom says to me as she hands me a stack of glass plates to set the table.

"Keegan's a baseball player."

"So that's why he's being so nice. I expected your dad to be stone-cold all night." I have to laugh at this; I thought the same thing. "Dinner's ready, guys. Please, come sit." As she introduces herself to Keegan, I hear him say that she looks too young to be my mother. *Yep, he's definitely a charmer.*

My mom and I set out the usual five placemats; Matthew is away at a sleepover, which means that Dylan will probably take his spot across from me, and Keegan will take Dylan's place next to me. I'm glad about this, because Matthew would be the one to say something embarrassing and ruin things before they even begin. Also because I'll be less tempted to hold Dylan's hand under the table with him sitting across from me.

"Hey." I feel Dylan sneak up behind me and place his hand on the small of my back, just like Keegan did a moment ago. I quickly remove his hand after giving him a what-the-hell-are-you-doing look. I can tell that he's uncomfortable, but I can't do anything about it. One, we're with our family, so I have to act like his sister. And two, I need him to be okay with this so that our relationship can continue undisturbed.

"He looks very comfortable," he whispers so only I can hear.

"Yeah," I whisper back. "He knows how to swim with them. He and Dad are already hitting it off with baseball talk." A small grin creeps onto my face as I watch Keegan mingle with my mom and dad. "This just might work."

"Just don't get caught up in the lie and forget your reason for doing this" is the last thing I hear him say before his natural scent of paint and soap leaves my side. With his hands crumpled into fists, he goes over to take his seat in Matthew's usual spot. The grimace on his face says it all: he's not happy about this. And as much as I want to kiss his perfectly pouty lips to reassure him, I can't. I know he doesn't like this, but for tonight, he's going to have to get over it.

At dinner, all I can think about is not embarrassing myself or letting anyone catch on to any romantic subtext here. For Dylan and me to keep things a secret, I need tonight to go as smoothly as possible.

"You ever been to the batting cages near City Park?" my dad asks as he takes a piece of garlic toast from the basket in the center of the table. "I used to spend so much time there after the injury. I knew I wasn't going to be able to hit like I used to, but I couldn't lose the skill, you know?"

"I know what you mean. When I broke my hand diving for a catch last season, I thought I wasn't going to be able to play again, but thankfully, I've recovered and I'll be back on that field when the season starts in the spring."

"Enough baseball talk," I say as I feel Dylan's foot tap mine under the table. He's not playing footsie, but rather warning me when I'm getting too close to Keegan, who's sitting on my right. I wish he would stop monitoring my every move.

"Yes, I agree. Let's talk about goals and ambitions," my dad says as he takes a sip from his wineglass. This was bound to come up sooner or later. "Graduation is approaching rapidly, as I'm sure you know. Now, Emma's keeping her university picks a secret—even though I'm sure UCLA is at the top of her list—so we're dying to hear someone else's post-graduation plans."

"UCLA, huh? Trying to keep it in the family, I see."

"We're trying." My dad and Keegan share a laugh, but I don't join in.

"Well, for starters, I'm going to go the college route, too," Keegan begins.

"Good job. I knew I was going to like you," Dad continues.

"I've been corresponding with USC, and I'm pretty sure that I'll be able to secure a baseball scholarship from them if I play a clean season. So that's where I'm putting all my eggs."

"Any thoughts on what you want to major in?" Mom asks with a smile. I'm sure she's just as happy as I am that we've moved on from the subject of baseball. "Emma's going to be an English major. She has her heart set on publishing a book someday."

"As smart as she is, I'm sure she'll have no problem getting there."

I see Dylan jealously snarl at Keegan's comment. "But to answer your question, business with a concentration in entrepreneurship. If I don't go pro, my buddy and I want to start up a sports rehabilitation center for injured players. When my hand was broken, I relied heavily on my trainer to get me back to where I needed to be." He pauses for a minute to finish chewing his food. "Plus, I look good in a suit." My mom and dad chuckle at his comment, and I think I even see a grin pass over Dylan's lips.

"You've got a good head on your shoulders, son. And I wish you the best in your endeavors."

"Thank you, sir. By the way, Mrs. Ellenburg, this pasta is divine." He's really turning on the charm, and my parents are swooning. Even I find myself falling for his alluring personality as the night progresses.

"So what about you?" he says to Dylan. "Are you into baseball, too?"

"Not really. I'm into the arts. Have been since before the Ellenburgs started to foster me."

"Fostered? I thought you were adopted."

"No. Not yet, anyway."

"Well, I'm sure a lot of people are rooting for you. Everyone at school loves you, from what I hear." I see Dylan's hard looks soften, and I can tell that he's getting sucked into Keegan's gentle ways, too. "There's been talk about asking you to paint a mural to commemorate those who died in the school shooting here a few decades ago."

Cedar Pointe fell victim to a school shooting back in the mid-eighties. At an assembly during my freshman year, we were told that three students ran through the school at lunch and killed eighteen students and permanently disabled five others. Another tragic random act of violence.

"Really?" Dylan's eyes light up when he hears this. I know he saw the video clip about the shooting during his orientation, and from what I heard, he was very emotional about it.

"Yeah. I heard Principal Reed and Ms. Portman"—she's the art teacher—"talking about it in the office the other day. They've seen some of your work in the art room and they're impressed."

"See, Dylan?" Dad interjects. "I told you. People are dying to see your work."

"He's waiting to hear back from the San Diego Museum of Art. Hopefully he'll get picked to exhibit his pieces in their teen art show-case in December." My mom is radiant with pride as she speaks.

"Oh yeah. I heard of that. My twin sister, Karmin, was saying something about that a while back. She interned at the museum over the summer, and helped raise the prize money for it." It still blows my mind that he and Karmin are twins. He had always looked older than her. "She says the turnout is amazing every year."

"Cool." Dylan slinks back into his quiet state, probably from Dad mentioning the showcase.

When dinner ends and when my mom and dad say their good-byes to Keegan, I know the night is almost over. He did a fantastic job selling himself to my parents, but now I have to seal the deal and get him to ask me out to homecoming. I don't really want to do it, because I know how much this is going to bother Dylan, but it's the only way that all of this is going to work.

"Sorry if they embarrassed you tonight or asked too many personal questions. I told them not to," I say as I walk him back to his car.

"Oh, it's fine. Your parents are pretty cool."

"If you say so."

"I do. And you're pretty spectacular yourself." We're halfway down the walkway when he pauses and looks in the direction of my room. "You guys have a pool house, too? That's it, I'm coming to live here." He laughs.

"That's actually my room."

I see Keegan's eyes light up with curiosity. "Can I see it?"

"Keegan Ortega, are you trying to . . . seduce me?"

"No, no. Not at all. I read that bedrooms can say a lot about a person. I'm not trying to seduce anyone. I just—"

He's pretty cute when he's flustered, too.

"I'm only joking," I say, scanning the walkway to see if anyone—namely, Dylan—is following us. "Come on." We enter my room, and I see his eyes fly from the guitar next to my bed, to my rose-colored curtains and wallpaper, to my bookshelf, to my shoe closet, and then land on me. "So what does my room say about me?"

"Well," he starts as he takes a seat next to me on my bed, "I gather that you can play the guitar, your favorite color is pink, and you love to shop almost as much as you like to read."

"Wrong, wrong, and half wrong. Nice try, though." I giggle. "I love antique furniture but most of it only matches with pink, not purple, which is my favorite color, and I hate shopping. I only go to hang out with my mom. But I do like to read. That one you got right."

"What about the guitar?" I see his eyes fall on the instrument that I haven't picked up to play in almost six years, and then circle back to me as a wide grin creeps across his face. "Do you play?"

To answer his question, I grab the instrument and pluck a few chords. It's rough and out of tune, and I'm embarrassed that I even picked it up to show him how horrible I sound. "After hearing a beautiful guitar ballad at a Justin Timberlake concert, I decided to try my hand at the guitar. I took a couple lessons and called it quits shortly after. The strings hurt my fingers, and my wrist hurt from holding it in an awkward position. It was just bad." I giggle nervously. "But I keep it around in case I want to give it another try one of these days." Before I can finish speaking, Keegan grabs the guitar from my hands and returns to my bed. "What are you doing?"

"Well, if you don't play it, someone should."

"You can play?"

He doesn't answer. I watch him quickly tune the instrument by ear, and before I know it, he's plucking and strumming away. Maybe it's just the vibrations of sound I feel pulsing through my body, but when Keegan begins to play, my palms start to sweat.

So this is how it's supposed to look and sound, I think as a flashback memory of my guitar lessons works its way through my mind. I watch Keegan intently, his fingers moving gracefully across the strings on the neck of the guitar, creating the rainbow of sounds that I hear in my ears. There are no words to his song for me to connect with, but when Keegan's gaze pierces into me, we're harmonizing with each other through the melody.

"Whoa" is all I can get out when he finishes, his last strum still trembling through me like leaves hanging from a tree on a windy spring day. "You're really good."

"Thanks. Maybe I can teach you how to play sometime."

"Yeah. I'd like that." It isn't until now that I notice how little space is between us. An inch, maybe half an inch. As much as I don't think Dylan would like it, I know I'm going to have to kiss him in order for him to ask me out.

I should kiss him. Now is the perfect time to kiss him, right? Keegan doesn't break my gaze, like I expect him to. *Yeah, I should definitely kiss him now. But do I initiate it, or do I let him lean in first?*

In the middle of me trying to figure out the perfect moment to kiss him, I hear Keegan say, "It's . . . um . . . getting late. I better start heading home."

"You're right. It *is* getting late, and you probably have z's to catch." *Get it? Catch, because you play baseball?* Keegan doesn't even chuckle. My attempt to make a baseball joke fails miserably, and the longer I let my words linger between us, the more I want to trade them in for something less lame. "Not saying that you look tired, because you don't. You look great, actually. I mean . . . I'm going to stop talking now."

Dammit! I mentally kick myself. *I missed my chance. That's my second denial in two months. Clearly this bed is Rejection Central.*

Keegan doesn't comment on the blabber coming out of my mouth. Instead, he just replaces my guitar and silently holds the door open for me to lead him out of my room. When we get to the end of the walkway, he leans up against the side of his truck, like he's expecting me to plant one on him now. *What was wrong with kissing me in my room, a second ago?*

"Thanks for coming. I know it was last minute, and I really appreciate it."

"Again, no problem. Truth be told, I've been trying to work up the courage to ask you out ever since I helped you with your car. I just didn't know the right time to do it."

I feel a shiver of excitement run down my back. *Really?* But the feeling dies down when my mind shifts to Dylan. For a moment I regret pursuing him instead of Keegan. With Dylan, it's complicated, but with Keegan, it could be so easy. My parents like him almost as much as I do. It would have been perfect. But I can't hurt Dylan like that.

"So," he says, "why *did* you invite me over? I'm sure it wasn't just to hear me strum on your guitar." Our eyes connect, and when they do, another chill crawls down my back.

"Because I like you." When I say it, it doesn't feel like a lie, like I told Dylan it was. It feels real.

"Good, because I like you, too." *Perfect*, I think. This is going to work.

"So where does this leave us?" I say, taking a step closer to him.

I'm waiting for him to say something about homecoming when I feel his hand grab the back of my neck and his lips press into mine. It's kind of weird to kiss him; I'm so used to Dylan's lips. But when he cups his hands around my face, I melt into him, just like I do with Dylan.

"Look, I like you, Emma. A lot," he says, breaking contact and leaning his forehead on mine. I feel the *but* coming on before it can even pass over his soft lips. "But I want to get to know you a little better . . . before we go any farther. What do you say we go to homecoming together?"

I don't even think about my answer. "I'd love to."

chapter 13

DYLAN DEFINITELY ISN'T thrilled when I tell him. It's not like I expected him to be, but still. I give him a play-by-play of what happened between Keegan and me, carefully leaving out the part about our kiss. He's already upset; I don't want to make him furious.

"Homecoming? I thought we decided not to go with anyone else. That was the arrangement we made, remember?" He doesn't look at me when he talks; he just stands with his back to me, flicking paint at a blank sheet of paper. He says he's cleaning his brushes, but I think he's looking for a way to release his anger about the Keegan situation.

"I'm sorry, but you should have seen how Mom grilled me the other day. I had to tell her something. And this is going to work. Want to know why?" He shrugs his shoulders, and I can't tell if it's because he wants to hear my answer or because he doesn't care. "Because I chose you. I want you. Keegan means nothing to me. It's all you."

This is the first lie I've ever told to Dylan, and I'm not even sure if it's a lie. Yes, Keegan and I had a moment after dinner, but what I feel for Dylan is much greater than what I feel for Keegan.

I see his shoulders relax and his grip on the paintbrush loosen. He's calming down. "Maybe we should just stop this right now. We have too much at stake." I can hear the resistance in his voice as he speaks. "Well, *I* have too much at stake."

"Are you worried that we'll get caught?" He goes quiet again. "Because I will never let that happen. I have our bases covered. You just have to trust me."

"I do trust you. I just . . . I wanted you all to myself."

"You *do* have me all to yourself. Keegan's just the decoy. There's nothing going on between us, I promise." My second kind-of lie. I give him a hug from behind, and leave him on that note.

It takes me a few days to get Dylan on board with the plan, but eventually he comes around. Not to the point where he no longer grimaces when I say Keegan's name, but, hey, progress is progress. And when I ask him to be my dress-up partner for Nerd Day during Spirit Week, he agrees to that, too. It's so un-Dylan of him—he's way too introverted to do something like that—that I have to question if I'm abusing my power as his girlfriend.

"The Willy Wonka Nerds costume you and Dylan wore for Nerd Day was so cute. The added suspenders and glasses were a great touch, too," Karmin says as we change into our dance team uniforms for the football game. "How'd you get him to agree to that?"

"I don't know. I just asked him, and he said yes. Simple as that."

"Simple? Please. Keegan and I may be twins, but he would never in a million years do something like that with me." A comparison of Dylan and Keegan was the last thing I wanted to hear about right now.

I'd been doing enough of that on my own, and apparently, so had Dylan.

Earlier, I made the mistake of mentioning to him that Keegan would be in full Cedar Pointe High gear at the game tonight to lead the student cheer section, and Dylan—through some deranged change in character—said he was going to do the same but "better." Now I'm afraid to see what ridiculous thing Dylan is going to do to try to show him up. But I don't have time to think much on it. With the game in half an hour, there's nothing I can do now.

"And speaking of Keegan," Karmin starts, pulling her hair into a ponytail, "I heard that you two are going to homecoming together."

Of course she already knows. "Yeah. He asked me a few days ago and, since we've been fishing around for a date for me, I said yes."

"Hmm" is all she says at first, but when I don't elaborate, she continues. "So was he the mystery guy you were talking about?" She's so open about things—unlike me—that I can't help but wonder why she's so adamant about adding me to her arsenal of friends. I'm a shy nobody, and she's the irresistible it-girl that gets voted things like Most Likely to Be a Celebrity in the yearbook. Why does she want to hang out with me all the time? I know she has better options to choose from.

"Yep."

"Well, why didn't you tell me? I could have set you guys up weeks ago." I'm glad she's taking it so well. With her being his twin sister, this could have gone south fast. "So do you *like him* like him or . . . what?"

"Yeah. I mean, he's cute. And smart. And did I mention, he's cute?" Again, it doesn't sound like a lie. *Am I really starting to fall for Keegan?*

"Really?"

"Yes, really." *What's wrong with me liking Keegan?* I wonder as I fasten a bright red bow to the top of my head.

"You just don't seem like his type. His last girlfriend, Lori, was feisty, flirty, and very *experienced*. She balanced that out with her smarts, though." Karmin must see my gaze fall to the floor, because she quickly edits herself. "Not saying that you're *not* feisty, flirty, or sexy. You're just not on our level."

"Our level"? What is that supposed to mean? "Explain."

"Guys like girls who are aggressive. You know, who aren't afraid to tell them what to do every once in a while. And they like girls who know how to embrace their sexy side."

"And his ex-girlfriend had that? A sexy, aggressive side, I mean?" As the question rolls off my tongue, I can't help but wonder if Keegan is a virgin. *Probably not.* He's eighteen, and from what I've read in magazines, most guys lose their virginity in their early teens. But I won't know anytime soon; I'm not bold enough to ask.

"Like I said, she was experienced. And everything I know about attracting guys, I learned from her. How do you think I got Sam?" Sam is Karmin's hot surfer boyfriend. The one I see pressing Karmin up against her locker to engage in an in-between-class kiss every day.

I check around the locker room to see if any other girls remain inside; there is no one in sight. I know I shouldn't ask her, but my curiosity wins me over. "Can you teach me?" I whisper. "You know . . . to be feisty and sexy?" I cringe as the words escape me. I know this is weird, but I have no one else to ask.

"I can't teach you to be feisty. It's just something you're born with. But sexy? I can help you with that." Karmin finishes applying her red lipstick and leads me to the big, floor-length mirror on the opposite side of the locker room. "Take out your bow, and let down your hair."

"But, I just put it in. Why—"

"Just do it," she snaps as she takes her hair down as well. I do as I'm told and wait for further instructions. I'm not sure if she's aware of how long it takes me to get the bumps out of a high-pony hairstyle, but I let it go anyway. "Sexiness comes from body movement. I'm talking hair, hips, and arms. So when you're out on the dance floor tonight, work your hair. Flip it, run your fingers through it, I don't care. But do something with it."

She demonstrates how to do it, adding in some sensual swaying and over-the-head arm movements, and I try to mimic her. "How was that?"

"Not bad, Em. A little more hips, and you got it down." We practice in the mirror a little longer, and then she starts rattling off other sexy things to do when I'm with Keegan: talk slower, bite your bottom lip, lean close to him when you're talking so he can catch your scent—you do have a signature scent, don't you?—and don't forget to giggle A LOT. After a while I feel like I should have out a notepad and pen to jot everything down. "Oh, and when you're slow-dancing and your arms are on his shoulders, occasionally play with the hair just above the back of his neck and stare into his eyes. That's a surefire way to get a guy to kiss you."

"Grab his hair and stare. Got it."

"Stick with that, and you'll have my brother under a spell. I just know it."

Again, I know I shouldn't ask her, but my curiosity wins the battle in my head again. It's like whenever the good parts of my mind command me not to speak, the stupid parts push forward anyway. "Why are you helping me get with your brother? Isn't this weird for you?"

"Nope. My brother was so hurt when Lori cheated on him, and

it killed me to see him like that. But he likes you, and I know you like him. So I know you won't hurt him like that. And you're so nice, you probably wouldn't hurt a fly."

Her words put a bittersweet taste in my mouth; a part of me likes Keegan and really wants to act on my feelings, but the other part of me is only using him to throw my parents off my trail. *God, I'm a horrible person. This is definitely my first-class ticket to hell.*

"Well, thanks for the advice. I'll be sure to use it tonight." I silently pull my hair back into a ponytail, and start for the door before she can rattle off more how-to-be-sexy tips, or flood my mind with more excruciating compliments.

"Not so fast. We haven't gone over your kissing technique yet."

"What do you mean—"

Before I can finish my question, Karmin grabs my face and starts leaning in, her red lips puckered.

I laugh as she moves closer. "I—I think I'm good on that one. Thanks, though."

"Suit yourself," she says with a smirk. "But if you ever need any tips, you know who to call." I watch her pick up her sparkly pom-poms from the bench by her locker and strut her way out the door.

The confidence coursing through her is invigorating, and as I follow her out of the locker room, I can't help but wonder what else she learned from Keegan's ex-girlfriend. She is so open with her sexuality and willing to kiss me that she must have gone a lot farther than that. But then again, that's none of my business.

We meet up with the rest of the girls outside the gym and start toward the football field; the bleachers and sidelines are filled with fans sporting our school colors, and the sight of it all fuels me with energy. When I get into position, I glance over at the student section. Keegan has painted his face half red and half black, and he's passing out noise-makers and foam fingers. In all fours years of going here, I've always wondered who the guy that always painted his face for games was, and now I know. He winks at me when our eyes meet.

"Emma, I know your future boyfriend—aka my brother—is in the crowd right now, but I need you to get your game face on," Karmin says before a band member blows his whistle and begins to play. I raise my sparkling red pom-poms in the air and begin doing the robotic arm motions that I've practiced a million times on the gym floor.

In the middle of our stand-dance with the band, I hear the student section grow rowdy all of a sudden, but I'm not allowed to look until the song is over. I imagine that Keegan is doing a crazy dance to get them going, but once I am able to look, I see that it's Dylan starting the wave in the middle of the students. He doesn't have a shirt on, but his skin is painted red with a big black *C* in the middle of it. He's trying to beat out Keegan and doing a pretty damn good job at it. For a second, I wish I wasn't on the dance team so that I could act as a buffer between the two, but it's out of my control.

Throughout the entire game, I watch the tension grow between Keegan and Dylan. At one point, I even see Keegan bow out in the bleachers and let Dylan lead the crowd chants. I feel the pit of my stomach twist, turn, knot, and churn; this is my fault.

"Did you have fun, sis?" Dylan says when I see him after the game is over. "I did."

"I saw that." I want to ignore him, but he's leaning on the side of my car, blocking my door so that we *have* to have a conversation. "Can I help you? I have to get ready for the dance."

"This is what you wanted, right? For me to fit in, act normal?"

"I didn't say become mortal enemies with Keegan."

"Mortal enemies? No. That was just a friendly competition."

"It didn't seem like it."

"Well, believe it or not, it was." He picks at the paint on his chest and frowns. "I've got to go home and take a shower. See you at the dance, *sis*." He backs away from me and starts toward his car. If my eyes were daggers, he would have two gashes in his back right now.

"You okay?" It's Keegan. "You looked pissed as hell."

"Oh, it's just my brother. He's always doing something dumb. You know brothers."

"Yeah. I, myself, find that I suffer from Douchey Big Brother Syndrome from time to time." He glances from me to Dylan and then nods in his direction. "He was stepping on my territory tonight." *And you don't even know the half of it.*

"Sorry about that. I don't think he knew that this was your thing."

"It's cool. I was kind of pissed at first, but I figure I need to pass the torch down to someone when I leave this place. Might as well be him." I like how cool he's being about this. Dylan was in full-on four-year-old mode tonight. But not Keegan. His maturity is kind of hot. "Well, I'll see you in about an hour."

"Can't wait." I smile as he backs away, showing off a toothy grin of his own.

I PULL THE DRESS, WRAPPED IN A PLASTIC COVERING, FROM MY BACKSEAT and head to the girls' locker room to shower. Though I've never attended a homecoming dance here, it seems stupid to have it imme-diately after the game; the players, school spirit squads, and band members don't have the luxury of going out to eat before the dance or getting picked up by our dates to take pictures. It's strictly game, then dance, which seems silly to me.

When I walk through the gym doors with the rest of the spirit squad girls, I imagine that Dylan is at home rinsing the red and black paint off of his body. I hate that I like him so much; I wish I could stay mad at him for longer. *He's just jealous of Keegan*, I think to myself. And I don't blame him. Keegan is able to flirt with me out in the open, while every feeling that Dylan has for me has to be kept inside and hidden from the rest of the world. I'm the only one he can share it with. I'm the only one who can know.

The sweaty and usually smelly gym that I've come to know over the past four years has been transformed to fit the Evening in Paris theme. There are streamers hanging from the walls and strings of balloons that come together in the center to create an Eiffel Tower tent look, and the floor is sprinkled with gold confetti. I don't see Keegan walk in, but when I feel his hand on the small of my back, I melt into a smile. No guy has made it his mission to seek me out in a crowd of gorgeous girls.

"Hello, beautiful." He's wearing an all-white suit with a red bow tie. He looks even better than he normally does, and the more I look at him, the more my insides squirm with excitement for what is to come tonight.

"Me? What about you?" I look down at my short, white dress, and then back to him. Because he already knew what color my dress was, he probably tried to match me, which isn't going to sit well with Dylan, but it makes us seem like a couple, and that electrifies me. He pulls a red rose corsage from behind his back, and I extend my wrist for him to fasten it on me. "Great minds," he says, gesturing to our matching ensembles.

When I see Karmin emerge from the balloon arc in her lavender dress—which makes her boobs look amazing, just like she wanted—I know the dance is finally beginning. She's the most popular girl in school, and everyone operates on her time. Whenever she arrives at her destination, everyone else is not far behind her.

Dylan enters the arc a couple minutes after her, but he doesn't advance toward me. Instead, he starts for a small group of art club students; he probably doesn't want to approach me with Keegan nearby. I glance up at the clock and am reminded that there are three hours left of the dance. *Plenty of time*, I think to myself. I'll get to him eventually.

A fast-paced song plays next, and Keegan drags me to the center of the dance floor. I glance back at Karmin as he does, and I see her mouth the words *hips and hair*.

Hips and hair. Hips and hair, I repeat to myself.

I finally understand what Karmin means after the second song ends, and that's when I really start to let loose. Before I know it, my arms are moving, my hips are swaying, and my hair is everywhere that I want it to be. Because I'm so busy dancing and having a good time with Keegan, I don't even realize that I haven't spoken to Dylan until he's pulling me behind the bleachers while Keegan gets some punch. The dance will be over in a half hour, and I've barely even looked in his direction. If Girlfriend 101 was a class, I'd be failing miserably.

"Forgot about me, huh?" It's dark in the gym, but I can tell that his eyes are clouded with disappointment.

"No, not at all. I'm just trying to make sure that Keegan gets to know me. He won't ask me out until he feels like he knows me well enough."

"Spare me the details of your love affair. When are you going to spend some time with me? I feel like I haven't really seen you in almost a week, and we live in the same house." I can't respond to his words; they're too true for an excuse. "Looks like you've made your decision."

He's so concerned about me, it makes me wonder if his possessive instincts are a bigger problem. I flash back to the way he flipped out on Dad when he had taken his painting without asking first.

"No, Dylan. It's all fake." I know we're at school, but I have to reassure him somehow, and I can't think of another way than to pull him close to me. His lips are soft and familiar when they touch mine, and I find myself smiling as I get into it. "I want you," I whisper between kisses. It seems to be enough, because I can sense him grinning as I continue to kiss him.

I feel his hand travel from my waist, up my back and neck, to touch my face. As his palm grazes my cheek, I notice that his hand is rougher than usual. "What is that? It's so itchy." I take his hand in mine, and squint to see what it is. It's a bandage. "What happened?"

"I cut myself." He must see my concerned expression change into a wide-eyed one. "No . . . not like that." He laughs. "I'm not masochistic. I was trying to get the can of paint open to paint my body red, and the lid slipped and sliced my hand. It's no biggie. It'll heal in about a month."

"It must be deep if you had to use gauze. Maybe you should see a—"

"Emma, I'm fine. I have this under control." His voice is calm, but he grits his teeth like he's hiding something. It isn't until I see him smile that I finally decide to drop it.

"Okay." I try to think back to when I saw him at the pep rally. Was his hand bandaged then? I was so worried about his feud with Keegan that I probably wouldn't have even noticed it if it had been.

"Your boyfriend is looking for you. You should get back." He pecks at my lips and then releases me back onto the dance floor.

He's not my boyfriend. You are, I want to say, but he's already walking away before I can get the words out. I try to push Dylan out of my mind so I can focus on securing Keegan as my faux boyfriend, but as I walk toward him, I find myself thinking about Dylan and his hand. *Was it bandaged at the game or not? I can't remember.*

"Emma?" Keegan says when he meets me in the center. "Everything okay?"

"Yeah," I lie. "I just can't believe I wasted four years hating this place, when I could have been doing things like this."

"High school is not as bad as people make it seem."

"Well, I know that now. I'm just trying to soak everything in so I can remember this night when I'm old and wrinkly." A slow song begins to play, and Keegan pulls me close so that we can sway as we talk. He places his hands on my waist, and I wrap my hands around his neck and twirl his hair around my fingers, just like Karmin instructed me to do. "I'm in this beautiful dress, surrounded by my friends and teammates. It's amazing."

"You're amazing," he says as he pulls me in tighter. "So how are you doing in your honors civics class?"

I squint my eyes at him. "Very random question, but pretty well, I guess."

"So you're good at remembering dates and stuff?"

"I guess so, yeah." I'm clueless to where this conversation is coming from, and why we're having it right now in the middle of me trying to encode this moment into my memory. *Maybe he needs help with his classwork or something,* I think to myself. *Oh no! What if this grand gesture is just to get me to tutor him?*

"Good, because I don't want to be the only one who remembers our anniversary next year." I'm so focused on trying to figure out where he's going with this talk about history class, that I almost miss him asking me out. "Or monthiversaries, if you're into that sort of thing."

"Wait, are you—"

"Asking you to be my girlfriend? Yeah, I am. You're beautiful, funny, and smart. Any guy would be so lucky to have you." These words sound familiar, and it takes me a moment to realize why. Dylan said something similar before he asked me out. *Do all guys read from the same relationship handbook or something?* "Emma?" Keegan says, bringing me out of my daydream. "So what do you say? Will you be my girlfriend?"

I know that this isn't the first time that someone has asked me to be their girlfriend—Dylan did it not too long ago—but I can't hide my delight from Keegan. "Is that even a question?" I reply, beaming like a star in the midnight sky.

chapter 14

Dear Catherine,

It's like the second I became Keegan's girlfriend, I started drowning in popularity. Before, when I would walk through the halls, no one even knew my name, and now everyone knows so much about me. People I've never seen a day in my life know who I am, what my car looks like, and where my classes are. It's weird being on the other side of the fence, but I like it.

As little time as I was spending at home before, I'm there even less now. And I feel horrible about it. Not just because of Dylan, but because of the rest of my family, too. My mom and dad only have this year left with me before I embark on my own journey into adulthood. I'm not being fair to them. But with all of my AP classes, dance team practice, and spending time with Keegan, I can't fit in much more.

Speaking of boyfriends, I have to ask something. Your situation, with marriage and all, is much more serious than mine, but I need to know: did you ever feel bad about abandoning Heathcliff? I mean, I feel bad for ditching Dylan, but a part of me feels like it's not my fault. I'm caught in the middle of two separate lives: Emma the sister and Emma the girlfriend. I can't swap roles at his beck and call—especially when one of them is supposed to be secret.

And I can see the disappointment in Dylan's eyes every time he looks at me while I'm clinging to Keegan's arm. I'm chipping away at what we have, and sometimes I think that one day, I'm going to look up and his heart's not going to be entangled in mine anymore. He'll end things and move on, and my first love will be gone before I get a chance to really enjoy it. I haven't been focusing on <u>Wuthering Heights</u> these days, but I'm sure this dilemma of yours gets resolved in the end. I just hope mine turns out the same way.

♡ Emma

When I make it home early on a Thursday evening, I'm greeted with confused faces as I enter through the back door. My mom is cleaning up in the kitchen, and my dad, Dylan, and Matthew are on the living room floor playing a video game. It's some racing game that Matthew got as a gift for his birthday, and judging by the smiles on their faces, they all seem to be enjoying themselves.

"Nice to know that you're still alive," my dad says when I sit down behind them. "I haven't seen you since you brought Keegan over. I liked him at one point, but now I'm not too sure."

"It's not his fault, Dad. Practice has been running late," I say as I raise my voice. Dylan has turned up the volume on the television, probably to drown out my excuse. "We're getting ready for competition season, and we have to extend practices. We have to run, stretch, then work out, then learn a new part of our dance, and finally practice it. I know it seems selfish, but I have been working very hard on this."

"I believe you," Matthew butts in. "I've been so busy trying to learn how to add and subtract mixed fractions that I've barely left my room either." Sometimes I forget that he's a freaky genius kid. I only remember it when he brings up his schoolwork, which is hardly ever.

"Oh, okay. Do you want me to help you practice?" I haven't spent time with Matthew in forever, and I don't want him to think that I don't want to be around him anymore.

"No thanks. Dylan always practices with me right before we read comic books together at night." I feel a twinge in my left side. I used to practice reading with Matthew before Dylan got here.

With the rejection from my brother still fresh, I turn my attention back to my father. "Dad, my dance tournament is in January. On my birthday, actually. You guys are gonna be there, right?"

"Do we ever miss any of your competitions or awards ceremonies?"

"Or birthdays?" my mom cuts in.

"Of course we'll be there." This makes me feel better, especially seeing as Dad was on the fence about me joining the team at first.

"Yeah," Dylan says, taking his eyes off the screen for a second. "We promise." I can taste the sarcasm in his voice, and I don't appreciate it. I know I haven't been around much, but I don't deserve to be treated so coldly.

"I'll, um . . . I'll be in my room. Good night, everyone."

When I finish showering, I climb into bed and immerse myself in schoolwork. My grades have dropped slightly since the new me took over, but at least I'm still at the top of the class rankings. As I pull my history textbook from my shelf, another book falls. It's *Wuthering Heights*, the limited-edition one with the gold pages that Dylan gave me. I've been so distracted that I can't even remember where I left off in it.

"I haven't seen you pick that book up in a while," Dylan says when he comes to my room. "Funny how time flies, isn't it?" He has a point. I've been so preoccupied with everything else that I haven't been keeping up with all the things that used to feel important.

I can't blame him for being mad at me. I've broken so many late-night art dates and hangout sessions that I'm not even sure if we're a couple anymore.

"It sucks that Cedar Pointe hired a new English II teacher. I kind of liked having you in class with me. We didn't even get the chance to finish out the semester together." When he doesn't respond, I change the subject. "How's your hand? Does it still hurt?"

"It's getting better." His bandage has a crimson-colored stain on it, and I wonder if it's just because he hasn't changed it in a while or if it's because the cut was so deep that it's still bleeding.

"You sure you don't want to go to the doctor? Mom and Dad wouldn't mind taking you."

"Emma, again, it's fine. I'm fine." His terseness slices into me. He never used to shut down when we first met, but now it's like he's holding everything back. "You haven't spoken to me in almost a week, and your only concern is my hand? Really, Em?"

"Well, we're not in the same class anymore, so—"

"That's not what I mean, and you know it."

"Look, I'm sorry if I've been busy, but I figured you'd understand. This was all for you, anyway."

"No, actually, I think it was for you. We were fine until you brought him into the picture, but he's changing you. You're breaking promises, missing dates. And this isn't you." His voice grows louder with every word he speaks, and he's starting to scare me. "He's even changing the way you look. Nice contacts, by the way." With a warm jolt sweeping across my cheeks, I sneak a glance at my reflection in the vanity mirror across the room. *He's right. I have changed.*

"Dylan—"

"You said that this *arrangement* was supposed to help conceal us, but all it's really doing is getting in the way of things. Of us."

"But, it *is* helping hide us, Dylan. I mean, I got Mom and Dad off our case, didn't I?"

"Yeah, but at what cost? He's got his tongue so far down your throat that you can't even think straight."

Okay, I might have deserved that one. I have been enjoying Keegan a little too much. I think in the middle of pretending to be with him, I actually fell for him. I'm a cheater.

"You haven't been the greatest of girlfriends, okay? I've had some stuff going on, and you haven't really been here." He breaks eye contact, and it makes me feel lower than low; he can't even look at me when he speaks. He's needed me, and I haven't been here. *I'm worse than a cheater. I abandoned him.*

"What's going on? Tell me." I urge him to sit next to me, and when he does, I inhale his soapy scent. I've missed it. "Dylan?"

I watch him with careful eyes as he raises his hand and places it on my shoulder. At first, I think he's trying to prepare me for the breakup bomb he's about to drop, but when he pulls back, holding a single strand of my golden hair between his fingers, I narrow my eyes at him. "Did you know a strand of hair is about twenty micrometers in diameter?"

What?? How could that possibly have anything to do with what we're talking about right now?

"No, I didn't know that. What's that got to do with—"

"Twenty micrometers, and we never would have met. I wouldn't have gotten the chance to get placed in a foster home, or even be put up for adoption. Twenty micrometers closer to my heart, and I would have died. Twenty micrometers, and my father would have been a murderer of two people . . . not just one."

This is it. He's finally going to tell me about what came before. "Dylan," I say, taking his right hand in both of mine. I have to choose my words carefully, but there's no other way to say what's on my mind. "Did your father . . . shoot you?"

"It felt cold at first. I guess that was the shock coursing through my veins. But as time went on, the cold turned to fire. In my chest . . . in my arms. Tell you the truth, I thought that was it, and then I blacked out, reflecting on the fact that I was leaving this world before I could put a good stamp on it. I woke up in an all-white room, blank and disoriented." I witness a wide smile break onto Dylan's face just before a chuckle escapes him. "The doctor kept telling me that I was lucky. He missed my heart by a hair."

"What happened to him? Did he go to jail?"

"No. They took him to a psychiatric detention center on account of his mental instability when he . . . did it." He pauses, I guess waiting for me to ask the question everyone else before me has asked when he's told them this story. But I don't, so he continues. "My dad had problems. You never knew which side of him you were going to get. Some days, he was all right. A loving husband and father just like anyone else. But on the other days—the bad ones—it's like a switch was flipped that turned him into this monster that me and my mom were afraid of." Dylan inhales deeply before speaking again. "He'd break things and threaten us and curse us out like we were after him, like he had no clue who we were. At least twice a month, my mom locked us in my bedroom until his episode passed.

"He bounced in and out of at least five mental hospitals while I was in middle school. We'd convince him that he needed help and he'd oblige, but every 'new beginning' quickly dissolved. Soon after his release, we'd be right back at square one, hiding away in rooms and closets waiting for him to return to . . . normal . . . so we could, too."

"Dylan, I'm so sorry. No one should ever have to go through that."

With his lips pressed together, he nods, trying his hardest to hold back tears.

I'm not sure if I'm supposed to play the role of his sister or his concerned girlfriend. Should I try to comfort him like a lover would do, or give him advice like a sibling? I don't know which one to be. I choose lover and scoot closer to wrap my arms around his waist. "So is this why you've been acting so . . . not you . . . lately?"

Untangling himself from me, he ignores my question. I don't think my words came out as uncaring or coldhearted, but from the look Dylan gives me, I'm not sure if I succeeded.

"Your mom and dad got a call the other day from the judge presiding over his case."

"And . . . ?" I'm so far on the edge of my seat that I almost reach down his throat and pull the words out myself. "What'd they say?"

"They've been trying to get him to sign his parental rights away since he's pretty much going to live out the rest of his life in a mental institution. He was given those papers before, when my group home parents were thinking about adopting me, but he refused to sign them. He has this idea in his mind that when he gets out, we're going to be a family again. Just me and him."

I remain quiet, not wanting to express my feelings on such a touchy topic.

"Your parents found out that he's moving to another place due to overcrowding, and . . ." I watch as Dylan balls his hands into fists and then opens them several times before continuing. "And I think I want to go see him. Maybe a visit from me will convince him to sign the papers. Convince him that the life we once had ended when he pointed his gun at my mom . . . and then me."

"Y-you're going to go visit him?" I ask as I try to remember the woman and boy in the portrait that he painted when he first moved in here. His mother was delicate and beautiful, and he's her spitting image, with almond eyes and dimples to match. It's hard to wrap my mind around the idea that someone who's had to endure unthinkable pain and heartbreak can still find a way to make beautiful things.

"Yeah, tomorrow actually."

"Why didn't you tell me what was going on?" I inquire gently.

"You haven't been the easiest person to track down." *Well, why*

didn't you text me? "And I would have texted you, but this isn't really a conversation meant for text message." I like how he still has the ability to read my mind; we haven't lost that piece of our relationship yet.

"I know, and I'm sorry."

He gives me a look. "Sorry doesn't make things better."

"I know that, too." I'm a half-second away from apologizing again, but that wouldn't help my case. "So how are you going to make this happen?" I ask, trying to get the conversation away from me and my horrible girlfriend behavior.

"I've set up an appointment to see him after he gets transferred to the new mental hospital." As he speaks, I feel my stomach harden and a burning sensation ripple through my chest. Switching into sister mode, I wonder, *Why?* He's been here for a little over two months, and, although it's not *official* official, he's a part of our family now. He's Matthew's and my brother, and my parents' son. I know that his dad is his closest living blood relative, but is it wrong of me to want to keep them apart? "I've been trying to catch you to tell you this for some time now, but you've had . . . other obligations."

"So you're sure about this?"

"Positive. But I'm not sure if I want to go alone." He's quiet for a moment, as if trying to pick his next words very carefully. I expect him to say that he wants to take Dad or Mom for parental support; that's what I would do if I were him. But no. He has something else in mind. "Do you want to go with me?"

I have to repeat his question several times in my head before I say anything.

The answer is a no-brainer: of course I want to go with him. I am his girlfriend. But something deep down inside of me tells me that I shouldn't go, and neither should he. This time, though, the kinder parts of my brain win me over, and I find myself saying, "What time do you want to go?"

"Right after school. It's a half day, and this place is in LA, about two hours from here."

"But I have practice tomorrow," I say, biting my lip. "It's competition season, and I can't afford to miss."

"You're right. I don't know why I asked you. You barely even speak to me anymore." He gets up to leave, and as he does, I grab his hand to give it a squeeze. The words are on his lips, I can feel it. *It's over, Emma*, I imagine him saying.

"I'll find a way to get out of it. This is really important to you, and I can't miss it. I'm in."

⊂◊⊃

OUR TRIP TO LOS ANGELES IS ALL I CAN THINK ABOUT, AND I BARELY GET any sleep that evening. *When I meet his dad, will he want me to go as his girlfriend or his sister? How will he introduce me?* I can't calm down all night.

We decide to take my car, but Dylan forgets his ID and wallet, so we have to return to the house before we leave, putting us fifteen minutes behind schedule. My dad is outside in the pool when we pull up. Lately he's been into water resistance training, which is a little off-putting because his chest is so hairy. But if it makes him happy, then who am I to knock his passion? I wouldn't want to do to him what he does to us.

When my dad sees Dylan run into his art studio, he climbs out of the pool and grabs a towel. "Hey, Dylan."

"Hey." Dylan's face crumples with confusion, and I know it has everything to do with the impending face-to-face he's about to have with the man who almost killed him. "What's up?"

"I know you didn't want to enter that art showcase, but I got a call today and they are really interested in your work. The deadline to accept is coming up, and I don't want you to miss out on this opportunity. Can you accept their invitation? For me?"

I see Dylan's mouth morph into a deeper grimace, and the sight of it all hurts my heart.

"They're not asking a lot. Just enter five original pieces made in the past two years. What do you say?"

Dylan nods, but it's not one of the cheery ones that I've seen him do at school sometimes. This one is slow and forced. I can tell that he still doesn't want to do it, but I'm sure he sees how happy it's making my father, and so he goes along with it.

That will be his fatal flaw, I think to myself. He's always so set on pleasing others that he pushes his wants and needs aside. I should know; he's been putting me before himself for a while now, letting me run around with Keegan and leave him at home. He's never going to be content in life if he keeps doing this, but I can't help him. Rather, I don't know how to help him. I admire his altruism, but I know it can be suffocating. Dance team saved me from that feeling, but Dylan never does anything for himself. He only operates on what others want him to do. I hope he breaks that habit before it breaks him.

We ride in silence for the first twenty minutes. It's only us and the music, but no one is singing to it.

"You don't have to do the showcase if you don't want to," I say to break up the stillness. "You could tell him no. He'll be disappointed, of course, but he'll get over it."

"I don't want to let him down. If he went through so much trouble to enter me, I might as well honor his request." He stares out the window as he speaks, and I envision him imagining how different his life would be if he felt he could say no sometimes. "Speaking of saying no, how did you get out of practice?" he asks after a while. "What did you tell them?"

"Well, first they were super pissed at me for skipping, but when they heard why, it was all fits and giggles," I say as I see a smile slither onto his face. "Don't laugh, but I told Coach Denise that I had a bad case of diarrhea and needed to go home." Before I can finish the sentence, Dylan is already bursting into a fit of laughter. "Hey, you said you wouldn't laugh."

"I did not," he says in between his hoots, the veins in his neck throbbing. "And what did she say?"

"Well, first she looked me up and down, and wrinkled her nose. Then she said to go home and rest, and not to return until I'm fully better because, and I quote, 'We don't need you giving us the sick shits.' Unquote."

"Nice," he says, throwing his head back against the passenger headrest again to laugh. This is the most I've seen him smile in a long time, and it's refreshing.

"Yeah, so you better be grateful, because I'm completely mortified."

"I am." He reaches down and grabs my right hand from my lap; it's a little sweaty, but I don't complain. This is one of the few perks of being a lefty; I can drive comfortably with the left, and do other things—e.g., hold Dylan's hand—with the right. One time, I remember Karmin saying that her boyfriend would kill for her to be a lefty— or ambidextrous, really—so she could give him hand jobs while she drives. I told her that wasn't really my style, and changed the subject. Her sexual openness makes me uncomfortable sometimes.

"What is this generic crap you have us listening to?" Dylan says, reaching down for the radio knob.

"Haven't you ever heard the shotgun-seat rule about not touching someone else's radio? It's the ultimate form of betrayal." I wasn't listening to the song, but I'm able to catch the end of it before he switches the station. "And that was Taylor Swift. She's, like, the queen of pop, rock, and country, you know?"

"You mean 'pocktry'?" Sometimes Dylan mixes words to create a better word to describe something. Another one of his creations is *lover-alls*, which he uses to describe a group of girls at school who love overalls so much that they wear them at least twice a week, even though overalls aren't exactly having a retro-chic moment.

"Yeah, I guess."

"I'm not a fan of the way she uses her music to whine about her failed relationships."

"Say what you want, but Tay Tay has gotten me through high school. I never dated anyone before you, but her music makes me feel experienced enough to know what to do in this relationship sometimes. And, by the way, she is not whining, she's liberating herself from the total assholes who've broken her heart."

"'Tay Tay'? Really? That's it. Now we're breaking up." He laughs again. "You already have a guitar—now go make a pocktry hit about me."

Good. I know he's only joking, so as of right now, we're still together. This is good.

I hear him humming a piece of one of her songs as he finds a new station. "Is that Tay Tay that I hear you humming?"

"It's catchy, and don't judge me." He chuckles, which makes me wonder if Taylor Swift is one of his guilty pleasures.

"So how are you feeling?" I ask after a while. "Are you eager to see him? Your dad, I mean."

"Not exactly eager . . . more like nervous."

"What's the difference?"

"Eager implies that I'm somewhat excited about any of this, which couldn't be farther from the truth. I haven't seen him in almost two years, and I have so much to say to him. So many questions to ask." He gives my hand a light squeeze, and I squeeze his back to tell him that I understand, even though I have no clue what he's going through.

"Well, I'm here for you. Whatever you need me to do, I'm here."

"I know." The gentle trust in his voice makes my insides heat up, and I almost burst into tears right there. *I've missed him.* But I can't make this about me; this is about him. "I appreciate it." He takes a minute to find a classic rock station, and then turns to me and says, "Now, *this* is what I call music." He keeps jiggling his legs, letting on that he really is nervous, and so I don't try to change it back. If it calms him down, I'm fine with it.

DYLAN AND HIS DAD DON'T LOOK ALIKE, BUT I CAN TELL THAT THEY ARE father and son based solely on their eyes. I've only ever seen those extravagant honey specks in their irises; never anyone else's. When his father appears in a white T-shirt and tan cargo shorts, I hear Dylan's breath shorten, his nerves setting in.

"It's been a while," the man says as he sits across the table from us. I notice that the strings on his dad's shorts have been cut off, probably to comply with the institute's regulations. "You're looking pretty good. Just like your old man."

Dylan doesn't acknowledge his father's compliment. He gets straight to the point. "I heard that you just got moved here, and I wanted to come see you."

"Yeah. The other place was starting to get a little crowded. More people equals more fights, and well . . ." He looks at his right hand, his knuckles glowing red, maybe from a recent clash with another patient there. "I mean, I'm happy to be here—the food's better and the nurses are a little nicer—but it's not home."

I see Dylan's eyebrows draw together, sympathetically. "Dad, you can't go home. You know that."

"But I'm better now. I really feel like myself."

Dylan swallows hard. "You killed Mom, Dad, and you almost killed me. You do know that, right?"

Mr. McAndrews doesn't say a word, and I think maybe it's because he has wiped that memory from his mind. *Maybe he is sick. No lucid person could sit before their son and pretend not to remember that they almost killed him.* I wiggle my fingers between Dylan's and squeeze his hand as hard as I can, letting him know that I'm still here for him.

"You were horrible to Mom and me, but you weren't always that way. You used to take us on family vacations and plan surprise birthday parties and take care of us when we were sick. You did all of that, and I know you loved us," Dylan goes on. "But then one day, you just . . . stopped. Like, you woke up and decided that you didn't want us anymore." He loosens his grip on my hand, giving me the chance to wipe the sweat off on the leg of my jeans. Though his hands say otherwise, Dylan looks awfully comfortable right now. "At first it was

Mom. You started accusing her of cheating on you, hiding your things around the house. Then it was me. You thought I was stealing from you and lying to you. Every argument spiraled into a fight, and you were violent." Involuntarily, Dylan rubs the scar above his left eyebrow. *He must have gotten that from his dad.*

"I came home from school one day, and the door was open, which was really weird. Mom never left our door open. She was adamant about that. 'Don't leave the door open unless you're okay inviting a killer into our home,' she would say. Little did she know she was sleeping next to the killer every night." Dylan isn't looking at his father or me when he speaks. His eyes are focused on the line where the wall meets the floor behind Mr. McAndrews.

"Anyways, I set my backpack down and went to the kitchen to look for a snack. And that's when I saw it. The blood. I tried to scream, but nothing came out." He focuses his eyes on his father's and stares for a minute, the tears sitting on the edge of his lids, waiting to be released. "You killed Mom. And when you saw me, you pointed the gun directly at my chest."

Dylan's dad looks up with empty eyes; he's muddled and scared, unable to recognize himself in Dylan's chilling words. After a minute, he nervously looks my way. "I'm sorry. How rude of me," he says, his eyes dancing all over my face. "I'm Aaron McAndrews. And you are . . . ?"

I open my mouth to speak, but Dylan answers for me. "This is Emma. She's my foster sister."

I'm thankful that he took over; I had no clue which title to take.

"You're gorgeous," he says with a smirk. "Are you sure you're only his foster sibling? The way you've been holding on to his hand so tightly, I would imagine that you guys are . . . maybe more than that?"

I retract my earlier statement; there's no way that this man is clinically insane. He is too observant for that.

"This isn't about her. This is about you, Dad. *You* tore our family apart when you ignored your mental illness. This is all because of you."

"I'm not sure what you want me to do now," Mr. McAndrews whispers after a while. The blank look on his face is too much for me to take. I have to say something, but what? "Look, son—"

"You don't get to call me that," Dylan snaps almost before his dad can even get the word out.

"Okay, Dylan. What do you want from me?"

I sense Dylan's breathing pick up in pace and before I know it, a warm pink tint crawls up his neck and settles onto his face. "Just one thing. In the next couple of weeks, some nice-looking people in suits are going to come and hand a pen and a set of papers with the words *Termination of Parental Rights* across the top. After reading over them to the best of your ability, I want you to sign and date at the bottom, confirming that you understand that your rights have been released. You haven't been anything to me in a long time anyway. This is just to make it official." The words come out hoarse and rough, as if Dylan is losing his voice. I imagine that it's because he's holding back tears he's wanted to cry for a long time now.

"Why would I do that? You think these people are going to adopt you? You think her family is going to want you to burden their lives like you did mine?" I flash back to the two boys who used to taunt Dylan at school, and how I stepped in to protect him. *Now's your chance, Emma. Save him.*

"Because that's what a father would do. He would realize his mistake, and try his best to make it right. And seeing as you haven't been a father to him since you took his mom's life, this is your last chance to do something for your only son, who almost died because of you. Do the right thing for once in your life and sign the papers, asshole." I rise from my seat, rage building up inside of me. I want so badly to slap Dylan's father, but I repress the urge when Dylan pulls me back down.

"I don't want to hate you," he says to his father through clenched teeth, "but I do. You're so selfish. You only think of yourself, and you always have. It was never about me or Mom. Only you. Always you. But not anymore."

"Dylan, you're all I have left . . . I can't lose you, too."

"Lose me?" Dylan shouts into his father's eyes. "*You* pushed *me* away. You never took your mood disorder seriously, and you let it break us. And now that I've found a family that wants me, you want to exert your parental claim to me? That's a load of crap and you know it."

It's at that moment that I realize that nothing we say will convince him to sign those papers, so I hop up again. "You ready, Dylan?"

Dylan hesitates, his eyes still focused on his father's and his breathing more frantic with each passing second. I imagine him cursing him out inside his head. *I hate you*, I can almost hear him say. "Yeah."

"Do the right thing," I say again before signaling to the guard that we are finished here.

After we exit the gray building, I pull him to the side. "You okay?"

"Yeah. Did you really just call him an asshole?" he asks, his mouth hanging open in an I-can't-believe-you-just-did-that kind of way.

"Sorry. I just got mad. I don't think he thinks he did anything wrong."

"He hasn't been able to make sense of the way he acts in a long time. . . . Hence the mental institution," Dylan says grimly.

"I'm so proud of you. That took a lot of courage, and I just want to let you know how proud I am to call you my boyfriend, and future brother." I don't have enough time to stop the tears from welling in my eyes; before I know it, they're forming salty trails down my cheeks and falling to the ground. *I'm sorry*, I want to say. He brought me here to be strong for him and with him, and I can't seem to hold it together. I have to wrap my hands around his waist and bury my face in his chest to conceal my breakdown. If anything, he should be the one crying, not me.

I feel his fingers run through my hair as he holds me close. "This meant so much to me, and having you by my side today . . . Words can't describe how grateful I am to have you in my life, Emma." With two hands, he grabs hold of my face and lifts it until our lips meet.

I try to think of something cooler and more meaningful to say in return, but when our lips disconnect, all I can come up with is "Me too."

chapter 15

I'M NOT SURE what to say to Dylan when we leave the dingy gray mental institute; he looks like Death. The guy sitting in the passenger seat of my car doesn't resemble the guy he was when we walked out of the building hand in hand. Everything, from his dark and glazed-over eyes to his trembling lips, screams *Boy, Interrupted*. It breaks my heart to see him like this, and what's even more painful is the fact that I can't do anything to help him. Not as his sister. Not as his girlfriend. Nothing.

"You okay?" I finally work up the courage to ask after riding in silence for a few miles. I know he said that he was grateful to have me by his side today, but that feels like forever ago. Now it's like someone flipped a switch and he turned into this sleepwalking being; he's not saying much, not breathing much, and his eyes have got to be drying out because he's barely blinking either. It's like he's crossed over into full-on zombie mode. When he doesn't answer my question, I focus my attention back onto the dashboard. The red needle on my fuel gauge is hovering over the E. If I don't stop now, we'll run out of gas in the middle of nowhere, and I'm not trying to star in the next based-on-a-true-story made-for-TV thriller. We're not that far away from the asylum—or the prison. There are weirdos out there.

"I'm stopping for gas," I say as I pull up to pump number one at the nearest Circle K.

That's his cue to volunteer to pump, but instead of getting out, he squirms around in his seat before settling even deeper into it, ignoring me completely. I have to contain my annoyance because I know his fit has nothing to do with me, but it's getting harder to tolerate his mood swings as he brushes off my efforts to make him feel better.

A thousand thoughts overload my mind as I wait in line to pay, none of them helping at all. *Why isn't he hungry? I mean, I'm starving! Oh, God . . . what if he's depressed? But don't depressed people eat a lot . . . to make up for them feeling so crappy? Maybe I should cook him something when we get back. Depressed people eat casseroles, right? But I don't know how to cook a casserole. Oh my God . . . he's going to break up with me after I poison him with bad casserole.*

"Sweetheart!" the man behind the counter half screams at me to get my attention. "You buying something, or what?"

"Twenty on pump one, and this candy bar, please." As I hand him a fifty-dollar bill, I glance out the glass doors to see Dylan walking around the car and opening up the driver's side door. I don't take my eyes off of him as I hold my hand out for what feels like forever, waiting for my change. I hear the man mutter the number of bills and coins he's giving me, and when he places them into my hand, I sprint back to the car so fast, any bystander would have probably assumed that I'd stolen the chocolate candy bar I'm shoving in my pocket.

"Not trying to take off without me, are you?" I inquire as I watch him reach down and pull the lever to pop the trunk.

"Wouldn't think of it." His words are short and sharp, and I fear that I might get cut if I ask another question, so I let him continue with whatever he's doing as I pump the gas myself. It's hard to see with the trunk door in the way, but I think I see him grab a black bag and walk back to his seat. I'm not sure if I should attribute his weird behavior to the shock of seeing his father for the first time in so long or to the pain he felt from opening up about the day his mother died, but either way, I wish it would stop. This trip was supposed to make things better, not worse. I want my Dylan back, my honey-eyed Dylan.

I keep the radio on the rock station he set it to on the way up here, hoping that eventually he'll turn to me and say something—anything—to end the taciturnity between us, but he doesn't. *It makes no sense,* I think to myself as he lets out a deep sigh. *Doesn't he want to talk about this? I mean, that's what couples do . . . they talk about things like this. It's supposed to bring us closer . . . or something.* I glance at him out of the corner of my eye and see that his eyes are closed and his chest is moving up and down at a steady rate. I've never seen Dylan sleep; he's always up painting, working, or playing with Matthew.

As I don't think I'll be able to stand another minute of his music, I press the play button on the CD player. A familiar female voice comes on the radio, picking up where I last left off in my audiobook.

It's been a while since I've listened to this in the car, but after the first few lines, I pinpoint our location to chapter nine. Catherine's famous "I am Heathcliff" speech—which I had to memorize as one of my AP English projects—is approaching rapidly, and as it does, I reach an epiphany.

Is Dylan my Heathcliff? Am I his Catherine? And is Keegan the Edgar wedge being driven between us? Dylan seems to know more about me than I do myself, just like Heathcliff. But Keegan is the more appropriate suitor for me, as Edgar was for Catherine. And on top of that, I have to stand by and pretend I can't see the jealousy that I put Dylan through every day, just to protect my own image. I am Catherine. I am Catherine!

I have to pull over to the side of the road to steady my thoughts and regain control, but the blood pounding in my ears makes it difficult to shake the spine-tingling feeling inside of me. I shift the car into park, and reach behind me to grab the frozen bottle of water I stashed behind my seat before we left the house, with hopes that it's not still rock solid. The crunch of the plastic bottle and the cool condensation dampening my fingertips are a hopeful sign.

With the cool liquid surging through my body, I look over at Dylan. Set against my frenetic self, he's never looked calmer; the slight smile on his face says it all. I imagine that he's entered a world where his mother hasn't been murdered, his dad isn't a killer, and he can have me all to himself. If I were in his shoes and I was having a dream like that, I'd grin in my sleep, too. As I place the cap back on my bottle of icy water, I spot the black bag that he grabbed out of the trunk earlier.

I know that I'm about to lose my nomination for the Best Girlfriend of the Year Award (who am I kidding; with all of the Keegan stuff going on, I was definitely kicked out of the running weeks ago), but I can't help myself. I have to know what he's hiding from me. Boyfriends and girlfriends don't hide things, but maybe he's keeping me in the dark for a reason. It's hard to think straight with my girlfriend label on, so I switch into sister mode and reach down to get the bag.

I silently thank God for knocking Dylan out so hard, because it makes it easier to grab the bag at his feet without waking him up. I pull on the drawstrings and open up the bag to find two transparent orange bottles of pills, both white and oval-shaped. They're so similar-looking that if I'd only glanced at them, I would have thought they were the same pill. The only difference, to me, is the size of the pills. In one bottle—the one with his name on it—is a set of thick capsules, and in the other—the one that has the label ripped off—is a set of thin ones.

I turn the bottle with the big pills over in my hands so I can read the label. *Ambien*. The prescription date says that these were issued to him back in September, when he first arrived at our house, so he's either not taking his pills or hoarding them. Or both. Or—I always feel the need to give him the benefit of the doubt—he's just using an old bottle for some strange reason. I don't know.

I continue to turn the bottle over to read the label. It sounds like a bunch of gibberish until I come across the word *insomnia*. Out of the corner of my eyes, I see him wiggle around in his seat—trying to find a comfortable position, I guess—and, out of fear of getting caught, I shove the bottles back into his bag and place it at his feet where I found it. When I turn my attention back to the road and shift the car into drive, I realize that *Wuthering Heights* is still playing; I was so focused on snooping without getting caught that I think my ears turned off.

At first, I want to get upset at the fact that Dylan's been keeping this from me, but then the idea that he might be embarrassed to tell me settles in. *Maybe he doesn't want me to think he's crazy or something? He did say that he hardly ever gets a full night's rest.*

"Cheyenne," he breathes, so low that I almost don't hear him. *I didn't know he talked in his sleep. And who is Cheyenne? His mom? Or maybe he lived there?* I try to think back to the conversations we've had, but I don't remember him ever mentioning a Cheyenne—person or place. Or maybe he did, and I was too busy with other things to listen intently enough to remember.

The dizzy spell I experienced back in September tries its best to reemerge, so I turn off the radio and drive in silence for the next hour and a half, listening to Dylan whisper pieces of his dreams while he tosses and turns in his seat. It isn't until I get into the lane for the off-ramp that he wakes, looking even more dead than when he went to sleep.

"Did I sleep the whole ride back?" he asks, smoothing down his hair.

"Sure did. But that's okay. The silence was good. Gave me time to sit back and reflect on a few things."

"That can't be good," he mutters underneath his breath. Obviously not low enough, because I still heard him.

"Why is me reflecting a bad thing?"

"Because I know women"—*Do you, Dylan? Do you really?*—"and I know that when you start to think and reflect on things, a reckoning awaits."

"Ha-ha, very funny," I say as I glance into his eyes as I stop at a red light. Looking at the clock, I assume that we only have about twenty minutes of daylight left before the purplish-blue sky settles in for the night. "But seriously . . . I started thinking about our big picture, and how this whole thing is going to work when I go off to college. I like you, but—"

"We'll cross that bridge when we get there." He doesn't say much after that; he just focuses his eyes on the road before us. He always knows how to shut down conversations that he doesn't want to have. "It'll be easier, though. Once I get adopted and you're away at college, we won't have to sneak around anymore." He grabs hold of my hand as he speaks, letting the butterflies out of their cage once again. *Leave it to Dylan to find a way to make me smile even when I'm slightly upset with him.*

"Do you know that you talk in your sleep?" He's been quiet for most of the ride back, and I have to keep the conversation going somehow; I can't take another second of silence from him. "You kept muttering the name Cheyenne over and over. Is that your mom's name?"

More silence.

"Dylan?"

"No," he finally says. "She was this girl who used to live across the street from the group home I stayed at."

Involuntarily, my fingers loosen their grip around his. "Did you used to date her or something?" *She's probably the one who taught him how to kiss so well. I bet it was her.*

"No." He laughs to himself. "But she did give me my first kiss." *I knew it! Is it possible for me to appreciate and abhor this mystery girl at the same time?* "She was my escape from everything. You see, my group home was run by a retired drill sergeant, and with eight foster kids in the house, he wasn't the most compassionate person to talk to. Whenever I could get away, she would listen to me talk endlessly about missing my family, or getting in trouble with Sir, or whatever problem I had going on at the time."

"Sounds like you loved her." Though I don't mean for them to, my words come out cold and reeking of jealousy.

"Maybe." *Damn.* "Then again, I'm not sure. I don't really know what it feels like to love someone, and I don't think I was capable of loving anyone with the state that I was in."

I pull into the driveway of our house and unhook my seat belt, but I don't get out of the car. Through the window, I see the sun resting just above the horizon as if it's contemplating whether or not it really wants to sink beneath it. "When my parents first got me this car, I didn't want to drive it because I was scared to damage it. I used to let it sit in the driveway, and every night I would come out, put the top down, and watch as the skyline gobbled up the sun and the stars appeared out of thin air right before my eyes."

As I speak, I press the button on the dashboard to let the top down, and another button to let our seats back. "I've never been in love either, but I've always had this idea that it's supposed to change the way you see the world. Like, all at once, everything is different . . . good different.

"It's where you want to go out of your way to see that other person smile. And when you get some really exciting news and they're the first person you think to call, because you know they're going to be proud of you and just as excited about your success as you are. It's where their passion is an indispensable part of your own, and you would do anything to keep that happiness in their heart."

"So that's love, huh?" he asks, his eyes sparkling as if he knows something I don't.

"My definition, yes."

"Sounds like you know it well. You sure you've never been in love?"

"I'm sure," I say after a moment. "I would have told you if I had been." Another noiseless minute flies by before either of us says anything. It's almost as if we're both trying to figure out if, by my definition, we love each other or not.

"Do you like Keegan more than you like me?"

I'm not sure if it's my imagination, but as he speaks, I think I can hear his heart pounding with anticipation for the answer.

A part of me wants to deny any feelings that I have for Keegan, but I can't lie to him. Not again, especially after he let me into a sacred part of his past today. "I like him." I cringe when the words come out; I can almost hear his heart breaking. "But that has nothing on what I have with you. It doesn't feel like some silly high school thing with you, like it does with him. It's more than that."

"You're right. It *is* more than that." He reaches for one of my hands that is resting on my stomach, and laces his fingers with mine. And even though we're out in the open, sitting right beneath my parents' window, I let him hold my hand, and he repeats, "Much more."

Dear Catherine,

Today I met Dylan's father. He's despicable, but I think the entire visit brought me closer to Dylan. The way he looked at me when we were sitting in my car, under the stars, enveloped me in this lightness. Like everything was right in the world at that moment. I don't know what it was exactly, but I think I like it. I think that feeling has always been there, simmering underneath everything else, but tonight, I felt it boil over.

Keegan doesn't ignite anything close to that kind of feeling. Usually it's just fun and flirty with him. I don't have the same deep conversations with him that I do with Dylan. But that could be a good thing. Maybe Keegan just wants to keep it simple, because after we're done with Cedar Pointe, the simplicity of our youth will end. He could just be one step ahead of me already. Or maybe I'm one step ahead of him, keeping just enough distance between us so that once Keegan and I go our separate ways in college, Dylan and I can finally have space to grow together.

Maybe I'm thinking too much about this, but tonight opened my eyes up to something I hadn't thought of before: What would have happened if you had gone back to Heathcliff after choosing Edgar? Would you have regretted it? Would you have lived and died happier than you did? As I look at my Dylan vs. Keegan situation, I can't help but wonder . . . what if?

♡ Emma

chapter 16

M ATTHEW ALWAYS CALLS the shots with our Sunday family activities, but for some reason Dad lets Dylan do it this week. I suspect that he's trying to make up for entering him into the art showcase against his will, but I'm not exactly sure.

"So what'll it be?" he says as he passes the plate of pancakes around the table.

"How does everyone feel about going to the batting cages for a little bit?" Dylan must be trying to apologize for blowing up at Dad eons ago. Men are so weird. They never apologize for their actions; they just find a way to make it up to the person that they've hurt. I, myself, have never heard Dylan or my father actually say the words *I'm sorry*.

"Sounds like fun," my mom says as she pours syrup over Matthew's short stack. "We'll leave in an hour."

I lace up my cleats and pull on one of Dad's old baseball jerseys and a pair of jean shorts. It's unusually hot for the end of October, and, though I typically don't like to show so much skin in public, I refuse to pass out from hyperthermia.

"You look ravishing, Emma," Dylan says as I sneak into his room and close the door.

"Thanks." I knew he was going to say something like that. Dylan can hardly keep his hands, let alone his eyes, off of me whenever we're alone. Since our trip to LA, he's gotten a lot more playful, and the flirting between us has been at an all-time high.

"Did you wear that for me?" Before I can answer, he puts his hands around my waist, and presses me up against the wall. I can't help but wonder what's gotten into him; he's usually not this passionate.

I let his kisses migrate from my lips to my neck, and as they do, I glance at the ground. His backpack is open, papers flooding from it. I follow the trail of papers to the balled-up piles by his trash can. On top of it is a chemistry test, a big, red F in the top right corner of it.

"How's school going?"

"Are we really going to talk about this right now?" He blows off my question and tosses me onto his bed. He tries to kiss me again, but I won't let this go.

"Are you failing chemistry?"

"What? Where is this coming from?" I push him off of me and pick his test from the top of his wastebasket. "Oh, that. I was gonna ask you for help, but we haven't been hanging out like we used to."

"Are you seriously blaming me for your failing?"

"No. I just have had a lot going on. Between you, the showcase, work, and everything going on with my dad, I haven't had much time for school stuff. But I'm not worried. I'll just study more."

"My parents don't take failing grades lightly. How do you plan to dig yourself out of that territory?"

"With these." He opens the drawer on his side table and pulls out the unlabeled orange bottle of thin white pills that I saw in his bag when we went to LA. "I got them from one of the art students at school. They're supposed to give me the energy I need to stay awake. He called them—"

"Study buddies, I know. The real question is why do you have those?"

"With everything on my plate, I'm getting burnt out halfway through the day." He pops the top on the bottle and tosses one of the tiny white pills into his mouth as if it's nothing. "These give me energy like you wouldn't believe."

"You shouldn't be taking those with your sleeping pills. That's extremely dangerous. I mean, anything could happen if you mix them. You could slip into a coma or have a heart attack or—"

"Who told you that I was taking sleeping pills? Nobody but your mom and dad knows that."

Uh-oh. I can't think of an excuse for why I know this and out of fear of getting caught, I tell the truth. "I saw them in your bag when we were on the trip." Before I can get a chance to explain myself, he's turning away from me, his hands on his head. *That's never a good sign.*

"You went through my stuff?"

"I was just worried about you, Dylan. You passed out cold in the passenger's seat of my car, and I had to figure out why."

"I didn't know it was a crime to want to knock out after a life-altering conversation with my killer slash father." When he turns around to face me, I can see the disappointment in his eyes. He thinks I don't trust him.

"I didn't know it was a crime to care about you." *There I go again, speaking before thinking. When will I learn?* My words must sting a little, because when my eyes gloss over his face, a shade of pink seems to rise from the neck of his shirt, as if I slapped him.

He bites his lip and takes a breath. "After the shooting, I couldn't sleep—PTSD, they chalked it up to—so I was prescribed pills to help relieve my insomnia. And when I moved in here, your parents were put in charge of my medication. So every night around nine or ten, your parents give me one pill and watch me take it."

But why do you have a bottle of Ambien pills if they are in charge of it? And why is the bottle expired?

"The guys at school want something in exchange for the study buddies, so sometimes, I hide my pills under my tongue and save them for trading." *There you have it, Emma. He's storing them in that old bottle to trade with the school druggies. Just great.*

"Why didn't you tell me?"

His brown eyes pierce into mine before he says, "You don't tell *me* everything all of the time."

The heat—fueled by embarrassment and irritation with myself—rising in my own cheeks makes it look like we've just engaged in a slap fight. "Okay. I get it."

"I'll share anything with you, Emma. But this"—his finger toggles between our bodies—"this has to be a two-way street when it comes to that."

As he leans down to give me a reassuring kiss, I catch sight of the unmarked bottle of pills on his side table; what I want to do is flush its entire contents down the toilet. I know he doesn't need them. "Okay.

Can you get rid of them, please? All of them. Both bottles. I don't want anything bad to happen to you. I wouldn't be able to live with myself if I stood by while you dug a grave for yourself."

"The chances of that happening are slim. But if it'll make you feel better, I'll flush them."

"Thank you."

"And you can help me, too . . . with school. If that offer is still on the table." That was probably intended to be in a much happier tone, but it sounds like he's spitting the words out, instead of gently floating them by me. *Sister. Girlfriend. And I guess I'll add tutor to the list of things I am to you.* "We better get going before they start getting suspicious."

He grabs a pairs of tennis shoes and bolts out the door, leaving me behind to take another look at the bottles of pills still on his side table. I don't want to have to nag him about keeping his promise to me, but I can't ignore the gut-wrenching feeling in my stomach.

⁓

WHEN I WAS LITTLE, I USED TO GO TO THE BATTING CAGES ALL THE TIME with my dad. He would pick me up after school, and we would stay out there for hours on end. Before he became crazy with competition, I loved going to the cages. It was a way for us to bond, and I was damn good at it. The bitter smell of the dirt always made me feel at home. And it still does.

"Who's batting first?" my dad asks as he unlocks the cage.

My hand shoots in the air. *Might as well show everyone how it's done.* Grabbing my helmet, I enter the cage as my dad sets the speed of the pitching machine to my old settings. I raise the bat and let it hover over my left shoulder as the click of the machine launches a fastball toward me. For a moment, I imagine it's coasting at fifteen miles an hour instead of hurtling at sixty. When I think I've timed it perfectly, I swing hard. Miss. *So much for showing them how it's done.*

"You're swinging too early, honey. Wait for the next one, and keep that elbow up." I adjust my elbow as the machine launches another ball at me, and this time when I swing, the ball and the bat connect with a high-pitched crack. "You still got it, sweetie." As I turn around to give my dad the thumbs-up signal, I see him walking toward a white truck. Keegan's truck.

"What's he doing here?" Dylan asks through gritted teeth as he shifts his weight from one foot to the other; Keegan's presence always makes him uneasy.

"No clue. I didn't invite him."

"I did," my dad says with a huge grin. "We need an all-star player if we're going to beat these guys."

"Yeah," Keegan chimes in, setting his baseball bag on the ground. "Your dad said that he called in some of his friends to play a quick game with us on the next field over." Keegan's eyes are bright and shiny; he loves baseball probably more than anything.

"And here they are," Dad says, motioning to the group of men with their sons walking toward us. "Let's get a few more practice swings in before we begin." I'm so mad at my dad that I want to throw my bat at him. We can't even have a family outing without him getting all competitive.

I don't say a word to my dad while we play the game. Partly because I'm furious with him for inviting Keegan, and partly because I'm trying to keep Dylan as far away from Keegan as possible. He was just starting to get used to me being back in his life, and Keegan's surprise feature at today's Sunday family outing has brought him back to the dark place he was in before we made up.

We end up winning the game by three runs, which makes my father happy, and it isn't until the end that I let my arbitrating guard down. Keegan and Dylan are going to go their separate ways, and everything will get back to normal.

"Great game. I had no clue that you were into baseball, too." Keegan reaches down for my hand and squeezes his fingers between mine. I want to pull away, but I know that I have to pretend, even though I'm fully committed to Dylan now.

"I used to play softball a couple years ago."

"Well, you still got it." He leans in to kiss me on the cheek, and when he does, I see Dylan's jaw tighten. He was getting in some post-game swings, and is bringing his gear in now. "Your brother wasn't as good as I thought he would be, though. Maybe I can come over and teach him sometime."

"Pass," Dylan says as he drops his bat at our feet. "We don't need you or your help."

"What's your problem, man?" Keegan has released my hand and is now an inch away from Dylan's face. They're the same height, but Keegan has more muscle, and I'm scared that a fight is going to break out between them. "I've been trying to be nice, but I can't ignore it anymore. If you have a problem with me, say it, and stop being an asshole about it."

"Right now, you are my problem. Why don't you just leave? Nobody wants you here."

I try to wedge myself between them, but they're like statues; two hot and sweaty Greek-god statues that won't budge. I see Keegan's veins start to rise from his skin. Would he actually hit Dylan?

"Apparently, *she* wants me here, and so does your dad." I see a pompous smirk crawl across Keegan's face. "Maybe if you were the

foster son he wanted, he wouldn't need me to come rescue your team."
Wrong thing to say. Before I can call someone over to break them up,
Dylan's fist has already connected with Keegan's jaw twice.

Keegan picks himself up off of the ground and starts toward
Dylan, but this time, my dad is there to break it up. After a quick lecture, he sends Dylan to our car and Keegan to his. I know what I have
to do now. This has to stop.

I meet Keegan at his car window. His cheek is swelling from the
sucker punches, but other than that, he doesn't look too bad.

"Can you believe him?" he says, spitting some blood onto the
ground. His eyes search for empathy in mine, but I'm unable to give
it to him.

"Yeah, I do, actually. That was a horrible thing to say."

"And what he said wasn't?"

"I'm not saying that he wasn't wrong, but he's my brother . . . kind
of . . . and I can't have you two fighting." He reaches down and tries
to grab one of my hands, but I lace my fingers together behind my
back. "I like you, but I can't have this tension every time you come
around. It's been there since the beginning, and I'm not sure I can do
this anymore." I see him look down and into his hands; he already
knows what I'm about to say. "I'm sorry, Keegan, but . . . we have to
break up." I want him to try to convince me to stay, but he doesn't even
try to contest it. The look of betrayal in his green eyes is the last thing
I see before he cranks his truck up and drives away.

It's almost eleven when the headlights of my dad's car wake me
from my slumber later that night. After he separated the fight, he
took off with one of his friends from the game, and we haven't seen

him since. As he advances toward the house, I can tell that he's had a few drinks, and although he isn't drunk, I know he's close to the edge.

Shortly after my dad makes it inside, my phone vibrates from my bedside table with a text. Thinking that it's a message from Dylan or Keegan, I rush to answer it, but when I pick up my phone, I realize that it's not from either of them.

Dad: Family meeting.

Uh-oh. Dylan's done it now. We hardly ever have family meetings, because they only happen when there's something big on the table that we have to discuss immediately. The last one was almost a year ago, when Mom and Dad told us that they were applying to be foster parents. The issue tonight must be too mature for Matthew's ears because they leave him asleep in his bed.

"I just want to ask one question," my dad says when he finally speaks. "What the hell happened? I thought you and Keegan were friends. I turn my back for three seconds, and you're pounding Keegan's face into the ground."

"Friends?" Dylan and I say in unison, but then I decide to let him have the floor; he *is* the reason that we're having this meeting right now. He might as well speak for himself. "I lost it for a second, I guess." He looks as if he has more to say, but nothing comes out. I don't know how he's going to cover this up.

"You 'lost it for a second'?" my mom interjects. "I think you did a hell of a lot more than just lose it for a second." *She's not wrong.* "I can't believe you would do something so stupid, Dylan. Violence is never the answer—"

"I agree," Dad says, cutting Mom off. "As of right now, we're not sure if Keegan's family is going to press charges, but quite frankly, I wouldn't blame them if they did. I talked to his mother, and she says he's pretty banged up. Nothing's broken, but he might have a zygomatic fracture." I see the corners of Dylan's mouth twitch a little as if he wants to laugh. "Now, I think that we need to get away to the lake house for a while so everyone can cool down. Lake Arrowhead is beautiful at this time of the year."

I think back to when I got in trouble for crashing Dad's car into a streetlight when I still had my permit. It wasn't my fault because I was only swerving out of the way of another car, but I still ended up hitting the streetlight and causing a blackout that lasted almost four hours. I don't remember Mom and Dad rewarding me for crashing their car by letting me take a vacation. But Dylan walks in, takes a few hard swings on my boyfriend—well, ex-boyfriend, now—comes within an inch of breaking Keegan's face, and embarrasses my family in front of everyone at the batting cages, and now Dad wants to let him take a trip to "get away from it all." *That's fair.*

Then again, except for the car incident, Matthew and I have never really put a toe out of line, so he probably doesn't know how to discipline us in situations like this. Maybe I should cut them a little slack. *Meh.*

"I'm sorry, but what the hell is going on here?" I ask before he can get another word in. Mom and Dad both look at me with wide eyes; they've never heard me curse before. "Are we *seriously* going to reward him for fighting? What happened to 'violence is never the answer,' Mom?"

"I think that we've all been under a lot of stress lately, which is why Dylan might have lost it today," my dad answers for her. "And I think we would all benefit from a mini vacation to the lake house. It's the perfect time. You kids are on fall break, and the weather is perfect. Plus, we might as well take advantage of it. It may be the last chance for us to go together as a family."

Dad is relentless. He threw that last bit in for me because he knows that I feel bad for wanting to go away for college. I'm sure he's still hoping that I'll follow in his footsteps and go to UCLA. I glance around at my family members' faces; their eyes are begging me to agree to the trip. "Okay, I'll go."

"Great," my dad says. "We'll leave in the morning." He dismisses us after that, and he and Mom retire to their own room without taking another look at Dylan and me. I wait until I hear their door close to jump down Dylan's throat, but before I can get my first word out, he's already headed out the back door.

"Dylan," I say as I take a seat next to him on the lawn in our backyard. He's been avoiding me since we came back from the cages, but I'm not going to let him get away from me this time. "Dylan, what happened today? I thought you were okay with me and Keegan."

"I was. At first. But somewhere between seeing you guys all over each other at homecoming and him crashing our family day, I lost it." He doesn't apologize, but when I look into his eyes, they are saying the words for him.

"Well, you'll be happy to know that I broke up with him today." I see his dimples flash across his face as he tries to hold back his smile. "I'm still willing to make this work, if you are."

"I know I haven't been the most patient person in the world. I've just been going through a lot. But I want you to know that I'm going to try. I don't want to lose you to something stupid." He grabs my hands and rubs them between his.

"Speaking of losing me—" I look away from him. We have to have

210

this conversation whether he wants to or not. "I know that this thing between us is growing, and it's so easy to cast away all our problems when we're together. But now we need to focus on reality." I take a deep breath before confessing, "I'm applying to some schools out of state. My GPA is high enough to shoot for the Ivy League, and I'd regret it in a big way if I didn't try."

Dylan's eyes narrow on mine and hold an unblinking stare for almost thirty seconds before he speaks. "Are you warning me that you're going to break up with me when you leave for college? Because if that's what this conversation is about, I don't want to have it. Not now, anyway." He gets up and storms into his studio in a huff. I hate that Dylan never wants to stick around to deal with things.

When I catch up to him, he's already at his easel, getting lost in the crimson background that he's painted. "Not at all. Don't get me wrong, Dylan, I want to be with you. But I'm trying to be proactive and solve our problems before they sneak up on us. I can't make decisions about *our* relationship by myself, though."

Before I can get my next words out, he's throwing his brush at the ground, painting it red in a few places. "Well, what do you want me to do?"

"I want you to help me figure this out." No response. "But college is a big deal, and I want you to be happy for me, too, like a brother would be."

"But I'm more than that!" he screams, his voice shaking my body like an earthquake. He's never really yelled at me, and he must see the shock on my face, because he calms himself before continuing. "Sorry. Let's just talk about this later."

"Why later? It's *always* later." My eyes burn with fiery tears as I lay into him. "You know, your hot-and-cold act is getting really tired,

Dylan. I'm not sure who you want me to be. Your sister, your girlfriend, your tutor, your mentor . . . what? Because I'm getting dizzy spells from spinning my wheels trying to figure it all out."

"Then why stay with me?" he spits, his voice cold and unforgiving.

"Because I . . ." *Love you.* "Never mind . . . Now is not the time."

"Maybe it's because you already broke up with Keegan, so now you're stuck with me. And you know that there's no one else waiting in line to date you."

The world around me freezes for a second, giving me time to process the malice in his words.

"I cannot believe you just said that."

He turns back to his easel, shrugging off our conversation as if there's nothing I can say to contest him.

"But if that's what you think, then fine." I leave his studio, and I purposely don't tell him if our relationship is over. I want him to worry about what will happen to us. I want him to worry that he's lost me for good.

chapter 17

W<small>E USED TO</small> go to the lake house every year for the Fourth of July. We would go fishing as a family and have a contest to see who could catch the biggest fish—Dad always won, of course. After we finished cleaning them, Dad would build a campfire and have us grill the fish over it. Mom used to put little pieces on my stick to make it like a kebab, and I would continue to roast and eat the pieces until my stomach grew heavy with satisfaction. Then at the end of the day, we would pull the fireworks from the basement and light up the night sky for at least fifteen minutes.

The lake looks the same as it always did to me. A little muddy around the edges, a deep greenish-blue in color, and filled with colorful fish. When I step out of the car and catch a whiff of the out-doorsy scent, I'm instantly reminded of all the good times we've had here. And that, at least for the moment, distracts me from my wither-ing relationship.

"Beautiful Lake Arrowhead, how I've missed you," my dad breathes when he exits the car. With his hands on his hips, he continues inhaling and exhaling until he's filled his lungs with the lake air. "Dylan, help me get the bags. Emma, can you go unlock the doors while your mother gets Matthew out? He's still asleep." I couldn't sleep the entire ride because Dylan had his headphones turned up so loud that I could hear his music through them, but somehow Matthew managed to sleep. How? I have no clue.

Dad tosses me the keys, and I race to the front door. I struggle with the locks, but eventually I hear the click and let myself inside. After hanging the keys on the hook by the door, I retrace my old steps to the room I've had each time we've stayed here. It's on the second floor, and it's the only bedroom, besides Mom and Dad's, that has a view of the lake.

My dad seems to already be in the mood for fishing and announces that he's going out on the lake as soon as he can grab his bait and rod, which gives us no time to unpack or change if we want to come with him. But I know my father, and I know he's going to go fishing at least three more times before we leave, so I'm fine to skip the first round and catch one of his later time slots.

When I finish unpacking, the sun is high in the sky, but my internal clock is screaming that it's time for a nap. The three-hour ride up here must have worn me out, so I crash on the sofa that lines my wall of windows. The last thing I see is a single cloud in the sapphire sky. It's shaped like a heart—a lopsided one, but a heart nonetheless. As the cloud continues to float along in the sky, I see it start to break down the center into two pieces. *Is the universe trying to tell me something? Are Dylan and I done?* For all I know, we might be.

When I open my eyes, it's Dylan that I see standing before me, setting up his easel by the windows as if this is his room. Even though he's not talking to me, I find it hard to hold back a smile. I knew he was eventually going to seek me out in my room; we can't stay away from each other for too long.

"We had a fight," he states matter-of-factly.

"Yeah." I run my fingers through my lightly greasy roots and sigh. "Yeah, we did."

"Still thinking about leaving me for college?" His brown eyes are cold as ice when he looks at me.

"I think I owe it to myself to see what's out there. Don't you think I deserve that?"

"Don't do that," he counters.

"Do what?"

"Make me out to be the bad guy. Like my anger is just an over-reaction. I mean, how am I supposed to feel about losing the only girl I've ever come close to . . ."

The only girl you've ever come close to . . . What, Dylan?

Shaking, he turns away from me. "You should just cut the cord now. Why continue this if it's only gonna end, right?"

"It might not end, Dylan. Just because I'm applying doesn't mean that I'll get in."

"It's hard to believe that when your name is sitting so comfortably at the top of the class rankings list." *He has a point.* The odds of me getting turned down by every school I apply to are unlikely. But I'm not ready to give up on us yet. We've already gone through so much. "It makes it hard to trust you, when you can look me in my eyes and lie to me every day. Telling me how much you care about me, but secretly planning to up and leave me once graduation is over."

"That's the problem. You never trust me. Not when I was with Keegan, not with knowing about your sleeping pills. Not with anything. You keep everything bottled up so tightly that I have to dig deep just to get anything out of you." He lets his head hang low while he searches through his bag of paintbrushes. He knows I'm right.

"You have no clue what I've been going through, Emma. Your life is perfect. And yes, you've had some social setbacks, but compared to mine, your life has been a cakewalk."

"Then tell me. Let me help you. That's what a relationship is. You help me when I fall, and I help you when you fall." I try to make eye contact with him, but he won't meet my gaze.

"Everyone I've ever cared about has left me somehow, someway. My mom was taken from me, my dad would rather rot in a mental institution than deal with anything . . . and now, you're going to leave me, too." I don't know what he wants me to do. If I stay here, I'll resent him for not letting me fly, but if I go, I'll resent myself for not sticking around to see if things can work. It's a lose-lose situation, just like he pointed out with Catherine and Heathcliff.

"Do you remember what you said to me when you asked me out over text message?" I grab his hand and help him to his feet. When we stand, I can feel the sunlight illuminating my eyes. I imagine them reflecting a mixture of purple, blue, red, orange, and yellow; the colors of today's sunset. "You said that you were always going to be there. Now I'm saying it to you. Dylan, I'm not going anywhere. No matter what happens—whether I'm two miles away or two thousand—I'm always going to be there whenever you need me." When his hands wrap around me, a small smile sneaks up on me.

He rests his forehead on mine, the eye contact between us and my breathing both intensifying as he does. I feel a warm, electric current pulsing in my fingertips, and before I know it, my fingers are tangled up with his like a bunch of old necklaces in the bottom of a jewelry box.

"And just for the record," he says in a low voice, "I hate fighting with you. It sucks."

"I agree. It totally sucks," I say as he presses his lips into mine. In that instant, my mind goes blank, and I let myself get caught in the moment with him. We've been so at odds with each other that moments like this have been rare. "So, come to draw me like one of your French girls?" I joke as I lift my arms over my head like the girl in the *Titanic*. "I'm ready when you are."

"Actually, no." *Funny; he thought I was serious.* "It's the sunset. The colors mix and mingle in a way that I've never seen before, even though I've seen a million sunsets and sunrises. For some reason, it looks different here." He pauses before continuing. "You want to join me? Should I set up the second easel? I brought it in case you wanted to fool around . . . with the paint, I mean. Not like . . . never mind."

I have to stifle my laugh.

"Dad's probably finished with the fish and should be calling us to eat any minute now." As if he heard me, my dad's voice rings through the house, telling us to come down for dinner. *I know my dad too well.*

My mom directs us outside when we arrive on the first floor. "This sunset is way too beautiful to pass up," she says with a wide smile. We arrange ourselves around the picnic table that I've sat at many times before. It used to look much bigger than it does now, but I assume that's because I've grown so much since the last time we were here.

"CAUGHT, GUTTED, AND GRILLED BY YOURS TRULY," DAD SAYS AS HE PASSES me a plate of fish. I feel like since he's been out of the pro leagues, he's been looking for a way to release his competitive side. But in doing so, he's made everything all about him. There is nothing spectacular about his fish, but he always wants us to praise him for these types of mediocre things. I think he has a problem.

"How did everyone's first day go? Mine was great, as you can all see."

"I caught a fish, too, Dad. Remember?" Matthew pipes up from across the table.

"And you did very well, son."

I feel bad. Even Matthew has to compete with Dad for attention from the rest of the family. It's ridiculous.

"Emma?" my dad says in an agitated voice—I guess for the second time. "What did you do today? I feel like I've barely heard from you."

Well, we are *on vacation. Doesn't that mean that I should get a break from you, too?*

"Oh, I slept all afternoon. Gotta catch up on all the beauty sleep I missed last night."

"You're already beautiful," Dylan whispers so low that only I can hear him.

Across the table, Dad, who must have heard a piece of his soft words, asks him to speak up.

"I said, I spent it painting." His cover is so believable that no one even pauses to question it. "The sunset captured me today." We all turn to admire the setting sun, and I think I hear a collective sigh.

"If I were you," my dad says, "I'd enter this one into the show-case. Everyone loves a good sunset."

I see Dylan flinch at Dad's words, and I don't blame him. He came here to escape reality and forget about his problems for a while. But it seems that as long as Dad is present, Dylan can't relax. I'm sure he is tired of me fighting his battles for him, so I hold my tongue.

Without a word, he drops his fork and excuses himself from the table. The rest of us remain outside on the deck, but we can hear his every move inside the lake house. Everything from the heavy thuds of his feet as he climbs the stairs to the gunshot-sounding slam of a bedroom door, probably his own.

I sigh as I push the food around on my plate. The more time I spend with Dylan, the more I'm starting to see flickers of his father crack through to the surface of his personality. I love how sensitive he is, but the mood swings and sudden fits of rage have been more frequent since our visit to the mental institution. And I'm worried it's going to get a whole lot worse before it gets better.

"I'll have a talk with him later," Dad says. I'm not sure what he expects Dylan to say to him. I mean, he's one of the reasons Dylan is acting out like this. "Oh, that reminds me. Keegan's mom called today. She said he had a bit of a bloody nose last night and now has a black eye, but overall he's fine. And Emma, Keegan wanted you to give him a call. He says it's important."

I swallow hard at his words. "I don't have anything to say to him, and I would appreciate it if you and Mrs. Ortega could stay out of this from now on."

"What? Why? Keegan's great, and—"

"Because we broke up, Dad." That sure shuts him up, but I can tell he wants so badly to ask why. I sit through the rest of dinner in silence, and when I finally escape, I rush to Dylan's door and turn the handle. It's locked. "Dylan, it's me. Open up." I hear him scrambling around in his room, closing containers and what sounds like a dresser drawer. Once the commotion stops, he opens the door, out of breath.

"I was changing my bandages." He's very jumpy and nervous, which makes me think that he is lying, but when I look at his hand, it indeed has a new bandage on it.

"What happened? Why did you leave like that?"

"You know why. Your dad's insistence is getting on my nerves."

"That's how he is. Eventually you'll get used to it."

"No," he yells a little too loudly. "I don't want to get used to this. This is not what I signed up for when I was invited to come live with this family." This feels tragically ironic. *Technically, we signed up for you.* "His pressure is going to push me over the edge. It doesn't matter how much I tell him to lay off, he doesn't quit. He's making me want to give up painting altogether. And once I get back home, I'm dropping out of this stupid showcase."

"You can't," I say as I smooth my hands over my shirt nervously. "Do you know how much that scholarship is worth? Enough to seriously help you pay for any in-state college you want, that's how much. My advice is to stick it out for two more years, and if you never want to see him again, go off and do your own thing at some faraway college."

I can see the wheels turning inside of his head when his eyes meet mine. "Is that why you're going away?"

I have to think before I answer this question. I'd never really thought about it before, but when Dylan says it out loud, I realize that it *does* look like I'm trying to run away from this lavish life that I've been given. A life that some people would kill to have. "I guess I never really had a good enough reason to stay."

Dylan leans in close and brushes his lips across mine. "Still don't have a reason to stay?" I watch as his mouth curls into a smile and his dimples appear out of nowhere.

I hate that he's making this a choice. As my foster brother *and* boyfriend, he should be excited for any big opportunities that come my way, but I don't think he has the capacity to do that. To see beyond only what he wants.

chapter 18

OUR WEEK AT the lake house goes by so fast that I feel like we just got here when it comes time to leave. I spend my time hiking, watching Dylan paint, and brushing up on *Wuthering Heights*. I'd been neglecting it for almost a month, and I figured it was time to get back into it—especially with the exam coming up.

Not once did I join Dad for fishing, and on the ride back, I don't feel bad about it at all. It's kind of sad how time has changed our relationship; when I was little, I used to always want to hang out with him, but now that I'm older, I can't really stand to be around him.

"I'll meet you guys inside. I'm just going to grab the mail," I say when we pull up to the front door. As I'm going through the letters, I see a red envelope from school. I've never received one of these personally, but I've heard some kids at school talk about them. It's one of the dreaded letters of possible failure that Cedar Pointe High sends out after midterm grades are calculated. I know it's not for me, but when no one is looking, I take the envelope addressed to my parents and stick it under my shirt.

When I finally get to my room and set my bags down, I pull the letter out and rip it open. It's not for me, like I thought, but it still isn't good news. Dylan has a D minus in chemistry and is going to fail unless he aces his next couple of assignments and passes the final exam with at least a B. I knew that he needed help in chemistry, but I wasn't expecting this much. Without a second thought, I grab my chemistry books, handouts, and notes, and head back to the main house.

His door isn't locked when I turn the knob, and when I burst in, I see him sitting on his bed, lacing up a pair of his shoes. "Thanks for knocking," he says sarcastically. "Do you need something?"

Judging by his tone of voice, it's a bad time, but I tell myself not to be angry with him. His body is probably agitated from stopping the study buddy pills cold turkey. That's a typical symptom—I looked it up. "Yeah, just wondering how long we're going to stay up studying tonight?"

"I'm fine. I don't need to study tonight."

"Are you sure? Because this letter says otherwise." I hold the letter out in front of him and let his eyes skim over the first three lines. When he's finished, he snatches it out of my hands, balls it up, and heaves it across the room at his trash can. It's overflowing with other balled-up papers, probably other tests and assignments that he's bombed. "You're failing?"

"You don't know what it's like to try with everything in you, and still come up short," he whispers. "To not be able to get it right, no matter how many times you go over it. Everything comes so easy for you."

"You've never seen me play tennis, and you'd probably change your mind if you had. I've played in over forty matches, and I've only won twice."

"Okay, so *one* thing gives you a minor setback. Boo-hoo. Chemistry is an entirely different entity. You can't fail tennis. You can, however, fail chemistry."

I scoot his shoes over and sit down next to him before grabbing his hand and lacing my fingers in his. "I believe you can do it. All you have to do is focus."

"It's not that simple," he says, pulling his hand from mine and bending down to rest his elbows on his knees. "I've dug my grave already. I spent so much of my time trying to convince myself that what you had with Keegan wasn't real, and working, and trying to come up with ways to get your dad off my back, that I let my grades slip. And that was before everything that's happened with my own dad." He starts to search the end of his shirt for a loose thread to pull, a habit that I've started to notice creeping up when he gets nervous. "Mr. Wright's chemistry test is going to be killer. Do you know how hard I'm going to have to work to pass that thing? It's nearly impossible."

"You said it yourself. *Nearly* impossible. Not *im*possible." He stares blankly at me for a long while, and I'm the one who has to break the connection. "I'll meet you downstairs in ten minutes if you want a real tutor on this. Bring your books."

I'm waiting on emails to refresh on my phone when I see Dylan appear at the top of the steps. He's changed into a new set of clothes— he probably took a shower—and has his book and notebooks with him. My phone has not yet refreshed when he sits down beside me at the coffee table, so I set it aside. It will ding once everything pops up.

"Ready?" I smile.

"Ready as anyone can be at eight in the evening." He winces as he sets the books down on the table, and I'm not sure if it's because he's ashamed or if it's because he doesn't want to do this. Either way, we're going to get through the material. I decide to start with the basics—the periodic table—and after an hour of studying, we've made progress in memorizing most of the polyatomic ions.

"$C_2H_3O_2$ negative?"

"Acetate."

"Correct, but these are ions, so you have to say 'ion' after its name. Otherwise Mr. Wright will count it wrong. Now, SO_4 two negative?"

"Sulfate ion."

"OH negative?"

"Hydroxide ion."

"Good," I exclaim, leaning in to give him a hug. I'm about to wrap my arms around his waist when he recoils. I try not to take his rejection personally, but I can't help it. "Everything okay?"

"No time for hugs. I have to get this stuff."

I like that he's eager to get this under his belt, but his dismissal stings a little. "Okay."

I'm in the middle of helping him draw sulfuric acid when I hear my phone ding. My emails have finally pushed through. "Good. Now try sulfurous acid on your own while I check my phone. I'm dying to see my SAT scores. It's the last piece of the puzzle that I need to complete my college applications." Lake Arrowhead is incredible, but I don't get an ounce of cell phone reception there, so I'm just now getting around to checking on my scores even though they've been up for almost four days.

As I wait for the page to load, a wave of fear washes over me. *What if I don't make a high enough score? Yes, grades are important, but SAT scores matter more than that. There is no room for error.*

Dylan must see the worry in my face, because when I look up at him, he's staring back with sympathetic eyes. "Bad score?"

I wrinkle my brows at him. *Why would he immediately jump to that?* "No. Not yet, anyway. It's still loading."

We wait for a minute longer, and when the page finally comes into a view, I squint at my score through one eye . . . 1420.

"Fourteen twenty! YES!" I scream, ignoring the fact that the rest of the Ellenburg house—besides Dylan and me—is trying to rest. In the middle of my celebration, I see his eyebrows grow pointy with frustration and his shoulders slump a little more than usual. "Something wrong?"

"What schools are you applying to?" He sets his pencil down and turns to look me dead in the eyes, his face emotionless.

"Huh?" I ask to buy myself some time. He doesn't have to repeat the question; I heard him loud and clear the first time. Given his reaction the last time we talked about this, I've been holding off on telling him that more than half my list is out of state.

"What, do I need to put this in the form of a test question to get a straight answer out of you? Where are you applying?"

"Whoa, Dylan!" I try to keep my voice as calm as possible, but all I can focus on is the warmth—probably from anger—emanating from his body. *I don't want to fight with him again. I'm tired of fighting.* "Where is this coming from?"

He peels a few scraps from his sheet of paper and rolls them into a ball between his fingers. "I feel like you're holding things back from me. Not telling me important stuff—like where you might be next year—to . . . protect me or something."

"But, Dylan. I'm not even sure if—"

"I don't really wanna hear your excuse. Just tell me."

"Well, there's Stanford, UCLA—to appease my dad—and Berkeley." I make sure to state these first, as they are all in California. "And I'm also applying to the University of Westminster, which is in London, Brown, Duke, and Columbia." I sit in silence, waiting for him to explode, but he doesn't. "Say something."

"I don't really know what you want me to say."

This is precisely what I didn't want to happen. "You're pissed."

"Yeah, well, it's hard not to be pissed when you're ditching me for a college across the country."

"It's just an application, Dylan, and Westminster isn't even in the US." *Not helping, Emma.* Déjà vu takes control of me for a second; I know we had this same conversation about my staying or going not too long ago.

He begins packing up his things, obviously finished with our tutoring session. "You know, it may just be an application to you, but to me, it's a pretty good sign of what you want for us, which obviously isn't very much."

"Wait, no," I say, rising to my feet. "Don't try to change my words around. This has nothing to do with us. This has to do with you and whatever happened before you came here." He stops dead in his tracks when he hears this. "What's really going on, Dylan? Because I can't keep fighting with you. I won't."

He sits on the bottom stair and puts his head in his hands. "Maybe I was better off in that group home."

But if you had never come here, wouldn't that mean that we'd have never even met? Wouldn't that mean that everything I'm feeling for you wouldn't have existed? That every kiss and hug we've shared never even happened? I have to take a couple of deep breaths to steady my thoughts; I don't want him to take this the wrong way. "Dylan, I think you should see someone. A therapist, I mean."

"Why?"

"You have all of these things going on, and I think you need to talk to someone about it."

"Isn't that what I have you for?" His question kills me. "No, I'll be okay. Just give me a little time to get my head on straight, and I'll go back to happy-go-lucky Dylan. I promise." He picks up his books and starts back up the stairs. "Don't worry about me. I'll be fine."

The optimistic sides of my brain want to believe him. But the rational bits of my brain know that something is wrong. That he's spiraling out of control, and that there's nothing I can do to stop it.

⁓

I KEEP MY PROMISE TO DYLAN, AND TOGETHER WE WORK HARD TO HELP him overcome his fear of chemistry. By the time his final comes around a few weeks later, he's mastered every section outlined in his syllabus.

"Are you nervous?" I ask as I take out the note cards we made so that he can get in some extra test prep this morning. We've gotten to school so early that we're the only ones in the library when it opens up.

"A little. I'm gonna have to repeat the class if I don't pass this thing." He looks off into the distance for a second. "But that's not what worries me the most. It's disappointing Mom and Daniel." *Whoa! When did he start saying that?* It's so weird to hear him call my mom "Mom," but my dad "Daniel." He must not see my dad as a real dad yet.

"You'll do fine, I know it. Stop worrying so much." I pull a card from the top of the deck and show it to him. "What kind of reaction is this?"

"Combustion."

"Correct. What is a substance that speeds up the rate of a reaction called?"

"A catalyst."

"Right again. You've really been studying, huh?"

"Up all night. And what can I say, I have a great tutor." He leans over, and our lips connect for a half second before I push him away. I don't want the librarian to see us.

"We've got to get through these. Your test is in thirty minutes." My eyebrows arc tense with determination, but I relax them before pulling another card from the deck. "Next question: the number of moles of solute per kilogram of solvent is called what?"

"Molarity?"

"Wrong. It's *molality*." I see him flinch when I tell him the correct answer, as if he wants to punch himself in the face for missing such an easy question. "It's okay. Those words are so alike in spelling that it's easy to mix them up. I still do sometimes. And besides, that was one of the first things we went over. I don't expect you to remember that."

"But you're not Mr. Wright, and I'm sure he expects me to remember that." He puts his head in his hands in frustration. I don't know why he's coming down so hard on himself; he just answered a stack of these correctly without much effort.

"Dylan—"

"Just leave me alone," he screams—even though he knows

that we're supposed to whisper in the library—and I recoil, burned. I'm only trying to help. *It's just his nerves talking,* I tell myself to brush it off.

In the beginning of our relationship, we established that those were our safe words. We said that if we ever got into an argument, those three words—leave me alone—would mean exactly that: leave each other alone and talk about it when we both cool off. Period.

So, without another word, I leave him and start for the pavilion to find Karmin. She's sitting where she normally sits, which makes it easier to find her. Keegan isn't too far from her, and I feel my throat tighten up when I see him. *When are we going to swallow this pill and talk about things?*

"Hello, stranger," Karmin says when she sees me. "You've been disappearing as soon as practice is over every day, and I hardly get to talk to you anymore. Is everything okay?"

"I've just been helping Dylan study for his chemistry final."

"He has Wright, doesn't he?"

"Yep."

Her face floods with sympathy. "I remember when I took his class two years ago. I almost blew up the lab because I forgot to dilute the acid before I added it to my solution."

"Wait, that was you?" I laugh, reliving the memory in my head. "You put the entire tenth grade out of the chemistry lab for three weeks. And that smell was awful." The laughing takes away from my thoughts, but when it stops, I'm brought back to the reason I came to see her. "Can we talk for a minute?"

I bring her over to a less crowded section of the school, and before I can even get a word in, she starts. "Finally taking me up on my offer to teach you how to kiss, are you?" I see her laugh as she pulls a tube of lip gloss from her pocket. Before she can start applying, I stop her.

"No. Again, I'm good."

"Aww. Well, if this is about Keegan, the answer is yes. Yes, he misses you." That definitely wasn't the question I wanted her to answer, but it's still nice to know that he thinks about me from time to time. "He took it pretty badly, you know?"

I look over at him from where we now stand. Keegan isn't the chipper guy I got to know earlier this year. Our breakup must have affected him more than I thought, and it kills me to know that I made him unhappy.

"This isn't about Keegan," I say. "It's about Dylan."

"Dylan? What's going on? Does he like me?" I see her eyes widen with excitement. *Has she forgotten that she already has a boyfriend and that he's standing less than ten feet away from us?*

"No." *He better not.* "Well, we don't really talk about you." Her face droops with disappointment, and then snaps back to reality as if he was easy to get over. "I think he's in trouble."

"Like, he got a girl pregnant trouble?"

"No."

"Oh, so drugs trouble?"

"That wouldn't be my business to tell, but . . . no." *At least I don't think so. I don't think he's used those study buddy pills since I asked him to flush them.*

"Weed?" I can barely get a word in over her eagerness to answer my question, so I grab her by the shoulders and stare into her eyes to get her to shut up and focus, but my plan backfires. "So, you *do* want a lesson. I knew it. No one can resist my lips." I want to shake her and tell her to shut up, but I hold back my urge.

"Karmin," I say, breaking up the syllables in her name so that she can understand my every word. "No, I don't want to kiss you, and no, he's not in any of that kind of trouble."

She leans back, I guess confused. "So what's wrong with him, then?"

"I think he's . . . depressed or something. He hasn't been painting much, he's always down on himself, and he's been more aggressive than usual."

"Oh, is that all?" *"Is that all?" What do you mean?* "Honey," Karmin says, placing a semi-comforting hand on my shoulder, "he's a teenage boy. They're moody and aggressive. It's just what they do. And plus, he's a painter. Artists are emotional."

"But he's failing, too. And he's one of the smartest guys that I know. You think I should tell my parents about it?"

"God, no! Trust me, it'll be a while before he forgives you if you do that. Once, when we were fifteen, I accidentally told my parents that Keegan skipped school with some of his baseball friends to go to LA for a Tame Impala concert. He got grounded for two months, and it took him an extra month post-grounding to start talking to me again. It sucked so much. I mean, not being able to talk to your brother is one thing, but not being able to talk to your twin? Now, that's torture."

I tune her out to be alone with my thoughts, and that's when it dawns on me: Dylan can be more trouble than he's worth sometimes. Besides Keegan, he's the only other guy to ever want to be with me. So while a piece of me feels obligated to stay with him, the other piece feels like I should listen to the voice in the back of my head—the one that urges, *Move away from Heathcliff*—and end things with him. I know it's horrible, but when I think back to my time with Keegan, sometimes I regret that I chose Dylan over him. Keegan was simple; with Dylan, I have to jump through hoops daily to keep him semi-happy. But I can't change things now. Dylan's in a downward spiral, and if I leave him now, it will only get worse.

"Maybe you're right, Karmin."

"I know." I want to tell her that she has a problem with humility, but after the conversation we just had, I decide not to. It's not my place. "And you're welcome. That's what best friends are for."

Did she say "best friend"?! My excitement instantly turns bittersweet. Of course, I finally get a best friend in the middle of my senior year, right before I leave for college. But then again, better late than never.

"So did Coach Denise hear back from the competition director yet?" I say to change the subject.

"Yeah. If we place in the top three at regionals in January, we can go to nationals in March."

"We'll qualify for sure. Our routine is as solid as can be."

"Yeah. Also, Coach Denise says that she's looking for two girls to enter into the solo category. It will help our team score if we can place in those as well."

"She have anyone in mind?" I try to come off as nonchalant, but what I really want to do is fall on my knees and beg her to convince Coach to let me have one of the spots. Karmin is the best technical dancer on our team, so she's basically guaranteed a solo. But I want the other one.

"Not yet, but we'll find out at practice today."

"I hope I get one." It's my senior year, and I want to be remembered for something. Not the shy bookworm who skipped two grades, but the cool, popular girl who could dance her ass off and win competitions.

☙

AT THE END OF EVERY PRACTICE, WE ALWAYS SIT IN A CIRCLE AND DISCUSS what we've improved on and what we need to work on. Today, Coach Denise says that if we don't place at the regional competition, it will be because of little things like our feet and our legs.

"Your feet should be turned out at all times, and when you kick, your legs should be so straight that it looks like you don't have knees." As she speaks, I try to think back to my performance in the routine we just finished practicing. *Were my feet sickled? Were my legs bent?* "I received news that we are allowed to enter two soloists into competition. They say that the average score of the two soloists will count for twenty-five percent of the team score, so this is kind of a big deal."

I look around the circle, and everyone has on a nervous face. Everyone except Karmin. She knows that she will get one of the spots, so instead of a worried look, she's wearing a tranquil one.

"I've given this a great deal of thought, and the first solo is going to Karmin." When she says this, Karmin's mouth falls open with surprise. *Save it for the Oscars,* I think to myself. I look around the room and try to size up my competition. Sophia's kicks aren't as good as mine, but her legs are longer, which gives them that wow factor, and Autumn and I are neck-and-neck for the second-best turns on the team. Will Coach Denise overlook my imperfect practice record and give it to me? *God, I hope so.*

"The second girl is going to be . . . ," she says, dragging out her words. She pauses dramatically, and when she feels like we are about to jump down her throat for the name, she finally says, "Emma."

I can't control my excitement in the same way Karmin did, and I throw my fist into the air, and scream "Yes!"

"It seems fitting, seeing as both of you are the only seniors on the team. Might as well go out with a bang, right?"

I feel my fire of excitement die down a little. She didn't pick me because I have great technique; she picked me because of my senior status. It's definitely humbling, but I have the spot, and that's what's important.

"Congratulations, girls. We'll start working on your solos as soon as we return from Thanksgiving break."

I stick around today to talk with Karmin. She has a ton of ideas about what kind of dance she wants to do at regionals and is hoping that Coach Denise will take her ideas into consideration when she choreographs our dances. I don't really care what I do, I just want to dance. I want my parents and siblings to be in the audience watching me finally do something that I love. And I want Dylan cheering me on and giving me roses because I was great, even if I don't win. Don't get me wrong, though. I want to win.

After practice, I race home to tell Dylan. I enter his studio to see his tongue sticking out the side of his mouth, a look of great concentration on his face. He's working on a painting. I stand there for a minute or two before he even notices my presence.

"Hey," he says as he sets down his paintbrush and stands to give me a hug.

"How did your test go?"

"I think it went well."

Good. "Good."

"Thanks, Em. For everything. I don't know what I'd do without you." The sincerity in his eyes makes my insides flutter. *I never thought I'd ever mean this much to anyone.* I'm not sure how I'm supposed to reply—"Thanks" doesn't sound good enough—so I change the topic.

"You're finally painting again. I haven't seen you create anything since the sunset." I sit on his lap when he reclaims his easel.

"Yeah. Now that I don't have chemistry clouding my mind, I can focus on my showcase paintings again." I take a look at his piece. It's an image of a blond girl sitting cross-legged in a pile of blush-colored flower petals, reading a book.

"Clearly, I can't get my mind off of you," he explains, and all I can do is smile.

chapter 19

Dear Catherine,

Just so you know, I don't have to keep this journal anymore—Mr. Lawrence stopped having us journal now that we've closed our unit on <u>Wuthering Heights</u>. But I kind of like it. Being able to tell you—someone who can understand—about the dramas of my life makes things a little easier to deal with. Karmin's my best friend, but even best friends keep secrets from each other. There are some things I can tell you that I wouldn't dare tell her. So, thank you. I can't tell you how much I appreciate your attentive—and never judgmental—ear.

Okay. Hallmark moment over. Let's get back to business.

Something's wrong. I'm not sure what's going on with Dylan, but he's been really off for the past couple of weeks. One minute, he's happy, and the next, he's sad, then he's mad, and then he's back to happy again. I don't get it! I mean, I understand that he's stressed that we might be apart this time next year, but I don't think this is normal.

How did you possibly handle Heathcliff's manic emotions? The temper, the self-destructive tendencies. . . . I try to comfort Dylan as much as I can and keep his temper at bay, but lately—with the stress of my college apps, normal parental pressure, and my dance competition practices—it's been a bit much.

With Keegan out of the picture, I thought that would help, but it seems like nothing I do for Dylan is enough to cure him of this dark cloud. Do you . . . do you think it could be because he's no longer taking the study buddy pills? I read online that coming off of that stuff could cause really bad mood swings and agitation, so maybe all of this is my fault? I was just looking out for him, but now I think I've created a monster that I can no longer control.

How can I help him without breaking his trust? Point me in the right direction, Catherine. I'm begging you.

♡ Emma

The smell of Thanksgiving food wakes me up, so I figure my mother must be doing some serious cooking. I pull on a set of pajama pants and a hoodie, and head across the way. She's at the chopping board when I see her.

"Smells good, Mom," I say, inhaling deeply through my nose. We've spent Thanksgiving in other places, but nothing beats having it at home. I'm always soothed by the smell of my mom's cooking, especially her stuffing and sweet potatoes.

"Thanks. Happy Thanksgiving, honey," she says without looking up at me. Her hair is in rollers, and she has on her robe. She's probably been up since five this morning cooking, cleaning, laying out her clothes, and doing her hair. She wants everything to be perfect when our family members arrive.

"Happy Thanksgiving."

"Have you picked out your outfit yet? Your aunt and uncle are going to be here at noon." I glance at the clock. It's a quarter to eight. "And can you go make sure your brothers are awake? I've laid their clothes out already, so they just need to eat breakfast, shower, and put them on, in that order."

"Sure thing. Do you want me to help you cook, too?"

"Oh, yes," she says, after taking a deep breath. "I'm finished with all of the dinner, but I still have a couple of desserts left to make. You can help me with those." She takes the cutting board and dumps the pecans she was chopping into a big bowl of what looks like cake batter. She turns on the mixer, and then gives Dad a thumbs-up through the window. He's outside checking on the turkey that he has on the grill. I hadn't even noticed him out there when I passed. He probably thinks I'm still mad at him, and therefore ignoring him. I haven't figured out how to make up with him yet.

After spending a couple minutes admiring the desserts that Mom has already finished making, I head upstairs to wake my brothers.

When I knock on Dylan's door, he's already awake, like I expect him to be. He hasn't slept in in a long time.

"Good morning," I say as he motions for me to close the door, which I do. "Mom wanted me to wake you up."

"Well, as you can see, I'm up." I sit on the edge of his bed and lean in to give him a quick kiss, which somehow turns into a full-on make-out session. "So tell me, Emma," Dylan says when he pulls away from me, "it's my first Thanksgiving in the Ellenburg house. Should I be prepared for anything unusual?"

"That depends on who's coming." I laugh, but Dylan doesn't join in. "I'm only joking, Dylan. Mom and Dad have probably invited every living relative they know, and it's most likely going to be a full house. But no, there's nothing that you should be worried about. It's a pretty normal day here, except there's a ton more people seated around the table."

"Okay, good." I watch as the anxiety in Dylan's eyes lessens for a moment. It's kind of cute that he's so nervous about meeting the rest of my family.

"I gotta go wake up Matthew, but you should eat breakfast, shower, and get dressed. 'In that order,' per Mom's instructions. Our family members should be arriving in a few hours."

"Okay, but before you go," he says, grabbing my face with both of his hands. When his lips press into mine, a swordfight between our tongues initiates. He hasn't kissed me this passionately in a long time, and it feels good to have the old him back. Maybe Karmin was right. He just needed some time to pull himself out of his mood.

"Emma? Is everyone awake?" my mom shouts from the bottom of the stairs.

"Yeah," I yell back. "I'll be right down!" I turn to Dylan, and kiss him on the cheek. "I'll see you in a little bit."

When I finally make it downstairs, my mother has laid out her frosting supplies on the counter. "Took you long enough," she says.

"Matthew was throwing a fit. You know how he has a hard time getting up. I told him he can sleep in for a few extra minutes, and then he has to get moving. Oh, and by the way, he's not too happy about having to take a shower either, so that'll be another battle."

"That boy would wear the same underwear for a month straight if we didn't make him shower every day."

"Let's just be happy that he's more into doing math problems and using proper grammar than eating dirt or bringing home worms in his pockets." That's what the boys used to do when I was his age. "So what are we decorating?"

"A cinnamon spice cake. I'm going to start that while you begin working on the pumpkin pies. We're making four of them. I can't believe I forgot all about them. My mom would kill me." A worried look passes over Mom's face. She's stressed.

I start down the list of directions, but I have to keep checking the paper to make sure I'm doing it correctly. It's my grandma's passed-down recipe, and my family will be disappointed if the pie doesn't taste exactly right. My mom finishes decorating the cake very fast—she's a pro—and when she comes to help me, I feel as if I'm getting in her way, so I hand her the reins and watch from the other side of the counter.

"I thought you were going to help me," she says when she slides the pies into the oven and removes the pan of stuffing. "You're just like you were as a kid. You would ask to help, and then get distracted and end up licking the bowl." I chuckle at her memory of me. I've been sneaking my finger into her now-empty bowl of pumpkin pie filling since she finished pouring it into the crusts.

The corners of her mouth twitch upward for a split second. I know what she's thinking: this is going to be my last Thanksgiving with them before I go off to college. "Don't cry, Mom. Please, don't cry. I'm always going to visit for the holidays."

"I'm ecstatic for you, I really am. I just don't want to miss you. Most parents get eighteen years with their child before they go off to college, but I only get sixteen. I'm happy for you, but it just seems unfair."

"I'm sorry, Mom."

She pulls me into a tight hug. I know she doesn't want me to leave at all, but I think she's been trying to convince herself that things will remain the same when I'm gone. "No. Don't apologize for being great. Most parents would kill for their kid to accomplish what you have, and we're not going to force you to stay because we can't handle it." She wipes her tears before they can fall from her eyes and gives me one last hug before telling me to go get dressed.

The feeling that I'm breaking my mother's heart is almost enough to make me want to stay, but I know that I'll never leave if I do.

DINNER GOES BY QUICKER THAN USUAL—PROBABLY BECAUSE EVERYONE'S so interested in getting to know Dylan that I get to coast for the first Thanksgiving in my life—and once I finish my plate, I sit down with my grandmother to talk.

"Emmy," she says when I wrap my arms around her fragile body. She used to call me that when I was a kid, and I guess she hasn't given it up yet. "How are you?"

"I'm fine, Gran."

"You're becoming such a pretty young woman. Do you have a boyfriend?" Leave it to my grandma to cut straight to the chase; she's always been frank. "You're glowing like you're in love."

"No, Gran. I *had* one, though. Keegan . . . his name is Keegan, but we just broke up." I look down into my hands as I speak these words. It's the first time I've opened up about Keegan to any of my family since our blowout at the batting cages. Then I think of Dylan. A grin too big for my face tries to break through to the surface, but I refuse to let it pop up and release the secret I'm holding inside. As much as I trust my grandma, I know I still can't tell her about us.

"He's an idiot. Got to be to give up a girl like you." As I look at her, I see that her blond hair has faded into a lighter shade of gray since the last time I saw her, and she has many more wrinkles in her skin, too, but her eyes are still as blue as the sky on a cloudless day. "Did you love him?"

I say nothing. I don't want to think of what I felt for Keegan. All that really matters now is Dylan. I shrug.

"I remember when I first started dating your grandpa."

"Papa?"

"Yes. It was hard for him to keep his hands off of me. He was a frisky one."

"Gran!" I try to delete that visual immediately.

"We fell in love as teenagers, and our parents let us marry when we were only seventeen."

"Seventeen?"

"Yep. Took some convincing, though. They said it was just lust clawing at our heels." She motions for her glass of water, and I give it to her to take a sip. "They had no clue that we could feel something so deep for each other."

"So then how did they end up letting you get married?"

"When they figured out that I was going to run away in order to be with him, they decided to give him a chance." She runs the back of her hand across my cheek, and I see her smile weakly. "Adults think that love isn't real when you're young, but I know it is. If I've learned anything over the years, it's this: Love is love is love. It has no limits. And from the look in your eyes, I think you probably know it, too."

Shaking my head, I set her straight. "Gran, I'm not in love with Keegan. I was never in love with him."

"Well, you're in love with someone. I can tell."

But how? I ask her inside my head. I have no idea if I'm really in love with Dylan. *How do you know?*

"Trust me, Emmy." She takes another swig from her glass and hands it back to me. "I can tell."

⌒◇⌒

WHEN I FINALLY GET A MOMENT TO LOOK UP AT THE CLOCK, IT'S TIME FOR our guests to leave. Being a show pony for my extended family is exhausting, so after I help my mom put the food away, I retire to my own room to relax. Dylan is waiting for me when I get there.

"Well, hello," he says as I enter. He still has his dress clothes on, and his hair is still slicked down, but now that everyone has left, he seems less tense. He, too, has started to return to his normal self.

"Hey," I say, distracted.

Dylan grabs my hand and gives it a squeeze. "You okay?"

"Yeah, just thinking about something my grandmother said to me after dinner." Out of fear that he will ask me to elaborate, I change the topic. "Do you mind helping me with this stupid zipper? I haven't taken a comfortable breath all night." I turn around for him to unzip me, and when he does, I disappear behind my dressing screen across the room, pushing my grandmother's words from my head. I pull a shirt over my head and slip on some pajama shorts, and then emerge to sit on his lap. "So what's up?"

"I just wanted to share one of my Thanksgiving family traditions with you."

"And what is that?"

"Going around and saying what we're thankful for."

"Okay. You first, and then me."

He picks up my foot as he begins. "I'm thankful for your ten little piggies, not only because they never smell bad, but because they are the tools that let you dance so gracefully. And, even though you hate the way that they look, they allow you to do something you love dance—which puts a smile on your face and, in turn, mine." He slides his hands up to my thighs and squeezes. "And your thighs, because . . . well, because I'm a guy and we like thighs. Same thing here," he says, his hands skimming across the top of my butt with a gentle tap. "I love this part of you, too." *There's that word again.* *Love.*

He continues to slide his hands up my body and stops at my waist and lower back. "I love your belly button and the little scar you have on your back from when you had the chicken pox, too. And then, of course, there's your boobs."

"Because you're a guy?"

"Well, that, and because if I were to get stranded on an island with you, I know I'd always have a soft place to lay my head at night." I giggle as his fingertips sweep across my arms and travel downward. "And then there's your fingers. I am thankful for these ten extremities because they are always there to remind me that I'm

245

not alone." He kisses them, and then laces his with mine. "Not to mention the way you run your fingers through my hair when we make out. That's kind of hot."

Thank you, Karmin, I say in my head.

"And I'm thankful for your neck for always smelling so good and holding up this beautiful blond head of yours. It reminds me of the sand on a beach I once painted. I'm thankful for your cheeks for giving you the ability to blush in that cute way you do when you're embarrassed or try to act upset. And then there's your lips. I could kiss them all day." He gives me one deep kiss before continuing. "Enough said, right?" I nod, and let him go on to compliment my hair and ears. "And finally, there are your eyes. God, those eyes. I am thankful for these sky-blue beauties because they allow you to see past all of the bull and into the real me. I've never seen eyes like yours, and from the moment I saw them, I knew they were something that I would never get tired of looking at."

He closes his eyes and kisses me once more before ending his list. "I'm so thankful that I have you in my life. You remind me of the happy person I used to be before foster care." He pauses for a moment and frowns, and I imagine him reliving the memory that got him placed here. Then he looks up at me to finish his soliloquy of flattery. "I wouldn't change a thing about you, Emma. You're perfect in my eyes."

I wrap my arms around his neck and pull him close. That is the sweetest thing anyone has ever said to me, and I just want him to hold me as I let his words continue to ring in my ears.

"Your turn," he whispers after my grip loosens.

"What? No way, I can't beat that. You set that bar way too high."

"Just try."

"Okay." I clear my throat, waiting for the words to come to me.

When they do, they don't sound as beautiful as his, so I just keep it short and simple. "I'm thankful that you haven't given up on us. I know our situation is complicated and that I haven't been the girlfriend you deserve, but I'm glad you're still in this. That means a lot to me. *You* mean a lot to me. And for all that you are, I am so very thankful."

"Not bad," he says after a while. "I mean, you could have said *something* about my good looks, but not bad." When I snarl in his direction, he bursts into laughter. "I'm just kidding, Emma."

"You better be." I tousle his hair to let him know that I'm not serious.

"But to add to what I said earlier," he continues, "I just want to say that what I feel for you is not ruled solely by my physical attraction to you. There's more to it. Something I can't quite explain. The surrealism of it all actually makes me think that I'm falling—"

I cut him off with a kiss. He's going to tell me that he loves me. And I love him. *Gran was right.* I've wanted to hear these three words all my life, but I don't want him to say it to me and ruin everything. I'm less than a month away from finding out if I'm going to stay here for college or leave, taking all of my feelings with me, and I don't want to say it out loud and then give us an expiration date. That would be cruel. No, it's better for the both of us if we wait to say those three magical words.

So instead, I whisper, "Me too, Dylan." It's not exactly what he wants to hear, but for now, it's going to have to do. "Me too."

chapter 20

As much as I want to spend time with Dylan during the Thanks-giving break, I can't because I have to study for my English final. It actually kind of works out, though, because Dylan is busy with work and putting the finishing touches on his paintings for the showcase.

When I exit my exam, I breathe a sigh of relief and head home to wait for him in his studio. I find that he has displayed every painting he has finished all around the room. Instantly, I'm drawn to his most recent piece—the one of a girl reading a book in a bed of flowers. Dylan hasn't openly said it, but I know the girl is me. I zero in on the book she's reading. The glittering gold-edged pages give it away. *Wuthering Heights.*

"I'm trying to figure out which ones I want to enter," Dylan says when he sees me in his studio. "I have to email them my list so they can print the labels for tomorrow night, but I can't decide. They're all pretty good, but I need to enter the absolute best if I want to win. I'll never hear the end of it if I lose."

"Want a second opinion?"

"Sure. Let's hear it."

"Pick the ones that mean the most to you. If you're passionate about it in real life, then that means you were probably just as passionate about it when you painted it. Those are the ones that will help you bring home the gold."

"And here I thought you were going to scrutinize each one for detail and accuracy. But this," he says, pulling me into a hug, "this is why I keep you around."

"Oh, that's why." He tries to kiss me, but I jokingly push him away. "No time for play. We have to pick your paintings," I say, though I let him sneak one kiss in before we continue to go through his collection. In the end, we pick the one of him and his mother, the one he did of my eyes, the one with the girl reading *Wuthering Heights*, and two scenic paintings, one of which is the sunset at the lake house. "'Everyone loves a good sunset.'" I quote my dad with a sly grin.

"Yeah, but a sunrise is even better." Dylan glances at the clock in his studio, and then motions to see my phone. When I hand it to him, I can see that his fingers are moving swiftly across the screen. "Sunrise is at six forty tomorrow morning, and let me tell you, it's amazing to watch. But the moments before it rises, when you can see the light from beneath the horizon, now that is truly spectacular. It's the overlapping—"

"Of night and day," I help him finish. "Where you don't know if it's morning yet or still night. It's my favorite part of the day." *The Middle.*

"Mine too. Meet me on the balcony at six o'clock."

"It's a date."

I toss and turn all night in my sleep, because I'm afraid that if I sleep too deeply, I'll sleep right through the alarm and miss the sunrise with Dylan. This is the happiest that I've seen him in a while, and I don't want to be the reason he slips back into a gloom phase.

When my alarm finally goes off, I'm already awake. Outside, I notice that Dylan has set a ladder up against the house so that I don't have to go inside and deal with the house alarm. *He's thought of everything.*

"Thought you overslept," he says when I reach the top of the ladder and swing a leg over into the balcony. He's set up two chairs at the edge for us to sit in.

"No. I don't break dates." He gives me a look, which makes me add, "Anymore."

"That sounds more accurate."

I watch quietly as he pulls items from the bag near my feet. "So what's all of this stuff?"

"Oh, just the essentials: blankets and hot cocoa. Just some stuff to keep us warm. I don't want you catching a cold in this cool morning air."

"Well, how very considerate of you." I grab a blanket and one of the thermoses of cocoa and wrap my cold fingers around it to warm up my hands.

"I try," he says as he takes a thermos in his hands to warm his fingers up, too.

Looking up at the stars, I remember something I heard my mom say after my grandpa—her father—had died. *The stars are how the angels watch over us at night time.*

"She's up there, you know? Your birth mom."

"You think so?"

"Yeah. Mom says that when we die, our souls get caught in the sky so that we can look down on the loved ones we left behind."

"Very nicely put." He silently looks up at the sky, and I can't tell if he's saying a prayer, or trying to figure out which of the fading stars is his mother. "Are you afraid to die?" he asks without looking at me. *What kind of question is this?* I think to myself. *How is anyone supposed to feel about dying and leaving your entire life behind?*

"More so of what happens after death than actually dying," I say after giving it a moment of thought. "No one knows what happens to us when we die, so we make up theories to fill the void. Of course, there's the whole heaven and hell theory and the reincarnation theory, but how are we supposed to know if those things really happen? We don't have a dead person to ask." I pick at my nails, not sure if I should redirect his question back at him. "Are *you* afraid to die?"

"No. My mom used to say that if we fear death, then we're already dead because we're not really living." *God, he's so smart.* "So . . . no, I'm not scared of death. When it's my time to go, it'll happen, you know?"

"That's just it. How can you know that it's your time to go? What if you don't get any warnings?"

"I'm sure there'll be someone or something that will let us know. Whether it's a doctor, God, or a pain in your upper chest. We'll know."

"I'd like to think that there is a point in the middle of us dying where we can choose where we want to go in our afterlife. As in, do we want to be a ghost and stalk our loved ones, or become a star to protect them, or go to heaven or hell, or whatever you believe in."

Dylan removes his hand from his thermos and laces his warm

fingers with mine. "I think that if you stick around as a ghost, you've chosen to live in the neutral ground. One foot in the real world, and one foot out of it."

"Neutral ground?" I ask as I tug at my ear in confusion. I've never heard that term before.

"Yeah. I read this book once and, because it was set in New Orleans, they would use a ton of colloquial terms in it, one of them being 'neutral ground.' It's what they call that piece of grassland in the middle of the road. You're not supposed to drive on it, but some people do anyway. Most places call this the median strip, or middle ground, but in New Orleans, they call it the neutral ground. It belongs to neither the left nor right side of the road, but it's its own entity."

"So, it's like us?"

Now Dylan is the one who's confused. "Explain," he says.

"We're stuck somewhere between siblings and lovers. Not belonging to either side fully, but rather somewhere in between them both. This territory is usually off-limits."

"And yet here we are."

"Yep," I say, turning my attention back to the growing light below the horizon. "And here we are."

Dylan follows my lead, and we sit in silence for a minute. "Life is full of choices, Emma. Life or death. Right or wrong. Cake or pie—by the way, for future references, I'm pro–lemon meringue. It's not always so black and white when it comes to choosing between those options. Take the colors, for example. There's white, which is the absence of color, and black, which is the summation of all of the colors. You're either painting with no color or all of them at once. But how boring would it be to paint with only black and white? What brings art to life is what lies between those two extremes. The different shades of red, blue, green, purple, yellow, and orange. It's everything between black and white on the color spectrum.

"This is the best place to be sometimes. Like us. We're not right, but we're not wrong, Emma. Our relationship lives and breathes in the off-limits, and I feel right being here with you even if everyone else thinks it's wrong. I just can't help the way that I feel about you."

"Dylan," I whisper, a little choked up.

"I really can't."

Blushing, I glance down at my phone and see that it's 6:32. "Less than ten minutes until this spectacular sunrise." The sky starts to reflect the approaching sun; there's a reddish-orange glow creeping up on the edges of night. "I think I like talking to you." I smile, wrapping the blanket a little tighter around my body.

"I *know* that I *love* talking to you." He reaches for my hand underneath my blanket and squeezes it a little tighter than normal.

"But what's going to happen to us if you get adopted?"

"I don't know." He loosens his grip a little, making me think that I've done something wrong. "I'm not sure I know how to be your brother, now that I've been your boyfriend."

"Well, first of all, the kissing, holding hands, long stares, and sappy speeches are going to have to stop. That's obvious. But that'll only be an issue if my parents have a problem with us being together. Maybe things will be different after we get through high school."

Dylan releases my hand and folds his across his chest. "I don't want to talk about this."

"It's a possible reality, Dylan. We have to be prepared."

"If that happens, we'll deal with it then. But I want to enjoy this right now."

"You're right," I breathe into the brightening sky. And he is. We don't know when or if this thing between us will end, so we might as well enjoy the moments while we still have them. "Let's do this again—just sit out here and talk under the stars. After the showcase tonight? Eleven o'clock?"

"I'll be here." We pull out our phones and synchronize our alarms to both ring at ten fifty.

"Oh, that reminds me," he says as he hands me a box of cards. "I talked to Mr. Wright about my grade yesterday after school."

I try to hold back my excitement, but I can't contain it. "What did he say? Did you pass?"

"B plus," he says with an ear-to-ear grin.

For a moment, I forget how chilly it is, and I throw my blanket off my shoulders and wrap my arms around him. "I knew you could do it!"

"Well, I had some help." Grinning, he reaches down and pulls a medium-sized velvet box from his bag. "It's just a little something to say thank you for helping me out this semester. Not once did you let me give up on myself, and for that, I am so thankful."

Now, I'm not really a jewelry kind of girl. I mean, I wear earrings and a couple necklaces here and there, but nothing more than that. Nevertheless, a gift is a gift. And what kind of girlfriend would I be if I turned it down?

I grab the box, and open it to see a small gold necklace with my name on it. "It's beautiful."

"I don't know where I'd be if you didn't have my back, Em. Thank you."

I lean across and kiss his lips. They are cold, but soft as usual. My mind can only focus on one phrase as his lips seem to devour me. *I love you, Dylan.* I feel the words crawl up my throat, but I swallow them back down. I don't want those words to ruin us. Not when everything is so perfect right now. *Later,* I promise myself.

As I pull away, I notice that the sun has broken the horizon. "I think we missed it." I giggle.

"Don't worry. We have plenty more sunrises to watch before you leave for college. We'll get it right one of these days." He presses his lips to mine again, and this time I can feel him smiling. It must be infectious because before I know it, the corners of my mouth stretch into a crescent-shaped grin, too.

"I THINK THEY REALLY LIKED THE ONE OF MY MOM AND ME," DYLAN SAYS as he takes a seat on the stool that the museum has given him. The showcase is over, and now he's finally getting a chance to breathe and take it all in before they announce the winner of the competition. The crowd of extremely well-dressed people has migrated from the showcase hall to the congressional room, leaving Dylan and me all alone now. And judging from the clock on the wall nearby, we should make our way inside soon; the winner is going to be announced in a little less than fifteen minutes. "If I ever become a famous painter, this is what my life is going to consist of. Showcases, I mean. And I could get used to this."

"Me too," my dad says, walking up behind us. "I took a look around at your competition, and there's no way that scholarship doesn't belong to you. Your work ran circles around those other kids."

"Dad," I cut in after seeing a look of aggravation appear on Dylan's face, "can't we just take this time to be proud of Dylan for getting this far? He's worked really hard, and you should be proud of him whether he wins or loses."

"I *am* proud," he says in a steady tone, but I can feel the hurt in his voice. "I just want you to win. That's what Ellenburgs do. We win."

"Well, I'm not an Ellenburg. I'm a McAndrews." I can't help but smile as Dylan finally says what he's been dying to say since he started this feud with my dad. "Stop pushing me to be like you. I'm never going to be like you, and quite frankly, I don't want to be. I don't care about the competitions and the stupid first-place trophies, Daniel. Can't you just accept that?" A chill runs up my spine as I hear Dylan's words echo through the now-empty hall.

My dad looks offended, but he doesn't say anything to refute Dylan's accusations. Instead, he turns to me and says, "We've saved you a seat if you want to join us, Emma," before shoving his hands into his pockets and walking away.

"It's about time," I say, opening my arms to embrace Dylan once my dad is out of sight. When I wrap my arms around him, his body is throbbing and pulsating, almost as if his heart is going to beat right out of his chest. "Are you okay? Your heart is beating really fast."

"I'm fine," he says, averting his gaze. "Never felt better, actually."

When our stares reconnect, a guilty grin emerges on his face, with his dimples following suit. "Dylan, tell me you didn't do what I think you did."

"What?" He shrugs. "I couldn't take a sleeping pill last night, or I would've slept through the sunrise. Actually, I haven't been able to take them for a week. The nerves have been getting to me."

"So, what are you saying?" He rolls his eyes and puts his hands on the top of his head. *Uh-oh.* The thought of him taking another one of those heinous white pills makes me sick to my stomach. "I thought you flushed the study buddies."

"I did, but a while back, I traded some of my pills for more. And I know you're mad, but without those sleeping pills in my system, I was dying. I had to start back up again."

"When?"

"Does it really matter?" *He's right. It doesn't matter. What does is the fact that he's been lying to me.*

I don't have the words to describe how disappointed and angry I am, but I hope that my pursed lips and balled-up fists are enough to get the point across. He's a smart guy. I don't understand why he can't see how dangerous those things are. Just a year ago, some girl in my history class who used them religiously had to be hauled off campus in an ambulance.

Before I know it, my feet are carrying me to the entrance of the hall, leaving Dylan standing there in his gray suit and tie all alone. I feel so betrayed that I can't even focus on the first half of the award ceremony. All I can think about is how upset I am that Dylan took another one of those pills behind my back. He probably wouldn't have even told me if I hadn't asked him about it directly, and that's the worst part.

From the third row, I try to focus on the woman onstage to ease the fury boiling inside of me. "As a past recipient of this scholarship, I am elated to be a presenter of it today," the woman says. The persistent thought of Dylan, who's sitting with the other finalists onstage, tries to plow through my mind, but I don't let it. ". . . and I am pleased to announce that this year's beneficiary of the San Diego County Exceptional Young Artists Award is . . ." I observe her as she pulls the tab off of a tiny white envelope—like we're at the Grammys or the Oscars—to reveal the name of the winner. "Dylan McAndrews."

The crowd bursts into deafening applause as Dylan stumbles up to the woman to accept his award and the big check for ten thousand dollars, which was raised entirely by the art museum. A wave of jealousy washes over me as he stands before all of the flashing cameras, holding his big check. I was the first-place child in the family; the trophies in the garage—or the ones that used to be in the garage before Dad cleared everything out to put Dylan's studio there—prove it. The feeling of being replaced hasn't surfaced for a while, but watching him hold his plaque and check brings all of that back, hitting me like a punch in the stomach.

I join in on the applause so I don't seem like a bitter sibling in front of my parents. My mom and Matthew, of course, are clapping their hands off, but when I look over at my dad, he's rising from his seat, his cell phone wedged between his right ear and his hand. I catch the end of something he says, and I swear I hear the word *adoption* leave his mouth, but I could be wrong. I look from him to the stage, where Dylan is standing, and it's almost as if I can see the exhilaration leave his body as his gaze follows my dad out the door.

My dad returns a few minutes later—just before the woman in red dismisses us—with a goofy grin on his face. I watch as he leans over to whisper something into my mother's ear, which cues the waterworks. My first thought is that my aunt Gertie—who my mom is sort of close to, but my dad hates—has died, which would explain his grin and her tears.

But that's not what he whispers into my ear when he leans in. Instead he says, "That was Ezra. Dylan's dad signed the paper, and his case is making its way through the system. We can adopt Dylan as soon as they give us the okay to do so." I feel myself smile from the inside out, knowing that as soon as he becomes an honorary Ellenburg, we can drop the charades and be open about our relationship. I mean, what are my parents going to do? Unadopt him? They can't do that . . . can they? I'll have to do more research before we make any moves.

As my father's words bounce around in my mind, I forget to be angry about the pills, and focus on us and the future of our relationship. I imagine Dylan and me strolling along in the park, holding hands and kissing openly, simply because we can. Simply because it's in our unwritten rights as an official couple. We won't have to hide anymore; we could do anything that any other couple can do. *Finally.*

Amid the hundreds of people packed inside the hall, my family and I make our way to the side door, where we parked in order to evade the heavy foot traffic at the main entrance. When we arrive, a seemingly hotheaded Dylan is already there, leaning up against the driver's door of our SUV, clenching and unclenching his teeth, with his arms crossed in front of his chest. From his body language alone, I know another argument is coming, but I can only hope that we can get the good news out before the fallout begins.

"Great news, Dylan. I just got off the phone with Ezra, and he said—"

"I did this for you, you know?" Dylan says, cutting my dad off in the middle of his sentence. "Do you have any idea how many hours of painting I put into this show? Thinking up ideas, mixing the colors, painting and repainting canvases, washing brushes?"

"Hmm," my dad says, slightly shaking his head in bewilderment. "I was not aware. But, like I was saying—"

"I stayed up late, spent my lunchtime in the art room, and called in sick at work sometimes just to push out paintings worthy of winning this stupid competition that I didn't even want to be a part of in the first place."

"I'm not sure what's wrong, son."

"'Son'?" *Wrong word.* "You are not my father. The last person to call me that nearly wiped me clean off the face of the earth. But you should be well versed on the story. I don't have to go into details, do I?"

Pulling the keys from his pocket, my dad shifts from one foot to the other. He's not used to anyone—adult or child—talking to him like this. "We'll talk when you're less worked up. At home. Lauren, get Matthew in the car."

My mom immediately jumps on his command while I just stand there, looking from Dylan to my family members and tugging down on my Emma necklace. I'm not sure which car I'm supposed to ride in: should I be a good daughter and ride with my parents, or should I be a good girlfriend and ride with Dylan? I hate that I have to choose between him and my family.

"Coming, Emma?" Dylan asks, stuffing the plaque and check into the trunk of his car. *Good girlfriend,* I decide. *I don't want him driving by himself, anyway. He's sleep deprived, thanks to those pills, and nobody in that state should drive alone. Or drive at all, really, but he's not going to let me behind the wheel of his car.*

You'd think I'd be used to riding in silence with Dylan, but the quiet picks away at me until I have to say something to fill the gap. "I know I'm the last person anyone would ever think to defend him, but when he took that call in the middle of the awards ceremony . . . that was for you."

His silence begins to slice into me again, and so I continue speaking in an effort to get it to stop. "It was Ezra. Apparently, the parental rights termination papers are being processed by the fostering agency, and it won't be much longer until we can adopt you. Isn't that great?"

I hear the plaque slide around in his truck as we pull into the driveway. My parents must have taken the scenic route, because they're not home yet when we arrive. He turns the car off, indicating that I should get out, but I remain in my seat. We're going to discuss this now; not later.

"Dylan? Did you hear what I just said?"

"I heard you."

"Well, aren't you happy that you'll officially be part of the family? I mean, that's what you wanted, right? That's what *we* wanted."

"I don't want to have anything to do with that man." He reinserts his key into the ignition, but doesn't turn it. "I'm not sure I want him as my adoptive dad."

I search for the light in his eyes, but he won't look in my direction. "Well, I mean, he comes with the territory. He's my dad."

"Look, Emma," he says, finally facing me. The thin, red lines in his eyes tell me that he's functioning on even less sleep than I thought. "I don't want to fight with you. I'd rather talk about this in the morning, if you don't mind."

"Actually, I do mind. Why are you acting this way? I've done nothing but support you and be there for you, and . . ." I trail off as I see him yawn, pull a transparent orange bottle from his glove compartment, and place a single white pill—I'm not sure if it's a study buddy or a sleeping pill—between his lips. "Are you serious right now?"

"I can't do this, Emma. Get out of my car." I hear the click of the car door unlock as his pointer finger presses a button on the side of his door. *My* parents *bought this car. It's not yours*, I want to say, but there are more important things for me to fight against right now.

"No! I'm not gonna let you drive like this. You could get in an accident and hurt someone or, even worse, severely injure yourself. I'm not going anywhere." Not listening, he leans over to put the bottle of pills back into his glove compartment. I reach for the container, and after wrestling for a little, pull it from his fingers.

"Fine. Keep it. I can always get more. Easy."

I want to cry, but I refuse to let the tears fall. "Dylan, why are you being like this to—"

Before I can get my last word out, Dylan is unbuckling my seat belt for me and reaching across to open my door. I expect him to push me out, but he doesn't. He knows better than to lay a finger on me. Instead he leans in so that his face is only two inches away from mine; he's so close that I can smell the cologne on his neck. "Get out. Leave. Me. Alone."

My bottom lip trembles when I hear the last three words come out of his mouth, our safe words. I have to respect his words and do as he requests. Even if he's taking away my option to fight for him . . . and for us.

I take one last look into his eyes, willing him to hear my silent thoughts, just for this one moment. *I love you, Dylan. Please, don't make me go.*

But he doesn't tell me to stay; everything, from the tight scowl stretched across his face to the deep wrinkles in his brows, indicates that he really does want me to leave him alone. And so I do. His bright red brake lights are the last I see of him before I start across the grassy backyard to the pool house.

chapter 21

When I get to the front door of the pool house, I try to call his phone four times—even though he just left me a little over a minute ago—but I'm sent straight to voice mail each time. So either he has blocked me, or he's turned his phone off altogether. With my stomach churning, I shake off the rejection and pull out my key to unlock the door. *I'll just have to wait for him to come around on his own.*

The first thing I do is pull the bottle of pills from my pocket and head into the bathroom to flush them. In my frenzy, I have to fight a little more than normal to remove the cap, but it finally pops off and the contents tumble into the toilet bowl. As they sink to the bottom of the basin, I realize that it's not just one set of pills but rather a mix of different-sized white pills. The tiny study buddy ones and the thick Ambiens. My stomach flip-flops like I'm on a roller coaster. This can't be good.

I take a shower and shortly after, I doze off. It isn't until I hear the alarm on my phone sound—the one we set for our stargazing date—that I realize I've fallen asleep. My eyes snap open with only one thing on my mind: Dylan. Pulling on some thick pajamas pants and wrapping my robe around my body, I step out onto the lawn. I know our last conversation wasn't the best that we've had, but I still expect Dylan to show up tonight. He's not the one who holds grudges; I am.

After several minutes of sitting in the dark, I open my phone to call him again. When I scroll to his name, I see that I've missed a call from him. It was about an hour ago, and because he never goes to sleep early, I expect him to answer when I call back. Straight to voice mail again. With the wind blowing strongly in anticipation of the upcoming—and very rare—storm, I have to slip inside the glass doors of the main house to keep from flying away. *I guess I'll go check for him in his room*, I think as I make my way to the staircase. His room is dark when I enter it. *Maybe the study buddies have worn off, and he's finally getting some sleep.*

"Dylan?" No answer. I don't want to flip on his light—in case he's asleep—so I have to feel my way to his bed. I pat all around the dark comforter, searching for his body, but he's not there. When I flip the light on, I find that his bed is still made. My blood chills and I race to the window to check the driveway. The black Camaro that is usually parked below his window is missing. *He isn't home yet?*

I'm making my way back to my room to try his cell again when I get the feeling that I should check our safe haven just in case. The light is on in his art studio, so I let myself in, as usual. I don't know why this wasn't the first place I checked, but that doesn't matter now. The wind is so strong outside that it takes all of my strength to close the door against it. When I finally turn around, the warmth of his studio melts away.

His studio is the same as we had left it. His paintings are still arranged in the circle around his easels, just like they were when we were picking the best ones to take to the showcase. Everything is right here, where it should be. Everything, that is, except him. As I inhale the scent of paint in the room, my heart sinks a little lower. *He's not here.*

Upon leaving the studio, I hear my father's voice boom as he makes his way across the lawn. "Emma," he says in a firm voice, "stay here with Mom and Matthew. I've got to go. There's been . . ." I don't need him to finish the sentence; I can do it myself. *There's been an accident.* Dylan.

I must be in total and complete shock—though I shouldn't be; something inside me saw this coming a couple hours ago when I watched him place that pill on his tongue—because when my dad says that Dylan crashed his car, it's as if my brain turns off all voluntary actions in my body. I can't move my lips to speak, I can't move my legs to walk, and I'm pretty sure that if my beating heart were under my control, that would have stopped, too.

"I'm coming with," I say, my voice suddenly steady and strong.

"No," he replies. "You're staying here."

"No. I can't. I won't."

Realizing that he's wasting time with this argument, my dad concedes and waves at me to follow him to the car.

It's not hard to find the site of the crash, because there are about six cop cars, two ambulances, and a fire truck packed within the intersection, their lights swirling and flashing in a quick pattern that would blind anyone if they stared at it long enough. When I hop out of the car, I forget that I'm standing in the middle of a four-way inter-section, and I think I've been transported to some junkyard. There's a ton of glass everywhere, big chunks of car parts lying around the pavement, and the three cars involved in the accident are all twisted and tangled in a knot so complicated that I'm not sure anyone survived it.

"Four severely injured. No fatalities. EMS is here," the speaker hooked up to a cop blares out for everyone at the scene to hear. As if on cue, tears begin their salty descent down my face. *It can't be. It just can't be.* I see my dad race over to one of the cops, where a man—or woman; I can't tell with the tears flooding my eyes—takes him to one of the ambulances. All the while, I'm inching my way toward the knotted cars and clutching my stomach, trying to hold it all together, though I know that I'm going to lose that battle any minute now.

"Dylan! Dylan!" I scream until my throat goes hoarse. The thought that I might lose him hits me out of nowhere, like an eighteen-wheeler smashing into a Volkswagen Beetle on the interstate. As I feel myself disappearing into a pool of tears, my screams turn into inaudible bawls until I, myself, can't understand what I'm saying any-more. All I can do is watch, through a veil of tears, as the scene unfolds before me.

Everything is a blur, except instead of moving at a super-high speed, like in the movies, it's as if everyone is underwater and every-thing is muffled and happening in slow motion. I see my father stagger when he closes in on the body they're lifting into the ambulance, and I see him hunch over to take some deep breaths as his mind registers what's happening. My tears obstruct my view of him, but it looks like his face is as pale and colorless as one of the cans of white paint in Dylan's art studio—I imagine that my face looks a similar color. When he gathers himself enough to stand up straight, I see one of the EMT's whisper something to him, and he mouths something along the lines of *Meet me at the hospital*. I'm not really sure what I reply; I'm too busy picturing us having to place the boy I maybe-love in an ivory coffin.

The sight of Dylan's seemingly lifeless body reinforces this thought even more, and the shirt on his chest soaked completely in his blood is almost too much for me to take, but a ray of light beams through the dark clouds in my mind. *At least he's alive*, I keep chanting to myself. I notice Dylan's hand resting on his stomach, just under where a few of his ribs have punctured the skin. The cuts and glass-filled wounds are distracting, but they can't divert my attention from the empty spaces between his fingers and my want to fill them with my own. *Me too*, I think, hoping that his time in the neutral ground has given him the ability to read my mind. *Me too*.

"Meet me at the hospital," my dad says again as they close the doors to the ambulance, and I take off running back toward our car.

THE SECOND I WAKE UP THE NEXT MORNING, I KEEP MY EYES CLOSED TO try to pull my thoughts together and shake off the nightmare of last night. I don't want to remember the sight of all that blood. Dylan's blood. *That was a horrible dream that I hope to never have again*. When I finally open my eyes, I realize that I'm sharing a sofa with Matthew in an unfamiliar room illuminated completely by sunlight. I try to say something, but my voice is so hoarse that it feels like knives are stabbing my throat. Then there's the constant beeping that resembles that of the tone I kept hearing in my head last night. The realization hits me like a sledgehammer: last night wasn't a dream.

I hear someone whimpering across the room, and when I see my mom's shoulders move up and down, I know that she's crying. "Mom," I try to whisper, but my voice is so gone that it comes out sounding like a croak. "Mom?"

As she rises from her blankets, I see that the skin beneath her eyes is red and puffy, and the bright azure blue of her irises is now dark and empty. Her hair, which is usually groomed to perfection, is messy and knotted in some places—like mine gets when I nervously twirl strands around my finger.

She wipes at her cheeks and then looks me in the eye. "Emma," she says in a half whisper. "The doctors said Dylan had small doses of amphetamines in his system. Did you know anything about this? Maybe you heard something at school . . . or . . ." Her voice cracks, and she places a hand over her lips, trying to keep it together in front of me.

Yes, I want to tell her. *Yes, I knew all about it. I could have prevented this.* But I can't. "No," I choke out like a coward.

"You sure?"

No. "I mean, I knew he was taking sleeping pills, but that's it."

Her eyes hold on to mine as if waiting for me to change my answer, but I don't. .

"I just had to ask," she says, looking down. After another moment of consideration, she lets her head fall into her hands.

"Mom, are you okay?" I question, my voice now shaky, too. She doesn't answer. Instead she just pulls me close to her, and we bawl into each other's shoulders.

I look around her in search of my father, but he's not beside her, like I expect him to be. "Where's Dad?" I ask, but get no reply. With only the *beep* of the heart rate monitor to fill the silence, I collapse into my mother and continue to sob with her. I try not to close my eyes as I cry because every time I do so, all I see are the deep gashes with

Dylan's thick red liquid oozing from them and his pearl-white bones sticking through his skin. Though I think that we're doing a great job of keeping our cries quiet, eventually our sobs grow so loud that we wake Matthew.

"Mom?" he says as he sits up on the chair.

"Good morning, Matt," my mom says, dabbing at her eyes with the sleeve of her shirt. "Mommy's going to be right back. I just need a minute in the bathroom." I watch her get up and lock herself in the bathroom without so much as a glance in Dylan's direction. I guess she doesn't want Matthew to see her cry.

"Emma?" Matthew whines, moving on to me in our mother's absence. "What happened to Dylan? Why does he have those bandages on?" He tugs at my shirt, and it takes every bit of self-control in my body to not ignore him. He just wants to know what really happened, but can I blame him? I'd be curious why we're waking up in a hospital, too. And I know he's a little young for the explicit details, but we can't lie. We have to tell him.

Turning to face him, I open my mouth to speak, but nothing comes out. I mean, how am I supposed to tell him that his almost-brother almost died last night in a car accident that he caused when he fell asleep at the wheel and drove into oncoming traffic? How can I tell Matthew that his hide-and-seek partner can't talk to us right now, and may never again because he's in a coma? How does anyone break that kind of news to a seven-year-old kid?

You just do it, my mind answers me back. *Especially since this is your fault.* It's true. I got out of the car and let Dylan drive away. I could have saved him. I could have told someone—Mom, Dad, the counselor, a teacher, anyone—that he was in trouble, but I didn't. I didn't physically floor the gas into the intersection, but I allowed him to get there in the state he was in. The drivers that he rammed into at eighty-nine miles per hour got hurt because of me. This is my fault. All of their blood is on my hands.

"Matt," I whisper, pulling back the curtain to reveal Dylan's heavily wrapped body. "Dylan's right here." Matthew makes his way toward the bed, where the constant dinging is coming from. It's hard for me to recognize that the person lying before us is Dylan, so I know it must be a stretch for Matthew to believe so as well. "Matt . . . um . . . Dylan's not doing so well. He got really hurt last night."

Placing his hand on top of Dylan's, Matthew looks him up and down, his eyes growing wide with curiosity. He's never been exposed to something like this.

"He looks . . ." *Like he should be dead?* ". . . so . . . calm." My seven-year-old brother almost brings me to tears in the middle of the hospital room, and I have to take a couple of deep breaths to steady myself as my mother rejoins us from the bathroom. Her eyes look even more swollen than when she left us. She's been sobbing again.

"Your dad is in the café," she says, running her fingers through my brother's brown hair. "I'm going to take Matthew to get something to eat. Do you want to come, or do you just want us to bring you something back?"

"I'll come down. Right now, I just . . . I just want a minute with him."

"Okay." She gives me a weak smile before grabbing Matthew's hand and leading him out of the room.

"Dylan, if you can hear me, I'm pretty sure you expect me to say 'I told you so,' and even though I have every reason to, I'm not. Actually . . . I'm here to apologize. I promised myself that nothing bad was going to happen to you, and I let us both down. I'm not sure if you saw the wreckage, but . . ." I will myself not to cry, in order to be strong for him, but then I flash back to the cars looped around each other and lose it. "Dylan, I'm not sure how you managed to stay alive after that, but I'm glad you did."

I slip my fingers into the spaces between his—the casts on his wrists making it more difficult than usual—but the electric current that normally pulses through me when we touch doesn't flow at all.

"I didn't think it would take almost losing you for me to express this. I would have never forgiven myself if . . ." I take a few breaths to hold back my tears. ". . . if I didn't get the chance to tell you that I am totally, completely, and undeniably in love with you, and I pretty much have been since the day you walked into my life." I give his hand two squeezes and, after waiting for him to return my gesture, give him two more. "God, I just need you to wake up, Dylan. Just open your big brown eyes so I know that you're okay. That *we're* okay, and that you're not going to leave me. Please, Dylan . . . for me. I need you. I don't know how to exist without you. Please."

I'm not sure why, but I expect his eyes to snap open at my request and his hand to give my hand a weak squeeze, but I get nothing. The only sign of life isn't even coming from him; it's coming from the heart rate monitor behind me. Unfortunately, the *beep, beep, beep* of the green line isn't the heartfelt rom-com-movie-scene response I am looking for.

chapter 22

Dear Catherine,

This isn't a normal journal entry, so brace yourself. Right now I'm sitting next to Dylan's hospital bed. On the night of his showcase, he fell asleep at the wheel of his car and drove through the middle of an intersection. The crash scene was like something from a horror film. He broke so many bones that the doctors had to practically wrap his whole body in a cast, but if I'm being completely honest, that's the least of my worries.

He's in a coma now, but the doctors have no clue when he'll wake up. "We're on his time now," they told us after the swelling in his brain went down. "It could be days. It could be months. It could even be years." Nobody knows, and that uncertainty, I think, is what frustrates me the most.

This unexpected break from Dylan has added another layer of complications to our love story. Colleges will begin mailing acceptance letters soon, and I've been looking forward to this moment for as long as I can remember, but Dylan and I were supposed to talk through my college decision together. Now I have to make the decision about our relationship for the both of us. I don't want to hurt him, but I don't want to hold myself back, either. I'm stuck.

Ever since the crash, my relationship with him has been put on pause. Right now, my parents never leave his room, and I can't really be his girlfriend, so I'm forced to think like his sister. And as his sister, I believe that Dylan wouldn't want me moping around waiting for him to wake up. I believe that he'd much rather I be out in the world, doing something that makes me feel alive until he's back. Something great, like going to the college of my dreams, wherever that is. But . . . with him still deep in a coma, it's hard to know for sure what he'd really want for me.

Oh, Catherine . . . what should I do? You've kind of been my North Star through everything with Dylan, but this is uncharted territory for the both of us. What should I do? What would *you* do? I need your guidance now more than ever.

♡ Emma

My parents make me stay home from school and dance practice for five days, and on the fifth day, despite my unwavering concern for

Dylan, I beg them to let me go. Not only do I have a dance solo to work on, but I have schoolwork to complete and finals to take, as well. Besides, sitting around in the hospital waiting for something that may or may not happen is—not to sound cold—depressing. The longer I sit around staring at him and hoping he wakes up, the more alone I feel. He was my best friend—even more so than Karmin—and without him, I'm not me. He's "on the road to recovery," as the doctors put it. "It'll happen when it happens." But it hasn't happened yet, and the uncertainty of his condition—and our relationship—is starting to wear on me. *I need to get away*, I think. *I need to go back to school.*

So on Wednesday evening, I pull my parents away from Dylan's bedside long enough to have a conversation about my returning to school. It went something like this:

Me: I want to go back to school . . . like, tomorrow.

Mom: Honey—*I hate when she honeys me*—I really think you should take the week off. I already called your teachers, and they're perfectly fine with you returning next week.

Dad: I agree. Don't you want to be here when he wakes up?

Me: *Sigh.* Yes, I do. But—

Dad: No buts. If they're letting you take a few days off, you might as well take them. Those don't come around too often.

Mom: He's not lying, you know?

Me: I want to be here, I do, but all this sitting around and waiting isn't helping anyone. I'm getting behind in my classes, and I don't want to be overwhelmed the week before finals.

Dad: Em—

Me: Please, Dad. I'm not asking to get a tattoo or some fancy body piercing. I just want to go to school. *Please* let me go.

They must hear the desperation in my voice because neither one of my parents attempts to respond. *I win.* And that's how I ended up at school bright and early on Thursday morning.

I feel like I'm going to see Dylan waiting for me in the parking lot when I pull into my usual spot, but his brown hair, honey eyes, and dimpled grin never make an appearance. I push him from my mind and try to focus on the day ahead, but with everyone giving me hugs and telling me that they are keeping Dylan in their prayers, it's hard to stay on task.

"HOW HAVE YOU BEEN?" KARMIN FINALLY GETS AROUND TO ASKING AT THE end of dance practice. Her voice is flat, which is unlike her, but it's probably because I ruined the routine several times today. All the missed practices are starting to catch up with me. With competition so close, I know my team and Coach Denise are starting to doubt me, but they have to cut me some slack. "How's Dylan?" When she places her hand on my shoulder, trying to comfort me, I almost lose it. But she thinks she's making me feel better, so I don't shake it off.

"Fine," I say dismissively. I got away from the hospital to escape my depressing thoughts about Dylan, but he's all anyone wants to talk about at school, too. I get it; they care about how he's doing and when he's going to wake up, but at the same time, what about me? Everyone wants to be there for him—the injured—but no one knows to be there for me—the hurting.

"What's with the decorations?" I ask, pointing to the purple ribbons that someone has placed on the lockers outside the gym. I've been in a blurry state all day, so I'm not surprised that I didn't notice them at school earlier today.

"Oh, we're holding a fund-raiser—a benefit, if you will—to cover some of the medical costs. Dylan's procedures must have cost a fortune, so we're putting together a fund-raiser so your family doesn't have to pay for everything yourselves, though I'm sure that it's not a problem for you guys. You're loaded. But still. We want to be supportive." Her words throw me a little off balance. It's not the fact that she's correct, but rather the image that surfaces when she says the word *procedures*. The casts on Dylan's arms, legs, and torso cover his stitched skin, but knowing that doesn't delete the internet images that I came across last night, when I couldn't sleep. The ones that showed the barbed-wire-looking threads sewn into the skin of patients who had suffered from similar car accident injuries.

"That's very nice of you all." I try to keep things short and sweet; the quicker I can get back to my car, the quicker I can begin to focus on something other than Dylan, and his wounds, and our fight before his crash. The more time she—and everyone else—gives me to think about him, the more I feel distressed and lonely in his absence.

Leave me alone. Those were his last words to me. He told me to leave him alone, but I never would have done so if I had known that it was going to end like this. With me seeing the crumpled-up mess of cars on the six-o'clock morning news two days in a row. I replay his words again in my head. His voice was so full of hatred and complete betrayal. And I can't even go back and change that moment. That was his last memory of me before the crash, and depending on his mental state when he wakes up—if he wakes up—that could be the only thing he remembers about me when he comes to.

I feel Karmin's hand wrap around my shoulder as she pulls me into a side hug. "Look, I know you've probably been losing sleep thinking about the accident—hell, we all have—but if you—"

"I'm fine, Karmin. Really."

"I know you are, but if you need a girls' night to take your mind away from it all, or if you just need someone to talk to, you know who to call."

"Thanks." The word comes out a little rougher than I want it to, but she either doesn't hear my tone or is ignoring it out of pity.

"That's what best friends are for. Plus, it's not healthy to keep things bottled up. Stress like that causes acne, and hair loss, and . . . dark circles." She swipes her thumb under my left eye and frowns. "You sure you're okay?"

My stomach bubbles at her words. *Just tell her,* my inner voice commands. Rolling my eyes, I pull her into a niche on the side of the building. "What I'm about to tell you is the biggest secret I've ever kept in my entire life. And you have to promise me that you're not going to tell a single soul, living or dead."

"Oh, dear God. Are you pregnant? Dammit, Emma. All you had to do was ask." She opens her dance bag, pulls a condom from it—I'm not exactly sure why she keeps her stash in there, but whatever—and hands it to me, the silvery foil wrapper glittering in the sunlight. With sympathetic eyes, she says, "I guess you wouldn't really need this now, but . . ."

"What? Karmin, no!" Frowning, I knock her offering away and rub my hand over my flat belly. *Am I getting fat or something?* "I'm not pregnant."

"Well, I had to ask. You never know these days." She laughs obnoxiously, as if she's trying to impress an eavesdropper, and I bury my head in my hands, the color red rising in my cheeks.

"I need you to be serious for a second. This is important."

"Okay, okay, okay. I promise." She traces an *X* over her heart as if to say *Cross my heart and hope to die.*

"All right." I take the deepest breath I can before saying, "Dylan and I sort of have . . . a thing." I feel the weight of a million elephants lift from my shoulders when the words exit my throat.

"What, like, you guys kissed?"

I bite my bottom lip, revealing the truth without saying a word. *More than that.* This sends Karmin into a fit of giggles so deep that I have to grab her by the shoulders and shake her to quiet her down. "That's it? That's your big secret? I was imagining so much worse in my head."

"Well . . . yeah. Foster siblings aren't supposed to be . . . *involved.*"

"Duh, Emma." She drags out her words as if this is common knowledge, but she isn't in my situation, so she can't see the gray area as clearly as I do. "So . . . did you guys . . . ?"

"No. We only ever made out, but I think . . . I think I was starting to fall for him. Like, hard."

"Well, he *is* quite the charmer." A thought occurs to her, and her thick eyebrows draw together in a straight line. "Wait, is that why you broke up with Keegan? For Dylan?"

"Yes. I mean, no. I mean . . . it's complicated. There's so many layers to the story, it'll take several days to get through it all. But I really did like Keegan, if that's what you are wondering. And it broke my heart to have to end things with him." She doesn't speak, and I imagine her fretting about whether it's against their Twin Code to keep this from him. "And it gets even more complicated." I walk her through the details of Dylan's current state, and tell her about the doctor's prognosis on his memory if . . . when . . . he wakes up.

"So, what are you gonna do if he wakes up and doesn't remember that you guys were *involved*?"

"I don't know." I open my dance bag and pull a white envelope from the inside pocket. It's a response from Stanford. I'm still not sure if it's my first choice, but it was the only one of my reaches with early action. "Him not remembering will make opening this a whole lot easier, though."

She winces. "Early action? That's a small envelope. Never a good sign."

My breathing picks up, the nerves taking over. "I know."

"Why haven't you opened it yet?"

"Well, I was *supposed* to open this with Dylan. I made a promise to him that we'd find out about my future together, but now, I'm not too sure if that'll happen anytime soon." I pause for a moment, and eyeball the envelope. "I'm not too sure about anything anymore. Dylan? Keegan? Whether I'm staying or going? Even the tiniest decisions throw me for a loop. And, obviously, Dylan wants me to stay close to San Diego, but—"

"But that's not what you want," she finishes for me. "God, Emma. And I thought *I* had problems."

"You have no idea." We laugh it off for a second before reality sets back in, bringing us both back to silence.

"My first kiss was with my cousin. I was thirteen, and we were playing a game of spin the bottle." I'm not sure if she thinks she has to pay for my secret by telling one of her own, but I let her continue anyway. "I mean, he was my aunt's second ex-husband's son. So, we weren't blood relatives, but technically, we were cousins at the time."

Three years ago, I wouldn't have even thought that Karmin and I lived on the same planet, even though we went to the same high school. She was a part of the exclusive elites at Cedar Pointe. Pretty, popular, perfect. And I was a nobody. But now I see that we've had more in common than I initially thought. We could have been each other's cushion to fall on all this time, but we didn't because I was afraid. So much lost time.

"And not even Keegan knows that," she says. "So you better take that to your grave."

"As long as you take mine to yours."

The apples of her cheeks rise as her lips form a pursed smile, her promise hidden within it.

"Well, I better get going. I've got a ton of work to catch up on."

"Emma," Karmin says, grabbing my arm before I turn away. "I know you've got a lot going on at home, so none of us would be upset . . . you know, if you didn't come to the competition. We've reblocked the routine to work with or without you, so if you want to sit on the sidelines until you figure things out, you can."

Practice the dance routine. I think, making a mental note to rehearse as much as I can before the big day. *You worked so hard for this, and you need the distraction.* "I'll be there. Don't worry."

THE BENEFIT SEEMED TO GO VIRAL OVER THE NEXT TWO DAYS, BECAUSE BY Saturday, it's expanded to a county-wide benefit to raise money for the medical bills of Dylan and the other crash victims.

I'm not sure how we were able to secure Balboa Park for the fund-raiser, but I'm glad that we got it; it's the only place that has been able to bring me peace since that fateful night of the art showcase. Something about the sound of the flowing river that they built a few years ago brings me serenity like no one else can—now that Dylan is in a coma, I mean.

When we arrive—and by "we," I'm talking about my parents,

Matthew, and me; I had to drag them all away from Dylan's bedside to attend, but that's beside the point—I see rows of big tents lining the walkways and tons of purple balloons. There are purple balloons tied to the bases of trees and purple balloons attached to the arms of benches. There are even purple balloons attached to some of the sculptures littered throughout the park, which I'm sure we'll get in trouble for later.

"It's not purple, it's *mauve*," Karmin reminds me once again, rolling her green eyes. "There's a difference." Purple. Mauve. Lavender. Violet. It's all the same to me. I didn't inherit the color classification gene that Karmin's so proud of.

"How much have we raised so far?" I ask her as I blow up yet another balloon and hand it to a small girl not much older than Matthew. "Do you know?"

"Can't see the money meter from here, but the last time I checked it, we had just hit four thousand." Karmin came up with the idea to sell T-shirts in the same ugly purple as the balloons, and the sea of noxious pity-purple—I mean, *mauve*—swimming around me is almost enough to make me puke up everything I had for breakfast this morning. "Might be up to five or six by now. I was over by the food booths earlier, and they had to send Keegan to get more steaks, hot dogs, and hamburgers. I'm not sure what they're doing over there, but they need to keep it up."

Her mention of Keegan's name brings a smile to my face; it's been a while since I've seen him, and with Dylan knocked out in the hospital, I just want someone to wrap their arms around me, and tell me everything is going to be okay, like Dylan used to do. If I were still with Keegan, he would have been there, but seeing as we're still not speaking, I can't expect him to comfort me.

"Man the balloon station for me. I'm kind of hungry."

"Yeah, sure." Karmin must only be half listening to me now because my mention of going to get food doesn't elicit the response I expect from her. But I don't have time to dwell on it. I'm hungry, and I want to see Keegan without making a big deal out of things. I grab a few dollars from my wallet, and, after shoving them into my back pocket, start toward the cluster of purple shirts gathered by the grills a few booths down. I'm barely out of our booth, when a piercing "Oh my God!" escapes Karmin's mouth. "OH MY GOD!" she says again, this time running toward me like I've just kicked the winning goal at the Women's World Cup. "You're getting back together with Keegan!"

"Um, no. I'm just going to get a burger. I swear my insides are going to start eating my outsides any minute if I don't get some food in me."

"But you just heard me mention that Keegan's there." Her statement feels suggestive.

"Correct. And?"

"And you've been avoiding him since the breakup."

"Again, correct. And?"

"And Dylan's unavailable right now."

"So?"

"So you're getting back with Keegan!"

"I think your logic is flawed somewhere in there," I say, which helps me understand how she has a C minus in Mr. Paloma's logic and reasoning class right now.

"Say what you want, but if you guys end up married six years from now, I expect you to let everyone know that I called it way back when."

She hands two balloons to a little girl with pigtails and looks my way. "I also expect to be your maid of honor."

"Okay, Karmin. Whatever." To be completely honest, I'm not sure if I want to get back together with Keegan. I mean, I still do like him, but after confessing my love to comatose Dylan a week ago, it would seem wrong to go after Keegan now, though his company would distract from this emptiness inside me.

The barbecue area is the most crowded part of Balboa Park. But I guess that shouldn't surprise me; people love food. Period. Especially barbecued food. Exclamation point. It's every vegetarian's worst nightmare out here; everywhere I look, there are people chomping and chowing down on hamburgers, hot dogs, ribs (pork and beef), chicken, and, of course, steaks.

I spot Keegan immediately. He's wearing a bright red apron and a backward baseball cap, a pair of metal tongs in his hand. The smile on his face helps one to appear on mine. It's been a while since I've seen that crescent shape frame his perfect set of teeth. It's as if he senses my presence, because as soon as I get in his line for burgers, his crisp green eyes find mine, and stare back with a tender softness only he can pull off.

There are four people in front of me, all wearing the ugly *mauve* shirts Karmin tried to get me to buy earlier. I have to assume that they all go to my school because I keep hearing Dylan's name spout from their mouths. After eavesdropping for a while, I realize that they are sharing memories of him.

"When I first broke my leg, he saw me struggling to hold my books and work the crutches, so he promised to help me to third period every day that he could. He was such a sweet guy," I hear one girl say.

"Yeah," another guy I've never seen before chimes in. "One time, he saw that I didn't have enough money to pay for my school lunch, so he bought me one. He told me that no one deserved to go hungry at school. He was a pretty generous guy."

As I listen to their stories, fury engulfs me. *Why are they talking about him in the past tense?*

"Excuse me," I say, tapping one of them on the shoulder. "You guys *do* know that he's not dead, right?"

"He isn't?" a girl behind me asks. She must have been eavesdropping on their banter, too.

"He's lying in a hospital bed, not a coffin, you idiot." My words come out louder than expected, and in an instant, all conversations around us stop, and twenty pairs of eyes are on me, including Keegan's.

"So, what's the benefit for? Isn't that for dead people?" She doesn't look dumb, but clearly appearances can be deceiving. I turn around, ignoring her, and move up in the line.

"That's called a memorial fund-raiser. But, *this*"—Keegan Vanna-Whites his barbecue tongs around in a circle—"is a *benefit*. We're raising money for the medical bills of everyone involved in the accident." As usual, he's come to my rescue, shielding me from anything and anyone who could cause harm. "And for the record, that's Dylan's sister that you're talking to."

Embarrassed, the girl jumps in front of me to grab a burger and scurries off into the crowd. Obviously, she had no clue who I was. Keegan starts to chuckle to himself and when a laugh unexpectedly escapes me, he looks in my direction. We haven't talked since that day at the batting cages, and I can feel the awkwardness pass between us.

"Hey," I say in a quiet voice.

"Hey, Emma." He hands the tongs to a bald guy standing next to him and grabs a hamburger without taking his eyes off of me. He nods in the direction of a vacant bench nearby, and I follow him to it. "I see you finally found your glasses again. You look good."

"Thanks." His compliment throws me a little, and we sit, awkwardly staring at each other for ten silent seconds before I speak again. "And thanks for that back there. You didn't have to . . . you know."

"People can be so clueless sometimes." He shrugs, handing me the hamburger that he apparently swiped for me, but not before pulling the pickles from the top of it. *He still remembers that I hate them.* "How've you been?"

I'm not sure if he's talking about how I've been since we broke up a month ago or how I've been since Dylan's accident, so I lie for both. "I'm fine." From his empathetic look, I realize that he's not talking about us, but rather Dylan, and so I add, "You know, besides the frequent hospital visits and all."

"Completely understandable. So, Dylan, he's doing all right?"

"Yeah. He's wrapped head-to-toe in casts right now, but aside from that, he's holding up. We're just waiting on him to wake up. Should be any day now." I'm not sure if this is a lie or not, because I really don't know when he'll wake up, but according to my mother, "positivity breeds positivity," so I'm trying to stay as optimistic as possible.

"Well, that's good. And, hey, at least you guys don't have to plan a funeral. That's worse than any hospital visit."

"I'll bet." Another silence passes through the space between us, and I take a bite of my burger while I have the chance.

"I just wanted to say that I'm here if you need anything. Someone to talk to, somewhere to escape to, or something to distract you from it all. Anything you need, just let me know." His speech sounds oddly similar to Karmin's and I marvel at the strength of their twin telepathy. Hopefully, she won't send him signals of my Dylan secret, though.

"Thanks." I look past him at the barbecue lines. In the pit, the bald man he handed the tongs to seems to be having a meltdown of sorts. "Your barbecue buddies are looking for you. I think that line is too much for that guy to handle by himself."

"You're probably right. I should get back."

"Yeah, I've got to get back to the balloon booth, too, but I'll see you around." He lingers as if waiting for me to hug him, but when I don't, he nods good-bye and returns to the pit.

I finish my burger in record time (for me, anyway) and start for the bathroom; I'm not sure when I'll be able to get another break from the balloon booth. I lock myself in the tiny room and instantly reach underneath my shirt to unhook my bra and reconnect it on the middle hook, allowing me to breathe a little easier. I've been trying to break in the new bra I just bought, and I haven't been able to decide if I like it better on the third or second hook yet. Or maybe I'm just looking for something else to focus on and stress over to distract me from the fact that my boyfriend—or ex, if he doesn't remember me when he wakes up—is lying in the hospital, unconscious for God knows how long.

I stumble over to the sink area and after splashing some water onto my face, run my fingers through my hair. I notice a purple—*mauve*—balloon bouncing in the background. *Nothing—not even the bathrooms—was spared by the benefit decoration brigade.* Using one of my earrings, I pop the balloon and a deafening bang fills the room for half a millisecond, helping me breathe even easier than my middle bra hook allowed a minute ago. With the reminder of Dylan out of the way, I glance back at the mirror and groan. I don't even recognize the girl looking back at me.

This isn't fair. Everyone else is having a great time here today. Everyone but me, that is. I bang my hands on the sink until I feel them start to bruise. It's not that I'm upset with Dylan, because I'm not. He just left so many unresolved things behind for me to deal with. Alone. This wasn't the plan that should have played out, and everything's messed up because of Dylan.

He was the one who mixed up his pills. He was the one who fell asleep at the wheel. He was the one who put himself in that coma. But now, I'm the one who has to sit here, waiting for him to wake up so my life can get back on track. I'm the one who has to hold it all together and stay positive, when all I really want to do is break down and cry at the fact that there's a possibility that the only boy I've ever loved may not remember me when—if—he wakes up. It's not fair. This wasn't what I signed up for when I gave him my heart.

"I love you, Dylan, and I need you right now," I whisper as if he's standing there and can hear me. I take off my glasses, lean over the sink, and put my face in my hands. "I'm so unhappy without you."

Over the past five months, Dylan stirred up some major strife in my life. He was complicated. One minute, I had to play his sister, and the next, I had to play his girlfriend. All of it made me dizzy and overwhelmed and a little resentful. But right now, there is nothing I want to do more than to curl up in his complications. He makes me feel safe and limitless. Now that we're apart I'm a ghost in a human shell, lurking in his shadow.

The hurt consumes me, and it isn't long before my cheeks are slick with my salty tears. "I'm sorry," I sob, my voice bouncing off the walls of the restroom.

I imagine Dylan wrapping his arms around me to let me cry into his chest. "It's okay," he says. "I'm here, Emma. I'm always gonna be right here."

I hear his voice echo in my head, refeeding me his Thanksgiving Day compliments in an attempt to cheer me up. "I am thankful for your hair; it reminds me of the sand on a beach I once painted." I envision him smiling so hard that his eyes are almost shut. "And your lips. I could kiss them all day. And your eyes. God, those eyes." I try to linger in the sugar-laced words he whispered into my ear not too long ago, but I can feel his memory fading away. "I wouldn't change a thing about you, Emma . . ." *Please don't leave, Dylan. I need you.*

"Stay," I plead once more, but when I open my eyes to find his amber ones, I'm alone again.

chapter 23

IT'S BEEN THREE weeks, and according to the latest brain activity scans, some parts of Dylan's brain that were initially inactive are starting to show activity again—so basically, he's doing better—but my family still isn't back to normal. We've skipped over Christmas and have begun a new year, but my mom is still crying, Matthew is still in denial—he keeps shouting "Olly olly oxen free" at the top of his lungs, trying to signal Dylan to come out of his hiding spot—and Dad has decided to occupy himself with yard work. He gets up early in the morning to pull weeds and trim bushes and hedges that have never really needed grooming.

They were all starting to depress me, so when it came time for me to leave for my regional dance competition, I was beyond ready for a break. I just didn't think my parents and Matthew wouldn't accompany me on my trip to LA to give Dylan's bedside a rest, especially on my birthday.

"What have you done?" Karmin asks on the day of the competition. Her green eyes are so wide that she looks like she's seen a ghost. Two days ago, when we arrived in Los Angeles, my hair was a long mess of golden locks, but now it's a dark chocolate brown and six inches shorter. "Who are you and what have you done with my Emma?"

"Y-you don't think it looks good?" I run my fingers through my shoulder-length brown waves, trying to get used to its novelty.

"No, I've just never seen your eyes look so blue."

She's right. My eyes were an icy blue color before, but now that I've paired them with a darker hair color, they're even more piercing.

"Yeah. They really pop now, don't they?" I smooth my hands over my hair to pull it into a tight, high bun. I don't want a ponytail to throw me off when I do my turns.

"You kind of look like the daughter from a show I used to watch with my mom. What was the name of it?" She starts going through the alphabet, making the sound of each letter as she says them to jog her memory. She makes it to the G's and it hits her. "*Gilmore Girls*! That's it! Oh, but what was her name?"

"Are you talking about Alexis Bledel?" I used to watch that show, too. I raided my mom's DVD collection and binge-watched all seven seasons two summers ago. Needless to say, I didn't get much of a tan that summer.

"Yes. That's who you remind me of. Looks great, Em."

"Thanks. I just wanted something different." *Lies. All lies.* Since the accident, I've forgotten what it's like to be happy, but this mini makeover was supposed to give me something to be excited about. Unfortunately, I'm still numb.

"Happy birthday, by the way. You're seventeen now, right?"

"Thanks. And yep." Karmin turns her attention back to getting ready for the competition. Now that the surprise has worn off, she can focus on perfecting her makeup again. "I hope my birthday luck kicks in today. Winning would be everything."

"Yeah, totally," she says as she finishes drawing on her eyeliner and begins to put mascara on her eyelashes. She's started responding in filler words, so I suspect she's checked out of this conversation. Dylan used to do the same thing to me when he would paint and I would go on and on about the latest episode of *Pretty Little Liars*, or something else that was of no interest to him.

But I know Karmin's reason for ignoring me is that she's completely focused on the routine. She's probably going over the choreography in her head. Every turn, every leap, every pointed toe. She's in the zone, which is where I should be, but for some reason, I can't seem to get there today.

After checking my tights for runs and holes, I slip on my jazz shoes and start for the door. "You ready?"

"Yeah. Let's do this." I'm so happy that I got my solo done and out of the way yesterday, when we arrived. Coach Denise said that it was clean and highly technical, and that as long as we dance a clean routine as a group, we are guaranteed a spot at nationals.

Backstage is filled with dancers from different schools going over their routines, stretching, and trying to shake out their nerves. While my teammates are huddled together, sizing up the competition based on their uniforms and makeup, I'm watching the dancers onstage intently, because that's what matters. Not how much glittery eye shadow they have on or how big the sparkly bow in their hair is. It's all about the dance itself. So far, no one seems to have as difficult a routine as we do, which is good. The more demanding our routine is, the more points we get, which gives us more room to make errors, though I know we won't have many.

As we wait for the announcer to call us to the stage, I overhear some of my teammates whispering about Dylan. *Why is it so hard for them to not talk about him around me? I already told them to stop on the bus ride up here. I don't think it's that difficult a request to follow.* I try to hum to the other teams' music to drown out their voices, but it doesn't work. Their high-pitched whispers still find their way to my ears.

"Why aren't her parents here? Did he die or something?" one girl asks.

"I heard that rumor, too," another voice says. "Any truth to it?"

"If so, he's probably looking down on us right now, wishing us and his sister good luck."

"No, I don't think it works like that," another girl says. "He almost killed someone in that car crash, so he's definitely going to hell."

"Exodus chapter twenty, verse thirteen, says, 'Thou shalt not kill,' and that includes attempted murder. God's not going to grant him admission into heaven for that act."

There's only one girl on the team who would say something like that. Peyton. She's extremely religious and takes it upon herself to remind us every moment that she can, especially by reciting verses from the Bible.

"Girls," I hear Karmin butt in, "don't you think you're being just a little inconsiderate? She's standing right over there." Even though I'm not looking at them, I know that their eyes all shift to me; I sense their gazes traveling from the dark brown bun on my head down my red-and-black uniform to my black jazz shoes. "Besides, you're all wrong. Dylan's not dead, and he's not dying anytime soon."

"I don't think we're being insensitive. I mean, her brother crashed his car, is now in the hospital—possibly on his deathbed—and I haven't even seen her shed one tear. Not even at the benefit." It's Peyton again. "As far as I'm concerned, she doesn't miss him at all. She's going on like he never even existed."

I hear Karmin scoff at her words. "We all grieve in different ways."

"Yeah, but she's not grief-stricken at all. It's almost as if she doesn't care whether he lives or dies."

"Well, how would you like me to act, huh? Do you want me to be sad and bawl my eyes out every day? Or curl up into a ball and lock myself in my room? Is that what you want me to do?" The girls have never heard me raise my voice at them or anyone else. Ever. "For the entire first week after Dylan's coma, I cried myself into a migraine. But it's exhausting, and I can't do it anymore." I hear the announcer welcome another team to the stage. We're next. "And by the way, he's not on his deathbed; he's in a coma. And his doctors are very positive that he will make a full recovery . . . one day."

"But what if he's not the same person he was when he comes to? What if he has no memories or develops a disability or wakes up brain-dead?" This time, it's Karmin who speaks. The upbeat confidence she usually has in tow is missing from her voice as her lips form the words on everyone's mind. "What if he doesn't wake up at all?"

"He will." *Positivity breeds positivity.* "He's going to wake up." I feel my chest grow warm with resentment toward all of them, especially Karmin.

"But what if he doesn't?" Karmin's voice is so low I almost can't hear it.

"Yeah, what if he dies," Peyton says, her eyes on the ground between us, "and you're not there when it happens? What do you think God would say about your actions?"

"Wait, are you guys seriously coming down on me for wanting to go to my dance competition instead of sitting by his bedside waiting for him to wake up?" I put my hands on my hips and stare directly at Karmin. She of all people should know how touchy this topic is for me.

"Just because my pain isn't visible to you doesn't mean I'm not hurting." I have to force myself not to cry in front of them, but the longer I face them, the harder it gets. "You have no clue what Dylan meant . . . means . . . to me, so stop trying to denounce me for doing something that makes me finally feel alive again." I hear the announcer call Cedar Pointe High to the floor, and I turn away from them. "That's us," I croak, wiping at the tears on the rims of my eyelids.

⌒◊⌒

WE COME IN SECOND PLACE, BUT IT'S A CLOSE SECOND BECAUSE THE OTHER team only beat us by half a point. When we get back to the hotel, all of the girls are celebrating, but I don't want to party with them. Not after the way they ganged up on me before we took the stage.

I throw on a jacket, and without letting anyone know, I leave the hotel in search of something to curb my rage. I end up getting ice cream in the mall across the street from the hotel, and, after finding a seat on the bleachers near the ice rink, I call my parents. They haven't returned any of my calls this week, and even though I know they're probably by Dylan's bedside right now, I can't help but be mad at them. *This competition was supposed to be about me, not Dylan.*

While the phone is ringing, I start to think of everything I want to say to them. Like, how I don't appreciate being forgotten on my birthday—the last birthday celebration that I will have with them before I head off to college—even if it is because of Dylan. I mean, I'm planning on taking a summer class or getting an internship before school starts, so I'll leaving in a couple months. They should be trying to squeeze as much family time in as possible. But no. The only family time that we've had since Dylan's coma has been family therapy sessions with Dr. Turner every Monday afternoon.

I'm not surprised when I get their voice mail, and I'm just about to leave a nasty message for them when I feel a hand on my shoulder. "Keegan?" I breathe icily as I pull my phone away from my ear and hang up. "What are you doing here? Did you follow me?"

"No, I was just in the area." He smiles, and I raise my eyebrows at him, looking for the truth. "I saw you leave the hotel and wanted to make sure that you were okay."

"Well, I am."

"I can see that. You're eating a bowl of ice cream and watching a rink full of people skate around to classical music. And you're all by yourself, even though your dance team just found out you guys will be headed to nationals in three months. You're right. You're perfectly fine."

"The sarcasm is really unattractive right now, Keegan. Just leave me alone." There he is again. Dylan. His last words to me before the crash echo in my ears as they make their way to Keegan's.

"Okay," he says, but he doesn't do as I ask; instead, he takes a seat next to me. I can feel his eyes all over my face, but I refuse to look at him.

"Can I help you?" I finally say after sitting in silence for almost ten minutes.

"Oh, no. I'm just going to keep you company until you return to the hotel. Think of me as your personal bodyguard for the night."

"I'm not a baby. I can take care of myself."

"Do you really think that I am going to leave you out here all alone? You're very pretty. Someone might try to snatch you up." His words are caked with charm, and I almost fall for it.

"Please, just leave."

He still doesn't move. "Okay, how about this: we skate for your freedom," he proposes.

"What?"

"Two laps. You beat me, and I'll leave you alone. But if I beat you, I stay."

I've only seen Keegan on skates once in my life, and it was last October. To raise money for our competition season, the dance team had an ice-skating fund-raiser. Keegan and his baseball boys could barely stand on their own, while I, and some of the other dance team members, skated circles around them all. There is no way he is going to beat me. "You're on."

We have barely taken two steps onto the ice when Keegan starts to stumble. He has his arms out to his sides, trying to steady himself like little kids do when they are first learning to skate.

"Do you want a couple of minutes to practice?" I offer as he holds on to the side of the rink.

"No, I'm fine. Let's start." I honor his request and line up at the center court line. At the count of three, we take off. Well, I take off. Keegan loses his balance and ends up falling before he can even get going. But once I start skating, I don't look back. I feel like I'm flying, and the rush of the cold air against my cheeks makes me feel alive again.

Keegan can't seem to get it right because when I round the corner for my second lap, he's still struggling in the starting area. I give him the thumbs-up and continue flying across the ice at full speed.

I take my time on my second lap, doing simple turns and tiny leaps, mimicking what I've seen the professional skaters on television do. When I finally make it back to Keegan, I guess he has given up because he's just sitting cross-legged on the cold ice.

"You should've gone for a practice run, like I told you to," I taunt as I skid to a stop beside him, sending an arc of shaved ice his way.

"Maybe you're right." He smiles back at me, extending a hand for help.

Hesitantly, I grab his hand and try to lift him to his feet, but I underestimate his weight and end up toppling over him, landing on his chest. I can't hold it back now. I have to laugh.

"There you are. I've been wondering where this version of you has been for the past couple of weeks."

"What do you mean?"

"You've been walking around in this funky mood. Snarling at people and giving them side eye."

"I have not," I say, playfully hitting his shoulder.

"Have so. Let me show you." He raises one eyebrow and puts on an ugly, hobgoblin grimace.

"Whatever. I have not been doing that." Another laugh escapes me, and he pauses to look at me for a second.

"I've missed your smile."

Don't fall for it, Emma. Don't fall for it.

"Well, you can miss it some more while I go take another lap. My butt's getting cold." I effortlessly stand to my feet and take off. When I look back, I see him wobbling toward me, trying to catch up. Needless to say, he never does. By the time that we make it off the ice and back to the bleachers, I'm freezing cold and my throat is raw from laughing and breathing in the frosty air.

"Did I ever tell you that I have a thing for brunettes?" he says as we reclaim our seats outside the rink.

"I was wondering when you would notice."

"Of course I noticed. I notice everything about you."

"Like what?"

"Like the fact that you get your hair cut four times a year, each time only taking an inch off. And when you're nervous, you chew on the left side of your bottom lip, and sometimes you bite the inside of your cheeks. And your hair always smells like strawberries and oranges. Oh, and happy birthday. How's seventeen treating you?" I feel the apples of my cheeks rise as his do the same. *He knew me even before I was suddenly popular on the dance team; he saw me when I thought nobody else did. He was always there.*

At first, I'm surprised that he's being so nice to me and giving me so many compliments, but then I realize why: Dylan. "You don't have to do that, you know? Be nice to me. It's not like he's dead or anything. He's going to wake up eventually."

"Yeah, my sister told me. And I've been meaning to ask you if you're okay. She said you had some sort of meltdown backstage earlier . . ."

I want to tell him everything. That I was . . . no, *am* in love with Dylan. And not only because he made me feel like I was the only girl who mattered to him on the face of this earth, but also because he fell in love with the version of me that no one else had cared to get to know. But at the same time, I want to tell him how upset I am with him for making me feel his love and then ripping it all out from underneath

298

me. It's like Karmin said earlier: he could die and take everything with him. All of the memories we made, kisses we shared . . . everything. And that's not okay with me. I'm not ready to give up my first love yet. But I can't tell Keegan these things. My brain can connect the letters to form the words to say it all, but my mouth can't make the sounds to go through with it.

"I don't want to talk about this." I turn away from him, letting my smile fade. I can never escape for more than a few minutes.

"Fine by me. Besides, you won the bet, so I'd better go take these bad boys off and return to the hotel."

"I should probably head back, too. Your sister will kill me if I sprain my ankle out here."

"She'd kill you, and then me for suggesting we do this. So in the end, we're both screwed." We chuckle, but then all of a sudden, things go back to being weird. This is our first real connection since our breakup—our chat at the benefit wasn't deep enough to classify as a connection—and I want to apologize for the way things ended between us, but I chicken out when our eyes meet again. "I've missed everything about you, Emma."

"Have you really?" I ask, playfully.

Keegan scoots closer to me—so close that I can see the bits of gold in his eyes—and says, "Of course. I hated how things ended between us."

They're so green, I find myself thinking, and before I can stop him, Keegan leans in to kiss me. I almost lose myself in him, but then I think of Dylan, and my body freezes up.

"I'm sorry," I say, pushing him away.

"No, *I'm* sorry," he answers bashfully.

"It's okay. You did nothing wrong. This mess is all me." I reach for the necklace hidden underneath the collar of my sweatshirt and rub the golden charm with my name on it between my thumb and pointer finger. *Forgive me, Dylan. I didn't mean it.*

"You okay?" Keegan says, bringing me back to reality.

"Yeah. Just . . . when you said you'd be here for me, I thought you maybe meant as my friend. Right now, I don't think I'm capable of anything serious." I don't tell him that it's because my heart belongs to Dylan, but I figure that's an ethical omission.

"Oh." I see a flush of color sweep across his olive cheeks.

"I'm sorry." My heart is heavy.

"No, no. Not your fault. I read the signs wrong." He scratches his head and scoots away from me. "But if a friend is what you need right now, then a friend is what I'll be."

chapter 24

With each passing day, somehow it's been getting easier. My heart still longs for Dylan, but I don't feel shrouded in sadness anymore. Keegan and Karmin pick me up when I fall into one of those moods. They, unlike my parents, understand that I need to keep up the distractions. My parents have been in this heartbroken trance for so long that it doesn't even affect me anymore.

When the last bell rings, I take the long way to the student parking lot. Earlier today, I made the mistake of passing by the "Get Well, McAndrews" table that someone set up in the middle of the hall. The school has embraced my mother's philosophy that positivity will breed more positivity, and so they placed a glass box on the table for us to drop notes into for Dylan. When he wakes up and is in recovery, they'll present the box to him so he can know that his Cedar

Pointe High family was thinking about him the whole time. When I saw the display earlier today, I felt a pang of sadness pierce through my lower abdomen. It took me a little while to get my breathing back under control, but Karmin finally settled me.

"I've heard that it's less dangerous to walk when you're looking up, but that could be hearsay," Keegan says when I finally make it to my car. I have to keep my eyes on the ground as I walk or else they'll wander to the empty space where Dylan's car used to sit every day. "What took you so long?"

"I wanted to go the scenic route," I retort with slight agitation. The way he constantly questions my actions is starting to get on my nerves. I get that he's checking up on me to make sure I'm okay, but sometimes I feel like he's suffocating me. My eyes meet his as he looks up from the school newspaper; his left eyebrow is raised, and I can tell that he thinks I'm lying.

"You don't have to lie."

"I'm not, I just . . ."

"Didn't want to pass by the table again? Don't worry, I understand completely."

"I'm craving a smoothie right now. Do you want to join me?" I say, trying to change the subject. Keegan knows that I don't like talking about Dylan, but he always seems to bring him up anyway. He nods stiffly, probably in reluctance, and then starts to make his way toward his truck.

Once we order our usual—a Strawberry-Kiwi Supreme for me, and a Very Vanilla Bean Shake for him—we grab a booth by the window.

"Where were you at lunch today? I was looking for you," he says. I try to avoid Keegan's stare, but he won't let up. His eyes find mine as he asks, "Well?"

"I didn't feel like holding any Spanish conversations with Señora Esperanza today, so I left before the late bell for third period rang and returned right after lunch." I can see the disappointment fill his eyes. He knows me as the good girl. The girl who never missed a class unless I was so sick that I couldn't crawl out of bed. The girl who got straight As with little to no effort. "It's not like it matters anyway. Since the accident, everyone has given me a free pass to use at my leisure."

"Since when did you become so badass?" he asks, his face twisting into a scowl. "This isn't you. I think that brown hair dye has gone to your head."

"Ha-ha, very funny," I say, pulling my vibrating phone from my back pocket and setting it on the table. "I heard that they updated the ranks again today. Did you swing by the office to see where you stand?"

"Couldn't. It was jam-packed up there. I guess everyone wants to talk about . . . you know."

"Yeah, I know." He's right. I haven't been able to get up to the counselor's office since Dylan's accident. It's actually kind of annoying. I mean, I was the one who was closest to him. If anything, I should be up with special access to guidance. Not the other students who didn't even know Dylan. "Can you believe that we're going to be Cedar Pointe graduates in just a few months?"

"I know. Sometimes it feels like I'm moving in fast motion. Like, I'm so focused on what's to come in the next year or so that I'm not taking enough time to enjoy these last couple of months at Cedar Pointe."

"I agree. But I actually want time to go by faster. I'm ready to leave this place."

"Given everything that's happened? I get that." There he goes again, trying to bring up Dylan. It's like I can't go five minutes without someone or something reminding me of his absence. It's unbearable.

"It has nothing to do with Dylan. I'm just ready for college."

Reacting to my terse words, Keegan can't change the topic fast enough. "I got my acceptance letter from USC last week. I'm one clean baseball season away from a full scholarship."

"That's great," I say, grabbing his hand from across the table to give it a friendly squeeze.

"I'm happy that I'm not going too far away, so that I can still visit when I get homesick."

"Or when you need your mom to turn your pink underwear back to white, right?"

"That was *one* time," Keegan erupts with a huge smile on his face. I can tell he's embarrassed by the amount of red that's overtaking his cheeks, but I don't comment on it. "I can't believe Karmin told you that. I'm gonna kill her."

"You can't." I play along. "Then who will I tell all of my secrets to?"

"Secrets? You keeping things from me, Em?" *Yes. Loads.* I purse my lips to keep my secrets from pouring out, and he must take it as a sign that he needs to change the subject again. "Anyway, what about you? Did you hear back from . . . where do you want to go again?"

Just open them, the voice in my head echoes. The dance bag at my feet holds the answers to the questions in my head. A few unopened envelopes are the only things standing between me and my future.

I gather the array of different-sized envelopes and spread them out across the table. Brown. Berkeley. Stanford. Duke. Westminster. Columbia. UCLA. Just looking at them, I can already tell that I got into Berkeley, Duke, and Columbia. They're all big envelopes. Colleges send out the big ones only to accepted students. Small ones either mean *No*, or that you've been waitlisted—from what I've read, anyway.

My hands brush against the Stanford envelope. Hopefully, I haven't thrown anything away in neglecting the initial letter that came when Dylan was first in the hospital.

"Well, what are you waiting for?" Keegan asks giddily, as if he's going to rip them open any second if I don't do it myself.

Dylan. "Nothing, I guess." I start with the big envelopes. They start out exactly as I expect them to: *We are pleased to inform you that . . .* blah blah blah.

I stack the remaining four letters and open them one by one. First Stanford and UCLA. *We are pleased to inform you . . .* (Okay. Maybe the small envelope theory is a myth.) Then, Brown and Westminster. *We regret to inform you . . .* (Okay. Maybe not.) The balloon in my heart deflates a little when I read these last two.

"So where do you think you're gonna go?" His question is so simple, but it feels complex when I actually start to think about my answer.

I was wrong. With what I told Karmin, I was so wrong. Dylan being absent for the opening of my college admissions letters doesn't make it any easier to process my feelings. I'm still stuck, rotating between the familial and romantic relationships that I have with him.

I push away all but two envelopes: Duke and UCLA. Both of them are offering me serious scholarships—nothing close to full tuition, but enough to pay for room and board—but UCLA's package includes a special first-year internship at L&B Books, a huge publishing house in Los Angeles. *It's simple, Emma. At Duke, you'll start out as a nobody, but if you go to UCLA, you'll at least have a foot in the door.*

I think back to my four years at Cedar Pointe High. For three of them, I was on the outside of it all, waiting on the popularity door to swing open and let me in. I don't want the next four years to be the same. If the door is open, I might as well step through it. *UCLA it is.*

"Earth to Emma," Keegan half shouts at me, waving his hands in front of my face as if he's trying to hypnotize me. "What are you thinking?"

"I need to talk to my parents." I grab my phone and dial my father's number as quickly as I can. *He's going to flip out when he hears this.* He answers on the third ring. "Hey, Dad, guess what? I—"

"Emma Leanne Ellenburg," my dad's voice booms through the earpiece. He's so loud that I bet Keegan can hear every word. "Where are you?"

"I'm—"

"Actually, I don't want to know. You just better be on your way to Dr. Turner's office. Therapy starts in ten minutes!" *Click.*

"Okay. Bye, Dad," I say, embarrassed, but Keegan doesn't buy it for one second.

"Emma, I'm sorry," he says, sympathy flooding his eyes. "Is everything okay?"

"My dad wants me to go to some stupid family therapy session. We go every Monday, and, after that call, I think I'm gonna skip that today, too."

Keegan's thick eyebrows crinkle with confusion. He doesn't understand my reason for not wanting to go, so I answer his silent question for him. "It's supposed to be for all of us, but my parents are the only ones who need it. They've been fighting a lot recently. Little things at first, but now they barely talk to each other, unless it's a fight. My dad doesn't go visit Dylan anymore, and it's been getting to my mom. I guess they think that therapy is going to fix us. Like we could ever get back to normal." I finish off my smoothie, slurping the last remnants through the straw, before grabbing his cup and taking a sip of it.

"The whole thing is stupid, though. I mean, the entire session is them debating who's to blame for our family falling apart, and each time we are left on a cliffhanger—'Will we find out who should be held liable? Will Matthew ever stay awake through an entire session? When will Dr. Turner give up the creases in her pantsuits? Find out on the next episode of *The Blame Game.*'"

I hope to get a small chuckle out of Keegan, but he doesn't give me that satisfaction. Instead, he says three words: "Go to therapy." After all of that, I was expecting him to be on my side and tell me that I'm right for wanting to skip. I wanted to hear him say that it isn't fair that my parents are making me go see a therapist every week, but he doesn't say any of that.

"Did you not hear what I just said? I don't need it, so therefore, I don't want to go."

"I think the reason you don't *want* to go is because you can't face Dylan. Like his accident hurt you in a way that you still don't understand and so to numb the pain, you ignore him." My stomach drops. *Did Karmin tell him my secret?*

"You don't know that."

"Really? Because I haven't seen your name on the hospital's visitor list in about a month." I feel his eyes all over my face, but I can't look at him. He's right. "Freshman year, Karmin and I lost our dad in a car accident." This is my first time hearing either of the Ortega twins talk about their father. I've been to their house many times, and I've noticed his absence, but I figured he was just absent, not deceased. "He was out drinking, and apparently, he was way over the limit. He ran off the road and crashed into a ditch in the middle of the night, and by the time the ambulance showed up, he was already dead."

I want to ask what his story has to do with me, but I keep quiet out of respect. I guess he sees the crash as the connector.

"I avoided my feelings forever, telling everyone that I was fine when I was really torn up. I missed him, but I was mad at him. Talking about it was too much for me to handle back then. Sometimes it still is. But do you know what I would give for him to be in a coma right now, instead of in the Cedar Pointe Cemetery?" His eyes start to fill up with tears that he probably didn't expect to still have. All I can do is watch as the stoic baseball player before me breaks down. "Go to therapy, Emma. It'll help you deal with whatever it is that you're not telling me, with whatever it is that you're hiding from everyone," he says in between sobs. "Promise me you'll go."

I don't see how my going to therapy just to conceal my real feelings from my parents is going to help, but when I look Keegan in the eyes, I feel a weight drop in my stomach. I don't think I've ever seen him look so serious.

"Okay," I say slowly. "I promise."

I'M ONLY TEN MINUTES LATE WHEN I ARRIVE AT DR. TURNER'S OFFICE. A light and familiar scent finds its way to my nose as I walk through the double doors. *Vanilla. Just like my mom always wears.* After having me sign in, the woman at the front desk ushers me to the room down the hall. I place my head on the door and listen before I go inside. My mom is speaking, and I can tell she's been crying because her voice is raspy and sounds as if she's struggling to form the words that she wants to say. On the door is a sign that reads SESSION IN PROGRESS, but I ignore it.

"Sorry I'm late," I say as I enter. The couch that we usually sit on is across the room, so it feels awkward to have to interrupt their conversation to find my seat. "Traffic," I lie. I've been getting good at lying to my parents lately. And because they're in some trancelike, depressive state, they believe my every word.

"It's okay," Dr. Turner says, turning to me. She's a tiny woman. Dark-skinned and undeniably beautiful, with big brown eyes that she keeps hidden behind a pair of dark-rimmed glasses. "Your mother was just telling us about how she's been having a hard time keeping hope when no one comes to visit your brother anymore."

I want to correct her and let her know that Dylan was not yet part of our family, but I swallow the mean thought. I can't have an outburst here. Not in front of my parents, and especially not in front of Matthew.

The way Dr. Turner has our sessions set up makes me feel like I'm in an Alcoholics Anonymous support group. Each of us goes around the room and says how we're doing now that it's been a few months since his accident, each trying to outdo the other with how bad we feel. It starts off with Matthew, then goes to my mom, then my dad, and always ends with me. To my parents' displeasure, I pass every time. I never say a word in here; to me, it's pointless. But since Mom and Dad are doling out a ton of money to have her help us, I can't tell them I don't believe in it. That would only add insult to injury.

As soon as I take my seat on the couch, I regret letting Karmin French braid my hair during PE today. I usually wear my hair down so that I can listen to low music through my earbuds; it helps the time pass by quicker than if I just sit here doing nothing. But now that my ears are exposed, I have to actively listen to the entire session, which is, by far, the cruelest form of torture I've ever had to endure.

"I guess I haven't been to visit him because I'm having a hard time dealing with what I saw that night in the ambulance. My wife didn't ride in the ambulance with him, so I don't think she understands why I can't face him." My dad sniffles.

"I'm very sorry to hear that, Daniel," Dr. Turner says robotically, almost rehearsed. "I understand that it's hard to face Dylan right now, but you have to realize . . . he didn't die. Whatever fears you have, you're going to have to let them go. Not only for yourself, but also for your children. You have to lead by example. If they see you being hopeful for his recovery, then they will also feel that way." For a moment, I believe in her words and sincere smile, but then I remember something that Dylan once said about therapists. *The longer they keep you in their office, the more money they make.* I bet she's secretly hoping that Dylan never wakes up.

My father's eyes meet mine and Matthew's as he shifts in his spot on the sofa. "I'm not sure I can do that."

"That's exactly what I'm talking about," my mom cuts in. "I don't know if I can take this much longer."

"Take what?" Dr. Turner asks, readying the pen in her right hand.

"His pessimistic attitude. It's hard being the glue that holds this family together. It's hard being the only parent who cares about Dylan's recovery."

"So, it's Dylan. You think he's the problem? The reason you guys have been . . . off?"

"No, no, no. Not at all. If anything, he brought us closer when he came into our family."

"Hmm." Dr. Turner's pen flies across the paper, noting something important. "What about you, Emma? Do you have anything to share in regard to this topic?"

"Pass," I say as I fold my hands over my chest. I just want her to end our session with an inspirational quote and tell us that she's going to see us next week, like always. But this time, my mom doesn't let me off the hook so easily.

"For God's sake, Emma. It's been almost two months and we haven't heard a word from you. We are here to figure out why we're not the same family we used to be and how we can get back to that. You passing every time is not helping us work toward that goal. Now, we are not leaving this room until you say something."

I see our therapist reveal, and then try to contain, a small smile, as if encouraging us to stay. She *does* get paid extra if we run over our time limit.

"Okay, fine," I say as I uncross my legs and arms. "I'm not mad at Dylan."

"But . . . ?" My mom drags the word out, aware that there is indeed a *but* coming, not sure what to expect after it.

"But I *am* mad at you guys."

"Why us?" my dad asks, his face shrouded in confusion.

"Because this is bullshit."

"Emma!" my mom and dad yell as they slap their hands over Matthew's ears.

"That's what I think of all of this. It's complete *bullshit*." I put emphasis on my words to let them know that I don't care to follow their no-cursing rule. When the words leave my mouth, I reach for my bag and head for the door. *I drove myself here and I can drive myself home.*

I'm one step away from freedom when my dad cuts in front of me. "Sit down, Emma." His voice is firm, so I know he means business. "Now."

I flash back to our phone conversation right before Keegan convinced me not to skip this. My dad's been so consumed with his fear about Dylan that I couldn't even share my good news with him. A few months ago, he would have been thrilled to hear that I'd settled on UCLA and was going to follow in his footsteps, but now, it's as if he couldn't care less. That's how it's been for a while. I should be used to it, but I'm not, and I think it's time that I stop choking down my feelings.

"Why? So I can listen to you and Mom recount Dylan's accident for the thousandth time, and then go back and forth about what's wrong with our family and what we can do to 'fix what's broken'? No! I'm tired of this. I can tell you exactly what's wrong here. It's you guys. The Dylan stuff has been rough on me and Matt, but you guys? You've been in the way of everyone's happiness for a long time, and I think it's time somebody spoke up about it."

I expect them to retort with a punitive comment about respect for adults and my current lack of it, but when they don't, I continue with my rant.

"I get that you're sad that Dylan's in a coma, but guess what? If you haven't noticed, you still have two children here, one of whom is leaving in a few months for college, and another who is struggling to get his schoolwork done in the middle of visiting the hospital just to watch you two pace around Dylan's bed. For two people who are regretting not spending enough time with the kid they were fostering, you sure aren't making an effort to invest time in your kids who are still walking and talking. You know, your *actual* birth children?"

For the first time ever in one of our therapy sessions, the room is completely silent. I can't even hear anyone breathe.

"Emma, I think we should discuss this at home—" my dad starts.

"No, Dad. Let's discuss this right now. And you want me to speak, right, Mom? Well, here I go." I take two short breaths before I begin. I've been holding a lot of anger in, and I know the pot is about to boil over now that they've turned up the heat. "Again, I'm not blaming this on Dylan, because I know it's not his fault, but ever since you brought him home, it's like you guys stopped caring about Matthew and me. Your every parental impulse has been spent making sure that Dylan is adjusting well, or that Dylan is taken care of, or that Dylan isn't over-whelmed by his past. Well, what about us? Did you forget that you had children before he came along?"

"Emma, how dare you speak to us in—"

"How dare I, Dad? No, how dare you! You completely bailed on my dance competition—we're going to nationals, by the way—you didn't even acknowledge my birthday, and when I called you to tell you about college admissions—the decision you've been waiting to hear for almost an entire year—you just blew me off like I didn't even matter. But I guess I haven't. Not since Dylan showed up, anyway."

My mom's lips tremble, and I'm not sure if it's because she's happy that I've finally made a decision about college or because she's flabber-gasted at my words. "Honey, I'm so—"

"Sorry? Yeah, you should be. Both of you, actually. In fact, you should be thanking me for coming forward now. If I hadn't, you both would have probably missed my graduation."

Stunned, my dad takes a second to process my outburst before speaking again. "We're sorry, honey. We've just been distracted with—"

"Distracted? Yeah, maybe just a little, Dad." I take another breath and look into his eyes before releasing the secret I've held in for far too long. "You both had no clue that Dylan and I were even dating."

A deafening silence falls upon the room, and I'm glad because I need a moment to gather my thoughts to continue with my emotional purge. "Since he came along, I've been on the back burner in your lives. How do you think that makes me feel? You haven't paid an ounce of attention to me all year, so how can I expect you to know what's going on with me now?"

"Emma," my mom starts, but doesn't finish. She probably can't find the words to do so.

"He was . . . is . . . my first love. The first person to make me feel like I mattered in this world. And I couldn't even share that part of my life with you." I feel the tears welling in my eyes again. It's been so long since I last cried that their saltiness stings my lids. "It's like you guys don't *want* me anymore. Like you've moved on already."

"What do you mean, Emma? We're right here."

"But you're not! You're only saying that because we're in front of Dr. Turner. If she weren't here . . . I doubt that you'd care."

"Adjusting to new siblings is hard, at any age," Dr. Turner says in a calm voice. "You know, it's okay to be jealous."

"Jealous?" I say, turning in her direction. "You think I'm jealous of Dylan? No. Wrong emotion. I tried to help it, but I couldn't . . . I'm in *love* with him." I hear my voice crack, trying to choke out another sentence. "But I'm scared that I'll lose him."

"He'll wake up one day, Emma. You're not going to lose him." My mom has finally found words, but somehow, I didn't think those would be the ones she would choose.

"Maybe. But what if when he wakes up, he doesn't remember us, huh? Then what was the point of all of this? What was the point of me loving him?" I crack my knuckles like I'm about to partake in the fight of my life as I walk back over to the stool by the door. "What if I never even get to hear him say the three words I've waited my whole life to hear." I can barely breathe now, and as much as I want to stick a plug in this heart-to-heart, I can't. "I hate this."

"Emma," my dad breathes as he places his hand on my shoulder. I shrug it off; I don't want his comfort now. He didn't care before, and I don't want him to now. It's too late for that.

"It's not fair. I was perfectly fine before he got here. I was going to go to college and leave these past four years—my worst four years—behind. But then he happened. I let him in and I fell. Hard. There was nothing I could do to stop it, not that I really tried. But now what am I supposed to do?" I scream at them again. I can't control my volume any more than I can control the words that are coming out of my mouth. Out of the corner of my eye, I see Matthew press deeper into my mother's chest, as if he's scared of me. "He can't just come in, make us different, and then disappear. That's not fair to us . . . that's not fair to me." I swipe the back of my hand across my face; it's wet with the tears that I'm finally letting myself cry again. *Now's the moment.* I reach for the door handle, and this time, no one tries to stop me.

chapter 25

EVERYTHING IS THE way he left it, just like the last time I set foot in here. Every brush, every canvas, every tube of paint. They are all exactly where he placed them. When I was dating Dylan, his studio was always the first place I ran to. I'm not sure if it was the smell of the paint or the way his arms always wrapped around me perfectly, but whenever I came here, it calmed me down. Now it's not the same. These four walls don't bring me the same comfort they used to.

I close my eyes and inhale deeply; the mixed scent of paint and soap are still here. This room still smells like him, even though he hasn't been here in months. There are drawers still open as if he just finished rummaging through them for a specific brush. He had a million of them, and I always found it hard to keep up with which ones he would use. Flat brushes, round brushes, thick ones, thin ones. *How did he do it? How did he always know which one would make the perfect stroke?*

"I blame myself." At first, it feels like I'm thinking aloud, but when I turn around, I see my father standing in the doorway. His face is long, and he's squinting as if the sun is shining in his eyes, though it isn't; the saltiness of his tears has probably dried them out. "I set him off . . . that night of the showcase. This is my fault."

"No. This all falls back on me," I say, looking down into my hands. Two bluish-green lines start at the edges of my palms and run up my pale arms, weaving together underneath my skin. "In addition to the sleeping pills you guys would give him, Dylan was taking study buddies, and I knew about it." I rub my hands together to keep them warm in the cold studio. "They're these little white pills that are supposed to keep you awake so you can cram for tests and stuff.

"When I found out that he was using them, I told him to flush them, which he did, but I guess he got more behind my back. He said that he needed them . . . because there weren't enough hours in the day. And that he was so busy with trying to balance our relationship and work and school and the showcase that he had no choice." I feel the guilt pulse through my veins as I speak, my dad unable to meet my gaze. "On the night of the showcase, after I got in the car with him, he took a pill before dropping me off, and I'm not one hundred percent sure, but I think he mixed up his pills and took a sleeping pill instead."

My dad opens his mouth to say something, but the words don't come out. *I wouldn't know what to say either.*

"So I knew about it. The pills. Even before the accident, I knew. I was just trying to protect him. I didn't want the social worker to find out. But had I known that things would end up like this—with you and Mom fighting, and Matthew saddened by his absence, and me lashing out at everyone—I would have never kept that secret from you guys. Please, believe me." I curl over and bury my head in my hands, trying to keep it together and hold it all back, but sitting in this room, talking about my part in Dylan's coma is too much for me to take. "This is all my fault."

I see a look of horror overtake my father's face before he settles on top of the other stool, Dylan's stool, and puts his own face in his hands, just like I'd done a second ago. "That damn showcase. I shouldn't have pushed him so far." This is the first time that I've ever seen my dad cry, and it's not something that I ever want to see again. He's supposed to be the strong one in the family, not the mess of a man who's sitting before me now. "I never should have entered that painting for him. I took the one thing that he enjoyed most in the world and turned it into something he grew to hate."

I don't say anything. Not because of the truth in his words, but because I don't know what to say to that. *Maybe he's right. If Dylan hadn't been in the showcase—killing himself to crank out paintings every night—then maybe he wouldn't be in this coma.*

"You can't blame yourself," I hear my dad say after a while. I pretend not to look while he wipes his eyes on the sleeve of his shirt. He probably hates that I'm here to see him like this. Weak and vulnerable. "It's not your fault."

For a long moment, neither of us speaks; we just sit there with our heads full of remorseful thoughts and our cheeks stained with bitter tears. "I guess we all played a part," I finally say.

We sit in silence for another minute, and I close my eyes to block out the image of Dylan that keeps popping into my head. The image of the glass-filled slits in his skin, bleeding out onto his clothes. With closed eyes, I can hear my dad sobbing, but I don't draw attention to it.

"Emma, I'm sorry," he says, still crying. "I didn't know I was . . . I mean, had I known that you felt the way you did, I . . ."

"It's okay, Dad." I lean over and lay my head on his shoulder. "It's okay."

"But it's not. I should have been there for you. And I know I've been a little absent, but I'm here now. Whatever you need from me, I'm here."

After a moment, I clear my throat and say, "Okay. What do you think of my hair? Do you like this color, or would you rather I go back to the blond?" All of a sudden, I hear my dad's sobs turn into chuckles. It starts low, but then grows into a full-blown laugh. "Dad, why are you laughing at me? I'm in serious need of your opinion, here."

"Leave it to my teenage daughter to ask my opinion about her hair while we're sitting here talking about your comatose foster brother," my dad says, wiping his eyes. This time I know his tears are from him laughing, not crying.

"Speaking of, I think that Dylan would hate it. My hair, I mean." I think back to his kind words on Thanksgiving night. He loved my hair. The length, the color, the smell. Everything about it. "All I can do is hope he doesn't wake up within the next few months, because that's how long the dye is supposed to last." I run my fingers through the tips of my hair and frown.

"To be honest, I'm not too fond of the brunette look on you. I thought it was one of those strange teenage-girl phases that you're supposed to go through, so I went with it."

I can understand why he would think that. He's never tried to keep up with trends. I mean, for God's sake, the man still uses a flip phone.

"He wouldn't be mad at you for changing your hair," he says.

"How do you know?"

"From what I hear, he doesn't hold grudges." I smile at his words. They could not be truer. No matter how mad we would make each other or how many stupid fights we would have, Dylan never stayed mad at me. I loved that about him.

"And, Dad," I say in a tiny voice. "About what I said . . . I don't think you ruin our lives. I was just upset, and—"

"Are you still on that?" he says with a confused look. "I was over that a long time ago. I've heard worse." He lets out another chuckle, and as he does, I feel a weight lift from my shoulders. The father-daughter bond we lost a long time ago is finally making an appearance. "So, I found this on Dr. Turner's floor when you left. Must've fallen out of your bag or something." From his pocket, he pulls a folded sheet of paper, the UCLA logo printed in big, blue letters across its top.

"Does this mean what I think it means?" he asks as he hands it over.

I nod my head. "They offered to help me land an internship at L&B Books on top of giving me a serious scholarship, and that's something I just can't pass up."

His face falls; I'm sure he was hoping that I'd say something about following in his footsteps.

"As much as I want you to go to my alma mater, I wouldn't be upset if you wanted to go somewhere else. You're free to go wherever you want, even if that means you'll be in another country for four years. Whatever you want, we'll go along with it."

"Well, Westminster didn't want me, so I'm US bound for now." I frown, thinking of all the wonderful things that I could have experienced in London. The sights, the food, the history, the accents. This would be an entirely different conversation had I gotten in. But I didn't. "No, UCLA will be just fine. It's only a two-hour drive—give or take a half hour for traffic. I could be back home at the drop of a hat if I needed to." *When Dylan wakes up*, I think to myself.

"So, you're sure about this?" He holds up my acceptance letter from UCLA with a notice telling me to confirm my seat by mailing in my deposit. "We can send this off today if you want."

"Nothing's ever felt more right."

"I'm so proud of you, Emma." His voice croaks as he hugs me.

"Me too." Years of living with his overinvolved parenting style made me develop a tiny pinch of hatred for my father. But now I see why he wanted to be so involved with us. It wasn't because he had no life of his own or because he wanted to embarrass me. It was so he could protect me. So that he could keep me safe long enough to experience moments like this one. *I get it now, Dad. I get it.*

I see him pull out his checkbook and his UCLA ballpoint pen. He used to tell me that he only uses it for special occasions, and I'm glad that my future in college is good enough for him to break it out again. "I've had this pen since I was a freshman at UCLA. My dad got it for me." He signs his name on the bottom of the check and begins to roll the sterling silver pen between his fingers, our last name engraved in calligraphy on the barrel. "Here."

"B-but this is your special pen! I can't."

"Yes, you can. I told myself that I'd give it to one of you if you ever decided to do what I couldn't: graduate from UCLA."

Sometimes I forget that my dad left college before he graduated. He went pro in the middle of his sophomore year and never returned, even though he talks a big game about UCLA being his alma mater. "Think of it as a late birthday gift. My most prized possession for my favorite daughter."

"I'm your only daughter, Dad."

"Exactly." He laughs, pulling me into a hug. "So you and Dylan . . . you guys were really dating, huh?"

Here we go. I knew this conversation was going to happen eventually, but I was hoping for a confrontation at a later date.

"Yeah," I say so low that it comes out as a whisper. "Go ahead and ground me for life."

"I'm not going to do that."

"Or report us, or whatever it is foster parents are supposed to do."

"I'm not going to do that either."

"Then what's my punishment? I mean, I did break one of the biggest foster sibling rules."

"We're not going to punish you." I see him tear the check from his book and dangle it before me. *Does he want me to disclose the secret happenings between Dylan and me in exchange for the deposit check he just signed?* "I don't want to know the details, but we are going to have a long talk about this when Mom gets home. Right now, I have to know one thing." *I knew it.* "You two, uh . . . You didn't . . . you know—"

"Dad, please don't," I say, holding my hands out in front of me to stop him midsentence. "I'm still a virgin."

I hear him breathe a sigh of relief and then let out a small laugh. "I knew I liked Dylan," he says, handing me the check. I feel myself blushing uncontrollably, and so I let my head fall into my hands again. "You okay?" he asks in a soft voice.

"I'm fine. Just mortified beyond belief."

"I meant with the whole Dylan thing. Do you feel better now that you've let everything out in the open?" I've disclosed enough about Dylan and me to my family that my skin no longer crawls with anxiety about keeping our secret. But even with that weight lifted, something still doesn't feel right.

"I'll be a whole lot better when he's no longer out cold in the hospital."

"Everything's going to be all right, you know?" *Positivity breeds positivity.*

"Yeah. I just hope he remembers me."

"Why wouldn't he remember you?" I open my mouth to answer his question, but before I can get a word in, he adds, "You're unforgettable."

"Corny!" I scream at him, rolling my eyes.

"Hey, I'm a dad. It's what I'm supposed to do." We leave the two stools in the center of Dylan's studio and walk back to the house, both of our smiles as wide as that of a blue whale.

chapter 26

Dear Catherine,

I feel like it's been forever since I've written to you—
seven months and four days, to be exact. You've always
been able to give me clarity in tough situations, and I'm
sorry to have forgotten about you in my time of need.
To be honest, though, you probably would have saved
me from dyeing my hair brown and cursing my parents out in front of our therapist. I mean, what was I
thinking??

A lot has happened since my last letter. But to
make a long story short: my dance team won the
national championships in Florida, and I pretty much
rocked the final days of the school year as valedictorian
of my senior class. Speaking of school, I finally decided

to follow in my dad's footsteps and go to UCLA. I don't think he's ever been more proud of me.

What else? Oh, I stayed away from boys, but not before Keegan tried his hand at getting back together. Don't worry, I didn't backslide, and we've remained friends. He's been keeping busy at a summer conditioning camp, but he still calls to check up on me from time to time. Also, did I mention that Karmin finally got her priorities together and hopped on the UCLA train, too? We're gonna be roommates, and she's prepping to move in during orientation week in September. Kind of awesome, I know. I'm not sure what'll be in store for our friendship in college, but I have a feeling I'm going to spend a lot of my time holding her hair back while she pukes up her party life in our dorm bathroom. That's just one of the challenges of best-friendship that I'm going to have to get used to, though.

As far as Dylan goes, I told my parents about us. I know that you're thinking: Am I asking for Dylan to get taken away? But no, my parents—as disappointed as they were in me—took it better than I anticipated. Dylan's adoption paperwork was already going through the court systems, so they couldn't go back on it, not that they ever would've done that. They did, however, give me an excruciating lecture—with a promise to give him one too, once he wakes up—and then they grounded me for the rest of the school year. Since then, they haven't brought it up again. I guess we're just going to act as if it never happened and move on.

Dylan is still in his coma, and I've been away in LA taking summer courses and interning at L&B Books—run by the legendary Ellen Bee herself—so it hasn't been something that they've had to monitor. I don't know what'll happen to us when he *does* wake up, though. I feel as if I've established my life out in LA now, but not a day goes by that I don't think of him and how much I miss talking to him and kissing him and just being around him. He was complicated, but I think that a part of me will always want to hold on to him.

Oh, and just so you know, this is going to be my last entry. It's not you . . . it's me. Ha-ha—I've always wanted to say that to someone. But really . . . I'm in college now, and I'm technically an adult, though not yet legally, according to my birth certificate. I think the time has come for me to leave you behind. You got me through my senior year and helped me survive my first relationship(s), but now I have to branch out and do things on my own, make mistakes and learn from them. Besides, I don't know how much time I'll have to write for a little while. I just registered for fall semester classes, and I'm not sure I'll even have time to sleep. I'll miss you, but now that I'll have Karmin 24/7, I'll just rant to her about my problems. I'm sure you'll appreciate the break.

Thank you for everything.

 Emma

"You come to visit us for the last time before you officially leave for the first week of classes, and *already* you're tired of us?" Laughing, my mom hands me a glass of lemonade and sits down next to me on my bed. I don't know why I expect her to look different, but when I see her, I try to scope out any distinctions between how she looks now and what she looked like when I moved out. No gray hairs in her head or wrinkles in her face, though. She hasn't aged a bit. When her vanilla perfume finds its way to my nose, I grin. Nothing has changed. "I can't believe you would rather journal than spend time with us. Then again, you're an English major, so I guess I can."

"Sorry. I got in a few minutes ago and wanted to settle in before I came inside. Where's Dad and Matthew?"

"They're at the batting cages. Apparently, Matthew learned something about how math is connected to baseball, and he and your dad have been at the cages all summer long. Matt's actually really good at baseball, which your dad is elated about. Obviously." I smile when her thin lips form a small crescent. It's good to see my dad and Matthew bond. They never really did before. "So, it'll just be the two of us until four o'clock."

I look around my room, and eye some of the things I left behind. Hanging on my dressing screen are my dance team uniform and my graduation cap and gown. Both of these outfits hold memories I wouldn't dare erase. On top of my desk is the copy of *Wuthering Heights* that Dylan bought for me. Looking at that book reminds me of the painting I have hanging up in my dorm room. It's the portrait of me reading *Wuthering Heights* that Dylan entered in his showcase last year. Being close to his art reminds me how grateful I am for our epic love story. Every kiss, every hug, every laugh, every smile. It all comes surging back to me in an instant.

"I've only been away for a month and a half, but already it feels weird to be back. Still, I'm glad to see that you guys haven't turned my room into a home gym yet."

"We're waiting on you to leave for good to do that."

"Very funny." I take a sip of my strawberry basil lemonade and wait. Any minute now, she's going to launch into a rapid-fire round of questions, wanting to know every in and out about pre-college so far.

"So how are you liking UCLA? Everything good?" She asks this as if we haven't spoken since I left, which could not be further from the truth. She calls at least three times a week to "check in" with me, but I know that she's really just checking to make sure that I'm safe in my dorm, instead of out barhopping.

"My internship has kept me pretty busy, but I'm having the best time there. My classes are amazing, the campus is spectacular, and the people—while they can be a bit eccentric at times—are pretty cool, too." My mom takes a swig from her glass and looks down. I imagine it's bittersweet for her to hear that I'm doing so well without her.

"That's great, honey. God, I'm so proud of you."

"Thanks." I adjust my dark-rimmed glasses and that's when I see a strand of my hair fall, featherlike, onto my jeans. "Oh, yeah. I went back to blond."

"I see," she says, running her hand over the top of my head before planting a kiss on my forehead. "We're like twins again."

"I tried to keep up with the chocolate brown, but having to constantly dye my roots drove me insane. Blond just feels right." I twirl my revived ponytail around my finger and chuckle to myself. Dylan would probably be a lot happier now that I'm a blonde again . . . if he could see me, that is. "One of the other interns, Casey, helped me dye it back. Her dorm is two floors beneath mine."

"I'm glad to see you're fitting in. Truth is, I was a little worried about you going to live out there on your own."

"Why?" I'm a little hurt by her words. *Did she think I was going to go to college and be a recluse?*

"You didn't have many friends until your last year in high school, and I was scared that you were going to go away and become a hermit. All work and no time for friends or play." Now that I've heard her explanation, I don't blame her. I was big-time socially awkward before I made the dance team; I didn't care for friends and had no interest in making them. As okay as I was with being that girl then, I'm so glad that I'm not her anymore.

"But you've come so far since then, and I'm sure Karmin won't let you go back."

"No, she won't. That girl is something else, but I love her." I flash back to the night we won the National High School Dance Team competition and chuckle. Karmin and I stayed up all night giggling about our futures together in college. I couldn't wait then, and I still can't wait now. "So, anything new with you guys? The last time I spoke to Dad, he said that everything was falling into place with the publisher for your book. Still true?"

My mom wrote a book about her experience fostering a teenager when she had two kids already, and while I was a little apprehensive about her talking about me and my life, I warmed up to the idea. And plus, she gave me her word that she wouldn't include anything embarrassing, like my secret relationship with Dylan.

"It's going well. I'm in my final round of revisions—hopefully—and after that we'll start the fun stuff, like picking out the cover and taking photos for the 'About the Author' section." As she speaks, she pulls what looks to be a long brown tube from her bag and hands it to me. I pop the top and rub my thumb over the edges of its contents. The laced texture feels familiar underneath my fingers. *This is a rolled-up canvas painting.* "I was going to use it for the cover, but I figured you'd probably like it to hang up in your dorm room next to the other one you have already." I unroll it to find a painted version of the family photo we took last year. We took the photo before Dylan arrived, but someone has painted him in to make it look as if he was a part of the original snapshot. "It just seemed fitting."

"Who did this?" I ask as I place my fingers over Dylan's face, and smile. "They did an amazing job adding him in. They captured his dimples and everything. I even see a bit of his hair sticking up in the back, like it always did." My mother doesn't answer, and I know why. *Dylan did this.*

I expect her to give me a hug or cry, like she used to whenever we brought him and his coma up in conversation, but she doesn't. Instead she says, "Let's take a drive, shall we?"

◦◊◦

"LISTEN, HONEY," SHE SAYS, TUCKING THE LEFT AND RIGHT SIDES OF HER hair behind her ears as she exits the freeway. This is serious. She only ever does that when she has something important to talk to me about. "I wanted to talk to you about your involvement with Dylan. Away from your dad."

I spoke—or journaled—too soon. We hadn't talked about this since the grounding after my outburst in Dr. Turner's office. I sit up straight and prepare myself for the lecture I know is coming. "What about it?"

I can see her struggling with her words, trying to choose them carefully. "I'm no fool." Her voice is low, but I detect a hint of laughter in it. "Did you really think I had no clue that you two were dating?"

She knew about us the whole time?? There is no way that my mother, the saint that she is, decided not to break Dylan and me up. There's just no way. "You knew? Why didn't you say anything?"

"I loved having him as a part of our family, and I loved how happy he made you. I had never seen you act so . . . blissful." A giggle escapes her as she continues. "And to tell you the truth, I didn't think you two would last. I figured you would go off to college and fall in love with someone else and eventually forget about that part of your relationship."

"Are you serious?"

"First relationships usually don't last forever, honey." I'm a little upset that she doomed us from the start, but she's just being honest and I can't fault her for that. "Yeah, I knew it the whole time. You may have been able to bamboozle your father, but not me." Another side smile sneaks up on me as her words echo in my ears. "You really loved him, didn't you?"

"So much, Mom. And it's not past tense. I still do." *You were right,* I want to say. She told me that I was going to love him back when they were about to bring him home for the first time. At the time, neither of us knew it was going to be a romantic love, rather than a sisterly one, that I would share with Dylan, but there's nothing I can do about the way I feel now.

"So why didn't you ever tell me?" she asks, taking my hand in hers as we wait at the light to turn into the hospital's parking lot. "We tell each other everything, Em. I was waiting for you to come to me with it, but you never did."

"I thought that if we put it out in the open, somehow it would get back to the fostering agency and they would revoke your license and take him away. And he loved being a part of our family. I couldn't do that to him." I can barely form a sentence because all I can think about is the fact that she knew about us the whole time and never said a word. "He was my first love, Mom. My first kiss and the first guy to make me feel like I was special. I couldn't give that up."

She goes silent, and I imagine her thinking about her first love. *It obviously wasn't Dad, since "first relationships don't last forever."* "Truth is, I kind of liked you two together, and in another universe, I would have loved you two to be an actual couple. He was a good kid—for the most part, anyway." A hint of delight floods her eyes, and I can tell she's reliving her memories of him. But then I see her expression change to a more serious one. "Your father doesn't know that I knew about you two. Don't tell him," she says with a wink.

"You're secret's safe with me, Mom." She parks the car and leans in to give me yet another hug, and we hold on to each other in silence for a couple of minutes. *I've missed this. I've missed us.*

"You ready for this, kiddo?"

I haven't seen Dylan in a long time, and my stomach fills with butterflies the second I think of seeing his face again. Every day, for the past month and a half in LA, I've dreamt of staring into his caramel eyes and hearing his goofy laugh. Knowing that I won't get to do either of those things kills a few of the butterflies, but I don't let my mom know that. "It's been so long, but yes."

It takes exactly four minutes and thirty-seven seconds to get from the hospital parking lot to Dylan's room. I've been here enough times to know that, no matter which way I take—the slower-than-molasses elevator or the five flights of stairs, which require me to go so out of the way that I don't make up the time I would have saved not taking the lethargic elevator—I will still arrive at the entrance of his room in exactly four minutes and thirty-seven seconds. On most days, this wait is nothing. A flash of time so insignificant that the events between me getting out of my car and me opening the door to his room vanish from my memory altogether. But not today. In the four minutes and thirty-seven seconds that it takes to get up to his room, my mind is as sharp as ever, alert to everything around me. Aware of my hands getting warmer and clammier by the second. Aware of the growing heavy feeling in my stomach, so much so that it feels like it's going to fall out of my butt. Aware that my throat feels as dry and itchy as my skin on the day I woke up with the chicken pox in the first grade.

Please be awake, Dylan. Please be awake today, I chant in my head when we enter the doors of the Extended Care Unit at the hospital. This may be the last time I get to visit him before Thanksgiving break, and I need to see his brown eyes before I go back. It's not a want anymore. It's a need.

Usually, Dylan's door is kept closed, but when we hit the corner, I see that it's wide open like the patio doors on a beachfront home. My mom doesn't enter. She stands by the side, waiting for me to go in first.

"Ta-da!" she screams as loud as she can when I cross the threshold.

But there is nothing to "ta-da" about. There are two nurses in there talking and giggling like high school girls as they change the sheets on the bed. There's a tray of half-eaten food in the corner, and a set of clothes that look to be about Dylan's size hanging on the back of one of the chairs. But no Dylan. He's missing.

"Um . . . Mom? What's going on? Where's Dylan? Mom?" In an instant, the weight in my stomach gains fifty pounds, and I have to sit down to keep the room from spinning out of control. *Where's Dylan? Why isn't he in his bed? He's* always *in his bed. Did he . . . die? He can't die!* My wild eyes search my mother's for answers, but she isn't the least bit worried about him, which is more than a little odd.

"Oh, shoot. What time is it?" She checks her watch, but I don't need to do the same. I already know that it's two forty-two. How? Because I checked it a million times in the four minutes and thirty-seven seconds that it took me to get up here. "Dylan must be in PT."

"PT?" *What's PT?*

Smiling from ear to ear, she sticks out her hand to pull me from the floor and brings me in for a hug. "Physical therapy. Dylan's awake. He woke up three weeks ago."

"Three weeks?" *Why am I the last to find out about this?*

"I'd never want to hide this from you but it was really rough at first, honey. He was having trouble with recognition and needed some time to find his words. Dylan begged me to wait until he was doing better before we brought anyone else in," she says, answering my question before I can string together the words to ask it. "I forgot that they changed his schedule to physical therapy on Thursdays now that he's regained enough muscle memory to stand on his own for a little while." She pulls back, placing her hands on my shoulders. "Well, say something."

At first, I don't know what to say, but then the words crash into me like a wave breaking onto an unsuspecting surfer.

"I'm so happy he's awake, don't get me wrong. But three weeks, Mom? I just wish I found out when you guys did." I'm a little hurt, but that doesn't last long when the thought of seeing Dylan races through my mind. "Now, where is he?"

"Physical therapy. Fourth floor."

I grab her hand and race toward the stairwell; the elevator is too slow to take one floor down.

When we reach the front desk of the physical therapy wing and sign in, my mom pulls me to the side. "I must warn you, he's still a little groggy some days. He didn't remember your dad or Matthew or me at first, but slowly he's re-mapping memories. And now he calls me Mom and your dad Dad." My jaw drops when I hear this. *Dylan never called Dad Dad.* "He even remembers that he and Matthew used to play hide-and-seek, and sometimes he talks about the best hiding places in the house. It's actually kind of cute."

"So, he could not remember . . . anything about me?" I knew this was a possibility, but I didn't think that it would actually happen.

"We show him pictures of you, but so far, he just hasn't said very much." I place my hand over my mouth, the tears ready to fall at my first command. "But you never know. He might. Only way to find out is to see for yourself." My mom opens the door and pushes me through it. There are two sets of people behind the doors of the physical therapy room. In the corner, there's a twentysomething-year-old guy and a teen-age girl at the parallel bars. With a black brace on her knee, she winces as she applies pressure on her leg and takes another step, the man cheering her on. And against the far wall is Dylan with a middle-aged man in scrubs. They're walking very slowly on the treadmills.

"Hi, Dylan!" my mom calls with a wave when she enters. Dylan returns the favor, his eyes passing over me, and then falls back into the exercise with the man. "I'm going to talk to his therapist to see how things are coming along, and find out what his plans for the future are. You guys should catch up, though. Remember, if he's not totally responsive yet, just give him some time. It may click once he starts interacting with you." My mom beckons the physical therapist over, whose name is apparently Jason, and they head to the tables on the side to talk.

Dylan switches off the machine and makes his way to one of the nearby wheelchairs to rest. He doesn't turn around when I approach but picks up a set of flashcards from the side pocket and begins saying the words out loud.

"Hey, Dylan."

"Hi," he says, without looking up at me. I rub away the goose bumps on my arms before sitting on the bench beside him.

"You want some help with those?"

"I guess. I can't believe they're making me do these," he jokes. For a moment, his brown eyes catch the light, and I almost melt in his presence.

He hands me the cards, and I show him the one on the top of the deck. *Water.* "Do you know what this word says?"

"Water."

"Good. And this one?"

"Elephant." I flash the next one to him, but he doesn't attempt to say the word. "I hate this activity. It's for babies," he says. "I like talking better. I just want to be a functional human again."

"One more, and then we'll stop." I show him the card again.

"House." *He's right. These words are silly and juvenile.*

"Very nice!" I try to make light of this, handing the cards back to him. While he puts them away, I check him out. He's lost so much weight in his arms, legs, and face that I have to try hard to remind myself what he looked like before. His dark hair is a bit longer   it now brushes against the tops of his shoulders—and his skin is a lot paler than the sun-kissed glow he used to possess, too. I'm so engrossed in what he looks like that I can barely focus on his words when he speaks.

"I think I used to do quizzes with someone else before the accident. A girl. But it wasn't words on the cards. It was something else—science?" His eyebrows wrinkle as he tries to extract the memory from deep within his mind, a coy smile slowly emerging on his lips.

My heartbeat picks up when he's says this. "Maybe it'll help if you describe her."

"She used to smell like . . . strawberries. And she looked like . . ." He stops, blinking his eyes a few times with a confused look on his face. When he turns toward me, I can almost see my name sitting on the edge of his tongue. "Emma?"

I'm already crying by the time his final syllable comes out, and when I wrap my hands around his fragile frame, I feel him do the same to me. "Yes, Dylan. It's me."

"Emma," he repeats, this time so clear that I can almost hear pieces of the old Dylan within it. His smile resurfaces, and I hold him tighter when I see it.

"You know, for a minute there, I didn't think you'd remember me."

"Forget you? I could never." He half smiles. "How have you been?"

I walk him through my summer at UCLA and tell him all about the craziness at the internship. I know that he probably doesn't understand why I'm so excited to spend my summer fetching coffee for the assistants and reading manuscripts of books that may never get published, but I don't care. Just talking to him makes me so happy.

"But enough about me. How have you been?"

"Fine. Considering." He motions to the wheelchair beneath him and sighs. "I can walk, but I get tired really easily, so I have to use this thing, too. I was told that I broke a ton of bones and was pretty slashed up, like a victim in a horror film."

"Yeah, you were."

"Well, that would explain the weird scars I have all over my body." He smiles at me, letting his eyes pierce mine, like he hasn't missed a beat between us for seven months. "I'm kind of upset that I missed the opportunity to get people to sign my casts. I mean, that's the whole point of breaking bones, isn't it?"

I can't help but laugh. I've missed his funny rhetorical questions. It's been far too long. "Mom and Dad wouldn't let anyone near you with a pen. They wanted you to have a 'clean cast.'"

"Probably for the best."

"Yeah. Mom would have majorly flipped out if she had walked in to see that someone drew anything lewd on your cast." Giggling, I raise a hand to brush my hair out of my face, but he catches my hand before I can do it.

"Let me," he says as he rolls his wheelchair closer and tucks the pieces behind my ears like he used to do all the time. "Your eyes are just as brilliant as I remember them." I feel his bony hand graze the side of my cheek and then take hold of the back of my neck before he presses his mouth into mine. Everything happens in slow motion: he lifts my chin, closes his eyes, and leans in before brushing his lips across mine, re-creating the first time he ever kissed me, in the middle of the not-so-crowded mall. A rush of energy surges through my body, making its way out to every extremity. *And your lips are just as soft as I remember them.*

"Wow," he breathes as he releases his grip on my neck. "Just like I remember it."

I look over at Mom, hoping that she didn't see us kiss. And as far as I'm concerned, she didn't. She's neck-deep in a conversation with Jason, a serious look in her eyes.

We're both quiet for a moment—I guess taking in the fact that our lips connected in the same way that they used to before the accident. The electricity from the kiss is still convulsing through my body when I say, "We have some things to discuss. About us, I mean—"

"I heard you," he cuts me off.

"What?"

"In the hospital room . . . I heard you. You told me that you loved me." I must give him a blank stare, because shortly after he asks, "Right? I wasn't just dreaming that, was I?"

"You weren't dreaming. I said that."

"Did you mean it?"

"Of course I meant it."

I was in love with him then, but am I still in love with him now? The escalation of the blood pounding in my ears answers for me: *without a doubt.*

"Hm." *"Hm"? What's that supposed to mean?* "So how is this supposed to work now that you're at UCLA?"

"I'm not exactly sure. In the car, Mom told me that they adopted you, so legally you're my brother now. Kinda makes things more difficult on top of everything else."

"Yeah. And I don't want to be the guy who holds you back or slows you down." My eyes inadvertently look at the wheelchair he's sitting in when he says this. "But I don't want to give you up that easily, either."

I look down at his hands and want so badly to wiggle my fingers into the spaces between his, but with my mom not too far away, I decide against it. "What *do* you want?"

"I want you." His words come out stronger than anything else he's said to me this entire time. "And I know I'm not supposed to because it's wrong, but I can't help that."

"I know."

He's quiet for a long while, causing the weight in my stomach to return with full force. In his silence, I think back to a conversation we had up on the balcony the night before the showcase. I have to wonder how much of his memories about me he has recovered, because Dylan's words now seem to echo that conversation from months ago. *"We're not right, but we're not wrong, Emma. I just can't help the way that I feel about you."*

It isn't until he speaks again that I'm brought out of my trip down memory lane. "You ever heard of this thing called 'the long game'?" It's sort of out of the blue, and that throws me off at first, so I shake my head. "I used to complain to Jason about never getting back to my old self again, and he told me we're playing the long game when it comes to this stuff. We don't focus on what's wrong right now, but keep in mind the good that will come from this later."

I bite the tip of my thumbnail as he speaks. "I'm not sure what you mean. And what does that have to do with us?"

"It's where you work toward a goal, but you don't know when that goal will be achieved. And it has everything to do with us." He wheels even closer and takes my hand in his. "I think we should be friends for right now."

"I agree. With college for me and physical therapy for you, there's not going to be a lot of time for us to spend with each other. And besides, I've already been your sister and your girlfriend, so being your friend shouldn't be that difficult." I try to pull my hand from his grip, but he won't let go.

"I don't know. It's going to be hard to resist wanting to kiss you whenever I see you."

"I know, but . . ."

His amber eyes capture mine, and a small crescent appears on his lips. "Play the long game with me, Emma."

"What?"

"I'll go along with this 'friends' thing for now, but what's going to happen when 'eventually' rolls around someday? Yes, for the next four years, you'll be in LA, and maybe I'll be away too, for art school after all this. But what's going to happen when our worlds collide again in the future?"

"Dylan," I gasp, as breathy as if I'd just run a marathon without stopping. "What are you saying?"

"I'm saying that we'll take it one day at a time as siblings and friends, but someday, I hope to end this long game . . . because . . . I love you, and I want to be with you."

The words seem to come very naturally to him. He speaks confidently. It's almost as if he's been practicing them in his dreams for the past seven months, waiting for his chance to say them to my face.

"I love you, too," I whisper into the space between us, tears flooding my eyes.

"I love you more."

"I love you most."

"Not possible," he responds, sparking my mind to recall the last text he sent me on the night he asked me out.

Not possible. You're never gonna lose me. No matter what happens, I'm always gonna be here 🩶

He's right. He'll always be in my heart. No matter where we are or what's going on in our lives, I'll know that he will always be with me, playing the long game until a day comes when every obstacle between us gets knocked down and we can be together once again.

"So, the long game?" he asks, wiping the tears from my eyes.

"Long game." I smile, scooting away from his body and extending my hand toward him, like I did on my last first day of high school. "Hi, Dylan. I'm Emma."

"Nice to meet you, Emma. I'm Dylan. Dylan McAn . . . I mean, Ellenburg. Dylan Ellenburg." A laugh escapes us both at the same time, his just as hearty as I remember it. "That's going to take some getting used to, that's for sure."

"Yeah, but now, you have the rest of your life to work on it. You're an Ellenburg for forever now."

"Forever," he whispers, his amber eyes smiling into mine. "I like the sound of that."

acknowledgments

Writing a book is never easy. I spent many hours hunched over my laptop crafting this story, but that is nothing compared to the time that so many generous people have put in to transform *Wrong in All the Right Ways* from an idea in my head to the book in your hands. I am eternally grateful for them all.

Thank you to my amazing agent, Jill Kramer, for taking a chance on me and having so much faith in me and my writing. I will never be able to repay you for your love, support, and words of wisdom throughout this journey.

Thank you to my publisher, Christy Ottaviano, and everyone at Macmillan who had a hand in bringing *Wrong in All the Right Ways* to life. This includes my production editor, Jennifer Healey, and the designer of my gorgeous cover, Danielle Mazzella Di Bosco. Thank you also to Ana Deboo, Regina Castillo, and Diane Miller for your attention to detail with this book.

A HUGE thank you to Jessica Anderson, my editor. Simply put, you are incredible (the Wonder Woman of editors, if you will), and words cannot fully express how lucky I am to have you in my corner. I am honored to have had the opportunity to work with such a hard-working and delightful person.

Thank you to my siblings for being my first beta readers (before I even knew what a beta reader was) and for not being afraid to call me out when my writing fell short. I love you guys! Will, I don't know how you've put up with me through this process, but your love and patience are deeply appreciated. And Mom, thank you for being my biggest cheerleader. You knew I was destined to "be somebody" since I was two years old. I love you, and I hope I'm making you proud.

And finally, thank you to my readers. Sharing this book with you is a dream come true!